Cast
of
Characters

A Novelists Inc. Anthology

Cast of Characters

A Novelists Inc. Anthology

Edited by
Lou Aronica

fiction studio books

The Fiction Studio
PO Box 4613
Stamford, CT 06907

Jacket design by Julie Ortolon

Print ISBN-13: 978-1-936558-50-6
E-book ISBN-13: 978-1-936558-51-3

Visit our website at www.fictionstudiobooks.com

First Fiction Studio Paperback Printing: April 2012
Printed in the United States of America

Special Free Offer:

Thank you for buying *Cast of Characters*, Novelists Inc.'s first short story anthology. We hope you love what you read here.

We have even more for you. You can get *Set Pieces*, a **free** e-book with more fiction from Novelists Inc. members by going to our site at www.ninc.com.

If you love exciting fiction, you're going to want this.

Contents

Introduction

by Lou Aronica

If you love reading fiction, there's a good chance that it's because of the characters. Sure, people read short stories and novels because of the plots and the settings, but if you think about the stories that you've loved over the years, there's a very good chance that what you remember most fondly is a character or a relationship that made the entire thing come alive. Characters make fiction real for us, and I think most of us who really love fiction do so because the best characters allow us to place ourselves in the work. Great characters transport us and make their situations our situations, teaching us something about ourselves at the same time.

Novelists Inc. is an organization that has been around since 1989. It is the only writers organization devoted exclusively to multi-published novelists. Our ranks are filled with tremendously successful writers, many of whom are *New York Times* and *USA Today* bestsellers, and I am honored to be the current president. When we decided last year that we were going to compile our first anthology of original short fiction, one of the first questions that came to mind was, "How do we tie it all together?" After all, Novelists Inc. has such a wide range of writers in its membership. How do you find a unifying theme in such a diverse gathering of genres and styles?

The answer, of course, is through the characters. There are stories in this anthology that take place today, a few years ago, in the distant past, and even in the future. They're set here, in foreign lands, and in mythical realms. There are love stories, suspense stories, fantasy stories, funny stories, profound stories, and several combinations of the above. Yet what unites them all is that they're all filled with characters that I think you're going to want to get to know. You're not going to like all of these people; if you did, the authors would probably be disappointed, because they weren't going for that. But I think you're going to feel some level of connection to all of them. That's because the authors in this anthology are true storytellers, and true storytellers always try to give you relatable characters.

I hope you enjoy this cast of characters. It's a distinctive lot.

Before you get completely carried away, you might want to take a minute to visit the Novelists Inc. site at www.ninc.com. There, you can download *Set Pieces*, a free e-book companion to this anthology.

Lou Aronica
February 2012

Between the Lines

by Victoria Alexander

Number one *New York Times* bestselling author Victoria Alexander was an award winning television reporter until she discovered fiction was much more fun than real life.

Since the publication of her first book in 1995, she has written twenty-six full-length novels and six novellas. With books translated into more than a dozen different languages she has twice been nominated for Romance's Writers of America prestigious RITA award. In 2009, she was given a Career Achievement Award from RT Bookclub and was named Historical Storyteller of the year in 2003. In 2008 she was the keynote speaker for the Romance Writers of America annual conference in San Francisco. Victoria credits much of her writing success to her experiences as a reporter.

During her journalism career, Victoria covered every president from Ford to Clinton. She knows firsthand what it feels like to be surrounded by rising floodwaters, inside a burning building and in the midst of a national political convention. She covered the story that was the basis of the movie *Boys Don't Cry,* and once acted as the link between police and a barricaded gunman. Her investigative work exposed the trucking of New York City garbage to a small town dump in rural Nebraska. When the Associated Press called one of her features "storytelling genius" it was the encouragement she needed to turn from news to fiction. She's never looked back.

Today, the former Air Force brat has settled in Omaha, Nebraska with her husband and two bearded collies in a house under constant renovation. Victoria laughs a great deal – she has to.

First of all, the Author character in "Between the Lines" is not me, although we do share a lot in common. She has always wondered if, when she's away from the computer, leaving her characters between pages or – as in this story – taking a break right before they are about to make love, disturbs them. With each book she writes, the characters she creates become real to her so it only makes sense that they live on even when she is not writing. They have their own lives, their own thoughts that she is not privy to. There's substance in the characters she creates. She molds their personalities, their likes and dislikes, who they are and what they want. Perhaps they live in an alternate universe that she is allowed to tap into. As much as she knows it sounds crazy, how can they not be real?

Oh, and the husband character? That's not my husband either but again they do have similarities. But my husband much prefers nachos to popcorn.

London, 1885

He swept her up into his arms and carried her toward his bed chamber. Desire quickened his pace and heated his blood. She was light as a feather, ethereal as an angel. Hair so blond it was nearly white drifted around a face that was surely sculpted in heaven itself. She was glorious and soon she would be his. He nudged the door open with his foot and strode toward his bed.

Cara glanced at the bed and shivered. Was it with appre hension or need? He set her on her feet by the side of the bed and looked down at her. Eyes, the colors of a summer morn ing, large and innocent and uncertain gazed back at him. His conscience nagged at the back of his mind. He was not used to defiling virgins, no matter how willing they may be. "You may change your mind, you know."

She stared up at him and raised her chin in determination. "No, Julian. I want this. More than I can say." She drew a deep breath. "I want you."

"That works out nicely then." He pulled her closer and slipped one arm of her silk wrapper off her shoulder to reveal flesh, creamy and inviting. He bent to kiss the side of her neck and her shoulder. "I have never wanted a woman as I want you."

"As that is the case… " She framed his face with her hands and drew his lips to hers. "You shall have me."

Her lips met his and fire flared within him. Still… He summoned all his strength, pulled away from her, then gazed once more into her eyes. "Are you sure about this? You will be ruined."

"Then it shall be a glorious ruination."

"Regardless…" He winced. This was not at all easy to say given his own rising need. "You should consider –"

"My lord. " She huffed. "You have a certain reputation. I was well aware of that before we reached this point. Indeed, your extensive experience with scandalous liaisons is precisely why we have come to this point."

He stared at her. "What?"

"One of the reasons," she said quickly. "At the beginning, not now of course. You were something of a challenge, you know."

He drew his brows together. "I was a what?"

"Well, no one ever imagined someone as inexperienced as I am could seduce a man as, well, *practiced* as you."

"*You* seduced *me*?"

"You needn't be offended." She shrugged. "It wasn't as if I have forced you here at the point of a pistol. Indeed, you have been quite amenable to my pursuit and most enthusiastic."

"Nonetheless, I was under the impression I was the one doing the seducing." Indignation sounded in his voice. Regardless of his own desires, the very idea that he had been manipulated was most annoying. Besides, she might well be the innocent here as the world judged such things but he considered himself a man with a certain sense of honor. And honor was debating whether or not to continue this course. Or at least it had been until a moment ago.

"Does it matter?"

"I suppose not." Still, if she were the seducer, there was really no need for hesitation at all. There might well be something to be said for manipulative women after all.

"Julian, I can't imagine being with anyone but you." She slipped her arms around his neck and pressed her body against him. He couldn't help but note how nicely they would fit together. "You're in my thoughts. In my dreams."

"Cara –"

"I do appreciate your consideration, I really do but…" Her lips whispered against his. "I want you, my lord."

He groaned. "You're making this exceptionally difficult."

"Then my plan is working." She pressed her lips harder against his. Her mouth opened and her tongue met his, demanding and insistent and not the least bit virginal.

Passion exploded between them. He pulled her nightgown over her head and tossed it away. She fumbled with the fastenings of his trousers, and pushed them down his legs. He kicked them aside, then paused and stared at her.

The dim light from the gas lamp cast a golden glow on breasts full and round, hips curved and luscious, legs long and shapely. His blood quickened. Those legs would soon be wrapped around him.

Her gaze met his, her eyes wide and dark with desire. "Are you going to join me, my lord?" A blush colored her cheeks at the brazenness of her question but she did not turn her gaze away. No, she wouldn't, would she? The little minx had planned this. All of it. Still, regardless of her words or actions or desires, no matter who was seducing whom, this would indeed ruin her. She was properly raised and of good family. Had she truly given the consequences of their union due consideration?

"Cara –"

"Shhh." She fisted her hand in his shirt and pulled him toward her. "This discussion is at an end." She tugged at him and together they tumbled backward onto the bed.

And his restraint vanished.

~ ~ ~

"Damn." I leaned back in my chair and glared at the computer screen. As if my innocent Mac was to blame. Well, I had to blame something.

"What's wrong now?" My long suffering husband – his description, not mine – uttered his comment without any serious thought, his attention still firmly on the college football game on TV.

"It's just not working."

"Maybe it would work better if you would go back in your office where you belong."

"Hey, I want to see the game too." Well, not this game exactly but the next one. My husband and I follow different teams and sometimes opposing teams. It keeps our marriage fresh.

College football is about the only sport I really like but I was on deadline and had to work. I write romance novels and I figured I could work on my book and watch at the same time. This is something that I've tried before. It never really goes as planned.

"So what's the problem?"

I glanced at the TV. Commercial. Of course. "Well, I'm just getting into a love scene."

"You do those very well."

"Thank you." My loves scenes were the only part of my writing that my husband could honestly claim to have read. "But my characters…" I blew a long breath."Well, he's an hon orable man and she's a virgin."

"You hate virgins."

"This is why. In historical settings, there are repercussion for even the most enthusiastic virgins." I sighed. "Anyway, they're about to make love and he's hesitant because it will ruin her."

"The sex, you mean," my husband said sagely. Or as sagely as a man in a thirty-year-old college sweatshirt could sound.

"Yes, I mean the sex."

"I don't see the problem." He turned his attention back to the TV. The game had resumed.

Not that I cared. "The problem is that he is an honorable man and, as a honorable man, he's not sure they should go through with this because it will ruin her."

"You mean ruin her reputation right? Not ruin her for other men."

I rolled my gaze toward the ceiling. "Exactly."

"I still don't see the problem." His words were directed at me but his gaze was fixed on the TV and his hand, apparently of its own accord, was dipping into a now empty popcorn bowl. And I thought women were multi-taskers. "He wants to sleep with her, right?"

"Well, he is a guy."

"And she wants to?"

"Oh, she's positively eager."

"Then no man in his right mind, fictionally or otherwise, is going to stop at that point."

I stared at him. "What about his honor? What about his conscience?"

He snorted in that derisive way he had perfected to an art form. "He'd do her first and deal with his conscience later."

He might have a point. "I suppose. You could be right. I'll have to think about it."

"While you're thinking about it…" He held up the empty popcorn bowl. "Why don't you take a break and, oh, I don't know, make some popcorn? I'd even share it with you."

"Sure, why not." I got to my feet. "How can I resist an of fer like that?"

"It wouldn't hurt to get away from the computer for a few minutes either. Clear your head and all."

I moved closer and took the bowl. "You are so thoughtful."

"I know," he said in an aw shucks, gee whiz ma'am kind of tone. "It's part of my charm."

"Lucky for you." I grinned. "But you're right, I do need a break."

~ ~ ~

Cara glanced down between them. "You can put that thing away, Author has left off writing."

"Now?" Julian's voice rose in frustration. "How can She stop now? This is not a good time to stop. What is the woman thinking?"

"She's certainly not thinking about us."

"How can She leave me, er, us like this?"

"Quite easily apparently. And I'd say it's your fault." Cara rolled away and propped herself up on her elbows. "She wrote you to be a man of honor and apparently honorable men do not boff virgins indiscriminately."

"It's not indiscriminate." He stretched out on the bed, folded his hands behind his head and stared up at the ceiling. "Not with you anyway. I love you. Even if I haven't realized that yet." He huffed. "She does this all the time you know."

"Leave us in the middle of a scene?" She sighed. "I know. It's most annoying."

"And usually it's a love scene." He clenched his teeth. "It's extremely frustrating."

"She doesn't like writing love scenes. She thinks they're hard."

"Not for long," he said under his breath. "I have a thought." He rolled over on his side and studied her. "There's nothing that says we can't, oh, I don't know, practice as it were."

She raised a brow. "Practice?"

"Or even better, call it research. She does like research."

"Research?"

"You know," he added quickly, "to make this whole thing easier for Her. "

"My, you are thoughtful."

"I think so." He smiled in a modest manner. "Well?" He tried and failed to hide an eager note in his voice.

"Well…" She paused and his hopes rose. "That's really not the solution to everything."

"It can be," he said. With any luck at all.

"Actually, I'm rather hungry at the moment. For *food*." She aimed a pointed look at him. "Do you think She wrote us something to eat?" She sat up, glanced around the bed cham ber and frowned. "She never remembers to write us anything to eat, as if we don't enjoy a bite now and then."

"She never lets us pee either," he muttered. "However, what She does do…" He patted the bed beside him. "She does rather well."

Cara stared at him. "Is that all you can think about?"

"It's how She wrote me." A defensive note he didn't quite like but couldn't seem to prevent sounded in his voice. It was a blasted nuisance to have one's nature determined by a woman with a knack for words and a nasty sense of humor. "I'm a…a…" What was the word? She'd written it accidentally on occasion. "A *guy* yes, that's it. Different century of course, but that's how She writes me. I'm a…" He raised his chin and squared his shoulders. "A 19th century *guy*."

Cara sniffed. "It's not at all appealing."

"It's completely charming and you well know it, as does She. Now, She may rarely feed us but this…" He patted the bed once again. "This She does quite nicely."

"Tempting but…" Cara crossed her arms over her naked chest, oblivious to the fact of just how delicious it made her breasts appear, like offerings on a platter, and directed him a firm look. "At the moment, I'd really rather have food."

~ ~ ~

I started toward the kitchen but a thought struck me and I stopped, turned and sat back down at my laptop.

"Popcorn?" my husband said hopefully.

"I could do fun with food," I said more to myself than him. I had written some interesting love scenes involving food in previous books. "Let's just put a bowl of strawberries by the bed…" I typed a line. "No, assorted fruit. " I changed a word. "And chocolates. That will give Julian a few more minutes to consider the consequences of his actions and something to work with if he doesn't."

"You talk about these characters like they're real."

"They are to me. At least while I'm writing them and I hope when they're read." I thought for a moment. "This is go ing to sound weird."

He gasped. "Weird? From you? Imagine my surprise."

I ignored him. It's usually best. "Sometimes I think they're a little indignant when I take a break in the middle of some thing important."

"Like sex?"

I nodded. "When I leave them, you know, right at the brink and then stop."

"I know I find that annoying when you do it to me. But you did give him fruit." He smirked. "That always makes me feel better."

"Hmph."

"And I'm sure when you get back to it, your character will do the right thing."

"I hope not." I got up and headed to the kitchen. "It's not as much fun when they behave."

~ ~ ~

"Thank God, fruit! There, on the table beside the bed," Cara said with a delighted smile. "Oh look, strawberries and oranges and some chocolates. How lovely. I can't imagine why we didn't see them before."

"I doubt they were there before."

She popped a chocolate into her mouth. "You think She heard us somehow?"

"She does talk about her characters talking to her but I doubt it. At least, She wasn't listening to me," he added under his breath. "If She had been, right now you and I –"

"These are wonderful." Cara took a bite of a strawberry. "You should try them."

"I will." He watched her for a moment. Author was right. There was indeed something most erotic about the combina tion of chocolates and strawberries. Although simply watching Cara eat was not exactly as exciting as any number of other things he could think of to do with chocolates and strawber ries. "You do realize She lies. Author that is."

"I believe it's called fiction, darling." She paused, the straw berry halfway to her mouth. "What do you mean She lies?"

"That business about you weighing little more than a feather." He eyed her in an assessing manner. "You've become quite a little plump pigeon since the last book."

She gasped. "I have not."

"Oh, you have definitely put on a few pounds."

"In the bosom perhaps! "

His brow rose.

"And possibly in the hips," she admitted reluctantly. "But this too is entirely your fault."

"How is this my fault?"

"You – Julian that is – prefers a heroine with a somewhat fuller figure than Author's last hero did. Therefore…" She opened her arms in a dramatic gesture. "*This* is what you get because *this* is what you want."

He swallowed hard. Cara had been written exceptionally well to appeal to Julian. He certainly couldn't debate that. "Yes, well you are exquisite."

"I know," she said smugly and finished the strawberry. "You're rather appealing yourself."

"She does write me well," he said modestly. Still, the chanc es of enticing his heroine back to bed right now were no doubt slim. Cara would do exactly as she pleased. Her independence and stubbornness called to him as surely as her beauty. Not that he could blame her. She was written that way. "Have you ever pondered the meaning of our existence?"

She selected an orange and peeled it slowly. "You mean the manner in which we only come alive while She is writing us? Or how the characters change from book to book but our, oh, I don't know, essence –"

"Souls perhaps?"

"Very well. *Souls* continue from story to story?"

"Exactly." He nodded eagerly.

"No, I haven't." She popped an orange segment in her mouth. "Nor do I care to. I see us more in the realm of actors. All the world is a stage and all that."

"Yes, but –"

Her gaze flicked over him. "You have never struck me as the type of man who enjoys intellectual discussions of the meaning of life."

"I'm not." He shrugged. "Not in this book."

"I don't like it."

He drew his brows together. "Why not?"

"Because it's not what I – or rather – what Cara wants," she said firmly. "Cara wants a wicked – in the naughty sense – dashing man of action and adventure. Now, in the next book, I – whoever I might be – might well enjoy a rousing discussion about the meaning of life. I might quiver at the very thought of an intellectual whose nose is pressed firmly in a book. I might well swoon in the presence of scholarly pursuit and academic accomplishment. But here and now…" She shook her head. "It holds no interest. "Indeed, I find the entire idea quite dull."

Indignation washed through him. "I'm not just a pretty face, you know. I do have a brain."

"Of course you do but –"

"And now and again I enjoy using it to consider the vaga ries of a literary life."

"Oh, come now, Julian. I find that hard to believe."

"I…I…" Bloody hell, he was sputtering. He never sput tered. He was not written that way.

She heaved a sigh of surrender. "There's only one way to shut you up isn't there?"

He narrowed his eyes. "What?"

She tossed the rest of her orange aside, licked her fin gers, then started toward him and cast him a wicked smile. "Research."

~ ~ ~

My team was on now and it was losing. It needed my emo tional support, whatever psychic waves I could direct toward the players through the TV. It didn't seem to be helping. Prob ably because my husband sitting next to me on the sofa was oh, so quietly sending his psychic support to the other team.

I heaved a resigned sigh. "I should get back to work."

"Yep."

"I still have no idea what I'm doing."

"You're working on a love scene right?" He glanced at me.

"Yeah," I said cautiously. It was always best to be cautious when my husband offered writing advice.

"You'll figure it out."

"Thanks for the vote of confidence."

"I'm nothing if not supportive," he said, his gaze firmly back on the game.

"Still…"

"You know what always clears my head when I have a problem." He stood up, pulled me to my feet and flashed me a wicked smile. The very same smile I usually wrote on the face of one of my heroes.

I stared at him. "That is not the answer to everything."

"Of course not." He scoffed. "Well, not *everything*."

It was obvious he didn't believe a single word of what he had just said. he was a guy after all. My guy. My hero.

We started toward the bedroom and somewhere, far in the distance, I heard the distinct sound of satisfied feminine laugh ter. Exactly as I thought Cara would sound. Weird. But now that I had started thinking about my characters living indepen dently of my words, I couldn't seem to get the idea out of my head. Either they were waiting in frustration for me to finish the love scene or they were cavorting on their own. Or I was just plain crazy. But I think you have to be crazy to work in a world you make up. At least a little.

"Don't think of it as sex," he said.

"Oh?" This should be good. "What would you call it?"

Again that wicked smile flashed. "Research."

Invidia

by Vicki Hinze

Vicki Hinze is the award-winning author of 25 novels, four nonfiction books, and hundreds of articles published in as many as 63 countries. Blending genres, she has won multiple trail-blazing awards: military romantic thriller, military romantic intrigue and by co-creating the first open-ended single title continuity series. She's mentored over 2000 other writers, hosted the acclaimed *Everyday Woman* radio show, and sponsors multiple benevolence programs. Vicki holds an MFA in creative writing and a Ph.D. in philosophy, theocentric business and ethics. Three years ago, she turned to writing Christian romantic thrillers and women's fiction. Her latest release, *Before the White Rose* (general fiction), was a bestseller in the U.S. and in the U.K. Her next Christian fiction release is book 3 in her Crossroads Crisis Center series, *Not This Time.* Visit her at www.vickihinze.com.

Gloria Rastin fascinated me, not for what she was, but for what she wasn't, and not for what she did, but for what she didn't do. Normal, everyday average, like most of us, she found herself in a situation not of her making but one that impacted her life and the lives of her children. We've all heard stories from other women about how they sacrificed their careers to help their husbands build theirs, put them through college, med or law school, only to be dumped on the street with nothing when those same husbands, typically going through some type of midlife crisis, engaged in affairs with other women and decided to ditch their wives. The good wives are left with few prospects, few options and few hopes of a decent future.

Gloria seeks a better solution, an unusual solution, and it too intrigued me. Fascinating woman, Gloria Rastin. So much so I find myself imagining where she'll go from here.

On the eve of the execution, I write this note to my daughters:

> When you're eighteen, the world seems small and the answers simple. Who you are and what you believe in focuses, well, on you. Whether you choose to conquer the world or the S.A.T. exam, you honestly think you can do anything.
>
> In your twenties, you will realize life isn't so black and white, but you'll push along, some times miring down in muck, sometimes sailing along like you have a strong wind at your back (you'll typically define as purpose), propelling you into the stratosphere. You will accomplish and achieve, or redefine your goals and com promise. Either way, you'll have the illusion that you're in control of your life, the mistress of your destiny.
>
> At some point, you likely will marry, have 2.1 children, buy a home, join the PTA and settle into a life. And while you'll recall fondly the per son you dreamed you'd be, you'll be anchored in the life of the woman you've become. And if you're not wholly content, well, you'll not be miserable, either. Not being miserable is pretty good in real life.
>
> And if your life goes as mine has, then will come the fall.
>
> One morning, you'll dry your hands in a rush on a slightly sour smelling dishtowel and answer

the ringing phone. Your husband, you'll discov er, has already answered, and he and a woman who is obviously his mistress are conspiring on how to best get you out of their way.

Trust in him shatters.

Your marriage and the life you built are over.

Betrayal stabs at the core of your heart and outrage echoes through its hollow chambers. But then comes the most dangerous reaction of all. The one that claws deep into your belly and fills you with bitterness, blasting apart all you believed, all you wanted and all you thought you had become. It is powerful, and second by second it grows stronger until it consumes everything. Devastated, you think of and then do things you never thought or imagined you would think or do. Devious, evil things. Deadly things.

To you, at the time, totally rational and justifi able things.

Then those things are done and suddenly the whole ordeal is over. Relief washes away any guilt or spears of remorse piercing your con science. You feel justified. Vindicated. Revived.

But all too soon, with the clarity of hindsight, you find yourself alone, looking through slat ted shadows of light that you're no longer in, and you shudder at what you have done. The truth is stunning, ugly, and you wonder, *"Who is this stranger in my mirror?"*

But you know her. Deep down in places you let no one else see, in places you don't visit yourself because to admit they exist inside you makes you sick, you know her. Just as you know that the most horrific aspect of it all is that you'd do everything you've done all over again.

You blame him. Her. You did your part. You were a good woman, a good wife and mother. You did no more or less than anyone else would do – you defended what was yours by all necessary means. And you did defend it. You did . . . de fend it. This is no time for regret. It's a time for celebration.

Yet you do not celebrate. Minutes before midnight – the official execution time – you'd have to be a monster to celebrate. You are a victim. One pushed beyond reasonable limits, beyond bearable bounds. You were pushed and shoved and kicked to the curb like yester day's garbage. So you rebelled. Of course, you rebelled. You showed them all that you can't command their love, but you do demand their respect. You were an ally; they made you an enemy. And you dedicated yourself to it with the same zeal and passion you dedicated to every thing else.

One thing drove you. Insidious, potent, con suming and powerful, that one thing seeped into your every cell. It wasn't love. It wasn't a cry for respect or honor or justice. It was envy.

And it worked.

Tonight, death calls.

And this time, it won't be you who answers . . .

~ ~ ~

After the Fall
Houston, Texas

"It's Monday." Gloria Rastin looked across the breakfast room from the stove to her daughters. They were dressed and ready for school. If she could get them fed and out the door in the next half hour, Gloria might just get through this without revealing that their world had crashed down around their ears. She needed to think. She needed to decide the wisest course of action to protect her daughters.

Tess, her eldest, paused, her forkful of French toast midway to her mouth. "I can't pick up Breezy, Mom. I have a mock debate right after school and then a prom committee meeting."

"So what am I supposed to do? Walk home?" Breezy glared at her sister. "You try walking home after you spend two hours in the pool."

Swim practice. Breezy had a shot at making the Olympic team, but that required support from her family as well as her own dedication, which she had in spades, if only for swimming. Gloria raised a hand. "Tess, you have an hour between the two. Use it to pick up your sister and get her home. I have a board meeting. I'm in charge, I can't miss it."

"But, Mom –"

Gloria lifted her egg-turner. "Cooperate."

Breezy grinned. Tess grimaced. "All right. But –" Tess looked at her sister with a warning that intimidated her debate opponents " – if you're not waiting at the curb, I'm leaving you there."

"No problem." Breezy snagged her dishes, rinsed them at the sink and then dumped them into the dishwasher. "Morn ing, Dad."

Marcus Rastin, tall and dark and still gorgeous, dropped a kiss to his youngest daughter's cheek and stuffed his cell phone into his jacket pocket. "Morning."

Texting her. Again. It all looked so normal. So typical of morning rituals in homes everywhere. But it wasn't normal, and Gloria knew it. The scent of another woman on him, late nights at the office, the sudden reduction of net pay going into their account, text messages back-and-forth in the dead of night. He was having an affair with "C." Shock had come first, then betrayal, and now . . . now Gloria was angry, and wondering what she had to do to protect her daughters and herself. The decision she'd made fifteen years ago to put her career aside and be there for her family had been the right one at the time. Now, because of his infidelity, she felt stupid for putting all her eggs in his basket. Stupid and used and, heaven help her, envious.

He'd have everything.

She'd have nothing.

And some other woman, the as yet unknown "C," would have her life.

"You okay, hon?" Marcus cupped her elbow.

Keep it together. "I'm fine, sweetheart." She dropped French toast onto a plate and placed it on the table in front of Marcus, forced herself to lightly kiss his temple when every thing in her wanted to rip out his heart.

He smiled up at her. "I've got a meeting scheduled at four today," he said, informing her he'd likely be late for dinner. "It could run long, but I'm hoping it doesn't."

"Not a problem." *Date night. Again. Third time this week.* If Gloria could just hold it together until she got him out of the house . . . Swiping at a nonexistent piece of lint on his suit jacket at the back of his neck, she planted the listening device and then lifted a pitcher from the table. "Juice?"

~ ~ ~

Two hours later, Gloria sat parked outside a posh Houston apartment complex watching her husband lip-lock the other woman. *Cara Jorge.* Gloria should have known. Marcus had taken over managing her financial affairs two years ago, after Cara's husband had died. She had it all. Looks – a tall, svelte redhead with classic beauty – brains and more money than she could spend in ten lifetimes. And now, Marcus.

Envy, bitter and hot, burned through Gloria, and she lis tened to their exchange without a sliver of remorse. Within minutes of entering the building, she followed them to an apartment on the top floor – 601, according to the shiny gold numbers on a discreet placket above the doorbell– and scant moments later, the volume changed, signaling Marcus had removed his jacket.

Gloria's heart beat hard and fast. She knew what that meant, and the sounds that followed proved it. They were in bed. Laughing and . . . *How could he do this to her? To them? To their children?*

It didn't matter. The reason really didn't matter. *What is, is.*

Cara's lighthearted voice carried through to the plug in Gloria's ear. "I'm weary of all this subterfuge, darling. It's gone on too long to not be boring."

"Mmm, what shall we do about it then?" Marcus's voice was stilted, as if his words were spoken between butterfly kisses.

Marcus was prone to butterfly kisses.

"You could get rid of the problem." Cara let out a little giggle. "That tickles, Marcus."The teasing continued between snippets of conversation that were chilling – to Gloria.

Couldn't he see the manipulation? Couldn't he sense her goading him into . . . She couldn't make herself think it.

"Divorce is out of the question. I'd lose my daughters – she's a good mother, even if she's a lousy wife. It'd cost me a fortune."

"Money." Cara grunted. "We've got plenty of money."

"I can't buy my children."

Cara paused, then said, "We've discussed this many times, darling. You know what you have to do."

"What?"

"Get more creative. Act with authority. If you want some thing, you must take it, Marcus. It's the way of the world."

"You're talking about killing her," Marcus said bluntly.

Gloria slumped against the wall, gasped, held her breath.

"If that's the only way we can move on with our lives, it seems we've no choice."

Reeling, Gloria lost their next few exchanges, but then forced herself to pull herself together and pay at tention – and almost wished she hadn't.

"I have put some thought into it," Marcus said.

Hope infused Cara's voice. "Really?"

"She gets her hair done at 2:00 every Thursday at Paleen."

"It's a busy area. Lots of activity," Cara said. "But wouldn't you be seen?"

"Highly unlikely. There's a bus-stop shelter across the street. It's the perfect place to hide in plain sight."

Does it have a good vantage point for you to see those entering the salon?"

"An excellent vantage point."

"But you can't be sure no one else will be there, wait ing for the bus."

"Trust me, sweetheart. No one who shops in that area rides the bus."

"And your exit strategy?"

"The bus arrives between 1:50 and 1:55. I eliminate the problem, hop on the bus, and I'm gone."

"And no one knows you've ever been there." She paused. "Mmm, obviously you're not going to strangle her . . ."

"I'll fire a shot from the bus-stop. The shelter will cover me."

"Oh, you clever man." Cara squealed her delight. "It's brilliant!"

"It is, isn't it?" Marcus chuckled, then growled. "Come here."

"No." Cara sniffed. "It's a brilliant plan but I'll believe it when I see it. You're not really committed to me, Marcus."

"I am," he countered. "Totally committed."

The debate went back and forth, and finally he said, "I'll be there. It's going to happen. If you doubt it, come watch."

"I don't believe you." Cara's voice went from light to daring. "But I'll be there."

"Good." He sounded satisfied.

"Marcus," she warned him. "Do not disappoint me in this. If you do, we're done."

"I won't disappoint you." Marcus spoke with conviction.

"What are you doing?" Cara asked him. "You're making a phone call *now*?"

"Texting my wife."

Gloria ran from the building. Her cell was in the car. She got in and collected the message. "Meeting will run late. Be home at 8. Love you. M."

Love you. *Love you?*

Her hands shook. She shook all over.

Marcus Rastin. Husband. Liar. And soon-to-be murderer.

No. No. How she would survive and make this right, she wasn't sure. But she was not going to die.

She would *not* die.

Flashes of agony, wistfulness and regret churned inside her and coalesced into one – envy. It burned deep inside her, and in it, a plan began to form . . .

~ ~ ~

Thursday. D-day. The day her husband planned to kill her.

Inside, Gloria was a tangled mass of live wires, each one frayed, frazzled and hissing. Outside, she was calm. Resignation fueled by determination could motivate a woman bent on protecting her children and herself in ways nothing else could.

For the last two days, she'd swallowed way too much coffee but had needed it, being locked in relentless internal debate. *Should she phone the police?* They hadn't protected her best friend, Jane. Paul had beaten her to death and had pinned the restraining order she'd taken out against him to her chest. The system couldn't be trusted. It had failed Jane then and it would fail Gloria now. *Should she tell someone else? Should she drain their accounts and investments, snatch the girls and disappear?*

In the end, she'd done none of that. She and the girls were Marcus's victims, and they shouldn't forfeit the lives they had built because he'd decided to abandon and kill her. The injustice in that was beyond anything they should have to endure. Yet if a man was determined to kill you, he would find a way, and after hearing Marcus herself, she couldn't deny that he was as determined as Breezy was to make the Olympic swim team. She'd do it, and so would he.

That eliminated running or any of the other thousand counteractions Gloria had mentally considered. If she wanted to live – and she did – then everything had to appear to everyone that they were still a young Ozzie and Harriet living and loving in Wonderland. Bearing that uppermost in mind, she'd pulled back, looked at the situation from a different perspective. Then she'd seen her first ray of real hope.

And on it she'd acted.

"So," she asked Marcus, reaching up to twist the brim of her hat then motioning down the length of her body. "It's all new. Do you like it?"

At the breakfast table, Marcus paused to look. "It's black." His gaze slid down to her feet. "Black top and slacks, black shoes, black hat – did someone die or something?"

She giggled, pecked a kiss to his brow and snaked his cell out of his jacket pocket. "Black is chic," she said, feigning an admonishing tone. "You should know that. Oh, don't forget," she tossed in, knowing it was the one thing not requiring a reminder. "I'll be at Paleen's this afternoon."

"Hair day. Right." He dabbed at his mouth with his napkin then slid out of his chair. "I'm late. See you tonight." He grabbed his briefcase, paused at the door and looked back at her. Doubt flashed through his eyes that sparked hope in her, but just as quickly, it died. "I, um, love the hat. You always did look great in black silk."

Bitter disappointment soured her stomach. "Thank you, Marcus," she managed, biting back tears, choking down anger and regret at what was lost and would never again be between them. "Have a good day."

"You, too." He walked out the door and didn't look back.

Gloria collapsed on the chair and cried until she ran out of tears. It'd been a wicked morning. She'd supposedly "gone for a jog" but actually had made an emergency run to Cara Jorge's apartment. Not in it, just to its door. Then she'd rushed back home, cooked breakfast, finally had gotten the girls out of the house, and now Marcus. Retrieving his phone from the silverware drawer where she'd stashed it, she texted Cara. *Look outside your door. I left you a present. Meetings all morning. See you at 1:45. Don't be late . . .*

The dye was now cast.

Gloria could breathe again. Pouring herself yet another cup of coffee, she sat back down at the table, stared at the clock, and waited.

Her life tumbled through her mind. The night she and Marcus met. Their wedding day. Oh, the look in his eyes that day. On the days that Tess and Breezy were born. Gloria sighed wistfully. How had they gone from there to . . . here?

She had no answers, yet on the memories came, assault ing her, mocking her. Now he looked at Cara that way. Now he was willing to do anything for her, including murdering his wife.

A sob broke loose in Gloria's chest and she buried her face in her hands. Wept and wept and, when she thought she had run out of tears, she wept more.

At 1:30, she sent Cara another text. "Can't talk. Still tied up. Did you get my gift?"

Minutes later, Cara responded. "You'll see at 1:45." A heart and a "C" followed. Dry-eyed, Gloria grimaced. "Perfect."

~ ~ ~

Just stay calm. Do nothing, and stay calm.

Gloria changed her clothes – white blouse, jeans and a col orful jacket – then drove to Paleen's, parked between a white minivan and a blue Lexus. She scanned the street for Marcus but first spotted Cara's car parked halfway down the block, fac ing in the opposite direction for a fast getaway. Swerving her gaze, she located the bus-stop shelter. A man stood under it sipping from a paper cup, but she couldn't tell if he was Mar cus. Surely he wasn't. Surely Marcus had reclaimed his sense and had forgotten this crazy idea.

The street in front of the bus stop was busy and people flowed in and out of the coffee shop behind the shelter. The man inside it stood alone, and his suit . . . was the same color as the one Marcus had worn that morning . . . It had to be him. Same suit. Cara here. Of course it had to be him. He was go ing to shoot Gloria on her way to Paleen's front door.

The last remnant of hope died and Gloria accepted the truth. He had not reclaimed his sense or changed his mind. And now Gloria knew the last piece of his plan she needed to know.

She pulled his phone from her handbag and then sent Cara her final text message. "You can't see from there. Cross the street and come closer."

Would she do it?

Gloria couldn't depend on it, and held her breath.

A minute later, Cara's car door opened and she got out, crossed the street in a throng of people, and walked right past the parking lot. Gloria ducked low in her seat. The gift had worked! It had worked! She wore the black hat. The black silk top and slacks. The duplicate outfit to the one Gloria had worn that morning with Marcus.

Oh my God. What have I done? What have I – no. No, he won't do it. He won't –"

A gunshot split the air.

It rang in her ears. For a second, Gloria couldn't move. Then she saw the bus coming down the street. He was going to get away . . .

Get over there, Gloria. Hurry! Hurry!

Gloria scrambled out of the car, so rattled she nearly fell. Righting herself, she rushed past where Cara lay crumpled on the sidewalk. Marcus spotted her, stopped dead in his tracks, stood slack-jawed and transfixed. He was in shock. But any sec ond, his survival instincts would kick in and he'd move for that bus. "Marcus!" she shouted to be certain everyone around her heard. Rushing him, she grabbed his jacket, slipping the phone into his pocket. "Why did you shoot that woman?"

Chaos erupted. People ran, pushed and shoved. "Glo ria?" Confusion fell. He darted his gaze to Cara, sprawled on the street. A wild look flashed through his eyes. The bus approached. He turned to run.

Gloria held fast to his jacket, holding him back. "You shot her!"

"Stop him!" a man shouted.

"Hey! Hey!" Pointing at Marcus, another yelled from the crowd. "That guy shot her!"

"Get the gun!" A third man shoved toward Marcus. "Get the gun!"

The crowd mobbed Marcus, pinned him to the ground. Gloria stepped back to the fringe. All of the fear and desperation and adrenaline that had carried her for days melted and sank. Her strength drained, leaving her knees week and her stomach empty.

"She's dead!" Someone shouted from across the street. "He killed her!"

"Marcus?" Gloria stood owl-eyed, lost and shocked and bewildered. "Why did you kill Cara Jorge?"

"No. Oh, no." He writhed on the ground, trying to break free. "I – I –"

"Oh my God." Gloria paused, let the horror set in. "She's wearing my hat. You – You thought she was me!" Gloria burst into tears. "You meant to kill me!"

~ ~ ~

Hours after the execution, I complete this note to my daughters.

> As this new dawn breaks, my darlings, you finally see clearly why despite your strident objections I have not divorced your father. You see why I have remained at his side through the trial and the countless automatic appeals he rejected, always wearing my hat and black silk. You see why I have not distanced myself from him. From the moment he saw my clothes on his mistress, he knew exactly what I had done, and I did not once let him forget it.
>
> Until this moment, I'm sure you thought my reasons were far different than they actually were. I'm sure you believed I acted out of some sense of obligation or commitment, or maybe out of devotion or love.
>
> Know that I did not lie to the authorities. Legally, I am guilty only of sending my husband's

mistress a gift. I didn't plot her murder. I didn't insist she wear the hat and black silk slacks and top. I didn't chamber bullets in the gun or point that gun at her, and I didn't pull the trigger.

Your father killed her. And now he has paid for that with his own life.

Yet while I didn't do any of those things, dar lings, I am not blameless. I knew there was a risk he would do what he and she had planned. And so I'm confessing my part in all this to you both for one reason – to spare you the agony with which I have lived in learning this truth:

Absens invidia.

Absent envy. My darlings, live your lives absent of envy. For when it resides inside you, even alive, you are dead.

Your father is gone now, and I am prepared to pay the piper. When you're ready, phone the po lice or do whatever you must do. I'll be waiting in the kitchen.

~ ~ ~

Tess and Breezy apparently had read the note. They walked into the kitchen together with it in Tess's hand. Not a word passed between them.

Sitting at the kitchen table, Gloria tensed, squeezed her eyes shut. The air felt charged with tension, sizzling on her skin. Would they hate her? They couldn't forgive her, but could they at least understand why she'd done what she'd done?

More terrified than she'd ever been in her life, she opened her eyes. They sat at their respective places at the table. Tess placed a large bowl between them.

Breezy held the note Gloria had written, stared her mother right in the eyes and said . . .

Nothing.

Tess struck a match. In silence, she set the note on fire.

They watched the fire until the paper burned to ashes.

Gloria darted her gaze between them, but neither of her daughters spoke a word. *What were they doing? What did this mean?*

Breezy picked up the bowl of ashes, dumped them into the sink, and then turned on the garbage disposal. She washed the bowl. Tess dried it, set it back down in the center of the table. Breezy filled it with fresh red apples, then both returned to their seats.

Tess reached out, covered her mother's hand atop the table. "*A bene placito.*"

Breezy stacked her hand on theirs. "*A bene placito.*"

From one who has been pleased well...

Pleased. She had *pleased* them well? Gloria's heart beat hard and fast, flooded. A lump formed in her throat, the backs of her eyes stung and tears filled her eyes, blurring her vision. She studied the women her daughters had become.

"We've lost Dad," Breezy said. "We don't want to lose you, too."

"Thank you for being honest with us." Tess blinked hard and fast. "That took courage."

Gloria nodded, struggled to keep her voice even, but it cracked. "Is there anything you'd like to say or ask before the authorities arrive?"

"We haven't called anyone, Mom." Tess glanced at Breezy, who nodded, and then looked back at Gloria. "The best judge on this is your own conscience."

They knew her well, and they knew this would grieve her more than anything else anyone else could ever do to her. But they still loved her. They would not shun her.

She had pleased them well.

Tears of gratitude streaked down her cheeks. Gloria looked at her daughters, lifted her trembling free hand and placed it atop the stack. "*A bene placito.*" She entwined their fingers. "*Ab sens invidia.*"

The Woman who Lied to Cats

by Rosemary Edghill

Rosemary Edghill made her first professional sale to *Creepy* Magazine in 1978. Since then, under her own name and a variety of pseudonyms, she has published more than 40 novels and more than 50 short stories, in genres from hard-boiled mystery, to technothriller, to romance. In addition she has edited two anthologies and has worked as a science fiction editor for Avon Books, as a freelance book designer, as a typesetter, as an illustrator, and as a professional book reviewer for the Science Fiction Book Club. *Mad Maudlin*, her third Bedlam's Bard collaboration, was a 2002 Voices of Youth Advocates (VOYA) selection as one of the best Horror and Fantasy novels of the year, and (under a pseudonym) she is a *New York Times* bestselling author. She lives in Maryland.

The original opening line of "The Woman who Lied to Cats" begins: "It was 1258 in the Summer Country..." Knowing when the story takes place is crucial: Mog is a bright and imaginative woman born in a time when a serf's daughter occupied the lowest rung on a very long social ladder. Serfs are considered to be little more than animals, and the nobility owns everything from the land around them to the people who farm it. Mog's dreams of a different life are seen as laziness and rebellion by her parents, and her curiosity and intelligence are only liabilities in the world she's been born into. But that changes as the Black Death sweeps across Europe. It kills over ninety percent of the populations in some areas, and suddenly, because of her imagination and her courage, Mog has the chance to reinvent herself and escape the trap of serfdom.

In the Summer Country, only ditching and dikes claimed the land from the sea. In the Summer Country, seed was sown beneath the surface of lakes that only dried to land in harvest time. It was a rich land, and in the spring of 1258 Death came to claim his entitlements. Death was a great lord, so great that he did not ask the tithe-tenth the Church claimed, nor the third part that King and Baron claimed. No, Death was a great lord.

He took all.

It began in the manor house, for stone walls and glass win dows could not keep out the rats, and the fever they brought. By sunrise the chapel bell tolled for the baron and his daughter. By noon the tolling bell had fallen silent, and within the keep the people lay where they had fallen, as if struck with sudden sleep.

~ ~ ~

Everyone knew what the tolling of the bell meant. It had harried them from the fields back to the village, where they huddled together and prayed Lord Death would pass them by.

Mog had been christened at the baptism in the name of Margaret, but Margaret Harald's-daughter became first Mogret and then Mog to a mother who had birthed and buried six Margarets and could have expected, in the ordinary course of things, to birth and bury six more. In secret Mog had dreamed of things impossible for a villein's daughter and called herself Catherine after the daughter of the lord temporal whose whim circumscribed her world; Aelfric Whitehand who owned her family and the land they lived on as the king owned him and his knights in turn. She was the first to fall ill.

A false clarity in her mind made her think herself as full of words as a tales-man. She got up from her knees and preached the words the angels whispered in her ears, until her father's fist knocked her sprawling in the mud. He saw the fever in her eyes, and would have driven her from the village, but her mother wept and begged and carried Mog away to the straw pallet in the sleeping loft. There Mog lay, her bones on fire with the words of angels, until darkness carried her away.

Thirst woke her, and her skirts were damp with piss. She did not know how long she had slept, but when she came down from the sleeping loft, there was nothing but silence and the stench of decay. She called out, but inside herself Mog already knew no one would answer.

There was no water in the house, and she was still too weak to raise the bucket from the well, but there was beer, and she drank her fill. Reeling drunk, Mog passed through the village. The people lay in their beds or before their hearths, beneath the open sky or in sketchy graves no one had time to fill. They were black and wasted or round and taut with decay: worms' meat, crows' meat, torn by dogs.

Dead.

It was something outside of Mog's expectations of life. If she had been dead herself she would have known what to do. If there had been someone else alive he would have bullied her, or Mog would have had someone to take care of. But she was quite alone.

She walked the five miles to the manor house. She had been here twice before: once on a Christmastide, and once when Aelfric's son had been born, but if she had not she would have been able to see it across the flat expanse of the Summer Country. It was a place as big as a barn, of stone and wood and bright white plaster and windows of real glittering glass: a place so large you could stay indoors all day and all night and never swelter in your own stink and itch.

As she approached, she could hear the howling of unfed dogs trapped in their kennels. Warily she circled the house, but there was no one to see and shout, to throw turds or clods or stones. The kitchen door opened to her, and there was no one there.

The kitchen bore the marks of a hasty looting, but even at the end of winter, an abundance of food remained. There was butter, still sweet, and last summer's dark rose honey. There was stale bread and hard cheese and half a sausage that had fallen into the ashes of the kitchen fire and been overlooked.

There was a stoneware crock of beer, and some dark bottles filled with a bitter liquid redder than berry-juice. Mog recognized it from the priest's cup at Mass: wine.

She was still thirsty. She drank.

~ ~ ~

She awoke again in such pain she was sure Lord Death had returned for her, but the hard black swellings in armpit and groin did not appear, and in a few hours the pain was gone as well. Sure now that neither Death nor Hell would claim her, Mog went from the kitchen – where she had the excuse if not the right to be – into the house, where she had no right to be at all.

No one stopped her. There was death and the stink of death, but these things had no power to harm her now. She passed through rooms beyond counting, until she came to where Catherine Aelfric's-daughter was laid out like a queen.

Her pale hair was brushed smooth and her braids were wrapped in embroidered ribbons. Her face was sunken in, hollowed like a skull; her eyes were blue and her lips blood-bitten and black. Maggots hatched under her tongue.

But she had died early enough for someone to lay her out with candles at her head and foot and her hands folded on a gold cross. Her room held treasures Mog had seen and heard of, and they were all here for her to touch. No one would know, and no one would see.

Mog ran amber beads through her fingers, each one red and clear as a drop of cider turned to stone. She held a silver cup bright enough that when she stared into its surface her own shadow stared back. In the clothespress there were four gowns – four! and Catherine already wearing one! – overtunic and undertunic and smock; wool carefully spun and as carefully woven, dyed with the deep enduring hues of colors bargained for in Flemish courts. There was a cloak so blue it was as if it were made of autumn sky or the hearts of flowers, and so thick that wearing it would be like wearing three dresses together. She left them all behind.

She still thought, if she took them, that there would be someone in all the world to see.

~ ~ ~

The penned animals still begged for freedom, but dogs bit and horses trampled, and she was afraid to go near enough to them to let them out. The cats were luckier. She saw one sleeping in a patch of sunlight in the mews; it saw her and ran toward her, calling her in a rusty voice, but to see a live free thing in that mortuary house was uncanny, and she fled from it.

~ ~ ~

There was a market town half a day's journey up the road, and Mog had been there – twice! – to sell and to buy. In ordi nary time, the town would have been the farthest bound of the world she could know, but the road did not end there. There was a grander city beyond, built at the edge of the sea. Her father had been there once and had spoken of it: a place vast beyond imagination, filled with the engines of weavers and the business of men whose trade was in yarn and fleeces, dyes and grain. It was a place she had dreamed of seeing, just as she had dreamed herself Catherine and not Mog, and so she went home again to dress herself in the best of her clothes, to make a bindle of the bread and cheese she'd brought away from the manor house, to wrap her feet in greased rags against the peril of the road. She still hoped someone would stop her – if not here, then somewhere along the way. Surely Lord Death had not taken all the earth for his teind.

There was no sense to starting a journey so late in the day, but the desperation of her solitude drove her to it – a quiet insistence she did not recognize as panic. It drove her from the village as the sun began to fall from the sky, and onto the packed worn earth of the road that led to a greater road that led to the city by the sea.

The hand of Man had always lain heavy on the Summer Country, and the spring had brought rain, as it always did. The first weir she passed was full to bursting with catch-water need ing to be let into the fields, lest it eat the weir away entire. She labored nearly an hour to raise the gate and ease the weir. And when she'd done that she went on, and the second ditch she crossed was just as full.

She looked down at the wood and leather gate. And then she looked all around, at a landscape as flat as the surface of a frozen pond, dry land called into being by the hand of Man, from which Man was absent.

She left the second gate unraised and went on.

She walked until it was too dark to see and lay down in the middle of the road to sleep. The morning light woke her and she walked on. And at noon day she reached the market-town.

It was empty of the living and choked with the dead.

She danced through the empty streets, singing and set ting fires. She howled like a brute beast and went on hands and knees. She passed through any door she chose and carried away what she chose, and by every art and defiance tried to summon someone to come, to care, to show Mog Harald's-daughter her true place again.

No one came.

She pissed in the church.

God did not strike her.

She wiped her bottom with the shewbread from behind the altar.

Satan did not come.

After, there was a time she did not truly remember later, but one day she found herself on the road again. It was almost summer, now, with berries on the bush and fruits setting on the trees and the bright flowers blooming. She lived on weeds and green fruit and raw eggs, and on what she could loot. The dead she encountered now were bare bones sheathed lightly in dried skin; mice and insects and birds had done their work, and what remained did not stink, let alone frighten. Panic had gone, and the first hot pang of fear had long since cooled. And now it was a whole season gone, and she had seen no other soul alive.

When she reached the sea at last, she gazed out upon a stretch of coast as unpopulated as the land at her back. That she had taken a wrong turning upon the unfamiliar road did not occur to her. All places were the same to her now; it seemed so much more likely that the town had withered to bone, to ash, that the dead and empty husk of it had been torn apart by the wind. She turned away from the bright and empty sea and headed north and east, as innocently and unconsciously as an animal. But she was not an animal. What she was she could not say: her definition had been in other people: Harald's daughter, Aelfric's villein, some day to be this one's wife, that one's mother. Now there were no other people, and she was only Mog.

(Catherine.)

~ ~ ~

In the summer of that year the fields were gold and heavy with wheat. The orchards were filled with fruit. The dogs that had not starved had gone wild; the few sheep the wolves had not taken wandered randomly across garden, meadow, and field; the cows and horses had long since died in stall and byre of burst udders, thirst, and starvation. But the cats remained.

In a village that looked much like any other (as empty, as silent), Mog found a mother cat suckling her kittens, and out of some sense of duty to the way things once had been took away the kittens, bundling them in her apron, and threw them down the well.

She watched, leaning over the lip, as the thin cries faded one by one and the last small warm furry head disappeared beneath the surface. When the water was calm once more she stood up. The mother cat was watching her; when she moved, the cat came forward, mewing, stropping itself about her ankles. She would have given the kittens back, then, but it was too late. The mother cat followed her out of the village, pendulous nursing belly swinging, but Mog (Catherine) only walked faster, and after a while she didn't see it any more. That night she thought she heard the kittens crying on the wind, but in time that, too, faded.

I shall become a cat, she decided later. *The world has not changed, for cats.*

~ ~ ~

The days shortened into autumn – haying weather, harvesting weather – and still she walked. For the sake of walking, for the sound of her feet on the road. She passed by farmsteads and villages without a second glance, but the unfamiliar trappings of wealth still fascinated her, and so, when she saw the Great House, she turned toward it. She was bold enough, now, to go to the front door. It was barred tight, as if that could keep Lord Death out, but the door to the buttery was unbarred.

Her feet had grown hard with a season's walking; they made sharp sounds on the stone floor as she crossed it. Cat inspected hanging hams and jugs of potted fruit with a grimy, knowing finger. Such profligacy no longer shocked her; the wide world was her town and everything in it; in a philosophic sense everything she saw belonged to her.

She passed on.

They had not been so long dead here as elsewhere. The Great Hall was filled with bodies; velvets layered with fustian, clogs and dainty embroidered slippers discarded together. In the summer heat the bodies had ripened and burst like berries; they glistened now with decay, webbed with corpse-mold, in sects quarrelling beneath their flesh. But she had seen dead be yond dead; more dead than she could count. She investigated the bodies, and picked up one of the slippers. It was white kid leather, only as long as her hand, and the toe was embroidered with pearls. Cat walked up the broad stair, carrying the shoe.

There were no cats here but one.

She found it in a cradle, dressed in baby clothes. It, too, was dead; smothered, perhaps, to make it lie so still and pretty. She touched it, picked it up. Beneath its clothes, the body was slick and slippery with rot, and the fluids of decay had seeped into the delicate embroidered garments, staining and stiffening them. She puzzled over why someone would dress a cat as a dollbaby, because she was a cat, was Queen of the Cats, and if cats could die it meant that Cat herself could die.

She left it there and wandered through the house of the dead, gathering treasures: a necklace of pearls, a great brooched hat with a long red feather, a cloak lined in the pelts of foxes, red shoes with silver buckles. Bright jeweled garments, too small for her and too hot for the season. She opened the seams with a silver knife and added the knife to her treasures, hers now, as the whole world was hers. At last she returned to the cradle, and picked up the cat, and carried it with her to the churchyard. There were empty graves here no one had lived long enough to fill. She spaded in enough earth to cover and walked away. Soon, the cat and the memory of the cat would both be gone.

But they weren't. The riddle haunted her dreams; a beast dressed in human clothes. Did that make it human?

If she took off her clothes did that make her a beast?

If she put on silks and jewels did that make her a noble?

If Death had killed God and Satan both there was no one left to see into her heart. All they would see was her body. All they would hear was her voice. She sang nonsense songs as she walked down the road wearing silk and jewels.

Harvest became Hallentide, became winter and then hard winter.

In hard winter one huddled by the fire to survive, eked hoardings into soup and porridge, fetched well-water with great reluctance. In winter one burned dung and hoped to live until the first green of Lady Day.

In hard winter she was Queen of the Cats and king of a town. Cold had driven her within its walls; after so long in open country the walls and lanes of made stone were as strange to her as Heaven and Hell. *I have wandered into Faerie,* she told herself. There was no one to contradict her; thus, everything she said became truth. And so Cat claimed the crown of Faerie.

She burned wood for her fire as if she were a lord and starved as if she were a beast: the getting of food required many hands to turn seed into harvest, into flour, into bread, and Lord Death had taken them all. The cats came to her and she shared warmth and melted snow. And in the darkest cruelest cold – perhaps even Christmastide, though she had lost count of Mass days and Feast days long ago – she saw the sign.

It was a curl of smoke, making its ladder to heaven against the ice-pale sky of Winter. She had been fooled in summer by lightning strikes that kindled trees to mock chimneys, but winter held no natural fires. She watched the smoke against the sky three days before she followed it to its source.

And there she saw a soul alive.

He was a tattered man, black as a tinker – black as Cat who was black as the Queen of Sheba, former queen of cats – and he sheltered within a copse of winter-stark trees in a swale cut off from the wind. He had a shabby cart with a shabbier pony between the traces and a tiny grudging fire.

"Man, mortal Man," the Queen of the Cats breathed to herself. The snow was hard-packed and windswept, silent to walk upon. She wore white velvet and a hood over her hair. She had heard him singing to himself and so knew to stop at the farthermost distance from which she could see him, to lie down upon the snow with her white cloak spread about her like a pool of frost; to watch.

The sight of him made angels whisper to her of forgot ten things, of catching goats and penning chickens, of plant ing corn and making cider. Of plain warm clothes and feather beds and fresh-baked bread, and the world turning predictably on its axis once more.

"Mortal man," Cat said to herself again, and slithered away.

After that she made no great fires; stopped up the chim ney with rags and endured the smoke for the sake of secrecy. And slowly a difficult thought hatched out in her mind – a strange, hard-edged thought, and entirely unlike anything that had come before it.

She did not want things back just the way they had been.

The sight of the man brought back memory of meekly keeping silent and doing as she was bidden. Of knowing the silks and velvets she now wore would never be for her. Of endless labor to the purposes of others – and, again, of nev er speaking out, never speaking her mind, always holding her tongue.

Cat looked down at the clothes she wore, and thought again of the cat dressed in human clothes. A great marvel, that; a cat taken for human.

What could Cat make of herself – and what could she be taken for?

~ ~ ~

Inevitably the man came to her town, but Cat had been given weeks in which to know its streets and alleys, and she easily kept herself from his sight. He staggered among the buildings like a blind man, leading his starving pony, and Cat watched him with a personal amazement. *What had been* said run to him, announce herself, draw the rags of the old world about them both. *What might be* said…

Wait.

He stayed through the hardest cold, looting what he could. The cats came to him and he drove them away with thrown bricks and curses. Cat took them in and promised them ven geance … but she lied.

She knew she lied when she spoke to them, running her fingers through their warm fur as they huddled with her before her small and secret fire. She didn't care for her subjects, only for the fact that they still lived. She would desert them for the chance to live herself, and so she did, for when the mortal man left the village, Cat waited a day and then followed after him.

She combed her hair with an ivory comb and wrapped herself in furs. She hung ropes of gold and pearls about her throat, set brooches to her gown and rings to her fingers, and took the road that he had taken.

She did not know yet what she meant to do, only that she must do it right when the right time came.

There was a green haze over the winter-black earth, and the red of returning life in the buds upon the hard branches, but the air was cold and raw, for Springtide was a false and faithless jade, promising a warmth and ease not in her gift to grant. But the Queen of the Cats was as cunning and clever as her subjects: she knew (as she knew true spring would come, and summer) that not even Death endured forever, and if she were to escape the last of his traps she must be watchful and valiant.

The man and his beast went north and east. He had nursed his pony through the winter on bark-scraps and straw that had once been bedding, and it accompanied him still. Cat wondered what sign that was, for there was Lord Death and Lord Christ and Queen Mary and the Queen of Cats, and in far London there was the England King, but there was no lord of horses.

Perhaps she would ask.

The signs of their passage were hoofprints in the road, bark peeled from trees, ash and bone. In the night, sometimes there was a distant spark of fire and the scent of roasting meat; scraps of tuneless singing to be heard upon the wind.

She passed with her quarry into a realm of great trees. Deer startled from her path, doves called from the air above, hares watched her as she passed. Here and everywhere the land raced into life, and still she waited for a sign.

Cats followed her in her dreams, ethereal as ghosts. The mother whose children she had slain, holding the power of Lord Death between her hands. The dollbaby who had been neither child nor cat, but a new thing, changed by the garments of its array. The silent army she had called to her hand as lord and king. Each had held knowledge in its jeweled eyes, knowledge that there was no one left to know her any longer. Knowledge that Death could not claim her, nor could the faeries strike her down. She was a queen.

And so when she dreamed in the night of an angel with wings of fire, she did not fear. His robes were the skins of leopards and his cloak was the skin of a lion. In his hand he held a bell of gold, and as she gazed at it the brightness of it grew more dazzling and more terrible–

Until she awoke to the sound of bells. Some charterhouse, some chapterhouse, some community of Godly men and women who worked and prayed, tolled a bell to mark the dark hours of prayer. And with that sound of life (of people, of the world she had left behind), the bounds of the world turned from mist to stone, and the things she had held as certainties were turned from true silver to dross and tawdry. Mog and Cat, the Queen of the Cats and the King of Faerie quarreled beneath her skin, and in her heart, Lord Death whispered to her:

Choose.

She sat sleepless through the rest of the night, and when she could see the branches above against the sky beyond, she got to her feet and shook the dirt from her velvet robes. She settled the cloak of fur and velvet about her shoulders and began to hurry toward where the man lay asleep.

~ ~ ~

He was shaggy and unkempt, and his eyes were wild at the sight of her.

"Hail, mortal man," she said. Her voice was rusty with disuse, as hoarse as a cat's cry. She watched as the man crossed himself, hands shaking with fear and wonder, and tightened her fingers on the silver knife hidden in the fold of her skirts.

"Lady," he said, his eyes filled with her jewels and her rich gown. "Are you body or spirit? I have seen no one living from high summer until this moment."

He had been squatting when she came, coaxing his small fire back to life, and had not dared to stand, but had fallen upon his knees.

"I am whatever I choose to be," the Queen of the Cats answered. "Call me as you choose."

"Lady, I dare not," he whispered, and to see fear upon the face of a man was sweet, and so she smiled.

"You have travelled long in the lands of Lord Death," she told him, and the words that had first found themselves in her mind in the days of fever, that had burgeoned and ripened and fruited during all the long days of her sojourn in Faerie, uncoiled now between her lips. "And soon you will pass once more into the lands of the living, reborn as if you were a suck ing babe. What guise will you put on in mortal lands? I tell you: Lord Death has slain your past."

He stared so long into her face that she thought the sight of her had stolen his voice, as the subjects of her kingdom stole the breath of children, but at last he spoke.

"Lady, I– I dare not be more than I am."

Cat reached up and lifted from her neck one of the chains she wore. It was of gold, long and intricate, relieved along its length by plaques of gold set with enamel. She held its heavy weight in her hands as she closed the space between them, and dropped it before him.

"Take it up," she said, in such a voice as Margaret Harald's-daughter had never dreamed to possess. He flinched away from the sound of it, but his hands closed upon the rope of gold. He stared at it as if he had never imagined such a thing could be in all the world, then lifted it up and set it upon his neck.

"I shall reveal to you a great secret," Cat said. "I am no mortal maid, but the Queen of the Cats, come out of Faerie to make you a great lord."

"Lady, I beg you!" the man cried. "Do not jest with me – I have little enough, but my soul is promised to Heaven!"

"I do not jest. I tell you truly: I am a great queen, and I have in my hand the power to raise you up as high as I choose. Tell me your name, man. Tell me who you were in life – master, servant, lord, fool? Who were you?"

"I am no one," she heard him whisper, and knew it for a prayer, a petition, a plea. "Tom. Tom son of Tom, a tinker as my father was before me."

"I say you are no tinker, no Tom," the Queen of the Cats answered gravely. "I say by the jewel about your neck that you are of noble birth, for who but a great lord might possess such a chain? Your kingdom is in a far land across the water, yet all you own has been stolen from you by a usurper, and in escaping his vengeance all your meine was slain. You travel now to seek aid from your kinsmen in the north, and all who aid you shall be richly rewarded."

She spoke the words as if they had long been true. She held the secret she had brought with her out of Lord Death's kingdom beneath her tongue like a pearl: seeming was truth. She saw his face as he struggled to believe, to learn in a morning the truths she had learned through the seasons.

"Of noble birth," he said doubtfully.

"I have said so, and so it shall be. Rise up, Lord Thomas," the Queen of the Cats said. She stretched out her hand to him, and after a long moment his fingers closed about hers, as gingerly as if the rings on her fingers were set with coals of fire.

"Lord Thomas," he said in wonder. He looked down at his stained and tattered clothes, at the filthy rags that wrapped his limbs from knee to toe. "This is no noble raiment."

"It is not important," Cat said. "Upon this road lies a religious house, and there we shall claim lodging, and robes fitting for a lord of another land."

"And horses?" Tom asked eagerly. "I would go a-horse, like– In the way I have been used to go," he finished, and the look upon his face was amazement and the beginnings of faith.

"They will not dare to send you forth afoot," Cat said with certainty. "But for now, I shall ride and you shall walk."

She stood unmoving as he scrambled to set a rope around the pony's neck and lead it to her side. There was uncertainty and adoration on his face as he put his hands upon her to lift her into place. She clutched at the pony's mane as it stepped forward. When they came to the edge of the stand of trees, she could see the monastery in the distance. Its bell began to toll, sweet and far, summoning the living to pray. Lord Thomas hesitated a moment, then began to lead the pony down the path that led to its door.

She knew Lord Thomas did not yet truly understand she had done a true thing, but he had shown her it could be so. Belief had made him kneel to her, speak to her in soft fearful words, do all she ordered. And as he had done, so would oth ers do. Lord Death had showed her there was only seeming. It took nothing more than courage to choose the seeming you desired, for the world was ruled by fear, and the fearful could not imagine courage.

They would believe. They would all believe.

And nothing else mattered.

A Child's Cry

by Heather Graham and Jason Pozzessere

New York Times and *USA Today* bestselling author, Heather Graham, majored in theater arts at the University of South Florida. After a stint of several years in dinner theater, back-up vocals, and bartending, she stayed home after the birth of her third child and began to write. Her first book was with Dell, and since then, she has written more than one hundred novels and novellas, including category, suspense, historical romance, vampire fiction, time travel, occult, and Christmas family fare.

She is pleased to have been published in approximately twenty languages and she has 60 million books in print. She has been honored with awards from Walden Books, B. Dalton, Georgia Romance Writers, *Affaire de Coeur*, *Romantic Times* and more. Heather has also become the proud recipient of the Silver Bullet from International Thriller Writers. Heather has had books selected for the Doubleday Book Club and the Literary Guild, and has been quoted, interviewed, or featured in such publications as *The Nation*, *Redbook*, Mystery Book Club, *People*, and *USA Today*, and appeared on many newscasts including "Today," "Entertainment Tonight," and local television.

Heather loves travel and anything that has to do with the water, and is a certified scuba diver. She also loves ballroom dancing. Each year she hosts the Vampire Ball and Dinner theater at the RT convention, raising money for the Pediatric Aids Society, and in 2006 she hosted the first Writers for New Orleans Workshop to benefit the stricken gulf region. She is also the founder of "The Slush Pile Players," presenting something that's almost like entertainment for various conferences and benefits. Married since high school graduation and the mother of five, her greatest love in life remains her family, but she also believes her career has been an incredible gift, and she is grateful every day to be doing something that she loves so very much for a living.

Heather's newest series The Krewe of Hunters has released, *The Evil Inside*, *Phantom Evil*, *Heart of Evil*, and *Sacred Evil* in 2011. Releases in 2012 include *The Unseen*, *The Unholy*, *The Unspoken*, and *The Uninvited.*

The character of Mallory Hampton was actually created by my co-writer on this project, Jason Pozzessere, my oldest son. Along with his siblings, Jason spent his summers going up and down the east coast of the United States, attending re-enactments, visiting battlefields and museums, and, considering that his friends thought he belonged to the real life Addams family, going on ghost tours.

As a family, we all fell in love with Harpers Ferry. The natural beauty of the place was enhanced for us by a wonderful woman named Shirley. She was the "ghost" tour guide at the time, taking visitors on voyage through time, lantern in hand, teaching history – the facts, just the facts – and then what people believed they had seen in the mists that so often haunt the junction where Virginia, West Virgina, and Maryland meet across rapid filled rivers and high cliffs and love valleys.

Mallory is at a cross – a place we all reach. Almost grown up, but not quite. Falling in love, and finding out it's not all it might be cracked up to be. Learning that family is the biggest pain possible – and the lifeline we're given when we're lucky.

For both of us, Mallory is special. We created her and flushed her out together, and we had an opportunity to look back at the past from two perspectives – life as I saw it, and life as he saw it. And, now, of course, as years have gone by, I can look back sometimes and see a zillion mistakes I made as a parent. And yet, as we wrote about Harpers Ferry together, it was remarkable to realize that yes, we did a few things right as well!

Mallory has a little bit of all of us in her, because the child struggling to become an adult continues to exist in all of us, long after we have reached the legal age of maturity.

"Will you play with me?"

The question sounded eerie; the tone of the voice speak ing the words seemed soft and oddly disembodied.

Mallory Hampton started at the sound of the voice, look ing around to try and discern who had spoken. She'd thought she was alone – alone at the top of a hill in a cemetery where a low-lying mist swirled around gravestones, but it had seemed the only place to be alone at the time she'd taken the steps up here.

"Play with me, please!"

A shot of fear swept through her, despite the fact that she wasn't generally unnerved; she wasn't afraid of shadows or graves or silly "scream" costumes, and, seriously, would a serial killer hang around a silly Civil War weekend where wom en were dressed up in long skirts and soldiers were running around with muskets?

A serial killer? A pedophile? Someone who knew that she was alone here, that no other tourists – or locals, for that matter – were here alone, surrounded by nothing but gravestones, monuments, and overgrown trees and foliage?

And, seriously, would a serial killer hang around in this cra ziness? Down the steep hill in the National Park, someone was giving a lecture as John Brown, the abolitionist who had tried to raid the arsenal, while someone else was giving a speech as Robert E. Lee, sent by the Secretary of War to stop the sedi tion. Surely, only historian crazies – like her father – would be running around Harpers Ferry today.

Mallory steeled herself, mentally and physically, and looked around. She saw no one at all. And it had sounded like a child's voice, curious, friendly . . . eager for companionship.

She took a deep breath and wondered if too much quality family time had finally made her lose her mind. Really – there was absolutely no one anywhere near her, and if someone had been hiding in the trees that surrounded the cemetery – except for the area that looked over the hill onto the beauty of the rivers rushing together below – that someone would have sounded quite different. The voice would have come to her across the space and be tossed on the breeze. No, no one was there. The pressure of *being her* was getting to her at last. She was cracking.

Still, a rivulet of fear seemed to swim through her veins.

Get a grip! she warned herself.

Maybe someone was playing a joke on her. Maybe even her little brother – capable as the next little brother of being totally obnoxious. And maybe he had followed her up here to torture her, just because she'd been freed from him for a while.

"Please, play with me."

The voice came again. A sweet voice, *a child's voice.*

"Jonah, is that you?" Mallory called out sharply. She set her hands on her hips, feigning a show of strength and anger. "If you ran off on mom and dad and followed me up here, you are in big trouble, little man!" she announced.

There was no reply. Nothing other than the soft rustle in the darkening line of trees and foliage that surrounded the lonely little cemetery at the top of the hill.

It's not Jonah! Mallory told herself.

It couldn't be Jonah; she had taken the long and winding walk just about straight uphill to the cemetery on the heights because she'd been allowed to escape her little brother – and ye olde big sister duty of carrying around her darling but poop-dispensing baby sister, Emily. Thank God her parents had decided that she needed a break. She really didn't even want to be here – here on a wretched family trip.

This was the first family road trip they had taken together since Anthony, her other brother, older by just one year, had headed off to college in New Jersey. Anthony had been truly freed from the family autumnal travel – except that the crazy boy would be driving south and meeting up with them later.

He was free . . . but he'd with them by tonight.

Then again, Anthony had always been a good kid – *the* good kid, when it came to the two of them.

A straight-shooter. Anthony had great grades, Anthony al ways dated nice girls, Anthony was responsible.

Still, even though she resented her older brother some times for being super-child, these trips had always seemed fine when he was with them. The two of them had found the ar cades, the shops, or whatever together, and she hadn't been the only one holding a baby half the day or dragging Jonah back to the dinner table at whatever mom-and-pop restaurant they had landed in. He would be there tonight; she was almost saved. Not that her parents didn't tend to their younger offspring, but, honestly, sometimes, Mallory felt heavy laden.

"I wish you were here now, Anthony!" she murmured aloud. If Anthony were here, would she be hearing voices? Yes, of course, Anthony's, as he chastised her for her latest fling, or told her that to be heartbroken over a high school jerk-jock was ridiculous.

A soft laugh rose on the breeze; again, it was a child's laugh. "*Hide and seek, hide and seek!*"

So, it wasn't Jonah. Some other little obnoxious kid was running around up here.

She turned around, trying to figure where the little kid was hiding, but she nearly tripped over a tombstone and looked down. Straightening and regaining her balance, she noted that she was by the gravestone of a Confederate soldier. The name on the tombstone was Jeremy Mason. He'd died at the age of twenty-three. She paused to note with a sad shake of her head that Jeremy had been killed in April, 1865, fighting with Lee's army of Northern Virginia. The soldier must have died right before Lee's surrender at Appomattox Courthouse. Now, that was tragic. A few more weeks of life for Jeremy, and the war would have been over, and he might have lived to a ripe old age.

She knew a lot about the American Civil War. God knew, she'd been dragged around to enough reenactments.

Mallory took a step and realized that she hadn't tripped over the stone; she had tripped over the remnants of a family enclosure. She saw the name *Mason* on a larger monument and realized that there were at least several stones with bits and pieces of the name remaining, though time had worn down the etching in several places.

"A family," she murmured, and then she paused. Sympathy filled her where fear had taken hold. One of the graves was for a childshe recognized the little cherubs on the small-sized stone as funerary art that identified the grave of a little on. She couldn't make out the first name, but the last name was Mason as well.

She knelt down and smudged some of the algae off the gravestone. The child had not survived hildhood – the date of death read October 17th, Year of Our Lord, 1864. That had been after 1859 – the infamous year here when John Brown had attempted to take the arsenal at Harpers Ferry. She knew the dates, of course, because she'd been attending lectures all morning with her parents – or, attending them, and then run ning after Jonah or sweeping up a crying Emily to allow her mom and dad to listen to the lecture. John Brown's raid had been a prelude to the Civil War; hanged, as the law decreed, he had become a martyr to the Northern cause. And, of course, once the war had begun, Harpers Ferry had become some thing of a ping-pong ball, changing hands over and over again throughout the years of fighting that began with the shelling of Ft. Sumter in April of 1861.

Sad – this was so sad. She found herself wondering if – and hoping that – the parents had other children beside those they had lost. How incredibly sad to lose them both!

She let out a soft sigh, having forgotten the voice for a minute. There was a little patch of wildflowers growing not too far away, struggling against the arrival of autumn. She walked over and picked two little white buds, bent down to her knees and placed them on the graves.

"Hello!" another voice called to her cheerfully.

She looked up. A young man in uniform – obviously com ing up from the various exhibits, speeches, and reenactments below – had made the climb to the misty cemetery. For a mo ment, he stood out against the golden red sky of dusk, and she thought that he looked very impressive there. He was her senior by a few years, she thought, probably college age. Or maybe he hadn't gone to college; maybe he worked in the one of the town's restaurants or was a visitor such as herself.

"Hello," she said.

She watched, frowning as he made his way to her; she wasn't sure what his uniform signified.

"Sorry to interrupt; I'm looking for a wayward child," he told her, grimacing.

"I haven't seen anyone, but I might have *heard* your way ward child," Mallory told him. "I keep hearing a little kid who wants to play."

He nodded. "That would be my brother," he said grimly. "I'm sorry if he's been a pest." He slid down to his knees by her, curious and friendly, and offering a hand as he introduced himself. "J.J. Pleased to meet you. You're visiting?" he asked.

"Mallory," she told him, smiling. "From Daytona Beach – Florida."

"Ah. Well, that's a fair trip," he said.

"Yes, well, it's a pain in the butt trip, really. For some rea son, my parents always want to make a fall trip. Yes, yes, the world is in school – it's nearly Halloween time, a nice time to be home, but . . . well, my parents like to take a fall trip."

He sat down in the grass next to her and chewed on a blade of grass. "Ah, yes, I know it well, the parental yoke!" he said. "They never wanted me leaving, but . . . "

"But you're here," she said.

"I'm here every year for these 'John Brown' days," he told her. "So, how did they get you to come along? Bribery? Threats?"

Mallory hesitated. "Well, it's true that I'm not at all sure I wanted to be here. But, honestly, so far, it's not that it's such a bad trip. But my little brother was really hanging on me and driving me crazy, so I've been reprieved for a spell. I actually used to love our little four-day autumn excursions. We'd start in the morning, make Williamsburg by the evening, have a co lonial dinner or do some such thing, hit an amusement park the next day . . . it's better when my older brother is along. Anthony. When we were younger, we'd do the amusement park thing, and the next day we'd spend at the Smithsonian, or hiking in the Blue Ridge Mountains, or heading off to a Civil

War reenactment. We ate at Civil War camps, learned about old weapons – it really wasn't all bad." She laughed softly. "But, my mom had to keep procreating. Jonah came along, and then Emily, and – as you apparently know – keeping up after little ones makes everything harder. Now . . ."

He laughed. "You still didn't answer. Bribery or a threat?"

Before she could answer, she heard the child's voice call out again. *"Come on! Let's play. Hide and seek, hide and seek!"*

"Bryce!" J.J. called. "No torturing the visitors! I'll find you in just a minute, you mark my words, young man." He looked at Mallory ruefully again. "So – bribery, or threat?"

She paused, thinking she should just lie to him. Tell him that she was a great kid, as good as her brother Anthony, and she enjoyed her family and knew that she was about to go out into the world, away from them.

She barely knew this guy. But, he was friendly, he was here, and he was really good looking, not that she really needed to flirt with someone twenty-something from West Virginia. But, he seemed honestly nice.

She let out a breath and laughed. "The truth? I suppose I could have gotten out of it. The truth? I decided to come, not that I was that good a daughter or anything. I was dating one of our high school jocks who turned out to be a jerk, and rumor is that he's been seeing one of my best friends, so . . . there's a big early Halloween party going on tonight, and I'm not sure if I cut off my own nose to spite my face, but I de cided just not to be there."

"Ah," he said, grinning.

"I had a really great costume and everything," Mallory said. "This sexy little 'Legs Avenue' Marie Antoinette. Oh, well, somewhere along the line I'll get to use it . . . I think I did cut off my nose to spite my face. Football jock and ex-best-friend will probably just be relieved that I'm not there, but at least I won't have to watch. And, while I have the little tormenters with me now – I ran up here for a few minutes of peace, my brother is seven and my baby sister isn't quite two – my older brother will get here tonight. Now, he's a fool. He's in college in New Jersey, but he must be a semi-masochist; he's driving down to be with us."

"Well, that's impressive. Maybe he misses you. You, and all the family."

"Anthony is a lot like my dad – a crazy history buff. And in all these years and all these trips, this is the first time we've come to Harpers Ferry. Seriously, crazy name, huh? There isn't even a ferry here."

J.J. laughed. "You know there was a ferry here, of course, at one time."

"Yes, yes, I've been through the history lectures and the reenactments all day long. It's really beautiful – the water, the hills, the mountains – whatever they really are. And I've enjoyed all the stuff going on. Most of the area right here is owned by the National Park Service, right?" J.J. nodded and she contin ued. "I've had a good time – except, of course, in the middle of the really perfect reenactor relaying his story as John Brown regarding the infamous raid on Harpers Ferry, Emily started crying, and for the moment, I did opt to be a good kid and let my mom – who seemed ridiculously enthralled – see the end of the performance or lecture or whatever, and I took Emily out of the group and over to the little café to try to get her to sleep. I was successful, and when they came back, my mom suddenly realized that I was there, and she told me to head out shopping for a while, to take a break. Then I thought that my seven-year-old brother had followed me, but now, I guess that it's your little brother, right? Bryce?"

"Yes, it's my brother, Bryce. He does this to me every sin gle year," J.J. said, sighing. "Except now . . . now I really don't mind chasing after him so much." He grinned. "So, you have a few minutes' grace, eh? Let me show you something."

He stood and reached down to give her a hand up. She accepted it. They left the cemetery area, walking toward the cliff. "We have some crazy fun stories here, too. There once was a man named James Brown who lived here; when he died, he wanted to be buried standing up, his head above ground in a glass dome. He paid a kid to watch it for a week; when he didn't come back to life and the seven days were over, the kid stopped watching the grave. The glass broke in time, and the skull became all imbedded with dirt and grass and local school kids crossing over at night would kick it around, like a ball.

Well, the authorities thought that it was *the* John Brown's head when they found it, and they mailed it to his widow in New York who indignantly sent it back. It's reburied somewhere."

"Sad and creepy!" Mallory said.

"Here's a beautiful one for you . . . come, come out to the walk, and you can see Maryland and Virginia and West Virginia, and the beauty of the river below. George Washington was the one to think that this would be an amazing place for an armory, and, of course, John Brown came here because of the weapons. Two Southern heroes, Robert E. Lee and Jeb Stuart, were with the Union army then, and they were sent out here to stop the fracas. Brown was a fanatic, and while he became a martyr, he was still a murderer, and that was pretty much so recognized at the time. But you know all that. I'm going to tell you about Potomac and Shenandoah." He pointed across the water. The light was fading, but it still touched upon the mounts and the rugged cliff lines and the dancing, sparkling water of the rivers below. "They were lovers. Shenandoah's father wouldn't let her marry Potomac; he wasn't of their tribe. Potomac tried to prove himself, and he fought a mutual enemy. Then, hoping he had earned a place in her father's heart, he tried to reach her, but as he traveled, a flood came, and he died in the river, crying her name. The river rose to become a great river, while Shenandoah, watching for her lover and then learning that he had died, threw herself over the cliff, and she was crying with such heartache that another river was formed, and now, they are forever together, forever touching, and forming a great and beautiful bond."

"Very romantic," Mallory told him.

"Hey!" called the strange little voice. Now it seemed to be coming from the direction of the cemetery. "I'm still hiding!"

The voice wasn't scary or creepy. Hearing it, Mallory laughed. "I think Bryce really wants to play."

J.J. offered her his hand. She liked his smile; she liked his sandy hair and the way he seemed to care so much about his little brother. "Want to help me find him? Whoops, sorry, I shouldn't be asking. You just escaped little brother duty."

"I don't mind at all," she told him.

She took his hand; she was glad that he was there with her. They walked back to the cemetery where, in the growing dusk, the graves and the past seemed sad. The golds of twilights were fading to mauve and gray, and the mist settled around the graves as if cloaking them in the shadow of history.

"You come back, you do reenactments," Mallory said to J.J. "What makes you do such things, do you think?"

He paused and looked at her. "Because, I think, it's just important to remember where we were, what we came from . . . the past is always important to the future."

"You could just quote the philosopher, George Santayana. 'Those who cannot remember the past are doomed to repeat it,'" Mallory said.

He looked at her in surprise. "Well, that's it, entirely, of course. Who said that?"

"You've never heard of Santayana?" she asked him, surprised.

He grinned. "No, but I like him! Bryce! Bryce, come on, you've hidden long enough, give us a clue!"

"Yeah! Find me!" called the little voice.

"There!" Mallory exclaimed, seeing movement behind one of the cherub monuments in the cemetery. There really weren't huge monuments here – it was a lonelier, old cemetery, and many gravestones were missing or broken.

"Ah ha!" J.J. cried, releasing her hand. She watched as he ran toward the little stone cherub, worn with age. A little boy, giggling, dashed out. J.J. caught him and lifted him into the air, and the boy squealed with happiness. J.J. set him down and came to her.

"Be a gentleman, now. Bryce. Say hello to Mallory. And be careful how you play – you scared her up here, you know."

Bryce was dressed for the occasion, too. He wore breeches and suspenders and a flannel shirt. A Civil War kepi – much like one her mom had just brought her little brother – sat atop his head at an angle.

"Hello, Mallory. I didn't mean to scare you; I just wanted to play."

"That's fine, Bryce," she assured him. "It was lovely to make your acquaintance."

He grinned, and he was off, running toward the stone steps that led back to the main street of the town and the his toric district.

"Well, I'm off, then, Mallory. Are you all right up here? It's getting dark – you should follow us down. You can trip up here, hurt yourself," J.J. warned."

"Sure; I'll come down with you," she said.

Bryce seemed agile and sure of himself, hurrying ahead of the two of them. As they walked down, Mallory was glad that he'd asked to escort her – shadows were falling thickly now. She could barely see the colors of the leaves that still clung to a few of the trees, while many had fallen, leaving the branches stark and skeletal.

"What's the uniform you're wearing?" Mallory asked J.J.

"Virginia militia," he told her, grinning. "There was no West Virginia, you know, until 1862. And this area changed hands over and over again." He paused for a minute. "Union soldiers held a little Rebel drummer boy one time. Right in the house you see there, behind the café. They actually came to love him, and they would play with him, tossing him back and forth. Once, they tossed a bit too hard, and he went crashing through a second floor window and died on the rocks below. It was sad and tragic to everyone – North and South. Kind of a lesson in really learning how to compromise and get along with one another, huh? He was a Southern boy, related to a family with soldiers fighting on both sides."

They were nearing Church Street. As they arrived, a "com pany" of Union soldiers was walking by, and they were laugh ing as they were joined by their wives and friends who were wearing Confederate uniforms. Whatever battle they had re-created, they were done, and the battle lines no longer stood between them. "Davey!" One Union soldier called to a Reb. "Meet us for a beer up at the inn?"

"You bet!" the one called Davey replied.

"Looks like everyone is getting along now," Mallory said.

"Hey!" J.J. shouted, starting to hurry through the crowd. Mallory realized that Bryce had taken off through the group and was heading down toward the John Brown engine house. "Sorry, Mallory! Hope to see you later. Enjoy your time here."

He stopped suddenly while others walked by him, seeming mindless of the man who blocked their path. "Enjoy your time here, and enjoy your family. It's really priceless, you know!"

She lifted a hand in goodbye, suddenly sorry not that she was here, but that he was leaving her. Quick as a whisk, he was off after his little brother.

She smiled and dodged between the "soldiers" filling the street now to make her way across to the café, where she was sure her parents were waiting for her, beginning to worry.

They were; her mother was standing anxiously outside the door, watching for her. She gave Mallory a smile. "I'm sorry; I was starting to worry. So many cliffs around here, I mean anyone could fall down and get hurt!" She was holding baby Emily, but seemed just as anxious about Mallory.

Mallory reached for her sister. "Your arms must be killing you by now," she said.

"Oh, I'm fine. She's been running around the dummy of the Civil War soldier in front of that shop; she's getting tired now. Are you ready for some dinner?"

Mallory's dad came up behind her. "Anthony is due any time now; he's going to meet us at the restaurant."

As her father spoke, Jonah raced up to her, tugging at her shirt. "Mallory, guess what? We're going on a *ghost tour* tonight. Mom is taking that pain-in-the-butt Emily to bed, and you and me and dad and Anthony are going on a *ghost tour!*"

Mallory looked at her mother. "I can stay with Emily; you go."

Her mother shook her head. "Frankly, I'm exhausted. Em ily and I will go to bed, and you four can traipse up and down the hills tonight. It will be great."

An hour later, they were at the restaurant, and Anthony had arrived. Her brother already seemed to have aged tremen dously from his month or so in college, and she realized that it was wonderful to see him, and that it was the family as it had always been.

She was startled when she went to the counter to pay the check for her father. The man at the counter was the young soldier she had met at the cemetery, only his hair seemed different and his eyes appeared to be green rather than blue. "Hey!" she told him.

He was startled. "I'm sorry; I don't mean to be rude. Have we met?"

"Up at the cemetery today," she said. "I was resting – from my little brother. And you were chasing yours around."

He shook his head. "Must have been my doppelganger. And that's highly possible; my family has been from the area since the days of Washington. I've been working all day – it's a big money day for us." He smiled at her. "Honestly, I'd have remembered if I'd met you." He said the words in a friendly manner, with appreciation. He wasn't trying to pick her up or come up with some kind of sexual or ridiculous line; he was just being nice.

She flushed anyway. "Well, your doppelganger was very nice," she assured him.

As he handed her the change, an older man came up be hind him. He smiled at Mallory and then talked to the cashier, who was evidently his son. "Brian, you need to get going. You're giving the eight o'clock tour, right?"

"Yeah, yeah, Dad, it's me," the younger man said. He gri maced at Mallory. "Got to go get ye olde lantern. Hey, you should take our ghost tour. Or our 'history and legends' tour. I'm honestly pretty good." He lowered his voice and rolled his eyes. "I've been here forever and ever. I know all the stories."

"We *are* taking the ghost tour," she said, ridiculously pleased. Brian was about her age. A good six-foot-two. He had a wiry build, sandy hair, and . . . he was cute. Really cute. It was truly absurd for her to think so, since they'd have one more day here, she'd be heading back to Daytona Beach, next year she'd be in New York, and she'd never see him again.

But it was nice to think that he'd be leading the tour.

"Want to come with me – I mean, if it's okay with your family. I just have to stop by our shop, grab my lantern, hat, and frockcoat, and wait for others to join us."

"Let me just see," Mallory told him. She ran back to the table; her father was already up. Emily had fallen asleep and she was in her stroller. Jonah had Anthony's hand.

"I've been invited to go ahead with our tour guide," Mal lory said. She thought that she should help; they had to get her mother and the baby and the stroller and the day's packages back.

"Hey, so that's our tour guide?" her father said. "Young, huh?"

"And probably good," Anthony said. He flicked Mallory's hair; it had annoyed her when they were always together. To night, it felt nice. "I've got this, kid. Go off with the Harpers hunk, and have fun."

"Go!" her mother said.

She did.

Brian was waiting for her at the door. "It's cool to see you here," he told her. "You are a . . . senior in high school? We usually get a lot of locals my own age but not that many from out of town."

"Yes, I'm a senior. My last year as an "at home" child.My older brother is in college now, but . . . he made it down. We've taken a day or two and added it to a weekend in the fall. It's a family thing."

"Nice," he told her.

She was startled when they reached the family store to which he had referred. There was a large sign that read, "Ma son's Historic Curios – find your old treasures here."

"Mason?" she asked him. "I saw the name on graves up at the cemetery today."

He nodded. "Yes, there are a lot of us in the surrounding area. Too many of us at times. You can get lost at our family picnics."

His mother was working the counter in the shop; she was nice and seemed pleased to see Mallory, offering her a cape for the walk, since it would get chilly at night. As they walked around to the meeting place for the tour, she learned that he was a senior in high school as well.

It was a busy night, and though there were several tours, Mallory discovered that she was extremely grateful to be on Brian's tour. He talked about the arsenal, he talked about John Brown, and he told stories about "Screaming Jenny" and oth ers. He gave a great tour, giving just the history of the place, what had really happened – and then, what others believed had happened since, and thus the ghosts. And then, from a place on Church Street, eerily dark now by night, he pointed uphill, beyond the steps, and toward the cemetery.

"If you haven't done so yet, when you get a chance, you have to visit the cemetery. The four acres were set aside by Robert Harper when he died, even though there were only a few houses here at the time. You can get a fantastic view from up there, and by Jefferson Rock, too, of course." He lifted his lantern and grinned at the crowd. "I'm not taking you up there now – too dark. We value our tourists. But I have a lot of relatives up there. And that brings me to another ghost story – that of my long lost little cousin, Bryce Mason. Bryce was a drummer boy with a Virginia regiment . . ."

Mallory listened to his words, but she wasn't sure she heard them. She felt the darkness and the mist that seemed to hover in the street now sweep around her. She tried to tell herself that she'd seen Brian himself in the cemetery that day, playing with his own little brother. This was all a huge joke on her; she was the outsider, coming to Harpers Ferry. She slid closer to her father, holding his arm.

"It was a sad time for our family; the family's oldest brother, Jeremy James Mason, was also with the Virginia troops. When he died – right before Appomattox – he was found with a letter to his mother, and in his letter, he promised her that he'd be home soon, and he'd play with his little brother then – James never received word that his Bryce had died in a horrible accident. James spent the end of the war praying that he'd be home soon. He was home soon but, of course, in a coffin. Now, as far as the ghost story goes, some people say that Jeremy returns and plays games with Bryce when the mist settles over the hills and valleys, and that he's forever trying to make good on the promise he had made in his letters home. Now, we also have an alligator that haunts the streets of Harpers Ferry. Yes, folks, an alligator . . ."

She listened to the rest, barely hearing. To make matters worse, in the midst of it – when she determined she was going to Google one of his facts to check it out, she realized that she was missing her phone.

When the tour was over, Mallory accosted Brian. She was scared; she felt something uneasy sweeping through her, and so she was angry and she accused him of playing a prank on her. He was a jerk, and she hoped he choked on one of his stories.

He stepped back, frowning, and she saw he was growing angry.

"Mallory, I have a little sister, but I don't have a little broth er, and I don't play games during the day; I work. I'm heading to college next year, and I'll need the money when I go to school," he told her. "I work, did you get that? You can ask half the tourists here who ate at our restaurant sometime dur ing the day!"

Most everyone else had left, heading up the hill to get back to their bed and breakfast inns or hotels. Her father waited with Anthony and Jonah, about fifty feet uphill.

"But – !"

"I tell history, Mallory, and that's that," he said.

Jonah came running back, slipping his hand into Mallory's.

"Mallory?" he whispered. He was worried about her.

"I'm fine," she promised.

"Goodnight; I'm sorry that you didn't enjoy the tour," Bri an said, and he turned to leave.

Mallory headed back with her family, still seething. The day had been annoying all the way around. On top of everything else, she'd lost her cell phone.

She was annoyed when Jonah announced that they were supposedly staying in the most haunted room at the inn. She was more annoyed when he crawled into her bed with her.

In the morning, she woke up ridiculously early. The rest of the family wouldn't be up and ready to head out for at least another hour.

Mallory walked back up the stone steps to the cemetery on the hill. Once again, she was alone. The morning was crisp and cold, and fog – of course – seemed to lie on the ground. She wanted to run back down the steps, she was suddenly so frightened. But she forced herself to hurry over to the graves of the Mason family.

Flowers had been left there, and in the midst of the flow ers, she saw her phone. She let out a little cry, and knelt down. With all the mist and fog, the phone should have been ruined. It wasn't. She started, nearly letting out a scream, when she heard footsteps. It was a Mason – Brian Mason, and he was coming from the area of the cherub.

"Thought you might come here sometime," he told her. "I didn't think you'd make it back to the restaurant, so I brought the phone here."

"Oh," she said. She felt foolish. *No, a ghost hadn't left her phone here.*

He came and knelt down beside her. "I've always wanted to see them," he told her. "I've heard stories that people do see them – Jeremy and Bryce – running through the crowds or lis tening to the bands or . . . just walking the street at night, hand in hand. I never get to see them. But," he said, smiling at her awkwardly, "I still love the story. I think about it every time I'm ready to tell my dad to run his own restaurant, or let my mom know that the 'hardtack' she sells at the store is as repulsive as it must have been to the Civil War soldiers. Mostly, I think about it when my little sister has just ruined one of my school projects, or tortures me when I'm with a girl. You can hate me; you can be mad at me. But, I think you were really lucky."

He was so earnest. She smiled at him and got to her feet. "I'm sorry. I don't know what I saw. Maybe you do have un known cousins running around and playing pranks on people."

"Maybe."

"Do you have to work today?" she asked him. "Maybe . . . well, it's a family vacation. Anthony is here. I want to spend some time with him."

He nodded. "But, today, I have a nice break for a few hours in the afternoon. I – I could take you, and your family, of course, rafting. I have all the equipment, and I know the best places."

She hesitated. "I have a baby sister. It wouldn't be fair to my mom."

He inhaled, grinned, and dropped his shoulders. "Well, you could switch off, watch your sister with other family mem bers. The river is great. And, later, maybe, when the little one is asleep, you could do the ghost tour again, and when it's over, some friends are having a party." He paused, grinning. "It's an early Halloween party."

She laughed in turn. "I didn't bring my Marie Antoinette with me."

"My mom has plenty of costumes. She'd be happy to set you up. That is, of course, if your folks would let you go."

"We can talk to them," Mallory said.

He stood, reaching down for her hand. It was a polite gesture; he was courteous, he was bright, he was . . .

She took his hand and stood. "Where are you going to school, by the way?" she asked him. "College, I mean. Next year."

"Pratt Institute. It's in Brooklyn. I'm majoring in graphic arts," he said.

She stared at him, smiling slowly. "Really? I'm going to NYU – their school of design."

"That's – that's great. Hey, you should put my number on that phone."

"The battery is dead."

"Okay. Can I put your number on my phone?"

She nodded slowly. "Yes, yes, of course." She gave him her number.

"We can email, Facebook, and Skype until then," he said.

Again, she nodded. "Yes, yes, it will be wonderful to keep in touch."

"Shall we go down – speak to your folks?" he suggested.

"That would be great," she assured him.

But as he started to walk away, she knelt back down quickly, and she gently touched the grave of Jeremy Mason, J.J., and that of little Bryce.

"Thanks," she said. She waited for a moment, and she thought she heard the sound of a child's laughter rippling softly through the breeze. "Thanks," she said again.

She stood and chased after Brian. Hand in hand, they went back down the stone steps.

She was suddenly anxious to tell Jonah and Anthony that they were going to go and have a great afternoon, river-rafting.

Little brothers were . . . well, they were pains. They were also precious. As precious as moms, dads, baby sisters, and big brothers.

Family.

Saint Agnes and the Black Sheep

by Jo Beverley

Publishers Weekly declared Jo Beverley "Arguably today's most skillful writer of intelligent historical romance." *Romantic Times* described her as "one of the great names of the genre," and *Booklist* declared her work "Sublime!" She is the recipient of numerous awards including two Career Achievement awards from *Romantic Times*. She is also a five-time winner of the Romance Writers of America RITA award and a member of the RWA Hall of Fame and Honor Roll.

She is the bestselling author of 35 historical romance novels, all set in her native England, and her books regularly appear high on bestseller lists. Her fiction is generally praised for being both entertaining and accurate to period, perhaps because of a degree in history from Keele University in Staffordshire plus an addiction to popular fiction, especially romance, from an early age. Her most recent novel is *A Scandalous Countess*, set in Georgian times.

One of the charms of short fiction is that the protagonists can have normal lives that don't have to be ripped apart, perhaps more than once, to provide a lengthy, complex piece of fiction. In this case, Agnes has a comfortable life and I can allow her to retain that with only one challenge to overcome. I enjoyed that, and I'm sure she's offering thanks that I didn't make her the heroine of a novel!

Readers familiar with my Regency novels will recognize I've used a few of my own cast of characters who people my Regency world. The Earl of Saxonhurst is the hero of Forbidden Magic, *and yes he is notorious for taking in hopeless cases. Meg, his wife, has to the cope with the consequences. The Dowager Countess of Cawle has appeared in a number of my stories as a goddess* ex machina, *wielding her indolent power, if she so chooses. My cast makes my worlds fun to play in, and my readers enjoy the recognition.*

Chapter 1

"Ready, dear?" Lady Martineux used the bright tone she always applied when preparing for another foray upon the ton.

"Quite ready, Aunt," Agnes Abbott said, rising from her dressing table and pulling on long, white silk gloves. As ready as she could ever be for yet another London evening.

She didn't want to be in Town, supposedly seeking a hus band, and her poor aunt didn't want to be hauling such an unpromising bundle around from rout to soiree to ball. The eligible gentlemen of London certainly didn't want to be com pelled to dance with a country vicar's plain daughter.

Agnes turned to the long mirror to make sure she was at least tidy – that none of her fine, mousy hair was escaping its pins, and that the maid hadn't scattered the powdered rouge onto her ivory silk gown. She'd tried to rebel against the rouge, but her aunt had wailed on so about her lack of color.

When Agnes had been worn down by her father's anxiety and agreed to this purgatory, she'd solemnly promised to obey her aunt.

In the case of the ivory silk and its fellows, she'd obeyed with good grace. She didn't want to marry a London beau and there was always the dread possibility that one would decide that her portion of three thousand pounds outweighed her lack of charms. However, nothing could suit her less than the pale, frilly fashion designed for youthful ingénues.

She was twenty-three, plump, and with a complexion coars ened by the sun. She loved to garden but regularly forgot her hat. And her gloves. Oh, how Aunt Martineux had exclaimed over the state of her hands.

She nodded at her reflection, satisfied by how unattractive she looked. She'd promised to spend six weeks on the Mar riage Mart and had survived four. She'd soon be home at Dux

Cherrymead, enjoying her books, her garden, and the company of her father and her friends.

She turned, but paused. Her aunt's thin, gloved fingers were tight on her fan and she might even be paler than usual.

"Are you quite all right, Aunt? We can stay at home if –"

"No! Not at all. It's only that.... Your grandmother is here!"

"*Here?*" Abby asked, squeaking from a tight throat. "In Town?"

"Here, " Lady Martineux repeated. "*In the drawing room.*"

"Oh my. Why?"

"To take command of your case. Agnes, I have begged you to apply yourself more!"

"More? Am I not in silk, with rouged cheeks and lips? Do I not attend every event you devise and do my best to be pleas ing? What more should I do?"

"Oh dear, oh dear. Do t*ry* not to speak like that to... But as always, you will do as you think right." She made that seem like a sin. "Come, come. She demands to inspect you before we leave. And," she added faintly, "she's staying."

"Staying?"

"In this house. For the next two weeks."

"I'm very sorry, Aunt."

"And so you should be! Oh, I'm sorry dear. I don't mean to berate you. But what Martineux will say when he finds out his mother's here I don't know. Come along, do, and try to placate her. If you could secure a proposal tonight, she might return to Lime Park tomorrow."

Agnes followed her aunt along the corridor rejecting that solution, even if it were possible. But, oh, she wished she weren't terrified.

It was ten years since she'd encountered the Dowager Lady Martineux, mother to Lady Martineux's husband; to Agnes's father, the Reverend Percival Abbott; and to a major general, an admiral, and two countesses, all of whom trembled before her. She'd terrified a thirteen-year-old girl.

The dowager ruled her family with dragon's breath, but by the grace of heaven, she mostly did it by letter from the dower house at Lime Park. No wonder Agnes's father had re jected a living close to Lime Park in favor of one three counties away. Lord and Lady Martineux didn't have a similar option, but they'd managed to find a great many duties that obliged them to be elsewhere, including a two-year diplomatic posting to Russia.

Agnes entered the drawing room tense with nervousness but determined not to be bullied. After all, what could the old tyrant actually do to her?

The dowager sat upright, thin hands on her carved wooden cane, mouth literally pursed – gathered tight amid wrinkles. Her wiry gray hair was frizzed into a nest crowned by a black widow's cap that had long lappets on either side of her scowling face. Her gown, though richly embroidered with jet beads, was a dense black, and given her thin body Agnes could only think, crow.

"Why's your bosom covered, girl?"

Agnes managed not to put a hand to her neckline. "For decency, Grandmother."

"What's decency got to do with it? You're on the Marriage Mart and should show off your wares! You look well enough endowed. Unless that's all padding."

"Certainly not!"

"Don't take that tone with me, girl. Something's amiss or you'd have a husband by now. You're an Abbott, and as your mother failed to produce any other child, your portion is respectable. You look healthy enough, and Claudia assures me that she's taken you to all suitable events."

"She has," Agnes said, hoping to deflect fiery breath from her poor aunt.

"Ineffectively," the dowager said, "but what else is to be expected?" The beady eyes fired at Lady Martineux then swiveled back to the main target. "You promised your father that you would apply yourself to your duty."

Had the dowager been behind her father's stubborn insistence on this plan? Had she harangued the poor man into it? Agnes's rare fury stirred.

"I have done my duty in all respects, Grandmother."

"Bosom!" the woman spat. "We'll have your gowns lowered tomorrow. Some width taken out of the skirts, too. That bulky thing makes you look broad in the beam."

"I am broad in the beam, ma'am, and plain as well. If being purchased from the shelves in the Marriage Mart depends on physical charms, I'm like to rot there. Except, of course, that I will soon be allowed to return home."

She threw it as a challenge, and the dowager inhaled, which made her nostrils narrow in an odd way. "So, you confess. You strive to return home unwed."

There was a neat trap.

"I do not wish to marry for the sake of it, Grandmother, and I've not yet encountered a gentleman for whom I have any tender emotions."

"Tender emotions weaken a wife. Marry for rank and fortune, I say. Those can be relied upon."

"I would not think that Christian, Grandmother."

"Christian! Folly to name you Agnes. What's amiss with Charlotte, Caroline, Anabelle and such? Puts a girl in the right way of things. Agnes, indeed. Patron saint of virgins and chastity, and always carrying around a lamb. Are you aware that the ton call you Saint Agnes?"

Agnes wasn't and her cheeks heated. She glanced at her aunt and caught a grimace. Lady Martineux had kept it from her.

"No, Grandmother, I didn't know that, but I see no shame in being likened to a saint, though I am, of course, unworthy of it."

The dowager smirked. "Are you confessing that you're not a chaste virgin?"

Agnes realized her hands were fists, but she couldn't think of anything to say that wouldn't be sinfully undutiful.

The dowager sniggered. "Not chased by the men, I'll be bound. Well, now that I see you, you probably are a hopeless case. I should have kept you to Lime Park when you were still a child and had the shaping of you. At least your saintly reputation can be put to use."

The change of tone should have been a relief, but instinct put Agnes on full alert. What was the old harpy up to?

"I have another reason for coming to Town," the dowager said. "Godson. I have too many godchildren – one's careless about such things in one's youth – and don't give them much heed. But Ned Ballard's mother wrote to beg my aid. Livia Ballard's become a limp twit over the years. Married for love, note. Nothing good comes of that, and in her case, her only son's a bad 'un."

Agnes glanced at her aunt and received a shrug. Lady Martineux was perplexed, too.

"Stop looking at one another as if you think I'm a lunatic. Livie's son is suddenly Earl of Riverstoke – he's from a twig far out on the Ballard family tree – and he's returned from America to take up his duties. She fears the ton won't like him, and she's doubtless right. She begs me to do something, and I suppose a godmother has some responsibilities. You, girl, will convey some of your saintliness to him. A dusting of his wickedness on you might improve your chances."

"What precisely are you expecting me to do, Grandmother?"

"Make mad love to him at Almack's," the dowager said, then snorted. "Speak to him, that's all! No chance of dancing with him, for I doubt any hostess will permit that. He'd come into contact with too many innocents. Walk with him, drive with him. Anything that will convey your saintly approval."

"I very much doubt I do approve, ma'am. What are his sins?"

The wrinkled face twisted into a sneer. "Sure you want to know?"

"I'm sure I don't, but if I'm even to consider this, I must."

"You will do as you're told."

Pushed to extremes, Agnes challenged her. "Or?"

The dowager straightened in outrage, and Agnes feared that there was some punishment available, but then the old woman sank back down. The dragon was a puffed up bladder it seemed.

"Ravished a young lady in Philadelphia and refused to marry her."

"Is that all?" Agnes said. A crack of laughter startled her, but it had been an unfortunate way to put it. "I mean, I expected a lifetime of vice."

"Ned Ballard's always been wild. Lived beyond his means. Consorted with Cyprians. Left England under a cloud, I'm sure. His mother writes nothing but complaints of him."

"A rake, in other words, but he won't be the only one in the House of Lords. I can't see where I'm needed."

"The American girl – Amelia Hurst, I think – made a great fuss about his behavior to her."

"Hardly surprising."

"Is it not? By making it public, she's ruined, whereas dis cretion would have preserved her reputation, especially as she miscarried the child at an early stage."

Agnes opened her mouth but closed it again.

"The chit lacks a father, but some other relative tried to call Ned out over it. The news about the earldom arrived and he took the opportunity to board ship and flee. Mrs. Hurst then took the matter to the British ambassador, Sir Augustus Foster. His mother, of course, is now Duchess of Devonshire. The short of it is that powerful people are against the new Earl of Riverstoke and I've promised Livie to try to at least gain tolera tion for him. You are my instrument."

"On which to play a very foolish tune, Grandmother. How can I weigh against a duchess?"

"Depends on the duchess. Elizabeth Foster was the duke's mistress for years. You must have heard about that, even in Muddlemead."

"Dux Cherrymead," Agnes corrected, but she had heard about the scandalous Devonshires. "It makes no difference, Grandmother. Lord Riverstoke is clearly a rakehell wastrel and my conscience would not permit me to try to whitewash him."

"No? Consider this, you uppity young madam. You've promised to remain on the Marriage Mart shelves for two more weeks and obey your aunt, and your aunt will obey me. I can make the coming fortnight miserable for you and perhaps even secure you an offer. Or I can leave you to your spinsterish devices."

It was a devil's bargain, and Agnes didn't try to disguise her opinion of it, but she was tempted. Though she hadn't directly promised to accept any respectable offer, it had been implied, and the dowager probably could drag some impoverished lord to the point.

On the other hand, she could see this as an act of Chris tian charity. Lord Riverstoke was a wretch, but even wretches deserved compassion, and his recent sin wasn't proved.

What's more, she realized, being seen in his company might smirch her sufficiently to deter any gentleman consider ing an offer.

"'Forgive one another,'" intoned the dowager, "'even as God hath forgiven you.' 'He that is without sin among you, let him first cast a stone.' 'The quality of mercy is not strained...'"

"That's Shakespeare," Agnes said, "not the Bible. But very well, Grandmother. Out of Christian charity I will not shun the soot-black sheep. If the Earl of Riverstoke then goes on to ravish some other innocent lady, on your head be it."

"Agreed," said the dowager in the manner of one who had gained exactly what she'd wanted.

Agnes and her aunt escaped and when they reached the hall, Lady Martineux murmured, "I'm so very sorry, dear. I couldn't think of a thing to say. You were very brave."

"I don't have to live so closely with her."

Maidservants came forward with their cloaks and they set off on the evening's round of amusements.

When first arrived in Town, Agnes had attended ton events in a state of nerves, but by now she was plagued only by boredom. What a great waste of time it all was. Tonight was enlivened a little by her grandmother's plan. Where would she encounter the black sheep? How would she arrange to smirch herself with his stains? In her experience, hostesses did not introduce ladies such as she to gentlemen such as he.

The coach deposited them first at Lady Chumleigh's rout, where they passed through the house, chatting briefly, but al ways in motion. A rout was the way a hostess fulfilled her obli gations to a great many people with the least effort, and Agnes thought them a waste of time. Why not a symbolic one? Lady Chumleigh could have sent cards to say, "Consider yourself to have attended my rout."

They went on to Mrs. Drummond-Burrell's drum, which was much like a rout except that one was supposed to pause to take tea. Consider yourself to have been drummed, she thought.

The whole of the season could be managed that way, by a shuffling of cards, saving a great deal of trouble and expense. People could even do it from the comfort of the country.

Agnes and her aunt, teacups precariously in hand, went to pay their respects to the hostess. Mrs. Drummond-Burrell was saying, "...Riverstoke. So unfortunate not to be able to attend Lady Saxonhurst's ball."

Agnes had previously approved of Mrs. Drummond-Burrell, who was not much older than herself but very much in control of her life and a great stickler for propriety. So many of the younger women, single or married, were flighty. Now, however, she detected something cold, even spiteful, in the woman's tone. Was Mrs. Drummond-Burrell using her influ ence to deter people from attending Lady Saxonhurst's ball?

Agnes liked Meg Saxonhurst. She was a little flighty, but she also had common sense and had been kind. Perhaps to make Agnes feel more comfortable, Meg had revealed that her father had been a scholar, so they came from a similar back ground. They shared a no-nonsense view of life and had en joyed some pleasant chats.

Agnes didn't know why the rakish Earl of Riverstoke would be at Meg's ball, but she didn't want her friend's en tertainment ruined. As her aunt said the right things to the hostess, Agnes remembered that the Earl of Saxonhurst had a reputation for eccentricity. He owned an ugly, cowardly dog and a peculiar parrot. Many of his servants were defective in some way, having lost an eye, a limb, or even their good name. Had he brought home a man lacking morals and conscience? Poor Meg.

"I assume we are to attend the Saxonhurst ball?" Agnes said as they put aside their cups and joined the stream going downstairs.

"I accepted," her aunt said, "but now I wonder…"

"Remember, Aunt, that I'm to apply saintliness to the sin ful Riverstoke."

"Oh dear, oh dear…"

When they were in the coach again, Lady Martineux said, "Is this wise, dear?"

"The dowager," Agnes reminded her.

"But where Mrs. Drummond-Burrell leads, many follow."

"Then she should lead along a more Christian path."

"Oh, dear, oh dear. I do hope you're not going to play the martyr over this, dear."

"I'm not going to play anything, Aunt. I'm going to speak to the reprobate, smile at the reprobate, and perhaps even go driving with the reprobate. Then, simple duty done, I shall return home and all will be perfectly as it was."

Chapter 2

Then, simple duty done…

When Agnes set eyes on the despicable Earl of Riverstoke, her words seemed like a devil's joke. Nothing to do with such a man would ever be simple. She'd met the occasional rake and reprobate and each had been disgusting in some way, whether it be slovenly, unhealthy, mentally loose, or showing even worse results of debauchery.

This rake did not disgust. He was talking to the Earl of Saxonhurst, a tall, tawny man, and another gentleman, a darker one, and was as impeccably dressed as they in dark evening clothes and white linen. To fit his role, Riverstoke should at least have the dark locks of a gothic villain, but instead his hair was an ordinary brown. A gothic villain should also have eyes that burned with vile passions…

Agnes turned away. She hadn't been able to tell his eye color, and thank the Lord, he hadn't looked her way and caught her staring. She should never have read that one Minerva novel in order to understand the folly of such works. This was reality, not fiction, and the reality was dangerous in a very ordinary way.

He was neatly presented, but she'd sensed that he was coiled dangerously tight. Hardly surprising given the reaction to his presence here, but a tight-wound coil could spring free, wreaking havoc.

She and her aunt had made their way to the ballroom and were speaking to acquaintances. A line dance was in progress, the music light and merry, but the atmosphere jangled. She heard "Ballard" and "Riverstoke" being mentioned all around, but the three men were isolated.

Anyone would think Riverstoke was a leper, when Agnes knew many of the gentlemen here behaved badly, and some of the women, too. Of course a gentleman should never seduce a lady, but to her mind he shouldn't seduce a maidservant either, or consort with whores.

Agnes disliked Riverstoke only for bringing his contamination here.

A contamination she was supposed to approach.

The task hadn't seemed so difficult when she'd imagined him a seedy wretch. Now, she felt slightly sick. What might people think of her? That she was drawn by his tarnished appeal? She slid another look in his direction. Yes, he was a handsome man.

She saw Meg Saxonhurst, looking determinedly cheerful, and made her way over there.

"An interesting event," Agnes said.

Meg rolled her eyes. "I could strangle Saxonhurst."

"I doubt it. Strong neck, small hands."

"You can be distressingly literal!" Meg complained, but her smile was genuine now. She wasn't a beauty, being in many ways as ordinary in appearance as Agnes, but her smile was lovely and she had a certain glow. Agnes had come to suspect it was kindled by the devotion of her husband. It was something to make a spinster turn foolish, except that a man like Saxonhurst would never come into her orbit.

"You're angry because he brought home Lord Riverstoke, I assume."

"Not quite home, thank heaven. Riverstoke has rooms somewhere, but Sax insisted he be invited to the ball. Half my guests have failed to attend."

"Is this his first appearance in polite company?"

"Yes! Why choose my ball for his debut?"

Agnes smiled at her. "Console yourself with the thought that it'll make it famous, and I'm about to enliven it even more. Introduce me."

"What?" Meg asked, wide-eyed. "Of course not."

"Why not?"

"I'd be condemned by all."

"Oh, I hadn't considered that. Then who could introduce me to him?"

"No one. Truly, Agnes, what are you thinking?"

"Christian charity. No one should be condemned out of hand. How can anyone know the story is true?"

"There is that," Meg said. "All the same... I *can't*, Agnes."

This was an unexpected barrier. "Who could?" Agnes asked.

"No one, honestly." Meg had been glancing around now and then, making sure her event was progressing as well as possible, and now she frowned at someone – an ample lady, peculiarly dressed in the wide skirts of a former age.

"Who's that?" Agnes asked.

"The Dowager Countess of Cawle…"

"Somewhat of an oddity."

"Shush. She's very powerful. What she approves is ap proved, and what she condemns is condemned, but she's ec centric about it."

Agnes looked again at the countess. She was probably of an age with her aunt, but what a difference in presence. No hint of anxiety there, which perhaps explained the generous curves and smooth, plump face.

"She might introduce me to Lord Riverstoke?"

"She's capable of it, but..."

"Then introduce me to her, please."

"Are you sure? She's a dragon beneath that smooth exterior."

"I'm familiar with dragons," Agnes said. "Yes, I'm sure."

The countess was ensconced on a sofa with three gentle men of various ages paying court. Meg waited her moment and then presented Miss Abbott, niece to Lord Martineux.

Rather sleepy eyes assessed Agnes, and then she was acknowledged. "Sit, Miss Abbott." To the gentlemen, she said, "I'm sure you should all seek partners for the next dance."

They went, and Agnes sat, saying, "I wish I knew how to do that."

Lady Cawle wafted a large fan. "At your age you should be more interested in gathering swains than dispersing them. The ton calls you Saint Agnes. Are you saintly?"

"No – except perhaps in contrast to the wickedness of some in polite society."

"Easy to be a saint on those terms. How can I help you, Miss Abbott?"

"You are willing to?"

"Not if you're desperate to find a husband."

"I'm not, I assure you. I'm rather desperate to return home to my tranquil life."

Those eyes studied her, and Agnes realized they weren't at all sleepy. "Safe, is it?"

"I suppose so, but that is part of its charm."

"What are its other charms?"

This wasn't what Agnes wanted to talk about, but she supposed she must humor the woman a little.

"The village, my garden, my books, my father's company, my friends. It's a pleasant life, is all, and I wish to return to it."

"No lovers or admirers?"

"I'm not that sort of woman."

"Nonsense, but if you believe it, it will doubtless come true. How can I assist you to return to your dull existence?"

Agnes wanted to argue various points, but she had a simple purpose here. "I wish an introduction to the Earl of Riverstoke."

The countess blinked. "You surprise me, Miss Abbott, indeed you do."

"It's not my doing," Agnes defended, knowing she was blushing. "It's my grandmother –"

A raised hand stopped her. "Aurelia Martineux. A thoroughly unpleasant woman. Don't distress yourself over how to respond to that for I'm sure you agree. What's her interest in Riverstoke?"

"He's her godson."

"Probably explains his predicament, poor lad – cursed at the font. What does your grandmother want you to do?"

"Acknowledge him. Talk to him. Be seen with him. I being saintly, you see, will dissolve some of his wicked ink."

Plump lips smiled. "Not a foolish plan, in fact. Unpleas antness does not equate to stupidity. In fact, I find stupidity distressingly common among the pleasant, don't you?"

She didn't wait for an answer, but gestured. A nearby gen tleman came over, eager to serve. How did she do that?

"Kindly request that Lord Riverstoke pay his respects, Knightly." The man went off and the dowager simply waited, observing the dancing. Agnes was tense from tete to toes, with a heart that raced rapidly enough to threaten light-headedness.

Here he came, moving with notable elegance and a super ficial relaxation, but he was alert, wary, and still coiled. For the first time she wondered how much courage it had taken to come here.

He bowed with grace. "Lady Cawle, how may I serve you?"

"Bring a chair over and sit, if you please." When he did so, Lady Cawle said, "I enjoy being the centre of attention, Lord Riverstoke, and you are distracting people from me."

Agnes saw his lips twitch in true amusement. His eyes flickered to her once, wondering at her part in this, but then returned to Lady Cawle.

His eyes were a light shade, grey perhaps, or a pale hazel, made striking by skin more sun-browned than hers. For some reason, that quick glance had tilted her world and set things all awry. What was happening to her? She remembered the play *A Midsummer's Night's Dream* and the potion that made the next person viewed irresistible.

She must resist such a wicked man.

Resist? He wasn't the slightest bit interested in her. Why should he be?

That hadn't occurred to her grandmother. That he'd not want her company at any price, no matter how saintly she was.

He and Lady Cawle were conversing about London and about his family tree. The lady seemed to know it well.

Lady Cawle turned to Agnes. "The previous earl was known as River Tick, from the extent of his debts."

"An unfortunate inheritance, my lord," Agnes said, having to look at him again.

"Not a blessed one," he agreed, "especially with duties in train."

Remember, this plan suits you, too. You want to become a minor scandal.

"Duties, my lord?" Agnes asked, attempting a fetching smile.

"I have a seat in the House and thus power, should I care to use it."

"And will you?"

"Of course. Who could resist?"

"Quite a number of peers, I gather."

"They probably have better things to occupy their time."

"Your estates, my lord?"

"All sold," he said, apparently undistressed. "River Tick broke the entailment and sold them off, and his son helped fritter away the lot before dying of drink. Now, now, Miss Ab bott, don't look like that. Everyone has loose fish on their fam ily tree, and I'm far removed from them."

"But not notoriously virtuous," she retorted.

Instantly she regretted it, and those eyes flashed coldly, but then he smiled, with lips at least. "No, I'm not notoriously vir tuous. Do you waltz, Miss Abbott?"

Agnes stared at him, shocked almost to dumbness. She knew how to waltz. In keeping her word she'd agreed to learn, and she had taken part in the scandalous dance a few times.

His brows rose, demanding an answer from her, and she recognized that this was his punishment for her remark. He didn't expect her to accept, so she would.

"I suppose the censorious would allow you to waltz," she said. "Not a line dance where you would touch hands and perhaps more with other ladies, but the waltz, where you will dance only with me."

"Precisely. Of course it's possible it will so outrage the censorious that everyone else will leave the floor, or even the house."

That image evaporated all Agnes's courage.

"Then we mustn't. I don't want Meg Saxonhurst's ball ruined."

"It'll make it the talk of the decade," he said, echoing her earlier thought. "What do you advise, my lady?"

Lady Cawle seemed genuinely amused. "Those who are here will stay, if only to be witness to yet further horrors, but there could be repercussions. You are *very* determined to remain a spinster, aren't you, Miss Abbott?"

"I'm committed to an act of Christian charity."

"That's a novel role for me," said the rake. He rose and offered his hand. "Shall we stroll as we wait for the waltz, Miss Abbott?"

Remember the plan, Agnes told herself, as she rose, curtsied farewell to the countess, and walked arm in arm with him around the room. She made sure to smile as if all was right with her world.

He smiled, too, as he said, "Now, what precisely is your plan, Miss Abbott?"

Agnes looked ahead. "To brush against scandal so that no man will offer me marriage."

"Intriguing. You are bedeviled by suitors?"

She ignored the implied insult. "Clearly not. There's always the danger of one desperate case, however. I do have a portion of three thousand pounds."

"You really shouldn't wave such temptation before a desperate man, Miss Abbott."

"Fortunately my father would not approve a marriage to you, sir."

"But you are of age. He has no say."

"He does with me."

"A dutiful daughter. How charming. I see that your plan is working. There are many scandalized looks, but to make the most of it you really should look more pleased with me, you know."

Agnes turned her smile on him, attempting to make it warmer. "A challenge, but I'll do my best."

Before she could react, he captured her free hand and kissed it, looking into her eyes with apparent devotion.

When she opened her mouth to protest, he said, "Just helping the cause. We could go even further if you wish."

He'd paused them, so she moved onward, cheeks hot, aware of being the focus of too many eyes. She tried to keep the smile as she said, "Don't be disgusting. If you want the full truth, I was ordered to this by your godmother."

"My godmother? Who the devil is she?"

"Don't swear, sir. The Dowager Lady Martineux."

"How odd. I'm not aware of her giving me a silver spoon, never mind sending Bibles and sermons, yet now she sends me a martyrish maiden."

"She sent you a saint. The ton has labeled me Saint Agnes."

"Why?"

"Out of foolishness. Your mother remembered the dowager's role as godmother, and the dowager commanded me to this in the hope that some of my saintly purity will brush off on you."

"Are you saintly? I thought saints were supposed to refrain from unkind remarks and turn the other cheek when attacked."

"They are also supposed to fight demons and face lions without fear."

"Or torture. I have always been deeply grateful not to be a saint."

"The reward for torment comes in the next life."

"So chancy, don't you think? We know we have this one, but the next is not proved, so why not enjoy life to the full? Ah, the waltz begins."

Agnes almost backed out. She hadn't enjoyed her previous attempts at the waltz, and she'd been uncomfortable with the turning step that brought the couple close together, face to face. Those dances had been with ordinary men, and Lord Riverstoke was not ordinary at all. She'd never met a man who could so easily make her unbalanced, or so easily anger her.

To retreat would show fear, however, and so she went onto the floor with him, yes, in a martyred frame of mind.

The first steps were much like an ordinary dance except that there was more hand-holding and the couples stayed together, but then the turn began. She had to face him, had to put her hand on his sleeve as his came to her waist as they turned, looking into one another's eyes. Their bodies almost brushed together at the front, and turning seemed designed to drive all good sense out of a woman's head.

When they separated to simpler steps, progressing as a couple with others in a big circle, she breathed again as she assessed reactions. A number of people still watched them, but many had found better things to do.

When they came to the waltz step again, she was determined to converse. "So, my lord, without estates, how will you live?"

"On my wits, Miss Abbott, as usual."

"Was Miss Hurst an heiress?"

"No. Doubtless why I didn't bother marrying her."

They separated again and Agnes regretted her challenging words. He made her so angry, and she wasn't sure why.

When they came together again, she said, "I apologize, my lord."

"Why?"

"Because I know nothing of you and Miss Hurst but gossip, and should not judge."

"Jupiter, you are a saint."

"Not at all."

They were loosed again, thank heavens, but inevitably returned.

"You're not a saint?" he said. "So how are you sinful? The seven options are wrath, greed, sloth, pride, lust, envy, and gluttony. I suspect all humans are guilty of them all. Even lust," he added, forestalling her. "It's possible to lust in the privacy of the mind."

Agnes became powerfully aware of his hand on her waist and of his fingers pressing on her back in a way that was surely unnecessary.

"I'm sure you have done so, frequently," she retorted.

"Rarely, as it happens. So much less exhausting to simply... lust. I wish your bodice were lower, Miss Abbott. Which is your primary sin?"

"At the moment, sir, wrath."

With that, Agnes could separate again, but how long did this devilish dance last?

Only one more turn to be endured.

"I suspect you're also prideful, Miss Abbott. You have a haughty way with you."

"Haughty? I do not."

"Secure in your prideful virtue."

Thank heavens the dance ended then, and they must part to curtsy and bow.

He amiably returned her to her aunt, who looked as if she sat on a pincushion, poor lady.

"There, duty done," Agnes said.

"Was it really necessary...? But indeed, your grandmother can't claim you've shirked your task, dear. Ah, here comes Mr. Wivenhoe. Thank heavens. I do believe he's going to ask you to stand up in the next set. I was so afraid…"

That after the scandalous waltz no man would dance with her again.

Agnes enjoyed an ordinary dance with an amiable partner. She resolutely did not look to see where Lord Riverstoke was, or what he was doing.

As her nerves settled, however, she realized she'd en joyed that badinage in the waltz, and yes, the waltz itself. Life had seemed more vivid for a short while, and Mr. Wivenhoe, though smiling at her, was very dull.

When that dance ended, Lord Pershall sought her hand. Agnes glanced around, wondering if this enthusiasm was some subtle punishment by the ton for dancing with the unwanted intruder. She'd never had partners come to her so willingly. Was everyone laughing at her? There was nothing to do but agree, however, and she did enjoy dancing of the ordinary sort. And waltzing, honesty insisted, especially with a dangerously wicked man.

He was. He was dangerous, and wicked, but in some way attractive and seductive. They said Lucifer could charm a soul to hell.

It had been the supper dance, so she was committed to tak ing supper with Lord Pershall, whom she didn't much like. He always seemed to be sneering and his voice was nasal. When they entered the supper room and Meg invited them to join her table, it was a relief. Until, that was, Agnes realized that Lord

Riverstoke was of the party. He was Lady Cawle's partner for the meal, and he was just going to select food for them both. Pershall seated her and went off to forage.

"Well done, Miss Abbott," said Lady Cawle.

"In what respect, my lady?"

"The waltz. I wish we'd had that dance in my youth. And it's served its purpose – that and my patronage. Many are not quite sure how to treat our black sheep."

"That still leaves Miss Hurst unavenged."

"Vengeance belongeth unto me, I will recompense, saith the Lord. So much easier to leave it to Him." Lady Cawle smiled at Riverstoke and a well-filled plate. "Thank you, my lord."

It was only when he sat that Agnes realized his place was between Lady Cawle and herself. Their arms were almost touching. When Pershall returned she had to try to eat while keeping her elbow tucked tightly to her side.

Conversation was general but Agnes was mostly silent. That wasn't unusual, for she wasn't a chatterer, and she neither knew nor cared about the latest on-dits. She was tongue-tied, however, by the man beside her, who seemed to...to send off something that made her want to relax her elbow so that it brushed against his, or even sway slightly in his direction.

"More wine, Miss Abbott?"

She had to look into his eyes, smile, say something. "Thank you, Lord Riverstoke."

He poured, which involved him moving just a little clos er, so a slight touch was unavoidable. A brush of soot and sainthood...

It must have been all too easy for Miss Amelia Hurst to be sucked into ruin.

Or perhaps...?

No, she wouldn't weave fantasies about the rake, fantasies in which he wasn't as black as he seemed.

Chapter 3

After supper there were musical performances in the drawing room until the dancing began again. Agnes strolled into a quiet anteroom with Lord Pershall simply because Riverstoke was escorting Lady Cawle to the music.

"You don't care for music, Pershall?" she asked.

"I don't care for sopranos, Miss Abbott. I am more drawn toward the larger sounds, to orchestras and large choirs."

"They are not much available in the country, my lord."

Agnes was thinking that she'd made an error. She did like sopranos if they were good, and a wind quartet was to play afterward. Riverstoke must be settled now, so easily avoided.

"If you don't mind, my lord..."

He grasped her hand.

"My lord?"

"Don't rush away, Miss Abbott. I wish to speak to you most particularly."

The words were warning, and his expression was confirmation. The dratted man was going to propose!

"Oh dear, my lord..."

"Come, come, Miss Abbott, don't play shy games with me. We have enjoyed one another's company, have we not?"

Instead of a blunt "no" Agnes said, "I wasn't aware of it being a *particular* enjoyment, my lord."

"Ah, I understand. Yes, Miss Abbott, I have not wooed you, but tonight, I see a new aspect to you. You are transformed in my eyes and I wish you to be my wife."

His manner of declaring that annoyed her, for he was so confident of her gratified acceptance, but annoyance was swamped by panic. Lord Pershall would be seen as a good match, so how could she refuse him? She wouldn't be able to keep the offer a secret, for she was sure he'd ask her aunt to persuade her.

"You're overcome," he said, smiling, "and I do understand, but you have only to say yes, my dear, and we will be delightfully happy."

"You… you've taken me by surprise," Agnes said. "Truly you have. I must…"

"Decline the kind offer," said a voice, and Lord Riverstoke strolled in, eyes bright with laughter. "What poor Miss Abbott is trying to convey, sir, is that she is already engaged to marry me."

It was as well Pershall was gaping at Riverstoke or he'd have seen that Agnes was too. By the time he looked to her for confirmation, she was attempting flustered embarrassment.

"I do apologize, my lord. We...we were to keep it secret un til Lord Riverstoke can speak to my father, you see. I do hope we can rely on you not to speak of it."

"You intend to marry *him*?" Pershall said, anger flushing his cheeks. "You are indeed much changed!"

"You claimed to admire that about me."

"I withdraw all admiration, ma'am." He bowed stiffly to her and stalked out of the room.

"I'd have knocked him out or challenged him for that," Riverstoke said, "but you wouldn't want to attract attention."

"Attention! There'll be enough of that, sir, when people hear about our supposed betrothal. What devil possessed you?"

"Gallantry. You were teetering on the brink of disaster, though why you didn't just dismiss him, I have no idea."

"It's none of you business," she said and walked toward the door.

He caught her hand and tugged her back. "No thanks?"

Agnes glared at him. She was by nature calm and forbear ing, but this man did indeed stir her to the sin of wrath. Be tween clenched teeth, she said, "Thank you, my lord."

He smiled. "I thought you'd come round to the idea. When shall we marry?"

"Marry? I'm not going to marry you!"

"You just accepted. A jilt, Miss Abbott? Tut-tut."

Agnes wrenched her hand free. "You'd be better engaged in restoring your reputation, Riverstoke, than in making a game of me."

"But I'm not playing games. I want to marry you, Saint Agnes, and I do think we will be delightfully happy together."

"We scarcely know each other."

"It only takes a moment, don't you find? You're brave and honest, clever and kind, and stirred to wrath in just the right way. I'm extraordinarily attracted to you, Miss Abbott, in all ways." A smiling glance flicked over her, truly like flame. "Don't you feel it?"

Yes.

"No. I'm plain and fat."

He laughed, but then sobered, frowning. "Do you truly think that? Is a lamp plain when the flame is lit within it? As for fat, God save me from a thin woman, but it's the other, the flame, that binds us."

When he drew her toward a sofa she knew she should ob ject – no, fight – but she let him seat her there, watched as he sat, turned toward her.

"You still doubt?" he said. "Let's test the power of the flame."

Agnes had only ever received mistletoe kisses, light pecks on the lips. When Riverstoke pressed his lips to hers it was different, and when he demanded more, cradling her head with one hand in a way that commanded her, it was, indeed, inflammatory.

Hot wetness made her jerk back, but a moment later she surrendered to it, swept out of her senses despite a distant small voice crying, *No, don't, don't!*

When his mouth released hers, slowly, then with a gentle farewell kiss, she glowed like coals in a hearth.

"You see?" he said, his voice hoarse.

"Yes..." But then she shook her head. "No, I can't, I can't. I love my home. I love my father. I don't want to go to wherever yours is. I'm sorry, but I can't."

He touched her cheek. "You don't have to lose anything for me. Remember, my predecessor was River Tick. Estates all gone, fortune drained down to mud. I, like the person in the Bible, will go where you go."

"Ruth," Agnes said, and bit back laughter. "Most inappro priate. But really, my lord..."

"Call me Ned."

"Ned, then."

"And you are Agnes. Agnes of the lambs."

"I'm no saint."

"And I'm glad of it, but I put hope in your fondness for sheep."

"I'm not particularly fond of sheep."

"Not even roasted?"

"Oh, don't."

"Will you believe that I'm not as black a sheep as I've been portrayed?"

After a moment, she said, "Yes."

"Why?"

"Because of Peggy Hopgood."

"I swear, I've never touched the lass."

"I'm sure of it. But you see, Peggy claimed the miller's son had had his wicked way with her and made her with child. Sam Miller denied it, but no one believed him, because he wasn't a pure white sheep."

"Few are," he said. "Much past birth, they're all grey. Which could make a parable, I suppose. What happened to Sam and Peggy?"

"I knew Sam loved Sukey Overstook, and I didn't think him black enough to seduce another, so I spoke to my father about it. He's the vicar, you see."

"A vicar's daughter. Perfect."

"I think you're mad. Father went to Peggy and her parents and asked when and where. She claimed it was too distress ing to think about, but he insisted, so she tried to come up with something, but it became clear she lied. In the end she confessed she wanted to press Sam Miller into marriage, him being a handsome young man who was going to own the mill one day. Nothing more was said of the imaginary baby, for in a village everyone knew the truth. Now she has to live with her more serious sin of deceit. That really should be marked as a deadly sin."

"For more harm's been done by lies than by lust, for sure. I wish you and your father had been to hand to deal with Amelia Hurst, though I must confess to having flirted with her. She's very pretty."

He was a true black sheep in many ways, with a wicked trail behind him. She shouldn't like him, but she did, more and more by the minute.

"Being pretty, she probably thought you'd not object. Peggy's pretty, too."

"Wise Agnes. You'll save me from further folly with pretty young women."

"Will I? Can a sheep change the color of its fleece?"

"I'm merely a slightly darker gray than most others, and I promise to try to become paler. Is it too early to claim that I love you?"

"Far too early," she said, but her heart didn't quite agree. No man had ever declared his love to her and it would be pleasant to experience, at least once.

"Then may I return with you to your home and speak to your father? I'm homeless at the moment, you see, so I might as well find a lodging in your locality so that I can woo you in a more regular manner."

Agnes looked away. That distant voice was trying to object, but Agnes was fighting an insane smile of pure delight. "I can hardly bar you from speaking to my father, sir, or taking up residence somewhere near Dux Cherrymead."

"Dux Cherrymead," he said. "How utterly delightful. Will you lead me into cherry meadows, my enchanting saint?" He rose, pulling her up. "We should return to company, however, before people talk."

Flustered, Agnes looked at the clock. "How long have we been here? Oh dear, oh dear... Drat, I sound like my aunt!"

He laughed and kissed her again. He linked their arms and led her out of the room. "I believe you'll always be saintly, for you have a true and kindly heart, but if female saints must be virgins, I hope to knock you completely out of the ranks."

"You really shouldn't say such things," Agnes said as they returned to the conventional world and the wildness of her behavior overtook her.

"Indeed I should. It's in the Bible. All that marriage and procreation stuff. I know that you'll insist on us doing exactly as we ought once we are finally man and wife."

Agnes did, too, and she didn't care what this tonnish world thought. Tomorrow she was returning home, with a black sheep in her arms, but one not as black as he'd been painted, and whom she knew her father would like and approve.

The only shadow on perfection was that the dowager might take credit for all, but Agnes would try very hard to be saintly about that, and even wish the old harridan well.

Don't Breathe

by Carole Nelson Douglas

Carole Nelson Douglas can't help it: she's colored outside the lines since she was three years old and never reformed. As an award winning a reporter and editor, she was "the first woman" in several newspaper and Newspaper Guild union positions. When the glass ceiling got confining, she became the first staff member to sell a novel in forty-five years and left the security of a well-paid union job to become the author of almost sixty genre-blending, line-crossing novels in historical and contemporary mystery/suspense, high and urban fantasy, and women's fiction. From the very first novel, she's been driven to explore the roles of women in novels and society. She was the first to make a woman from the Sherlock Holmes stories a protagonist of her own series. Her reinvention of Irene Adler as a woman of integrity, not a larcenous minx or mistress, is drawn from the Conan Doyle story and debuted with the *New York Times* Notable Book of the Year, *Good Night, Mr. Holmes*.

Carole currently writes the "epic" Midnight Louie feline PI mystery series, nearing a final 27 entries, and, more recently, the Delilah Street, Paranormal Investigator, noir urban fantasies. She's been on mystery, fantasy/science fiction, and romance bestseller lists. Eight of her mystery stories have been in "Year's Best" anthologies. Among her awards are *RT Book Reviews'* Lifetime Achievement awards in Mystery, Versatility and for being a Pioneer of Publishing. When reviewers note that she combines moral complexities with entertaining stories, she is a very happy writer.

What do women want? I'm with Dr. Freud in asking that question. My generation of girls was prized for naiveté. We weren't expected to be independent or to achieve, so I've been fascinated all my life by examples of both older and younger women who have trouble "owning" their talents and lives yet are admirable survivors.

I think society has been slow to understand the silent struggle of many women because boys are expected to act out and express, while many girls turn inward and suppress. My story imagines how one such girl-woman might wander into dark and deep waters, and how she could wake up and find the courage to defend – and become – herself.

The Hunt

I'm in need of some serious hiding.

Behind a garage or a garbage can won't do.

My thumping heartbeat tells me I've wasted way too much time considering options.

My eyes scan the familiar neighborhood.

The houses' front landscaping is the first place they'll search. They'll also go for the massed ferns on the north walls, although I love the earthy, medicinal smell there, where in the past I've hunkered on my belly like a cat, feeling safe and reas sured. No, not safe in the back yards. Even the jungle-thick plantings around Mrs. Menard's hidden fish pond are too obvious.

I hear their deep voices calling, coming closer. Any sprint of more than fifteen feet will give me away. *Think*, Cathy!

I've hidden myself all over this neighborhood and I don't care about getting dirty. I must hide completely. I can't be found. I can't be found.

Right now, I've boxed myself into the alley. I hear them tromping around the houses' side yards. No fences in this neighborhood. I'm still standing in the late afternoon daylight, feeling naked and visible.

Must disappear totally. *Fast.*

There! Fresh-trimmed brush by the Heinz's dented alumi num garbage can. Barbed-wire sharp branches top a huge pile of grass clippings turning sage green.

I fling the thorny branches aside and burrow like a bone-hungry dog into the dying grass clippings. I'm small, but need to dig deep to cover myself. I can feel the ground pounding from their running footsteps, my heartbeat becoming one with the rhythm of my pursuers.

Shifting deep, facedown into the underlying dirt so moist, cool, and damp, smelling of earthworms, I shovel soft barbered shafts of grass over me, grabbing sharp branches last. Their large, wilting leaves fan to hide me.

The pounding ground is under me now, my heartbeat sandwiched between that deep, sweet darkness and the dan gerous light of day above me,

I hear them stop, the branches stir, their voices muffled.

"She's the last one."

"*Ow!* Not even a rabbit would get into those thorn-bushes."

"Rotten little four-eyed brat. Thinks she's so smart."

A boot kicks the air and leaves above. If they find me now, I'll really pay.

Be quiet. Lie Still. Don't breathe.

This is supposed to be a game, but it isn't. If I win, I only make them madder and meaner. If I lose . . . I don't want to think about that.

Why can't I just become invisible when I need to? Maybe if I think about that harder, some day I will. I can't always freeze like a rabbit. Rabbits think they can't be seen when they can.

Be quiet. Lie Still. Don't breathe.

They've gone, but I wait until twilight to be safe, until the mothers in our small town walk to their front doors and call their kids home for dinner.

~ ~ ~

"How'd you get so filthy, Cathy?" mine asks as I slink through the back door.

"Playing hide and seek with the neighborhood kids."

"The others have come home already."

"They didn't find me."

And when I grow up and get out of this town, they'll never find me.

The Pool

I am trapped.

My toes curl around the round ceramic tile piece that edges the high school pool. Shouts echo against the high, opaque glass windows. Boys somersault off the diving board, scream ing "Geronimo." Ropes of beaded water lash me like liquid pearls as the boys disappear, leaving the waves lapping six inch es below my clutching toes. I could hide in the water, but not now, not here. Because I won't move, I won't.

I stand on the brink of the deep end, shivering. Everyone is staring at spindly me, arms crossed over my embarrassingly big chest, wearing my ugly brown tank suit that bags in the rear. I won't go in the water, so I can't warm up and the other kids' splashes just assault me, like they're doing it on purpose.

"It's required that every student swim, Cathy." Mrs. Apple baum looks silly in her coaching shorts and huge sweat shirt, maybe even sillier than me. "You did fine on the shallow end. You know your strokes. One dive off the deep end and I can pass you."

"Water will go up my nose. I can't stand not breathing."

"For heaven's sake. Don't be such a . . . . Look. It won't if you exhale as you dive. Or you can hold your nose or your breath. I don't care which you do. You'll be back up treading water within ten seconds and I can pass you. Just jump." She moves on, tired of waiting for me to be ready.

I'll never be ready. I gulp down a huge breath, bend my knees and hold my arms over my head, clasped as if praying. My elbows skim my ears, as instructed. I'll have to fall forward straight down, down, down, into the dappled blue water shak ing like Jell-O, shivering like me.

~ ~ ~

My eyes squinch shut behind the swim goggles as I finally push off, hitting water that hits me back – an icy slap in the face . . . then, then I am pushing down, down, my fingers graz ing the slightly rough plaster at the pool's bottom. My body rebounds to arrow up, up, breaking back into a breathing world I view through water-drop blinded goggles.

It. Had. Been. Easy. Fun. Exhilarating.

I thrash to the side, climb the cold metal staircase that hurts my bare feet, poise on the pool's edge and . . . plunge again. And again thrash and climb and plunge.

"Good girl, Cathy!" Mrs. Applebaum yells before my ears hit water and shut out everything but the sound of silence underwater.

I'm used to being told I'm a "good girl." My record is saved, I can graduate and go to college like a . . . good girl.

Now, though, I want to claim the element that had frightened me, to tame it. I fight to stay longer at the bottom, gazing up through the cool blue Beyond shimmering above. I can hide here, float. Yet the need for air always pushes me back into the noisy, echoing splashes, pushes me into visibility into the tiny tidal basin of everybody's pool.

Not mine.

~ ~ ~

Now they can't keep me out of the water. I discover the pool's off hours, then spend lovely hours alone there. I dive and remain submerged, my eyes open. My new, wet womb is my exact body temperature. I stare at my light-dappled sky, spread my arms and legs and float, hidden and safe from everyone.

I remember the pretty blue satin lining of my grandmother's coffin lid, gathered into watery ripples, rusching it was called. I'd been ten and decided I wanted a pale blue-lined coffin of my own some day, like a limitless sky of new possibilities.

"Where's she gone, Cathy?" I was asked, and was supposed to answer, "Heaven."

"Blue heaven," I'd said instead.

Now, I can glimpse that endless blue peace again . . . .

On land once more, dry and parched for buoyancy and a universe only I can see, I cruise the Internet for information on holding your breath under water.

Pearl divers can do more than six minutes.

Be quiet. Lie Still. Don't breathe.

Stunt athletes established a world record of more than nine minutes.

Be quiet. Lie Still. Don't breathe.

Magicians inhale pure oxygen beforehand and manage seventeen minutes. If I could have held my breath like this during hide and seek . . . .

Be quiet. Lie Still. Don't breathe.

At last, I master the final test for utter comfort under water.

I dive, relax, recline on my back on the pool bottom and look up. It can be done if you don't thrash, if you don't panic. Anything can be done. Some people freak at reaching, much less maintaining this position. I clasp the waterproof wrist watch over my stomach with my other hand and count as I hold my breath and stare at blissful nothing.

Be quiet. Lie Still. Don't breathe.

~ ~ ~

My parents ask what I want for a graduation gift from high school. They're so pleased with how well I've done the last two years, with my grades, my college scholarship, my maturity, they say. Our family is not in the "car for graduation" bracket.

"One perfect pearl," I say.

And I get it, not large, but on an eighteen-carat, fine gold chain.

I am a pearl diver.

Be quiet. Lie Still. Don't breathe.

The Professor

My parents try not to show their disappointment when I pick a college in Florida. One night, I hear them comforting themselves with the hope that it might hone my "social skills."

But I'm not after a "party" school. I'm after a place where pools are common. I take Psychology 101 in freshman year and self-diagnose. I'm a cliché: smart but shy and from a shel tered background. You live your life the way you have to and don't analyze it until you must.

Being smart had gotten me bullied, and I'd found the older neighborhood boys big, crude and threatening. At least in col lege that kind were confined to the locker room and I was meeting guys who wore glasses and read books and liked to talk about the wider world. I'd decided to major in psychology, but in senior year I had to get a passing grade from a professor who made the heartless anti-mentoring sharks I'd heard popu lated law schools look like guppies.

This was far trickier than diving into a pool of water, but my unique form of stress relief had given me some survival and coping mechanisms by then. I knew how to hide in class.

Professor Shark affected tweed jackets and a flashy bow tie. He was in his late forties, lean as a new manila folder and about as sharp-edged. He wore his thinning gray hair in an autocratic Caesar cut that curled around the front edges, ready for any possible impending laurel wreath.

The girls who were sent to college for other reasons than degrees or knowledge competed to line the front row of the theatrically raked classroom, all wearing short skirts and cross ing their legs.

I kept to the middle seats in the side sections and always wore jeans. I may still have been shy beneath the studious aca demic air I was developing but I wasn't stupid. The professor was vain, overbearing and liked to manipulate women.

The writhing wannabes in the first row were an annual fix ture, so he adored calling on me.

After reading from what he considered the worst of the weekly papers, he took glee in singling me out as Miss Perfect.

"Miss Carlson, however, avoids illiteracy as well as igno rance. Why can't you bozo boys and bimbo girls figure out how to parse a graceful sentence, not to mention pose a convincing argument?"

He then would wave my sheaf of white bond with the kind of flourish that passes for a wave from Queen Elizabeth to the crowd. "Stand up, Miss Carlson, and take your bow."

I would be forced to rise and smile painfully. Again.

"Class, perhaps you will consult Miss Carlson afterwards for tips on getting a passing grade. That's all."

Of course, they avoid me in droves.

One day as I shuffle out with my laptop bag at my side, someone jostles me. Not unusual. The other students, baited, often do that, punishing me in their mute, herdlike way.

"Wait."

The voice is unfamiliar. I turn to recognize the profes sor's runner, the teaching assistant who never gets a chance to speak, only to sprint up and down the aisled tiers to deliver the papers to their owners . . . after the professor has dusted them off his manicured hands and spiral-bound mind.

"Cathy." He pulls me out of the crowd and against a wall. "You left your paper."

I look at it, seeing the large A-plus in red on the cover page. Might as well have worn that grade as a scarlet letter. The students around us glimpse it too, and give me poisonous looks. I clap the paper facedown to my chest.

"Thanks," I tell the guy, not meaning it.

"Eric. I'm the prof's T. A. All the T.A. he's interested in is the tits and asses in the front row. Come on. I'll buy you beer at Rizzo's."

"I like wine."

"Wine it is."

~ ~ ~

"So." I sip the chardonnay. Eric nurses a pale ale. He's the opposite of the professor. His thick, curly brown hair brushes his earlobes and the back of his corduroy jacket, his features are even and open and fully shaved. "You're saying the prof does this every semester?" I ask. "Picks a class brain to turn into a pariah?"

"Pretty female class brain." Eric grabs some beer nuts to gnaw from the plastic dish in the center of the tiny table.

"I'm not . . . pretty."

"Sure you are." He glances at my necklace. I'm relieved his eyes ignore my chest. "Pearly white skin, coppery hair and green eyes, like a mermaid."

Wow. Eric knew how to make pasty skin, limp hair and murky hazel eyes sound good. His eyes are chestnut-brown, robust and energetic like him. Maybe he actually likes my . . . type.

I sip more wine. "And the only way the other female class members can get a passing grade is to line up in the front row for a turn in his bed? Ugh. That is borderline personality disorder."

"Yeah. He's a psychology professor. They're all crazy."

"Also a sexist, narcissistic sociopath."

Eric grins. "You'll go far in your chosen field. But I gotta get my thesis past that old bastard. I could use your help. He's stealing from everybody's papers for his own articles anyway, including yours and my rough-draft thesis. It would be fun to manipulate *him* for a change."

Fun. I hadn't had any in college yet. Eric's smile is mischievous. "Want to visit my crib and cook up some academic revenge?"

The Teaching Assistant

That's how it started, and if my ghostwriting was good for Eric's thesis, he was good for me too. My eyes did look more greenish than griege when I got contact lenses, started using green eye shadow and rinsed my dishwater-blond hair "Copper Shimmer 74."

I discovered that Eric was also an artist who cast found objects – leaves and seashells and acorns – into incredible silver and brass accretions that lined his walls like metallic barnacles. They were impressive.

"The master's degree in psych is just to fall back on," he told me, making a face, "so I can teach if I have to."

I discovered that sex was not only possible, but fun, like diving. Eric was pulling me into a free-wheeling kidhood I'd never had. We moved in together in six months. First requirement was a big living area he could use as a studio. I needed a pool.

"A pool? Cathy, you never allow the sun to touch a cell of your white skin."

"I swim after dark."

"*Hmm.* Weird but somehow sexy. OK. Whatever you want. But you've got to let me cast your hands."

"My hands? They're kinda big and bony –"

"Sculptural, hon. I don't know where you got this inferiority complex, but you're about to graduate so you should have the expertise to shake it, and if you don't, I'll shake it out of you."

He takes my hands and kisses them. "I want to memorialize the hands that make me happy and play me like a computer keyboard. Besides, I have great news. I can afford to put your hands in bronze."

I feel myself blush. Eric can go overboard, but that's what I love about him.

"I have some news too." His smiling, quizzical look encourages me to go on. "I'm thinking I'll go for my master's too."

After a tiny pause, he says, "Great. Two almost-'doctors' in the house."

I'd seen the quickly concealed shadow behind the smile. "What's your news?"

"First the white wine." He jumps up to fetch glasses of chardonnay. "A toast to your forthcoming thesis. May you get any advisor other than Old Ironsides. My news? The Vann Sommer Gallery wants to do a one-man show for me next year."

"But . . . that place is pricey and all the artists it handles are from the coasts."

"Exactly. I'll have to work like a demon. I need signature pieces. Bigger, bolder. It'll cost, Cathy, mostly in time and materials, but the rewards –"

"Oh my God, Eric! That's amazing." I bite my lip, seeing what he concealed. "Your T.A. money ran out with graduation and my job at the flower shop isn't enough to live on."

"I'll figure something out. Maybe my father up in Lake City could help out financially. The farm has him rolling in money. Shit sells, but I'm 'just' idling away in fine art."

"You're estranged from your father."

"Yeah, but I'm the only son. Maybe he'll melt. Don't worry about it. The show is months and months off. Anything could happen."

~ ~ ~

Something did. Two months later, I got pregnant.

"I don't understand. We were so careful."

Eric stops my distraught pacing with an embrace. "Well, you can't use the Pill because of the family blood-clot thing.

Diaphragm and foam is like something the Etruscans used these days. Not reliable."

"You're not angry?"

Eric shrugs. "Not in the plan, but, to be honest, I'm kinda excited. Everything is new for us, our degrees, my gallery show and now our baby."

"But the money!"

"Maybe my father will be an ecstatic grandfather. He has a patriarch complex. Maybe we could move up to the farm while you're pregnant."

Maybe not. The old man sounded like the kind of tyran nical parent who'd ridiculed his daughters and spoiled his only son. My baby was not going to be born under the likes of him.

Listen to me. Dawning motherhood had given me the spine of a shark. Or maybe at least a cuttlefish.

The House

Eric is right about his father. Once we got a city hall quick ie marriage (that disappointed my parents back home) and he told his dad that I was pregnant, the old man signed over a house he owned near the university to his son. The roomy two-story had once been grand, but is shopworn from being chopped up into rented student housing. A monthly mortgage payment comes with it. The only perk is a pool put into the wooded back yard to attract students. A wooden fence keeps the neighboring hordes of undergraduates out.

I get a job with the city social services department serving indigent clients. The pay is twice what I got in the flower shop, but it's high summer and the smell sits uneasily on my pregnant stomach. On the other hand, the position keeps me off my swollen feet. And my evening solo dips in the pool ease the pressure of my swelling stomach and breasts.

Eric always has a glass of sparkling water waiting for me when I get home from work. He's making major metal work sculptures now, and his muscles are ropy, his hair curled from sweat. He's not making any money, spending a lot instead, but you can't say he's not working. He's never looked hotter. It burns off of him like an aura of gas-blue welding-torch flame.

"Come on, hon. Feet up, sit back, and tell me about the weirdoes you saw today."

"They're clients, Eric. People who've fallen through the cracks and have never had their physical or psychological needs fulfilled. And it pays our way."

"Yeah, yeah. You're Mother Teresa. Speaking of physical needs . . ." He pulls a light chair forward so he can take my now-bare feet into his lap for a massage. "I got an idea."

"*Umm*. Only one?"

"I want to cast your tits."

"What?" I'd seen my metal hands lying around his studio and they gave me an odd feeling.

"Come on, Cathy. They've always been your best feature and now they're really pumped." His voice is almost a whisper, seductive.

"Come on, Cathy. I work with inanimate metal all day. Be ing pregnant puts a crimp in our sex life. Let me work with soft flesh for a change, immortalize your killer boobs, have something to polish while you're away at work."

He's never said such things to me. I'm both repulsed and . . . turned on.

His laugh sounds for a second like Professor Shark's. "I take it those nipples trying to punch through your T-shirt are a 'yes?'"

~ ~ ~

The process is damp, cold, and feels slightly perverse. The wet plaster clothes draping my chest seem more medical than sexual and I suddenly panic at being pinned down, frozen, exposed.

Be quiet. Lie Still. Don't breathe.

"Wish I could give you some wine to relax, babe," he mur murs, working over me like a doctor with a patient on a table. "Bad for the baby, though."

"Is this going on display?" I fret.

"On my studio wall, sure. But I'm thinking of making a multi-piece sculpture of 'Woman.' You're my muse, why not?"

"I don't want my body parts in an art show."

Eric shakes his shaggy head. "Cathy, Cathy. Don't worry. Nudes are anonymous in art."

~ ~ ~

I do worry.

I slip out of my bedroom with the unit air-conditioner at night. Now that I'm pregnant, Eric sleeps in the bedroom "stu dio." We can only afford only two window units, and he works forging cold casts into hot metal assemblages all day. My breast cast hangs on the living-room wall beside one of my hands and I shudder every time I pass it. It resembles the remnant of some long-gone ship's figurehead, found encrusted with bar nacles on the sea floor.

It's so damned *detailed*, a body cast. I feel as if pieces of me have been peeled off, like rinds, leaving my nerves exposed. It's probably hormones, so I cool off in the pool. I don't dive now, but slip into the water as silently as a seal and paddle my way to the bottom. I may feel like a whale on land, but here deep in the still water I am graceful and supported, my baby learning to be a water creature, like me.

One night, like a spider sensing prey in its web, I feel the surface agitated by tiny tugging ripples. I let myself float up to see four bare feet dabbling in the water at the shallow end.

Only my face breaks the surface as my hand clings to the ladder on the deep end.

It's two silly coeds, a bottle of wine between them as they sit, clothed, on the pool edge.

From the house next door, I hear the blare of an all-night party our air-conditioners drowned out.

"We shouldn't be here, Bree," one says. "I scratched my calf scaling that wooden fence. And actual people live here. I mean, not students."

"Footz on you. Listen to the air-conditioners hum. They're asleep in their separate bedrooms. Isn't this peaceful and *quiet*? We could skinny dip and no one would know."

"No. The guys might catch us."

"Don't be such a wuss, Kelly. Those undergrad guys are so gross and immature."

Speaking of shallow ends, “Bree” and “Kelly” are perfectly placed. I hear them whispering and giggling, Bree singing the praises of “bronze gods” obviously not present at the neighbor’s party, and Kelly taking long swigs from the wine bottle between worried glances at my house. Neither one thinks to glance at the other end of the pool.

I take a deep, deep breath and silently submerse. My underwater training will make delivery room breathing patterns a walk in the park. Now I feel mature, in control. Superior.

Be quiet. Lie Still. Don’t breathe.

~ ~ ~

A touch of autumn crisps the air. Soon I’ll have to switch to the Y pool two miles away.

When I come home one day, there’s no Eric, no glass of sparkling water.

The door to his studio is shut and the music is cranked up to a deafening roar, even over the air-conditioning.

I run to open the door, but it’s locked. Pounding, pounding on the thick old wood until my palms sting and my knuckles skin.

Then Eric stands there, bare-chested and gleaming with sweat, an empty whiskey bottle in his hand. He shouts four-letter words at me in repetitive strings. The room is dark except for night lights. I stumble inside to feel for the stereo cord and pull it out of the wall.

Eric is pounding the thick whiskey bottle base on his wooden work table, punctuating every blow with a foul word.

“Eric! What is it? What’s happened.”

“The old man. He died.”

“Died? I’m . . . sorry. Today?”

“Sorry? Sorry! Three weeks ago he died. My so-called sisters didn’t even let me know when he went into the hospital for the last time.”

“He did have a brush with cancer last year, you said. You didn’t call.”

“I was busy with the pieces for the show. Those damn bitches didn’t want me to know, didn’t want me there. I get this letter from a Lake City lawyer and he left everything to them. Like the cliché. The whole freaking farm! They snatched it from me on his deathbed. Do you know what it was worth?"

"A lot, you said, but you still have all the work you've done for the show, the baby is coming, we have the house . . . "

"The house is a liability, a piece of shit. It's underwater, do you know what that means? You're doing a crap job for crap money and I am screwed. The baby. The show. I . . . I just can't do it."

His anger drives me out of the room and he slams the door shut in my face.

I almost go for the chardonnay, but grit my teeth and stop myself. And here I'd felt mature and superior compared to those two party girls just a couple weeks ago. Bree was right. It looked like separate bedrooms for now, and maybe forever.

Be quiet. Lie Still. Don't breathe.

~ ~ ~

"Cathy?"

I wake up in the tangle of my bedsheets under the hum of the air conditioning unit.

"Cathy." I feel a weight depress the side of my mattress.

"I'm sorry," Eric says, only a slumped shadow in the dark. "I went nuts. I'd been counting on that inheritance and so ab sorbed in doing the pieces for the show. You're right. I've still got the show." His hand rests on my mounded belly. "And the baby. And you. I'm going to work even harder, because that could get us the financial security we need. Okay? We okay? If you'll just bear with me – ?"

"'Bear?'" I repeat with a smile in my voice.

"Oh, right. I'm a doofus." He lays the side of his face on my belly and I pat his cheek maternally. Men can be such chil dren sometimes. All tantrums and regretful aftermath.

The Mask

"Pretty please," he says.

Eric has dedicated himself to his studio work. He said the gallery owner came by when I was working to see the new stuff and had been bowled over. Eric showed me a sample of the invitation, classier than any wedding invitation I'd ever seen, on handmade rag paper with exquisitely transparent sheets in side. Eric's name and the gallery's were set in embossed silver-metallic type.

I felt like I was nine-and-a-half months' pregnant, but it was only eight months.

So when Eric sits me down and tells me Leon Sommer had been enchanted by his bronzes of my body parts, I can only blink with disbelief.

"It's the human touch in all this inanimate metal, Cathy. I need to do the pièce de résistance. The face."

"People would recognize me. It'd be like stripping for them."

"No. It's art. It's revelation, yes, but in the cosmic sense."

"I'm not an artist's model; I'm your wife."

"I don't want a model and neither does Leon. What makes it work is it's a real person, a person who means something to the artist, to me. Please do it."

"I'll have that heavy wet plaster cloth covering my face for how long? And how will I breathe?"

"Like they do for life masks in art classes. Straws, simple drinking straws, small enough for your nostrils. It only takes a few minutes, and you know how to be patient."

"Yes, I do, and since this pregnancy, I *really* do. It's a big decision. Let me think about it."

~ ~ ~

Eric is as delighted when I say, "yes" – as when I agreed to marry him.

He brings us ceremonial glasses of chardonnay. Studies showed pregnant women could drink occasionally, so I sip half of it. Then he poses me in the living room reclining chair with a big ottoman under my feet. Eric lards my face with Vaseline, especially the eyebrows and my closed eyelashes.

I'm already feeling a bit uneasy, but he squeezes my hand before he begins laying the wet cloths over my features, the same way a cast is made for a broken limb, only my face isn't the part of me that's broken.

The Vaseline-coated straws probe my nostrils. A tentative inhalation works. I try another, deeper one.

"That's fine, Cathy." I hear Eric leave my side and almost panic. I'm blind and gagged. He's back soon. "This will keep you warm." A heavy winter coat descends on me from neck to knees. My pregnant belly must look like foothill. Blind, gagged, and . . . bound.

I can't move. I can't speak.

I feel the fine hairs inside my nose tickle as Eric draws the slender Vaseline-coated straws through them.. Narrow red-striped drinking straws you can find in any grocery store. First in, and now . . . out.

"Don't worry, Cathy," Eric whispers over my shrouded ear. "I won't hang your face cast next to your boobs. No one will ever know the boobs are yours."

Those are the last words he says to me.

The wine has made my face tingle under the oppressive wet weight of the hardening plaster. The jacket he's thrown across me is as heavy as a leaded x-ray guard pinning me to the dentist's chair.

I can barely move a finger, but I don't want to struggle any more. Particularly not with him. This last betrayal has been too much.

Be quiet. Lie Still. Don't breathe.

"Why isn't she fighting? The voice is new, and female, but I'm not surprised that it's Bree's.

"I told you to stay out until it was over."

"I thought it was too quiet in here. Guess the wine worked."

"With the Xanax, really fast."

"The baby . . . ?"

"What about it?"

"It's half yours. Don't you feel guilty?"

"I'm not the baby-wanting kind. That kid let me down. It was supposed get my father's financial support. Consider it a late abortion. You've done that already, haven't you, Bree?"

"But it wasn't yours."

"Doesn't matter now. *You* are mine. And that's forever, baby."

"I never could figure out," Bree teases, "why a bronze god like you saddled himself with such a stupid wife."

"She wasn't stupid in one way, just in the wrong way. Just a stupid cow with great boobs."

"Creepy. Nothing's moving, not even the coat. She's a gon er. I could use a drink."

"I'm done drinking that pale-piss chardonnay. On to something full-bodied, babe. Merlot. We can drink a toast to my show and my new muse."

"You *are* a bad boy. Don't we have a lot of scutt work to do first?"

"Later. Tonight. Once this ole house is burned down. I'll be out from under it, and from her too."

That's right, my drowsing brain registers. His father's leg acy is now an overpriced mortgage. The house is underwater too, under the shirred blue satin of the coffin lid too.

Be quiet. Lie still. Don't breathe.

The Floater

Eric and Bree's voices segue into a louder, echoing babble. They seem to have panicked, poor things, something I haven't done, and will not do

When one doesn't breathe, I found out very early in life, when one is invisible, even when one is just treated as invisible, everything becomes so much easier to hear.

Some girls don't eat until they disappear.

Some girls cut themselves until they don't bleed inside.

Some girls hide inside themselves, out of sight to everyone else.

All such girls have nerves of naked awareness.

Poor Eric.

He mistook quiet for acquiescence.

My nerves are screaming now, shrieking violin strings mourning the absence of air.

Even that ungodly noise fades into the dark behind my eyes, the oxygen slowly evaporating from my cells. Our cells.

Be quiet. Lie Still. Don't breathe.

Then a confusing battery of sounds penetrates my shroud of heavy coat and suffocating face mask.

The weight on my body vanishes like a stage curtain jerked aside.

The hardening ghost of my own features is peeling away.

I am the center of all attention, the leading lady.

I can hear Eric and Bree providing a chorus of protests at the far edges of my perception.

"CPR," a voice shouts.

"No. I think she's still breathing, very shallowly."

"Be quiet. Lie still. Just breathe," a voice counsels me.

"It's a good thing she didn't panic."

"Or we got here just after this started."

Another stranger's voice calls from a short distance away, "Here are the nasal straws. The bastard put them in the ashtray *fifteen feet* away."

"What's your name, hon?" a woman asks. I don't mind the familiarity.

My stiff lips move as hoarded air eases through them. Slowly. Always come to the surface slowly. "Cath-Cathy."

Tending hands and voices surround me, urgent and kind. I sense their trembling triumph at finding I can still breathe.

I'm pretty happy about it too. That they arrived in time.

"Okay, Cathy. Inhale again. You're going to be okay. Just breathe. Slowly. Just breathe. That's a good girl."

I manage a tiny smile.

Someone pulls my cell phone from under my fingertips, from slightly under my body, concealed by my right palm and fingers.

"Somehow she managed to text 911 and send it after they pinned her down."

"It's a miracle. Can those creeps be charged with more than attempted murder?"

"On two counts? Don't worry," the man answers. "Any jury that hears the sheer sadism of their plot to kill mother and fetus will give that pair life without parole. Plenty of time to reflect on their sins."

"Poor woman. To lie there, absolutely defenseless, and hear, realize, what they were doing to her, and the baby . . . ."

"They're lucky she was still breathing when we found her."

"Why, I don't understand. Almost six minutes elapsed be fore we got here and pulled off the mask. It must have been the maternal drive to protect her baby."

Oh, yes. My baby is floating in amniotic fluid, attached to a swaying tube of sustenance like someone in an old-fashioned diver's suit, one with my body, breathing underwater. We all came from water.

Oh, my baby. *Be quiet. Lie still. Don't breathe.*

Not right now. Not quite yet.

Small Sacrifices

by Jodi Lynn Nye

Jody Lynn Nye lists her main career activity as "spoiling cats." When not engaged upon this worthy occupation, she writes fantasy and science fiction books and short stories.

Since 1987 she has published 43 books and more than 100 short stories. Among the novels Jody has written are her epic fantasy series, *The Dreamland*, five contemporary humorous fantasies, and three medical science fiction novels. *Strong Arm Tactics*, a humorous military science fiction novel, is the first of Jody's new series, *The Wolfe Pack*. Jody also wrote *The Dragonlover's Guide to Pern*, a non-fiction-style guide to the world of internationally best-selling author Anne McCaffrey's popular world. She has also collaborated with Anne McCaffrey on four science fiction novels. Her newest books are *Dragons Deal*, third in the *Dragons* series begun by the late Robert Asprin, and *View From the Imperium*, a humorous military SF novel. Coming soon is *Myth-Quoted*, the next novel set in Asprin's Myth-Adventures universe.

Perri Closson is a determined young woman. Her dearest dream, that of going on the Mars mission with her then-fiancé, Ethan, was dashed by a bout with heart disease. She underwent heart valve replacement with a bioengineered vessel from a genetically modified piglet. As a scientist, she had not previously considered the value of farm animals' lives. Now that one possesses her DNA, she has engendered kinship with it. Perri wants to wean humans away from eating pigs, by inventing a fully plant-based bacon. Her success throws her into contention with Ethan, whose family fortune and his own dreams of space travel depend upon bringing pigs on the mission as both food and scientific subjects. Perri, naturally, is conflicted. She doesn't want to destroy Ethan's family, but she does not want humanity to use live animals in the callous way it has. No matter what she does, someone is going to be unhappy, but her bacon is delicious.

Dr. Perri Closson watched as Dr. Ethan Miller chewed, trying to guess what he was thinking by the expressions on his long, mobile face. Her own smaller, rounder face she kept guarded. The small testing room, one of sixteen in a row in the Cropworth Corporation facility, had clean, white enameled walls, soundproofed to keep out ambient noise, comfortable but nondescript white furniture, all designed to make the sub ject focus on the samples at hand and nothing else.

"Well?" she asked at last.

Ethan swallowed. "Better than the last batch," he said. "I like the color more too."

"Good," Perri said, glancing at the platter in her hands. The crisped red-and-white striped slices, browned from the pan, were markedly more inviting than her lab's earliest at tempts. "So what's not right?"

He ran his tongue around his lips. "I'm not sure. It's sweet and salty and crunchy. You got the chewy part just right. And the smell is good, really good. Maybe it's because I know it's not really bacon."

Perri groaned. Ethan threw up his hands.

"I'm sorry! Ten generations of pig farmers, you're just not going to fool me with fakin' bacon."

"I will one day," Perri said firmly. She set the tray on the sample table and picked up her pad computer. "So, do you think this is 85% to approximating real bacon, 90%, or less? Your previous estimation was 80%."

"Oh, ninety," Ethan said. "You're getting really close."

Perri went down the list. She tapped the entries that were flashing, filling in Ethan's responses. Her white lab smock could have doubled for a chef's coat. Sometimes she thought she was turning into more of a cook than a biochemist.

"Thanks, Ethe. I don't know anyone else who would be so honest with me."

He eyed her, his round blue eyes fixed on her hooded brown ones. He hadn't changed much in the six years since they had graduated from their master's program. She had, and she knew it. "Why is this so important to you?" he asked.

She refused to meet his gaze. The real reason sounded silly when said out loud. "Sustainable resources are more easily met through plants than animals. Taking pigs into space is a bad idea."

Ethan nudged her arm. "C'mon, it worked for the Muppets."

Perri glared at him from under her brows. "I'm serious!"

"Why not?"

"Well… it's inhumane to raise them in such small spaces. They like to roam as much as the next animal. And they compete with human beings for the same food."

All humor went out of his expression and he became serious. "I know all that, Per. I was born knowing it. That's why I'm going on the mission. My family has always tried to provide sufficient room per animal on our farms, but we don't go crazy measuring every millimeter. Healthy pen space has been calculated into the generation ship floor plan for the working herd. We've got plenty of sperm, eggs and implantable zygotes in cryostorage, waiting to load. Pigs will be useful animals to have with us. They convert leftovers and scraps into edible tissue and organic fertilizer. We use every part but the squeal, and I'm working on a process for that, too. I will take care of them, but they are a vital resource."

"You know we shouldn't be eating pigs any more," she said.

Ethan scowled. "All right, that's it. You've changed since you got sick."

"I know. I did."

"You used to love bacon. You used to eat it all the time. You loved it when I brought packages to college from home."

Perri felt her conscience sting. "I still love bacon! I just don't think we should get it from pigs any more."

He threw a scornful hand at the tray.

"Where else? Your plants? That's not really a viable alternative. Why else do we raise pigs?"

"But they're intelligent!" She clutched the front of her lab coat. It covered the eight-inch-long scar that was a constant reminder of the change in her life. "And…when they did the bypass, they gave me a new heart valve from a pig."

"I know. I remember. It came from our facility. So that's it? That's your reason?"

"Yes! I can't eat pork any more. It would be cannibalism."

"How could it be cannibalism? You're not a pig."

"But some of them are partly human now. We hybridize all the time. We already share a lot of DNA with them. Especially me. While I was waiting for the operation, they integrated my DNA into a strain of pigs so the valve would be a genetic match."

"Oh, yeah, I knew that," Ethan said. "Herd #506HU, our best all-purpose animals. I think it was sow AM-09."

"No! Her name's Daisy. She received my DNA. Then she had Muriel Piglet who gave her life for me. She was only nine weeks old."

Ethan's face turned red, and his eyes flashed fury.

"Stop that. Don't anthropomorphize them. They're pigs. Swine. Meat on the hoof. They're used all the time for medical research procedures AND food. Having your DNA doesn't make them human."

"We're blurring the lines!"

"You know, you've turned into a real hypocrite," Ethan said. "You still eat other meat, don't you? How can you still eat beef and chicken if you've sworn off pork?"

"I'm not *related* to them."

He loomed over her angrily, his six-two overwhelming her five-four.

"You know, I really shouldn't even be helping you. If you get your way, you'll take away my dad's contract. That means half a billion dollars over the next ten years. Why do you even call me?" He stepped away, his expression rueful. "And why do I answer?"

She made the same face. Dear Ethan. It was never easy for either of them to stay mad at the other. "We always checked each other's work in Ag school, she said. "Old habits. I trust you more than anyone else."

"Well, don't," he said curtly. "We're rivals now. Don't call me any more. It was one thing when only grades were at stake. My whole future – my family's whole future – could be in the trash if your company gets the NASA contract and ours doesn't." He strode away. "See you on the launch pad, Perri."

With sorrow, she watched him slam his way out of the room. She felt terrible for him, but she knew she was right, both morally and ecologically. It was hard to separate herself from her work, even when it was appropriate or necessary. In a way, Ethan was right, too. She had to learn to be more dispas sionate, just not where pigs were concerned.

Her assistant, Dr. Asif Reylani, waited just the right amount of time before coming in to retrieve the ceramic tray.

"How'd it go?" Asif asked, as if he hadn't been in the next room listening. She had hired the fifty-something biolo gist from a lab in Great Britain purely on his reputation for precision, and had been pleased that he came with a wealth of tact and kindness.

"I think we're almost there," Perri said. She had to pull herself together. She forced the butterflies in her stomach to stop fluttering, and smiled at him. "That's a great batch. I think if he hadn't known, it might have fooled him. I don't know. We're almost there, I know it. Maybe just a little tweak to the next batch. Let's try cooking it in a different oil. The texture was great. I made notes. Go a little heavier on iron in the feed ing water. That ought to help incorporate just a little more meatiness. Tell everyone, good work."

"I will." He cocked his head. His deep brown eyes were framed with sympathetic lines. "You look depressed."

"I am. I pretty much lost my best friend. And it's only go ing to get worse. There's so little time left to make this work."

~ ~ ~

The chamber of Congress was packed with politicians, reporters and representatives from dozens of supply compa nies. Every one of them, like Perri, was hoping to make their mark on the upcoming long-range joint space project between NASA, the European Space Agency, and the Chinese space agency. It was the first manned mission since the Obama administration had pulled the plug on the budget over twenty years before. This one was for all the marbles, as Perri's CFO put it. A massive ship, to be built in space, that would take twenty months to make the transition to Mars. Once there, it would go into orbit around the red planet for a multi-year study. If the results were favorable, the engineers on board would begin the process for a planetside station, the first ever permanent domicile for human beings outside the confines of Earth. It was an incredibly exciting project, worth billions of dollars to companies lucky enough to have their products utilized. That meant a multi-year process of patenting designs, submitting offers, conferences with NASA/ESA/CNSA, tweaking and adjusting, then having to testify before Congress, all before getting the final go-ahead to receive funding. The last was the most tedious part, requiring endless repetition and explanation of data from documents submitted multiple times to men and women who were not engineers or scientists. Perri was prepared to smile and repeat herself over and over again, if it meant her company would succeed in getting Cropworth on board.

Senator Emmett Tolfield of Maine turned over a strip of Perri's best and latest version of the vegetable bacon on the platter before him before bringing it to his rather large nose for a sniff. His huge white eyebrows flew upward in surprised pleasure. Perri kept her smile noncommittal.

"I'm impressed, Doctor Closson. If I didn't know for certain, I'd have said this was good old hickory-smoked bacon. Nice work. You're sure it's made from sugar beets?"

Perri leaned into her microphone. A score of small recording devices from the various reporters lay on the table around it. "Yes, Senator. One of eight strains we've been working on for several years."

She was no longer concerned that anyone would glean enough information from her testimony to duplicate her company's work. The Patent Office had already granted the initial patents, and she knew she had fulfilled the 'first-to-file' requirements on all subsequent documents.

"Where'd the colors come from?"

"Red and white were already present in ordinary cultivars," Perri said. "You can see on your briefing the cross-breeding that we did to give the tubers vertical stripes instead of horizontal rings. We selected for higher protein so it has the equivalent of meat bacon without the cholesterol." A pleased hum rose in the room.

"One thing, though," said an African-American congressman from Oregon, raising a finger. "When my wife cooks beets, they always bleed red all over everything."

"Well, nothing's perfect, Congressman," Asif said, with a little smile. "But since you're frying and not boiling, the cell walls do a better job of containing the pigment. And we have also selected for stronger fiber. It gives the bacon that nice crunch without as much red staining."

Senator Melita Soukos (D-Va) waved a dismissive hand. "Explain why we should take this instead of what we understand? This is genetically modified, isn't it?"

Perri groaned to herself.

"Yes, of course, Senator. Just very small changes, but necessary ones."

Soukos frowned. "You expect us to send food into space that hasn't been proven safe?"

"It is safe, Senator. Beets have been eaten by humans for millennia. We have been running FDA-approved trials up to the human-subjects stage on our cultivars. We have had no problems whatsoever. I eat samples from various batches every day." She felt the perverse urge to cough, but knew perfectly well it wouldn't go over, and she could expect to see the clip on YouTube for the rest of her life. The congressional board had no sense of humor, and they were all too aware of the cameras. All of them hoped to score points with their constituents. She looked hopefully at the left side of the panel, where two senators and a congressman sat. They were known to support scientific advances, and had some imagination.

"What about this file? The fellow who went into insulin shock?"

Perri knew that case was going to come up, and she was ready for it. "He was an undiagnosed diabetic, Senator. I couldn't foresee that. He didn't know, either."

"You've got to know that we are reluctant to send anything on this long-term mission that might kill everyone six months out, even for the sake of a spaceborne BLT. Terran animals make a better food source for Terran explorers."

"But, ma'am, these take little care and far less room."

"Just tell me again why we should go with your GMO beets instead of good, old-fashioned meat. Just the science. We've heard from the animal rights activists. I don't want to rehash that with you. Why should we waste any more time on bacon?"

The senator wasn't really looking at her, but preening for the news cameras. Perri composed herself to look friendly and approachable. "Well, it's one of the most popular foods in the world, ma'am. We've taken multiple surveys and done over a hundred taste tests. One of the largest studies asked what would people miss most if they turned vegetarian. The answer was almost always bacon. Not other meats or cheeses. Bacon. The smell of cooking bacon provokes emotional and neurological responses that are not duplicated by other foods. Since our people are going to be away from home for a long time, we hate to see them deprived of food that gives both pleasure and comfort. A taste of home far away."

"Lust for junk food isn't a good reason, Doctor!"

Tolfield shifted to face Soukos. "I've got to tell you, I agree with the study. I feel the same way. Stop hammering her, Senator."

Soukos put her chin up, annoyed. "All right, but I hate to put anything on the ship that isn't organic in origin, pesticide and antibiotic free. They can't come back to Earth for emergency medical treatment. It would look bad if people started to die because they couldn't live without a BLT."

"It's more likely to be the mayonnaise that kills them, Senator," Asif said, leaning forward with a charming smile. The audience laughed.

At the other end of the table, Mission Commander Shirley Fisher pulled her microphone close. "We want this product on board, folks. All my crew are big fans of Cropworth. It's the first time I can feel good about eating bacon that isn't *traif*."

Tolfield chuckled and banged the gavel.

"All right, Doctor Closson. You're excused. We'll get back to you."

Perri kicked back her chair and made for the door, smiling and nodding to the reporters who clustered around her, shouting questions. Behind her, Ethan and his contingent took their places.

"Well, that went well," Asif said, putting a protective arm around her to guide her through the crowd.

Perri felt as if her heart was in her shoes. "No, it didn't. What's the hold-up? It's not like genetic modification is that new any more."

"Hard to get old habits out of their minds. You know what food substitutes have tasted like in the past, and they're all afraid of genetic monstrosities. If they allow a wheat-avocado hybrid, what's next? Glowing kittens and spider-snakes, that's what."

"You ought to work for Hollywood," Perri said, diverted in spite of herself.

Asif winked. "And you think they haven't asked me? I have to beat them away from my inbox with a stick."

"Even if Congress does give us the go-ahead, it still doesn't solve my basic concerns."

Asif patted her shoulder. "Well, desperate times call for desperate measures. But if you want my advice, you won't take any."

~ ~ ~

That evening, she wondered whether she should have taken Asif's advice. As she had been instructed by furtive text messages, Perri left her company vehicle at the main entrance to the shopping center and walked all the way through to the loading dock. It was dark in the stinking, concrete block. She heard shuffling sounds in the shadows. Her heart pounded so hard she could hardly breathe.

"Password?" a harsh whisper demanded as bodies crowded around her.

The very absurdity of the question made her gasp.

"*Really?*" she asked, her voice dripping with scorn.

"No," the voice said. "But if you weren't who you're supposed to be, you'd try to snow us." A cell phone illuminated under her chin for a moment, highlighting the people around her with neon. It snapped off before she could identify any of them clearly, but she knew who they were.

Back in college she used to get incoherent with rage at the animal rights protesters who broke into the school's labs and set the experimental animals free. She sat smugly with her fellow science majors and ate bacon sandwiches, making loud 'yummy' noises, across the street from the Animal Protection Society group. Now she'd do anything to save Daisy and her… well, for lack of a better term, she had to call them family. She couldn't be squeamish about it. They *were* her family now. And these horrible people who had interfered with her research, whom she had taunted and testified against, were her only potential allies.

"You said you could help us prevent live animals from going on the Mars mission," the harsh whisper said. "How?"

"No violence," Perri said. "The owners are my friends."

"No one who violates the rights of animals are anyone's friends," a female voice growled.

"Look, I'm not pretending I'm one of you, but I am concerned for the well-being of those pigs. I want to help you keep them – or most of them – from being taken away."

"How? By rendering them unfit for human consumption? Adulterating the meat?"

"Not more than they've already been adulterated," Perri said.

The cellphone flashlight glared into her eyes.

"You're another one of those filthy industrialists. Why should we help you? You just want to make billions on the space program. And weren't you engaged to the senior researcher for MegaPig?"

"No! It's not that." She tore open the collar of her shirt, showing the long scar that dove from just below her throat, between her breasts, almost to her navel. It elicited gasps from the unseen mob. She told her story.

"You're one of the damned," the growling female said. "You caused the death of one of those animals for your own selfish reasons!"

"I didn't have a choice. I didn't want to die," Perri said. "I've been grateful ever since. I visit Daisy once a week. I want to buy her, but they won't let me. I've been trying to make it up to them, by providing viable substitutes for what we get from pigs."

She opened the box she had with her and offered it around.

"That's bacon! You traitor!"

"No," Perri protested. "It's all plant matter, I promise."

Most of the protesters backed away, refusing to touch it, but the delicious aroma overwhelmed the scruples of several of them. Perri listened hopefully to the sound of munching in the dark.

The growling female voice softened to a coo. "Oh, my God, that's yummy! But what's it made of?"

"Mostly sugar beets," she said. "It's a hybrid of a number of plant species. You can have as much as you want, forever, if you help me. And expenses. In untraceable credits."

"Okay," the harsh male voice said. "But what's in it for you?"

"You're a moral coward, you know," the female voice said. "You have no more compunction about using us than you did that poor pig."

"I'm trying to prevent traumatizing those animals in outer space when they have no way to understand or escape."

"How is that different from having them killed for meat?"

The shadow figure of the tall male held up his hands.

"Small changes. We can't win all at once, but we fight enough small battles, we win the war in the end. All right, Bacon Lady. We're in. What do you want us to do?"

~ ~ ~

Perri rolled down her window to hand over her identification at the gate of the MegaPig campus. The blue-uniformed guard hardly glanced at it. He had known Perri since she was a student.

"Here for your weekly visit?" he asked with an indulgent grin.

"That's right," Perri said. "I hope to take Daisy home with me today." She always said that.

"Yeah, right," the guard said. "Make sure you check her out with me when you go." That was his eternal reply. Perri smiled at him.

I mean it this time, she thought. She drove along the long frontage road past a dozen identical, long, pale blue structures to Building D and parked in a nearby spot in the central lot.

Perri found the industrial complex itself depressing, but MegaPig kept its animal environments spotlessly clean and pleasant. Except for very recent deposits, the stalls never smelled like manure or urine. The effluvia pools were man aged like a high-tech septic system, processing the waste into top-grade fertilizer and clean water. Soft music played over the public address system. The lights ran on seasonal sunlight schedules. Day was just giving way to night. Shadows were deepening in the stalls. The animals were beginning to settle down. One quarter of the big building was separated by glass walls from the rest. Within, the score of pigs destined for the Mars mission lived together in a single enormous stall. Most of them were gilts, pig-heifers, with one or two senior females. A second, smaller stall held a large, black-spotted boar segregated from the rest. He surveyed his harem with a proprietary eye. Perri patted the syringe in her pocket. All she needed was five minutes, but she wanted to visit Daisy first.

The pink-and-white sow raised her head at the sound of Perri's footsteps on the polished floor. Over the past months, she had learned to look forward to visits. Her blue eyes, so intelligent, looked eager. She always looked freshly scrubbed. Even though she had been a mother twice, her flanks were slim. Her snout was light pink, as were the inside of her ears and the double row of teats that ran along her snow-white underside.

"Hi, lady, how are you?" Perri asked. She slid so her blue jean-clad legs dangled under the lowest rail and over the lip of the sunken stall where Daisy lived. She leaned in to scratch between the tall, peaked ears. The pig's straw had just been changed. The scattered golden stalks smelled of meadows and fields. “Mmm! Nice. You’d love the real thing. Wish I could show it to you. Don’t your eyelashes look lovely today? I wish mine were thick like that. And so white!”

Daisy slitted her eyes. Her heavy breathing told Perri she enjoyed both the compliments and the attention. Perri could tell by the sow’s bulging sides that she was pregnant again. Another brood to be sacrificed to science. Her heart sank.

“Hey, honey.”

Perri looked up. Ethan’s dad, Gilbert, slid down to sit beside her. He never dressed the part of a CEO, preferring the chambray shirts and jeans he had always worn. Steel-toed boots clanked against the inner edge of the pen.

“Hi, Gil.”

“Having your little chat?”

“Yes,” Perri said. She scratched around the stiff ear cup. Daisy ground her bristly jowls into Perri’s knee with pleasure. “We were just talking about beauty. I think she understands more every week.”

“She ain’t no more human than she was a week ago,” Gil said. It was a warning.

“I’ll double my offer for her.”

By the look on his face, she knew it was a fruitless request. He shook his head gently.

“Not for sale, honey. You know that. She’s one of my most valuable animals. She’s worth over two hundred thousand, not counting those piglets growing in her belly. You understand. Her time with you was like a doctor’s appointment. She gave you what you needed. It’s all small sacrifices for the greater good.”

“Another heart patient?” Perri asked, miserably.

“Nope. Skin rejuvenation experiment. Look, honey, she’s moved on to other people who need her, and so should you.”

“I can’t, Gil,” Perri said. “I’m part of her now. I really want her out of here.”

Gil took a deep breath. “Let’s not start that argument again, honey. She’ll never go for slaughter and I promise I will take good care of her, but she stays here. I’m sorry you’re not going with Ethan. He would still love to have you on the mission."

Perri touched her heart, where Muriel's tissue rested. "I lost my chance when I got sick. It's better that Ethan finds someone in the mission crew. I'm afraid I'm earthbound. That's fine with me. I'm still making my mark on the program."

His eyebrows went up. "So you got the approval for your bacon-beets? Congratulations!"

"Not yet, but the crew's pulling for me."

"Well, I got sponsors for over eighty million dollars worth of experiments. Mostly environmental. But only if Congress gets off its fat butt and gives us the go-ahead. They're just spinning their wheels, so I have to, too. Costing this company a fortune every day they delay and making it easy for other companies to catch up. Wish you luck."

"I wish you the same," Perri said. "Maybe something will shake them loose."

An electronic version of "Turkey in the Straw" burst out from Gil's pocket. He withdrew his phone. "Miller. Uh-huh. Keep 'em there. On my way."

He got up to leave. "Stay as long as you want, Perri. See you later."

"Thanks, Gil."

"No problem, baby."

Perri sat scratching Daisy's ears. So the press release Asif had e-mailed had done its work. There would be a dozen news crews on the doorstep of MegaPig, clamoring for confirma tion of the rumor, which she was about to make come true.

She pulled herself up and tiptoed toward the confinement area. The syringe in her pocket contained antibiotics, the kind usually given to breeding swine before they reached maturity. She wouldn't have to dose all of the pigs, just enough to cast doubt on MegaPig's claim of drug-free, antibiotic-free animals for the space program.

The door had a digital lock, but the combination never changed. Perri touched 1-2-3-4-5, and the latch clicked open. She slid into the room, trying to look as if she was just idly snooping. The boar was well fed and placid. Perri was experi enced at giving injections into the heavy back-fat. He wouldn't feel a thing. She leaned over the pen and gave the huge animal a scratch on the scalp. He turned in surprise, then let out a croon of pleasure. With her other hand, Perri reached for the syringe.

The boar had on a black, studded dog collar. To go around his immense neck, it had to have been made for him. She grabbed for it and heard a jingle.

A tiny charm hung from a loop under the animal's jowls. It was a silver miniature of the *USS Enterprise* from *Star Trek*. Perri jumped back. Then she noticed the silver plaque on the back of the collar. It said, "Kirk." The boar's name was Kirk. Pigs in space. All of Ethan's hopes and plans were tied up in this herd. If she went through with her plan, he would probably be thrown off the program. She was about to destroy his dream.

Her eyes filled with tears. She couldn't do it.

She stuffed the needle back into her pocket and dashed out of the room, back to Daisy's nonjudgmental presence. Perri was ashamed of herself. She would take the consequences, whatever they would be.

Robotic drones on tracks ignored her as they went about their business. The pens were cleaned, the piglets weighed, the gravity feeders were checked and replenished, then silence. Perri waited. The digital clock over the door slid over to five-thirty. Five-thirty-five.

Five-forty.

A klaxon erupted overhead. All of the pigs jumped. Some of them broke into hysterical squealing. The doors concealing the AI workers opened, and the drones plowed out, seeking the source of the disruption.

"Attention! Intruders in the complex!"

Perri stood up. Two of the robots grabbed her and dragged her out of the room. Behind her, Daisy whinnied her distress. In the anteroom, two security guards snapped plastic ties on her wrists. She recognized the guards as long-time employees who were contemporaries of hers and Ethan's.

"Luis, Candy, what's this?"

"Hi, Doctor Closson. We're sorry, but we're going to have to take you in custody," Candy said. She waited while Luis locked Perri into the rear of their van. Perri had never been to jail or detained. She was frightened.

"What's going on?" she asked.

"All hell's breaking loose," Luis said. "There's a bunch of people who came over the fence in about five places. They're bashing in doors, letting the animals run loose, and there's a big group of reporters in Mr. Miller's office. The whole thing's live on the net. Mr. Miller told us to round up anyone who doesn't work here. Sorry, but that's you."

~ ~ ~

"We're protesting the illegal treatment of an intelligent species, sending it on a potentially deadly trip without its consent!" a masked man shouted on one of the screens in the main MegaPig office building. He gestured to a pair of similarly masked people holding a makeshift battering ram. They used it to batter the steel door of one of MegaPig's habitats. A horde of protesters flooded into the breach. In moments, pigs came hurtling out.

As Luis had said, pigs of every size thundered around the enormous campus with smock-clad technicians, uniformed guards, and office workers racing after them. Perri almost laughed as a woman in a tight pencil skirt leaped on a half-grown pig, bringing it down to the ground. Both of them squealed angrily until a technician shoved the piglet into a portable cage. The news crews didn't know which of the two stories to cover, the protest, or the rumor.

Senator Soukos, who disliked anything that wasn't pure and organic, was at the head of the mob, leading the interrogation.

"We hear that the pigs that were set to be placed on the Mars mission had been treated with antibiotics, against what you told Congress, Mr. Miller. Did your son tell us lies under oath? We want the truth!"

"Where did you get that stupid idea, Senator?" Gil demanded.

"We heard it from Doctor Perri Closson's office."

"Perri? She knows better! Of course those pigs are organically raised! I've got records of every moment of their lives, going back nine generations! No drugs, no pesticides, and

NO antibiotics!" Gil Miller looked up as Luis escorted Perri in. "You keep a good hold on her," he snapped, and glared at Perri. "I'll talk to *you* later." He met the senator's imperious gaze. "You come with me this minute, and I'll show you. Faked records, hah!"

He strode off across the campus, the press corps in pursuit.

Perri walked behind, with Luis holding her arm. She had caused this firestorm. It was for a good cause, the best cause possible!

They saw the damage before they reached Building D. Gil started running.

"My pigs!"

Inside, the protesters had done their job, exactly as they had agreed to. Three quarters of the room was empty.

"Was this all arranged for our benefit?" Senator Soukos demanded.

"No!" Gil boomed. Then he saw that the isolation room was intact. He flew to it and put in the code. As the report ers crowded in behind him, he counted them. Perri watched his lips move, then purse in a soundless whistle. They were all there, including Kirk the Boar, all serenely eating or rolling in their straw.

Recovering his wits, Gil thrust his records into Soukos's hands. "All there. No adulteration. Organic feed. The best conditions."

She wasn't so easily pacified.

"We'll see about that. I brought a veterinarian with me to run blood tests."

"Fine," Gil said. "Run it right here on camera. I don't want to see any hokey tricks."

It took time, long enough for Senator Soukos to take a brief tour. Gil stood over the shoulder of the vet, watching every slide go under the microscope. When the last sample got the nod, Soukos turned to the cameras.

"Except for being nearly devoid of livestock, this is a handsome model facility, Mr. Miller. We are very sorry to have come here and disturbed you on the strength of a malicious rumor. But I am very impressed by what you have done on behalf of our very exciting upcoming mission. I am prepared to give my approval here and now for your funding. I will have to confer with my colleagues, but I think you can expect to hear within the week."

She swept out, reporters at her heels like swirling leaves. Perri stared after her.

"Well, it's an ill wind that blows nobody good," Gil said.

As the entourage departed, Ethan arrived, his face crimson.

He turned on Perri. "There are pigs all over the place! The fence is in shreds! Nobody's working! The whole facility's a hot mess. What did you do?"

Perri shrank away from him, but his father came to her rescue.

"It looks like she got Congress to approve us, son," Gil said, putting an arm around her.

"Half the pigs are missing! Where are they?" Ethan demanded.

"How should I know?" Perri countered. "I've been right here all the time!"

He came to loom over her, just the way she hated. "You will pay for every animal that we can't account for. I don't care how many!"

"All right, son, all right," Gil said, grabbing him by the shoulder and pulling him back. "Let's get out there and see how many are missing."

It was after four o'clock in the morning before every an imal still out running the campus had been herded back to their pens and stalls. A few had cuts and scrapes from dashing through hedges, but most of them were none the worse for their adventure. In the end, there was only one pig missing.

"Daisy," Gil said. "Where did you take her?"

"I don't know where she is," Perri said, with total honesty.

"Get her back, right now."

"I can't!"

"You mean, won't!"

"Son," Gil said, stepping between them. Ethan glared at Perri over his shoulder. "It looks like all this was a big misun derstanding. We've made a lot of sacrifices so you can go into space, not the least of which is that I'm risking *you*. It looks like the whole thing's finally a go. And if it takes one more little ex pense to make it happen, well, I'm willing to pay it. Daisy's dis appeared, that's all. What's one pig when the rest are all safe?"

"I'll pay you for her, of course," Perri said.

"No need to," Gil said. "You've already given up plenty for other people's dreams. This foofarah might even have cost you your chance to send your goods in the ship. Least I can do is make my own contribution."

"There are more important things in life," Perri said. "At least Ethan's still going." She glanced up at him shyly. "See you on the launch pad?"

Ethan laughed. They never could stay mad at one another. He gathered her in a huge hug.

"I'll take your bacon with me," he promised, kissing her on the top of her head. "It'll remind me of you. Sweet, good for your heart, and nothing at all like a pig."

Ghostel Montenegro

by Patricia Rice

With several million books in print and *New York Times* and *USA Today* bestseller lists under her belt, former CPA Patricia Rice is one of romance's hottest authors. Her emotionally charged contemporary and historical romances have won numerous awards, including the *RT Book Reviews* Reviewers Choice and Career Achievement Awards. Her books have been honored as Romance Writers of America RITA® finalists in the historical, regency and contemporary categories.

Marie-Celeste Montagne hears ghosts. She hears ghostly orchestras in old ballrooms and listens to spirits complain and laugh in her head. In another era, she might have been locked up in the attic as someone's crazy maiden aunt. In this modern era, she joins a Psychic Paranormal Society and becomes its secretary.

I write about psychic characters because I truly believe our brains are capable of a great deal more than we're willing to acknowledge. I know several people who have always been receptive to the spirit world. One has trained herself to interact with ghosts. I'd rather be able to read minds or the future, but I haven't reached that level of understanding yet!

At midnight, Marie-Celeste Montagne leaned against the Hotel Montenegro's carved double panel ballroom doors and listened to the ghosts dance.

Well, she supposed she was actually listening to ghost ly musicians since dancing wraiths made no sound, but she sighed in delight, imagining the ball being reenacted inside. She longed to spin in graceful circles in an elegant gown from a more gracious decade, twirling about the parquet floor in the arms of a gallant gentleman.

Ghosts were easier to believe in than gallant gentleman, but if she was dreaming, she might as well go all the way.

She peered through the crack between the doors and thought she caught the flash of diamonds and the flicker of red silk swaying in accompaniment to the music, but that could just be wishful thinking. She heard voices of the dead but sel dom actually saw specters.

That would be a problem with the Psychic Paranormal So ciety. They thought they could photograph ghosts. They might be right, but she couldn't *see* ghosts, so she couldn't tell the photographers where to aim their cameras.

And she really needed to convince the Society that she was worthy of the Director's job – the only salaried position in the organization. Without that salary, she'd starve and become a ghost, which would certainly make Fathead happy. Maybe she could come back and haunt her ex.

Realistically, she'd just go back to being a minimum wage secretary who got no respect – one heck of a lousy part for the girl voted Most Likely To Be a Movie Star. She'd married a drama queen. That ought to be close enough.

Fretting over how she would prove that the Montenegro had ghosts, she turned around and walked straight into a solid wall of pristine gray suit and red tie – Jack Terwilliger. Damn.

The hotel owner tilted his square jaw to look down at her. Celeste held her breath, hoping he wouldn't recognize her. She'd known Jack ran the Montenegro – the boutique hotel had been in his family for generations, after all. But she didn't think he'd seen her since high school.

"A little midnight stroll through the renovation zone, Miss Montagne?" he inquired with a cool distance she didn't remember from the good old days, when he'd been her college nerd tutor and she'd been high school prom queen and cheerleader.

"I heard music," she said defiantly, daring him to laugh.

He scowled instead, striding to the doors and unlocking them. "I've told the workmen not to leave their boomboxes up here. It's bad enough we have the constant racket of hammers and saws all day."

He halted in the doorway, frowning. "I don't hear anything."

"Just my imagination," she said brightly, although she could still hear the lilting strains of a waltz. "Are you returning the ballroom to its original grandeur to encourage dancing again?"

He closed the doors, locked them, and tucking away the key, cocked his head to study her as if she were an alien from Mars. "You want rap music ringing over your head? I'll be using this floor for a conference hall. Shall I escort you back to your room? Perhaps I can determine what disturbed your sleep."

"Oh, stuff it, Jack." She stomped down the uncarpeted upper hall toward the gilded elevator. The Montenegro was known for its historic authenticity, but the elevator was from the 1930's, not the hotel's origins in the 1800's. Some exceptions had been made for convenience. "You're not a paid tutor and I'm not a stupid rich kid anymore. You don't have to pretend to be polite."

"Since you're wandering the halls of my hotel, I have to assume you're a guest. I am always polite to guests."

Jack opened the manual elevator gate, catching a hunger-inducing whiff of musky gardenia perfume. Celeste had always worn the damndest scents and dressed in the most provocative outfits… Tonight she was merely wearing jeans and a T-shirt, but the V-neck revealed the years had only improved her impressive cleavage.

"I'm here with the PPS," she acknowledged stiffly. "I'm just a flight down. I can take the stairs."

She was irritated with him, although he didn't understand why. Story of his life. He'd bend over backward to help a female, and she'd step on his toes and kick him in the shins. Or higher. Celeste was the worst of them all. She'd ripped out his heart and ridden over it on a Harley.

He supposed that had saved him a lot of shock and grief later when his fiancée had done the same. He'd pretty much expected it by then.

"PPS?" he inquired, although he had a pretty good idea what she was talking about. Stringy-haired, bearded psychos from a weekend convention of ghosthunters had been wandering the halls all afternoon. He just couldn't place beautiful, blond and blue-eyed Celeste in their company.

"The Psychic Paranormal Society. I've been their secretary for the past two years." She grudgingly waited for the ancient elevator to level off before stepping inside and facing him as he entered. "We hold a conference in New Orleans once a year. People from around the world come to take our ghost tours."

"Ghost tours," he said flatly, thinking of the executive from the International Religious Institute arriving tomorrow to check out the hotel for their spring conference. He had a niggling suspicion that religion and ghost hunters did not mix well. "The Montenegro does not have ghosts."

"Of course it does," she said brusquely, as if telling him that he had carpets. "Most of the buildings in the Quarter have been around long enough to have collected any number of phantoms, but the Montenegro is one of the best. French duelists, American generals, abused slaves – they've all stayed here and died here. Their ectoplasm is part of the walls."

Jack considered stepping out of the elevator, closing the gate, and letting her go down by herself. Obviously, silly rich girls had a penchant for even sillier hobbies.

But she looked so ticked at him that he couldn't resist intruding upon her madness for a while longer. "Our walls are plaster," he said solemnly, pushing the button for the next floor. "I'm sure the building inspector would complain if they were of anything as insubstantial as ectoplasm."

The elevator had only a small crystal globe overhead for light. He could still see her reflection in the mirror. She looked tired. And the charming smile she usually used to flirt and de stroy was gone.

"Poke fun," she said. "My ex used to do the same, only he was meaner about it. I accept that most people don't have a sensitivity to spirit forms, so I can excuse your ignorance. But I demand that you respect and not laugh at my different perceptions."

"You mean it?" he asked incredulously, turning to look down at her honey-blond hair. "You really believe in ghosts?"

"I *hear* them," she said. "You may call them anything you wish, but I hear spirits who have passed beyond this life into the next."

"You want to dial up my father and ask what he thought he was doing when he replaced all the antique bathroom fixtures with fake 70's brass?"

She graced him with a haughty look. Her eyes darkened to indigo, and Jack thought she might stomp his foot now. He waited expectantly.

He watched in surprise as she visibly throttled her anger and looked at him in consideration. With any other woman, he would have known to flee, but Celeste had always been sweet-tempered. She hadn't needed to be manipulative. Any man who saw her would do her bidding just to hear her speak.

She'd broken more hearts with that oblivious sweetness than if she'd been a virago.

"Did your father die in the Montenegro?" she asked.

The elevator rattled to its awkward stop, and he slid the gate open. "Heart attack on four while shouting at a mainte nance man. And no, his spirit is not haunting that floor. We just completely renovated it last year and not one chain rattled."

"I don't hear rattling chains." She stepped off and marched down the Belgian-woven carpet of blue and gold fleur-di-lis. "If the dead want to speak, they seek me out. They don't need chains to be heard." She turned on the high wedge of her san dal heel and glared up at him. "Good-night, Jack. I'm sure the waltz you don't hear won't disturb your guests."

She keyed in her card, entered, and gently closed the door in his face, leaving the scent of gardenias hanging in the air like one of her ectoplasmic haunts.

Jack straightened his tie, listened half a second for music, and wondering if it was too late to steer the Religious Institute committee to another weekend, he aimed for the stairs. He'd learned he could travel them faster than taking the aging elevator.

~ ~ ~

Celeste checked the buttons of the crisp bolero jacket she'd worn to look authoritative, straightened the silk bow at her throat, and marched out to the podium in front of fifty of the Society's most established members. *Be firm,* she told herself. *Don't be a doormat. Ask for what you want.*

But the firm, professional executive she wanted to be smiled at her audience and said, "Good morning, ladies, gentlemen, and ghostbusters."

Her mostly male audience snickered appreciatively. The women didn't like her so well, she knew. That could change, if she could help them establish their ghost-hunting credentials.

"The Hotel Montenegro has an old and illustrious history, as the pamphlets in your welcome bag will tell you. There's been a hotel on this lot since the late 1700s. In the rough and tumble early days, the site saw pirates and duels of wealthy French and Spanish aristocrats. After the Montenegro was built in the early 1800s, slaves were sold on the front steps. Andrew Jackson was said to have slept here during the War of 1812. And the wounded were hospitalized here during the Civil War. In fact, there has been so much emotional turbulence attached to this land and these walls that it's almost impossible to walk through a corridor without brushing against the past."

Murmurs of approval rose, and Celeste drew in a breath of confidence. She knew her material. She knew her audience. "What the pamphlet does not tell you is how many people have died here and whether their spirits linger. The current owner's father could well be one of those restless spirits roaming the fourth floor." She silently apologized to Jack for using that tidbit he'd fed her. "The ballroom on the top floor has been closed for decades, but I heard unseen musicians playing a waltz just last night. I mean to research the events up there as soon as I am able, but for today, I'd like you to talk with the spirit inhabiting Room 260. She's young, apparently a girl who died in the yellow fever epidemic in 1847."

"What about murders?" Bobbert shouted from the front row. A young photographer out to make a name for himself, Bobbert was dressed in black leather. If he ventured out of the air conditioning into New Orleans July humidity, he'd steam in his own sweat. "We ought to investigate any murders. How did the previous owner die?"

"Heart attack," Celeste said grumpily, disliking having her planned presentation disrupted. "Obviously, with a history that goes so far back, there have been mysterious deaths. But so far, the spirits of those victims have not reached out to us."

"That won't sell membership," Hugh Carson protested. A former Society director, famous for his long gray ponytail, he was more concerned about keeping membership up and the cost of dues down than in actually contacting the spirit world. "We need to find new ghosts, solve murders, photograph pol tergeists. Marketing is everything."

Celeste had thought laying spirits to rest was everything, but that might be why she was a minimum-wage secretary. She smiled brightly. Always smile, her mother had advised. It keeps angry people off balance.

Celeste thought hitting them upside the head with a skillet would do the same, but that wasn't how she'd been brought up.

"You know perfectly well the Society welcomes new find ings. That's why we're here. I can only direct you to known specters. If anyone picks up on different energy, we will inves tigate, of course."

Ignoring any murmured squabbles, she produced the old-fashioned key to Room 260 and stepped away from the po dium, lecturing into her wireless mic so her listeners could pick her up on their earphones. "The hotel has caught fire on sev eral occasions. The basement is the oldest part of the hotel still standing, but the kitchens and storage are down there, and we don't have access."

She clipped along in her heels, heading for the staircase. She'd chosen a second-story room so she didn't have to wait for fifty people to ride up in an elevator that held four. "The back part of the hotel pre-dates the Civil War, and that's where we'll find Room 260. These stairs are original, so let's have quiet and open ourselves to possibilities."

She was already half way down the second floor hall, with her membership following behind, when the elevator opened ahead of her.

At that same moment, Bobbert shouted something indeci pherable in back and began flashing the enormous camera he carried around his neck.

Celese spun on her heel to watch in horror as Grace, one of their older female members, began shrieking and batting at her graying chignon. Instantly, all focus turned to the per formers. Fifty society members huddled around Bobbert and Grace, blocking the corridor. The two men stepping off the elevator – Jack and a somber man in an expensive tailored suit – were prevented access to the rooms.

As anxious as the rest of the crowd to see what was hap pening, Celeste acknowledged their presence with a nod but stood on her toes to see past taller heads.

~ ~ ~

Upon seeing the horde of long-haired, unshaven weirdoes in the hall, Jack would have closed the elevator door and taken the Religious Institute's executive to a different floor – except it appeared some woman was being attacked.

Excusing himself, Jack shoved past Celeste, cutting through the sea of T-shirts and khaki jackets while radioing security.

What was wrong with these damned idiots that they simply stood around taking pictures while a woman screamed?

Jack put his hands on the shoulders of a leather-encased photographer and shoved him aside so he could step into the clearing around an older woman with her coarse gray hair sticking out like a bag lady's. Terrified, she was swatting at the air around her head.

Jack's first thought was *bats*. They'd had a problem in the attic some years back. He didn't see any of the flying rodents, and given the current state of hotel finances, he wasn't about to inform the public of a possible bat infestation. Not seeing any other reason for the woman's hysterical antics, he simply walked up, captured one of her hands, and introduced himself.

"Madam, may I escort you to your room?" he inquired when she stopped screaming to stare at him. "Is someone here bothering you?"

He heard security approaching from the stairs but he didn't acknowledge them while he waited for explanations.

"It's all right, Grace," a quiet voice said from behind him. "She simply wanted to admire your combs. She didn't mean to disturb you."

The woman called Grace instantly relaxed and began patting her hair with curiosity.

Jack swirled to confront Marie-Celeste. He'd known she was in the crowd but hadn't realized she'd followed in his wake. He should have. Her gardenia scent wafted seductively around him. "You would like to explain the meaning of this disturbance?"

She looked at him with amusement, much as she had as a teenager when he'd tried to explain Socrates to her, and in return, she'd attempted to explain the lyrics of some absurd popular song. He was no longer charmed by a sultry laugh.

"Let us simply say we are more sensitive to your hotel's history than most of your guests," she replied. "That way we can both pretend we understand each other, and all is well. You can tell security we're fine, and thank you very much for coming to Grace's rescue."

"Let's get my computer and take a look at these shots," the photographer was saying while Jack stared into the laughing blue eyes that had haunted his teenage dreams.

The crowd began to disperse of its own accord, the older woman now quite eager to relate her tale to her fellows as she followed them back to the stairs.

"If you would kindly keep your *sensitives* from screaming in my halls, I would be most appreciative," Jack said stiffly, aware of the executive impatiently waiting by the elevator.

"Celeste, hurry it up, we need the key to the conference room!" one of the crowd shouted at her.

Jack considered grabbing the fellow's gray-haired ponytail and giving him a lesson in speaking to ladies, but he refrained. He didn't play noble knight to pretty damsels these days.

"If you've discovered the secret to muzzling drunks and rowdy revelers, I'll happily employ your technique to silence the society." She lowered her voice to a whisper. "But I don't think your friend over there would appreciate muzzles and I know your ghosts won't."

"He represents a religious organization," Jack replied in the same low tone. "I doubt that they'll be screaming in the halls."

She looked at him sympathetically. "You still really don't understand people at all, do you? This is New Orleans, not Boston. That's Arthur Glenn back there. I wouldn't call what he represents *religious.* He's ranted and raved on the radio for years. I wouldn't put it past him or his followers to proselytize in the halls. Get with the program, Jack, savor our differences!"

She sashayed off, not looking back. Impatient Ponytail huffed and hurried ahead of her instead of waiting for her to catch up.

Jack still had the unreasonable urge to bop the rude jerk in the jaw, but behaving like his temperamental, egomaniacal grandfather wouldn't do the hotel's reputation much good.

"Sorry for the disturbance, Mr. Glenn," Jack said, returning to the elevator and brushing a piece of – glitter? – off his arm sleeve. "The Montenegro entertains a wide variety of organizations throughout the year. These are dramatic performers. I've asked them to contain their performances to their assigned conference area."

"We might want to take a look at the other conferences scheduled for our weekend," the executive said stiffly. "Our members require a little more decorum."

Burned by Celeste's insult about his lack of understanding, Jack fought the wayward desire to ask why a religious group had chosen New Orleans. Despite Celeste's insinuations, he knew perfectly well that even the stiff-necked let down their hair at conferences in the Big Easy. It wasn't his place to question why, but to book the money.

An icy hand tickled his nape and he ignored it, as he always did when he hit the hotel's cold spots. The air conditioning in these old buildings tended to be inconsistent.

~ ~ ~

The camera and computer experts set up the wall screen to project the images of the morning's sighting. They were currently fiddling with adustments to enhance Grace's moment of terror.

As always, the screen pictured a whitish fog between the camera and the subject, but no one could prove the fog was ghost or just bad photography. Celeste had *heard* the specter speak, but she had no way of recording the voice inside her head to use as physical proof.

"What did the phantom say, exactly?" Grace asked again. "All I felt was icy hands and my hair being shredded."

Grace had gone to the ladies's room and returned her chignon to its normal uptight arrangement, with ornamental sticks poking from the sides, Geisha style. Celeste suspected Grace had probably worn pencils there in her younger days as a stenographer.

"Ghosts seldom say anything useful," Celeste reminded her. "I heard *pretty* and *please* and *sorry*. I merely interpreted her meaning in hopes of distracting the hotel manager."

"You can't sell a story like that to the public," Hugh Carson grumbled. "You've got to give us something more explicit."

Celeste's anxiety kicked up a notch. Was Carson angling to take back the director's position? He'd get the vote, if so. He'd always been a creative marketer. She merely reported what she heard and did what she was told.

Tell him Sister Sarah had long black hair and loved pretty hairpins a voice whispered in her head – with a touch of cynicism?

Grace blinked. She *heard* ghosts, yes, but none had ever spoken directly to her, and certainly never this coherently. She squeezed the bridge of her nose and tried to concentrate while the others talked in the background, pointing out shapes on the screen and speculating about form and density.

"Who is Sister Sarah?" she asked aloud, attempting to focus.

A kleptomaniac prostitute, if you want that much detail, the voice replied with a hint of amusement. *The old goat is right. Pretty stories are better.*

"Who are you?" she demanded, vaguely aware that the people around her had turned to stare.

Lillian St. John. Ask Jack sometime.

Celeste immediately sensed the loss of the vocal presence, as if she'd just sneezed and cleared her head.

"Who were you talking to?" one of the newer members asked.

Amazed, rubbing her temple, Celeste looked around at expressions avid with curiosity. "Lillian St. John," she said in a sense of wonder. "I was talking to the spirit of Lillian St. John."

"Lillian St. John," Carson crowed. "We have a name! Let's research."

Carson was such a desperate twit, Celeste thought in exas peration. All he'd had to do was ask her if she recognized the name.

If he had, she could have told them that she'd been talk ing to Jack's great-grandmother, the woman who had single-handedly turned the Montenegro from rundown flophouse to the most famous hotel in the city during the Roaring Twenties.

Had her memory for history simply pulled that name out of her subconscious? Now that the membership had happily latched on to a clue to explore, she didn't dare spoil their fun by voicing her doubts.

Perhaps a little performing to the crowd really didn't hurt.

~ ~ ~

Jack turned off the flickering images on the computer monitor. If they didn't book a good-sized convention every weekend from now until eternity, the hotel was going under. Hurricane Katrina, the bad economy, the oil spill, everything had contributed to a growing deficit. He'd already cut his own salary rather than lay off loyal employees. He could invest what was left of his own wealth in the old hotel, but he feared it was a losing proposition. Without an astounding turn around in fortune, a lot of good people would be out on the street in another year.

He thought about heading home, but the day had left a buzz of agitation in the back of his head that he needed to work off. Arthur Glenn hadn't signed a contract yet. The psychos from the paranormal society were last seen haunting the room beneath Glenn's. Celeste's laughing eyes mocked his concerns. He couldn't let her know the precarious state of the hotel's finances, but perhaps he could appeal to her southern hospitality and persuade her to keep her people away from the humorless executive until he left.

Hearing a mob of voices echoing up the open atrium of the rotunda, he stopped at the third floor railing overlooking the lobby. Below him, on the lobby level, the shabby psychos, dressed now in various versions of evening black, were jockeying for position in a rough circle – with Celeste in the center.

The whole scene was surreal against the lobby's rich maroon and gold carpet. He'd had the carpet replicated exactly when they'd replaced the threadbare original. The gilding had been reapplied to the columns supporting the rotunda and matched the ornate French-style chairs. The paranormal society's black rags were as out of place as a bunch of crows against the jeweled elegance.

The weird memory that a gathering of crows was called a *murder* set his pulse racing.

A photographer finished setting up his equipment inside the circle. Another geek in a black Metallica T-shirt fiddled with an instrument with dials. At a signal from Celeste, the house lights abruptly dimmed.

Jack was about to race down the stairs and shout at his staff when Arthur Glenn stepped out of the elevator, into the murder of crows.

~ ~ ~

Celeste blinked in surprise as the lobby lights dimmed. She wouldn't put it past Carson to have rigged the effect. Brushing aside that thought, she focused on the spirit who had guided her here. "Lillian, you have our full attention. What is it you would like to say?"

She felt a bit of a fool, as if she were performing a private act before an audience, but she was desperate for the director's job, and Lillian had whispered in her ear. One thing had led to another… And here she was, pretending she was a medium. Which she was not. She had no cohorts beyond the veil. She was simply a receptive radar for spirit voices.

Lillian St. John's voice was rather loud.

The grand staircase, the ethereal voice said gleefully inside Celeste's head. *Really, you have no sense of grandeur these days.*

"The staircase," Celeste repeated aloud. "What about the staircase, Lillian?"

Eyes closed, she was aware her audience had turned their attention to the wide, semi-circular stairs on either side of the lobby leading to the next floor. Enormous crystal chandeliers imported from France in the 1800's hung above each landing. In its heyday, the hotel had entertained kings and queens, welcomed party-goers in tuxedoes and long, satin gowns.

Even today, weddings were held here simply so the participants might be photographed beneath those chandeliers, on the fabulously woven carpet protecting the mahogany stairs, framed by the gilded banister.

But most days, kids in shorts raced up and down, shouting obscenites. Lillian was right. They lacked grandeur.

Let's give them their money's worth first, my girl.

How the devil did she translate that?

The crystals in the chandelier over one landing began to tinkle and chime. Opening her eyes at the noise, Celeste blinked. One of the heavy fixtures was *swaying.* Was there an earthquake? But the other chandelier was perfectly still.

All around her, the Society members froze. The gong of the ornate clock over the sprawling mahogany lobby desk began to chime into the sudden silence. Under her breath, Celeste counted the chimes and noticed Grace, standing beside her, did the same.

"Twelve rings," Bobbert shouted, focusing his camera on the landing. "It's only nine now."

A thrill of anticipation rippled through the crowd. Staticky gramophone music began to play a song from long ago. Celeste frowned, trying to recall the tune… "Ain't We Got Fun?"

she whispered to Grace, who nodded. A song from the 1920s, she was fairly certain.

"That's not funny, Lillian," Celeste shouted. "That chandelier can hurt someone. Stop it!"

Ghostly laughter rang overhead, and heads swiveled to search the atrium for apparitions. Bobbert and several others rapidly flashed their cameras. The IT equipment guys gestured excitedly at their meters.

And Jack Terwilliger stalked down the stairs with a grim look warning they were about to all be tossed out on their heads.

That's when Celeste noticed Arthur Glenn by the elevator, glaring at their antics and speaking sharply into his cell phone. She feared Jack's hope for a religious convention was toast. Ghosted?

Bubbled, Lillian murmured in amusement. And suddenly, soap bubbles floated upward, dancing in colorful translucence on air currents as if blown from an invisible machine. *Remember that trick, honey. The audience loves it. Now watch this.*

"Arthur, baby," a seductive voice crooned out of nowhere, echoing through the atrium. "I'm waiting. Hurry upstairs, Sexy Boy."

"Lillian," Celeste groaned aloud, but the dour executive on the other side of the lobby, unable to hear her protest at the ghost's mocking voice, turned an unhealthy shade of purple.

As Jack increased his pace down the stairs, Arthur Glenn shook his fist at him. Without waiting for explanations, the executive retreated inside the elevator and yanked the door lever. Celeste assumed he'd never be seen again.

I hate hypocrites, Lillian whispered. *The Montenegro is for fun.*

The chandelier continued to sway. Perfuming the air with jasmine, bubbles popped against gilded columns. And the expensive stair tread carpet Jack rushed down abruptly loosened and undulated as if invisible hands grasped one end and shook it.

With a cry of fright, Celeste raced across the lobby in an inane attempt to save her teenage crush from a fall. Jack caught the banister and righted himself, stepping to one side as he watched in astonishment while the carpet rippled, then separated on the stair where he stood.

Relieved that he was safe, terrified of someone else being hurt, sorry that she'd lost Jack his client, Celeste kept on running, up to the landing beneath the swaying chandelier. She'd never learned to be assertive, but apparently a ghostly riot was the kick in the butt she needed. Director's job or not, this scene had just become too dangerous to continue. "We are endangering the hotel guests," she shouted over the cacophony rising below, removing a shoe and pounding the heel against the banister to catch their attention.

Just the fact that Celeste had actually shouted at them brought startled glances her way. She pointed at the unhaunted stair on the opposite side of the lobby. "Go back to the meeting room before we disturb any more spirits. We're here to study them, not arouse their anger. I believe we should have sufficient evidence of ghostly habitation without requesting more."

Celeste heard Lillian chuckle inside her head, whisper, *Good luck, dear*, and then felt her abrupt departure as before, like a sudden emptiness.

The chandelier stopped swaying. A bubble popped on Jack's nose. He stared at her as if she'd grown horns and hooves.

The Psychic Paranormal Society gathered up their equipment and, murmuring in discontent, departed by the far stairs.

"You could have done that a little sooner," Jack said wryly, crouching down to check the carpet's separation. He'd paid a lot of money to have this sewn properly. It shouldn't have come apart, but he was relieved he'd been the only one standing on it when it had.

"I'm sorry," Celeste whispered, dropping down to sit morosely on the stair below him. "My ex always said I was crazy. Maybe he was right. But I didn't cause those bubbles or any of those other things."

Jack frowned as his toe located a loose floor board, but realizing it wouldn't do any good to take out his problems on her, he joined her on the stair. Except for the separated carpet, the lobby had settled back to normal. He'd have to have a clockmaker take a look at Old Ben. It hadn't run since his great-grandfather died. He didn't know what had inspired it to chime tonight.

"I can send security to hunt for a bubble machine," he said, "but it's not worth the effort. I've only been fooling myself thinking I could keep this grand old place open." Looking down at Celeste's beautiful, drooping lips, Jack couldn't resist one small kiss to perk her up. To his surprise, she returned the kiss with more enthusiasm than he had any right to expect.

She backed off first, glancing with embarrassment to the now quiet lobby below.

A little off balance by the sudden surge of awareness between them, Jack tried to behave as if nothing had happened. "If Lillian was really here, she was probably trying to get rid of Arthur Glenn. She detested the religious hypocrites who tried to shut down her speakeasy in the cellar."

"She was definitely here." Celeste clasped her hands in her lap, then glanced up almost angrily at him. "I don't want any more men who think I'm crazy. My father thinks I belong in an institution. The fat bastard I married thought he'd get his hands on my trust fund if he agreed with my father and tried to lock me away. I let him have the money in exchange for a divorce. Skeptics are not high on my list of favorite people right now."

She was warning him to back off. Jack shoved his heel against the loose stair tread and tried to paste together the image of the careless teen angel he'd admired from afar and the poised female sitting beside him now. They no longer fit in the same frame. She'd grown into a woman who'd known adversity but had grown through it without letting it dim her spirit. He wanted to kiss her again, but she'd thrown up a shield of defiance he would have to breech.

"A crazy lady would have played to the drama and encouraged whatever in hell was happening here tonight," he said, thinking aloud. "But you thought of others before yourself, and even though it will probably cost you grief with those knuckleheads you threw out, you did what was best for all. Did the voices in your head tell you to do that?"

She shrugged, and he noticed how slender her bare shoulders were in that spaghetti-strap gown. He was falling into Sir Galahad mode again, wanting to save another damsel in distress. He would probably only get his shins kicked for his efforts, but he dropped down a step to put his arm around her and pull her head against his shoulder.

Celeste didn't fight but answered wearily, "They probably won't make me director, that's for sure. Just because I hear spirits doesn't mean I have to listen to them any more than I do anyone else, I guess."

Jack laughed. "There you go. From what I know of my great-grandmother, that's probably why she likes you."

She glanced up uncertainly. "You believe I hear Lillian?"

He used his heel to loosen the unsafe tread, and the board clattered to the next step down. "Her antics saved someone from a nasty fall on that loose step. I'll not look too deeply into the whys and wherefores."

She glanced thoughtfully at the opening he'd created. "Did your great-grandmother like drama?"

Jack rubbed his hand over her slender, silk-clad curves, enjoying the company, even if his ship was sinking around him. "Lillian used to dance down these stairs leading a marching jazz band. Her parties were legendary. They brought this place back to life. And when Prohibition arrived and nearly wiped us out again, she installed a machine gun in the basement windows and defied the Feds to find the entrance to her speakeasy."

"And what did your great-grandfather think about all this?" she asked with curiosity, leaning over to explore the opening revealed by the missing board.

"He carried the money to the bank and kept the books. They had six kids, so I'm thinking he was okay with his drama queen." Unwilling to let her go, Jack leaned over to see what she was doing.

Celeste produced a gilded invitation on heavy ivory stock, handed it to him, and returned to rummaging. "Lillian's parties turned the financial tide, didn't they?"

Jack stared at the elegant invitation to a masked ball dated 1929. "They did." Reluctantly releasing Celeste's waist, he grabbed the remaining board in the loose tread and ripped it off.

Inside were aging photo albums, wrinkled newspaper ar ticles, and a feather-and-rhinestone headdress.

The phones at the lobby desk began to shrill, and a camera crew strode in past the beveled glass front doors.

Beaming, Celeste donned the feathered headband. "I think Lillian was trying to tell you something."

"Mr. Terwilliger," his receptionist called up in puzzlement, "We have a TV network and two radio stations on the line, and these gentlemen say they're from a magazine." She nodded at the crew who had just entered.

Celeste practically twinkled as she leaned over to kiss his cheek. "Carson will make a better director than I will. He's a whiz at attracting media attention. But I know how to throw really great parties. Want me to help?"

If he'd had any fireworks right then, Jack would have set them off. Instead, he settled for hauling his guardian angel into his arms and sucking off her candy lipstick while cameras flashed from the lobby below.

"If you'll be Guinevere to my Lancelot, the palace is yours," Jack murmured against her mouth.

"I remember you telling me that tale." She kissed his jaw and tickled his chest beneath his tie. "It didn't end happily. Let's just play your great-grandfather and Lillian and see where that takes us."

"Six kids?" he asked warily.

She laughed, and for a moment, he thought he heard the ghosts laugh with her.

Waiting

by Barbara Bretton

Barbara Bretton: telling lies for a living since 1983. Nine words that sum up the last twenty-eight years of my life. It isn't easy to write a bio when you've spent almost three decades playing with your imaginary friends.

I'm a *USA Today* bestselling author. I've written forty-five books, some of which have won awards. Currently I have more than eleven million copies in print around the world in different languages. I've been featured in articles in *The New York Times*, *USA Today*, *The Wall Street Journal*, *Romantic Times*, *Cleveland Plain Dealer*, *Herald News*, *Home News*, *Somerset Gazette*, among others, and I've been interviewed by Independent Network News Television, appeared on the Susan Stamberg Show on NPR, and been featured in an interview with Charles Osgood on WCBS. I can't sing or dance or act or sell cars or explain nuclear fission. I doubt I'll ever broker peace in the Middle East. I have one talent, one skill, and I was lucky enough to turn it into the life I always wanted.

I'm a writer. That's all you need to know.

For me, the most interesting characters to write about are those who understand that life is lived between the lines. The woman you see standing in line at the bank, the man pumping gas at the corner station, your boring next-door neighbor with the yapping dogs – they all have stories to tell, stories of love and loss that might break your heart if you stopped long enough to listen. That's where "Waiting" was born: standing in line at our local bank one afternoon, not long after my husband and I moved from Long Island to bucolic central New Jersey. I was going through a bit of culture shock at the time, and for a split second I thought I saw a woman I knew from the old neighborhood. I was wrong, of course. Nobody from the old neighborhood was within one hundred miles that day but that split second of mistaken identity triggered a story fragment that lingered.

The thing is, once you reach a certain age you begin to understand that the White Hat/Black Hat concept of hero and villain doesn't apply to the real world or the people who inhabit it. The woman in my story lives a life cast in shades of grey. Brought to her knees by the loss of her only child, she finds comfort with a man who isn't her husband. A man who at any other time in her life would be invisible to her. Taken at face value, it's a black-and-white situation, a clear-cut case of right and wrong. But nothing is that simple: not love, not loss, and definitely not life.

You are standing in line at the bank on a sunny Wednes day in the middle of your life. Behind you, two aging preppies compare golf scores and vacation plans in plummy tones that make you think of old money and Ivy League schools. This is Princeton, you remind yourself as you duck your head to hide your smile. Back in the old neighborhood it would have been fast cars and clubbing but it's still the same game.

The old neighborhood. You haven't thought about it in years even though your own speech still carries traces of the place where you started out. You try hard to push away the memo ries but they have their own agenda. For a long time you were happy there and then you weren't and it was when you weren't that danger slipped in.

You scan the light-washed bank as the preppies behind you debate the relative merits of merlot and shiraz. The dark-haired teller who lives down the block waves at you as she stifles a yawn. To your right, a woman you know from Friends of the Library blows out a gentle sigh as she waits her turn with an assistant. A double stroller is parked to her left but all you can see is an explosion of yellow blankets tumbling over one side and onto the pale beige carpet. You acknowledge each other with a nod and a smile.

You don't know all the names but most of the faces in the bank are familiar. This is home now, but there was a time when this new life seemed as foreign to you as the dark side of the moon.

You crossed two rivers to get here. This is where you ran to put the past behind you, to see if all those early dreams could be brought back to life. You left the sorrow and the secrets be hind with the fridge, the washer/dryer, and the window treat ments and you haven't looked back.

And that's when you see him. His back is to you as he speaks with the bank manager and for a moment you can't breathe. The broad brush strokes are all there. Medium height, thick chestnut hair, graying slightly, shaggy ends skimming his collar. Leather jacket that has seen better days. The jacket strains across muscles that are clearly the product of physical labor, not hours at a designer gym. You don't want to notice any of this but you do. Sometimes – not often these days, not ever these days – you can still feel those muscles beneath your fingertips.

Not that you ever think about him anymore.

The guy in the leather jacket turns around. His features are too weathered, the expression in his eyes too weary to be the man you once knew but you watch anyway as his eyes move over you then past you, as he pushes his way out the heavy glass doors and into the sunny afternoon.

You are both relieved and disappointed in equal measure.

The funny thing is you dreamed about him a few days ago. You were walking down Nassau Street and you stopped to toss an empty coffee cup into the trash and when you looked, up he was walking toward you. The man you knew was hidden inside someone you barely recognized. He held the hand of a small child who looked much the way he must have looked when he was three years old. That afternoon in his sister's living room seemed very far away.

He was twenty-eight the last time you saw him. He'd no ticed the For Sale sign staked in your front yard and he caught up with you at the car wash one soft spring morning.

"You're moving?" he asked with one of those looks that used to lift you up and out of sorrow.

"Yes, we're moving." You couldn't hide your smile. Just saying the words out loud made you happy in a way you hadn't been in a long time.

He told you he was engaged and you wished him well. To your surprise, you actually meant it. He told you he'd miss you when you were gone and you laughed.

"You'll live," you said. "We haven't spoken in almost three years and you've managed to survive quite nicely."

He gave you one of those quizzical looks that defined the time you spent together and a rush of affection, unbid den and unexpected, filled your chest. He loved you once and you'd let him, even though you knew you could never love him back. You had tried to tell him how it was with you, what you hoped for, your dreams, but he never did understand much of anything you said and, to be fair, you hadn't much interest in anything he said to you. You knew that his dark hair gleamed slightly auburn in bright sunlight. You knew he had a freckle beneath his right eye. You knew that he was almost as bad as he thought he was and that was considerable. You knew all you needed to know.

At first you took small risks and when the world kept turning those risks grew bigger, more frequent, infinitely more dangerous, until the snowy afternoon when you find his car angled across your driveway and you invite him inside. He stands there – too big, too male, too everything – in the middle of your tiny kitchen and all you can think about is his old Chevy angled across your driveway with the motor running.

He pretends he'd stopped by for a brochure, an advertising tract for a drama school you'd told him about. (If he'd been gifted in the art of irony, he would have known just how funny that was.) You pretend to search through the desk drawer for it but your hands are trembling and you see the flakes of snow melting on the shoulders of his battered leather jacket and you want to press your tongue to them one by one by one and melt them against your heat.

You find the brochure and hand it to him. Small talk, empty talk, and then it's time for him to leave. You are leaning with your back against the edge of the sink in your smaller-by-the-second kitchen. You feel the dampness seeping into your silk shirt. Your shirt is the color of amethyst after midnight. You will never see that color again without seeing him the way he looked that snowy afternoon in your kitchen. You wait and you don't know what exactly you're waiting for but you do know what you want. You want him to take you right there in your hallowed kitchen, maybe right there on that table by the window where the highchair used to stand, where the neighbors can hear you cry out when you come, where they can see him taking you the way you'd dreamed he would take you, with no preliminaries and no talk, offering nothing but the deep drug of forgetting.

Because that's what you want. You want to forget, even if in the process you burn your life down to the ground.

It will be a few more months before he takes you in his arms, a few more months before you feel his hands snake under your sweater and cup your breasts, a few more months until you find out just how far you'll go in search of oblivion.

~ ~ ~

It's a windy day in early spring. You take the long way home from the gym, the way that leads you past his sister's house where he has a room in the basement. He told you it was a temporary arrangement until he found another job. You never take the long way but today the pull is almost magnetic.

You're not surprised to see him standing near the mailbox. He looks up at the sound of your car and his smile ignites a longing you can't ignore. You glide to a stop. He motions for you to roll down your window. He peers in at you and grins at the wet hair pulled back into a ponytail, the sweatshirt zipped up to your throat. He's barefoot, in jeans and a tee. Neither of you is dressed for seduction.

Hello, traveler. Stop awhile.

You talk about megabucks movies and lost chances, lottery tickets and the weather. Meaningless talk that wraps itself around the two of you in ways you still can't understand. All you know for sure is that today is the day.

You hesitate when he asks you in. Not because you don't want to – you want it so much it scares you – but because this is your last best chance to make the pain go away.

You've been on your way to this moment for months. Today you will let him do all the things he's promised. Not in the motel room you've joked about. Not in the sweaty darkness of his back seat. Not in the sheltering woods by the lake.

But there, in his married sister's house, a place where plastic philodendrons melt at the kitchen window.

On any other day, that alone would have stopped you cold but you are too far gone now to care.

The living room is small and dark, dominated by an enormous black sofa angled in front of the TV. Golden Girls reruns splash against the oversized screen.

His skin smells hot and you feel dizzy with longing. There is nothing gentle or romantic about the way he makes you feel. You aren't naked yet but you might as well be.

He leans close and kisses your cheek – you feel stubble against your skin and shiver – and you hear yourself laugh softly and say, "You know you can do better."

Your head falls back and you bare your throat to him. He presses his mouth against your flesh, the faintest scrape of teeth. His hands cup you from behind, over the curve of your back, up and under your sweatshirt. His hands are flame. He leaves scars. His hands glide across your rib cage, then gentle as a whisper to your breasts. Unexpectedly gentle. But you don't want gentle. Gentle you can get at home. You want darkness. Oblivion. You want to forget.

Somewhere in the distance you hear a car door open then close and for an instant everything else falls away and you are a mother without a child in a house where you don't belong, naked in the arms of a man you're not sure you like, less than a half mile away from the place where you live with your husband and memories that linger in the shadows like ghosts.

He asks if you're crying and you shake your head no.

"Good," he says.

"Good," you whisper.

He brushes a lock of hair, still damp from the shower, off your cheek then kisses you again – open mouth, wet and hot – and you know you are exactly where you need to be.

Clearly you have lost your mind and it will be a very long time before you find it again.

~ ~ ~

And then you blink and it is six years and a lifetime later and you're standing in line at the bank when your friend the teller beams you a smile and motions for you to step up to the window. You move your baby daughter from your right shoulder to your left and get on with your life which is, you're sure, exactly what he did.

A Walk in the Rain

by Kate Kingsbury

Kate Kingsbury grew up in London, England and as a small child told stories to her school friends while huddling in bomb shelters during WW II. She moved to the U.S. in the early sixties, and published her first book in 1987. She is currently working on her sixtieth. Kate lives in Oregon with her husband and a rat terrier who thinks she's a Great Dane.

Women like Holly Fraser so often stay in an abusive relationship, even when the road is clear for them to leave. A controlling, vindictive husband can make a woman feel worthless, undeserving of a better life. She tells herself she loves this man and will stand by him, whatever the pain, when the truth is that she's afraid that if she leaves, she will lose everything – her home, her security, and maybe even her life.

It took something remarkable to happen for Holly to make a move. I know the desperation she felt, and what drove her. She knew the risk she was taking, and where it might end, but she had reached a point in her life where there was no turning back. No matter what the cost might be.

I knew something bad had happened when Holly Fraser didn't turn up that day for lunch at the diner. At first I was just annoyed that she'd kept me waiting. I kept watching the door, looking for her to come rushing through it, her face all flushed behind her sunglasses.

Holly always wore sunglasses, rain or shine. Those big, round lenses that cover half your face. I'd hidden enough bruises when I was a kid to know why. I probably wasn't the only one in Pine Bay who could figure that out. Holly's husband, Wayne, didn't hold onto his temper too well, and now and then he'd let fly with his fist.

While I waited for her I thought about the first time I'd met Holly. We don't have a lot going for us in Pine Bay. It's a small town, halfway down the Oregon coast. One main street with souvenir shops and a handful of restaurants and that's about it. The post office is in the back of the general store and our library has to borrow books from the one in Seaport. Most of our side streets lead to the beach and our houses are constantly losing their paint to salty winds and rain.

Our scenery, however, is tough to beat – rocky beaches with white sands and jutting cliffs topped with gnarled, twisted pines, wide swaths of blue ocean and frothy bays and views that stretch for miles. We get our fair share of tourists in the summer, thanks to the new resort hotel that opened a couple of miles farther down the coastline.

It took me a long time to get used to living at the beach. I grew up in Portland, and was working for a chiropractor when I met Sam Clarkson. Sam had problems with his back and Jim, my boss, seemed to be the only person who could give Sam some relief from pain. Sam was big and loud, and always smiling, in spite of the cracking and snapping that went on when Jim went to work on him.

I liked that. The smiling, I mean. Sam made me laugh and I fell for him hard. We were married for twenty-six years when

Sam decided to retire from the construction business and buy a fishing boat. The sea took him from me three years after we moved to the coast. That's when I met Holly.

She worked in the shop that provided the flowers for the funeral. I was drowning in grief, and everyone around me did their best to console me with fake smiles and contrived optimism. Not Holly. She took one look at me and tears started rolling down her cheeks.

"You must have loved him so much," she said, her voice all broken up and trembling. From that moment on we were soul mates.

My two sons live in L.A., and I hadn't had time to make many friends in Pine Bay. I leaned on Holly a lot in those early days even though I knew she had troubles of her own. Sometimes I would catch glimpses of a bruise behind those sunglasses. As the pain of losing Sam began to ease, it was replaced by a terrible anger.

How could a man who abused his wife so cruelly live on, when my warm-hearted, generous, fun-loving husband had so needlessly lost his life? What kind of justice was that?

Holly got me through those dark days. We met for lunch two or three times a week. I asked her over to my house for dinner many times, but she always made some excuse. I even told her to bring Wayne with her, but I could tell by the look on her face that was never going to happen. I got it. Wayne didn't like her going out without him and he didn't like me. Probably because he knew that I had him pegged for a bully. I've always hated bullies.

When the loneliness got to be too much for me, I took a job serving behind the counter in the general store. It gave me something to do, and I met a lot of nice people. Holly came in now and then, and we still met for lunch. In all that time, she never once said a bad word about her husband. Come to think of it, she never said a word about him, period. It was like he was off-limits. Although we shared a lot of secrets, her life with Wayne wasn't one of them.

I told Holly about my dad, and what he did when he got drunk. I had never told that to another living soul. Holly talked about her parents, too. I sometimes thought that if Holly had

had the experiences I did when she was a kid, she would have been able to stand up to Wayne, or better still, she might have found the courage to leave him.

To this day I'll never know why she stayed with him all those years. It's not like they had kids to worry about. She never talked about that, but I got the idea she wanted kids and Wayne didn't. Good old Wayne always got his way. In the end, I was glad she didn't want to talk about him. I might have told her what I thought of her jerk of a husband.

Then Wayne had his stroke, and everything changed. He was in a wheelchair after that. He couldn't even stand without someone there to help him.

Holly gave up her job at the flower shop and devoted herself full time to taking care of her husband. She had a nurse call in on the days she needed to take care of errands. I did offer to shop for her, but I think she was glad to have an hour or so to herself now and then.

I even offered to watch Wayne while she was out, albeit reluctantly. She blew that down right away. "He gets on well with the nurse," she said, implying that he wouldn't do so well with me. She was right about that. I'd have a tough time keeping from lashing out at him about the way he'd treated his wife.

Then Holly called me out of the blue. Said she wanted to meet me for lunch and that she had something real important to tell me. She sounded different – excited almost.

That's why I waited nearly an hour at the diner before ordering my sandwich. Holly never did turn up. I figured something must have happened to Wayne. I couldn't imagine why else she would let me sit there without even bothering to call me on my cell. Holly was real particular about not letting people down.

I worried about it all afternoon, and as soon as my shift ended at the general store I drove straight to Holly's house. It was raining as usual. We get an awful lot of rain here in Oregon.

Gladys Hopper opened the door. She was Wayne's nurse. She didn't look too happy to see me. Then again, she never did. I don't think she approved of Holly going off and leaving her husband to have lunch with me. "I've been waiting over three hours to leave," she snapped. "Where is Mrs. Fraser?"

"That's what I came to find out," I said. My stomach was tied up in knots. I was pretty sure now that something bad had happened to Holly.

The nurse looked over her shoulder, then back at me. "She's not with you?"

She wasn't helping my frazzled nerves any. "Does it look like she's with me?" I started through the door. "I need to talk to Wayne."

"He doesn't want to see anyone right now."

She grabbed my arm and I shoved her away. "He'll see me."

"Mrs. Clarkson!" Gladys was shouting now, trying to hold me back. She was a hefty woman, and younger than me by at least ten years. Helping Sam remodel our home had given me muscles. I kept going.

I'd dragged her to the door of the living room when she yelled again. "One more step and I'll call the police!"

I turned on her then. "That's a very good idea," I said. "In fact, if you don't call the cops, I will."

Gladys's jaw dropped and she let me go.

Wayne was sitting in his wheelchair, staring out the win dow. He turned the chair around when I spoke to him, and I could see the fear in his eyes. "Where is she?" he demanded, rolling the chair toward me.

"That's what I want to know." I looked at the clock. "She was supposed to meet me for lunch four hours ago."

He shook his head, and covered his eyes with his good hand. "Holly left to meet you before Gladys got here. I thought maybe the two of you had gone shopping after lunch."

He didn't look good. His hair was mussed up, he was wear ing an old robe, his shoes needed cleaning and he looked as if he hadn't shaved in days. I looked around the room. Ev erything seemed normal enough. Holly's knitting bag sat by the side of the couch as usual, and the newspaper was neatly folded on the coffee table.

Yet I had the distinct feeling that something was off. I just couldn't figure out what it was. "Did she say anything to you before she left? About what it was she wanted to tell me?"

I watched his face carefully, and saw the nervous twitch at the corner of his mouth. "She wanted to tell you something?"

"Something important." I moved closer. "Are you sure you don't know what that was?"

"Of course I don't." He was on the defensive now, his face turning hard with temper. "Just what are you getting at, anyhow?"

The look in his eyes made me nervous. I glanced at the door to make sure Gladys was still there. She was, but looking like she was ready to bolt at any second.

"I'm just trying to figure out what happened," I said. "Something must have happened to Holly. She would never have left me sitting there without calling to let me know she couldn't make it."

"I have to go," Gladys said from the doorway. "I'm already four hours overdue. I have to get home."

Wayne made an odd little whimpering noise, as if he'd suddenly realized the predicament he was in. His face was all crumpled up and he mumbled so badly I could barely understand what he said. "What am I going to do without Holly? I'm helpless without her."

"Who says you have to do without her?" I looked back at Gladys. "He's going to need someone to take care of him until we find out where Holly's gone. Can you arrange it?"

Gladys sighed and pulled a cell phone from the pocket of her uniform. "I'll call the agency. We may have to put him in a nursing home until he can make other arrangements."

"No!" Wayne's answer was an anguished cry for help. "I'm not going into a nursing home. I'm staying here."

"You can't stay here alone," Gladys said, in her brisk, professional voice. "You can't get out of that chair without help. How are you going to wash, dress and feed yourself? You'll have to go in a home." She looked straight at me. "Unless you know someone who can stay with you for a while."

It was a good thing Wayne answered her, because I had no breath left to speak.

"I don't know anyone," he whined. "I don't have any family."

"Well, I'll see if maybe I can get you foster care –" Gladys broke off as whoever she'd called answered the phone. "Yes. This is Gladys Hopper."

She started talking rapidly into the phone, while Wayne kept muttering and shaking his head.

I didn't like where this was heading. "I need to get home," I said. I looked hard at Wayne. "I think we should call the hospital. Holly would never have left you alone like this. She must have had an accident."

Wayne nodded, answering me in a whisper. "Okay, go ahead."

I called the hospital. No one of Holly's name or description had been admitted. The woman I talked to was real helpful. She checked with hospitals all the way to Portland. Holly was not in any of them. After that, I called the police.

Vic Moretti is our local police chief. He was a cop in New Jersey, until his wife divorced him and he transferred to Portland. When the job for police chief opened up in Pine Bay, Vic was first in line to apply. He and Sam used to go fishing together. It was Vic who broke the news to me about Sam. I'll never forget how kind he was that day.

Anyway, I asked for Vic and he answered right away. He listened to what I had to say, and told me not to worry. "People take off all the time," he said. "Maybe Holly had enough of taking care of an invalid and decided she needed some time to herself."

Thinking about those sunglasses, I wouldn't have blamed her if she had. I knew Holly, however. She'd put up with a lot from Wayne – more than anyone should have to, and she'd stuck by him. Now that he was a helpless invalid, I just couldn't see her abandoning him without making sure someone was there to take care of him.

I was convinced something bad had happened to her and I told Vic so. "If Wayne hasn't heard from her in a couple of days," he said, "I'll look into it."

Gladys left and I stayed with Wayne until the relief nurse arrived. I didn't say much to him. He talked about Holly as if she were already in the past, which didn't help my state of mind. I was glad when the new nurse rang the doorbell.

She was younger and a lot thinner than Gladys. Wayne cheered up considerably when she showed up. She said her name was Rachel and that she was there to get Wayne into bed. Then he'd be alone until Gladys could get there in the morning.

She looked at me as if expecting me to offer to stay the night. I soon put that idea out of her head. I left while she was in the bathroom with Wayne.

Vic came into the general store the next morning. He took me into the back room and told me they'd found some things belonging to Holly. I knew at once by his voice that it was bad.

"We found her shoe on the beach," he said, pretending not to notice the tears chasing down my cheeks. "Wayne identified it as hers. Her sunglasses were hanging from a rock, halfway up the cliff. What with the rain and those sunglasses, most likely she didn't realize she was that close to the edge. She'll probably wash up somewhere in the next few days."

I hadn't cried that much since Sam died, but that day I soaked Vic's shoulder with my tears. It was comforting to have a man's arms around me again, but I wished it were under different circumstances.

It wasn't until much later that night when my brain clicked back into gear and I started thinking. The more I thought about it, the more uneasy I got. I called Vic the very next morning and asked if he could call by my house.

The sun was shining for a change, and I made a pot of coffee to take out on the veranda. It was the first real warm day of spring and normally I would have thoroughly enjoyed sipping coffee out in the fresh air with Vic.

He's a big man, like my Sam, but his voice is quieter and he's more intense about things. Sam would have laughed at my silly notions. Vic listened, his face all serious, not saying a word.

"What was Holly doing up on the cliffs when she was supposed to be meeting me for lunch?" I said, trying not to let my voice get all shaky, the way it does when I'm upset. "She called me and said she had something important to tell me. What was so important she couldn't tell me on the phone? Why would she change her mind and go walking in the rain without calling me to let me know?"

Vic folded his hands between his knees and kept his head down. "Those are all good questions," he said, sounding in credibly sad. "Maybe we'll never know the answers."

"There's something else." I leaned forward to make sure he understood. "Holly would never get close to the edge of those cliffs. She was afraid of heights."

He looked up then, and his eyes were as dark and gray as a stormy sea. "She told you that?"

"Yes, she did. It's the reason she never flew anywhere. She was terrified at the thought of being that far off the ground. She didn't even like crossing bridges. I remember once when we went to that new restaurant that opened in Seaport. She shut her eyes and scrunched up her body as we drove over the Bayside Bridge."

Vic got a funny look on his face. "What are you saying, Rosie?"

I had to take a deep breath before I could put it into words. "I don't think Holly fell from those cliffs."

"Are you telling me you think Holly jumped?"

That thought hadn't even occurred to me. "No," I said, raising my voice to emphasize my words. "Holly would never do that."

He was looking at me and I could tell he was feeling sorry for me. Trying to humor me. "Like I said, we may never know all the answers. "

I got angry then, and thumped on the table, making the coffee spill over the side of my mug. "Can't you at least take a look up there? See if there are any signs of a struggle or something?"

He reached out and closed his fingers over my fist. "Take it easy, Rosie. We did take a look up there. The grass is long on that stretch of the cliffs, and it had been raining all night. There was nothing to see. Right where we think she went over, that's where the ground slopes down toward the edge of the cliffs. The grass was wet and slippery. I had trouble keeping my footing there."

I started to cry again. "You don't understand –"

He squeezed harder. "Yes, I do. You've lost a very good friend, and it's tough to accept. You're trying to figure out why it happened. Losing someone you love is so much harder when there are questions left unanswered. It takes time to get over something like that. It'll get easier."

Disappointed in him, I pulled my hand away. "I never knew what happened to Sam," I said, and now I couldn't stop my voice from shaking. "Only that his boat ended up on the rocks. Believe me, it doesn't get easier."

Vic looked as if I'd socked him in the jaw. "I'm sorry, Rosie. I miss him, too. I can't imagine how hard it is for you. But this thing with Holly, all I can say is that she was a very unhappy woman. Maybe she fell, maybe she jumped, we'll never know. All we can do is try to remember her in the best of times, and hope she's at peace."

After he left, I kept thinking about his words, and I did my best to come to terms with them. Maybe that's what Holly wanted to tell me – that she couldn't stand being around Wayne anymore. That she'd finally had enough and was going to leave him. Maybe she'd been so eaten up with guilt about that, she'd gone for a walk to think about it before telling me.

Then what? If Holly had ever intended to kill herself, she would not have chosen that way to go. Jumping off a sixty-foot cliff? No way. Neither would she have gotten that close to the edge. She couldn't even look down from that height. So I just couldn't accept the idea of her falling.

That left only one thing. Someone must have helped her over that cliff. But who? Who did Holly know who would want her dead? That didn't make sense, either. A random act of vio lence? It was possible, of course. A lot of disturbed people are running around out there.

Still, something kept niggling at the back of my mind. Something that I knew was important, if only I could bring it back into focus.

I kept thinking about being in Holly's house, talking to Wayne. How the room looked. Something that wasn't quite right. I thought about it as I was falling asleep, and woke up in the morning still trying to figure it out.

I was getting dressed when it hit me. Of course. I had been so upset about Holly I hadn't realized the significance of it at the time.

The more I thought about it, the more certain I became. I didn't waste any time getting over to Holly's house.

Gladys answered the door and I didn't give her a chance to tell me Wayne wasn't having visitors. I pushed past her into the hallway. "I've come to keep Wayne company for a while," I said.

She seemed relieved. "The full-time nurse will be here in about an hour. Can you wait until she gets here?"

I told her I would and she left. Judging by the way she scurried out the door, I think she was happy to go.

Wayne was in the living room, sitting by the window, as usual. He looked as if he'd aged ten years. His shoulders were hunched up to his ears, and his eyes were puffy and bloodshot.

For a moment I felt sorry for him. Questions soared through my mind. Was I wrong about all this, after all? Had I wanted answers so badly, I'd let my imagination play tricks with me? I thought about what Vic had said. *Losing someone you love is so much harder when there are questions left unanswered.* Could it be that I'd wanted answers to Holly's death to make up for the questions left by Sam's?

Wayne stared at me as if he didn't recognize me. "What is it?" he asked, his voice sharp and suspicious. "What do you want?"

I didn't know what to say. I started stuttering and stam mering like an adolescent on his first date. "I came to offer my condolences," I said, "and to offer my help with the funeral arrangements when they find Holly's body."

I listened while Wayne told me that Holly would be buried in the graveyard in Seaport, since Pine Bay had no burial place of its own. Then I offered to make him a cup of tea. Holly always used to make him tea in the mornings. Alone in the kitchen, I noticed my hand shaking as I lifted the teabag out of the cup and dropped it in the trash can under the sink. There was something else in the trash can. Something that confirmed all my suspicions.

Wayne seemed touched that I would go to all the trouble of making him tea, until I told him it made me feel closer to Holly. "She was my best friend," I said, walking toward him, the steaming hot tea in my hand. "She didn't deserve to die."

He looked startled, and I saw his hands clench on the arms of his wheelchair. "Of course she didn't. It was a horrible ac cident that took my dear wife away from me."

"Oh, it was no accident." I paused in front of him, the mug of tea just out of reach. "Holly was murdered. She didn't fall from those cliffs. She was shoved off there."

Wayne's eyes were round with shock. "What are you say ing? Who would want to kill Holly?"

"You." I leaned forward and dropped the mug right in his lap.

His scream of pain was music to my ears. I stepped back as he leapt from the chair, frantically scrubbing his crotch.

I backed away some more, toward the kitchen. "You killed Holly. She knew you could walk, and that you didn't need her any more. She was going to leave you."

His face turned red with a terrible rage and he came at me, forcing me all the way back to the kitchen sink. "After every thing I did for that bitch, I found out she was writing to some *bastard* she met on the internet. I figured that as long as I was in the wheelchair, she wouldn't leave. That's why I didn't tell anyone I could walk again." He moved closer. "This is all your fault, you know. She changed after she met you. She'd still be here if it wasn't for you filling her head with your big ideas."

There was a wooden block holding a set of knives right by his elbow. He must have read my mind, as he reached out and grabbed a carving knife. I've never known such cold fear as I looked into his murderous eyes.

"Holly's gone because of you. Now you can join her." He raised the knife and I jerked back, knowing there was nowhere to run.

At that moment, the back door opened behind him. He swung around, and I saw Vic standing in the doorway, gun drawn. All the strength flowed out of me and I sagged against the sink.

Wayne gave up without a word. Just dropped the knife and sat down on a chair, his face buried in his hands.

It was the shoes, of course. I'd noticed Wayne's shoes needed cleaning. It wasn't until later that I'd asked myself how a man confined to a wheelchair could be wearing muddy shoes. He must have cleaned them after I'd left that night. He left the polishing cloth in the trash can under the sink.

Good thing I'd had the presence of mind to call Vic before I confronted Wayne. He'd taken some convincing before he let me go through with the plan. I'd left the back door to the kitchen ajar so he could come in. He'd overheard everything. I shudder to think what might have happened if he hadn't been there.

They never did find Holly's body, and couldn't prove that Wayne murdered her. They got him on attempting to murder me, instead. Vic came to tell me that he was going to jail for a long time. He also told me that he'd been thinking about what might have happened if he hadn't made it there in time. He asked me to marry him that night. Of course, I accepted.

About a month after Wayne went to prison, I got an Email. I can't tell you what a shock it was to see the signature.

Holly wasn't dead after all.

Now that Wayne was in prison, she said, she felt safe in writing to me. She knew he could walk. She'd caught him at it one night. She'd made it look like she'd gone over the cliff be cause she was afraid he would come after her if he knew she'd left him for another man.

She didn't tell anyone she was leaving, not even me. She was real sorry about that.

I'm not.

Wayne got what he deserved, after the way he treated her. I hope he thinks about that while he's locked up.

An Arrow for Sebastian

by Greg Herren

Greg Herren is a New Orleans based author/editor who has published 16 novels, including the award winning *Murder in the Rue Chartres* and *Sleeping Angel*, which recently was awarded the Moonbeam Gold Medal for Outstanding Young Adult Mystery. He has published over fifty short stories in markets as varied as the anthology *New Orleans Noir* and *Ellery Queen's Mystery Magazine.*

The character of Sebastian in my story "An Arrow for Sebastian" was inspired by a chance meeting with a beautiful young 19-year-old boy from the Midwest while visiting friends in Florida. He clearly had serious issues with his sexuality, primarily because he was from a deeply conservative small town. My heart went out to him, because I could see a lot of myself in him – as I too grew up in a conservative small town in the Midwest with deeply religious parents. I've wondered about that young man a lot in the three years since I met him – and in fact, I started writing the story that very weekend. I hope that he has come to a better end than Sebastian; but so many times young men in that situation have not.

"So, just how did you two meet anyway?" Lorita Godwin asked into a sudden silence that had dropped over the dinner party. Her words were only slightly slurred. She was on at least her fourth glass of red wine since we'd sat down at the table. She'd had a couple of whiskeys before dinner, and God only knew how much she'd drunk before her guests started arriving. Her eyelids were starting to droop a bit – which didn't go particularly well with the bad facelift she'd had since I'd last seen her.

Bless her heart, Lorita's parties were always rather ghastly – a fact I always seemed to forget. It was like there was some kind of curse on her. She hired the right caterers, got the right flowers, and always invited interesting people. Yet somehow things never seemed to come together properly for her. The food the caterers were serving us at this party, for example, seemed to be either undercooked or overcooked. The salad was wilted, and the vinaigrette seemed to be mostly vinegar.

But she always got the liquor right.

I turned my head from her to the couple she was addressing. Jake Lamauthe and his young companion, Sebastian Dixon, were sitting to her left, and directly across the table from me. I hadn't really paid much attention to either of them, frankly. Lorita always insisted on eating by candlelight, and I really couldn't see them through the long tapered red candles in the center of the table. I'd spent most of the evening listening to Lorita ramble on about this or that. The woman on my right was a bore, so I'd ignored her for the most part.

Jake was just as used to Lorita's awkward conversational gambits when she was drinking as the rest of the condemned unfortunates gathered around her dining table. He merely smiled in that strange way he had and said, "You know, Lorita, I was after him for quite some time, but wasn't getting anywhere.

Finally, I just had to hit him with my car to get his attention. That did the trick, and we've been together ever since."

Everyone laughed at this, and conversation around the table started up again. From the corner of my eye, though, I'd noticed that young Sebastian's laughter seemed a bit forced. As soon as everyone's eyes had turned away from him and Jake again, he compressed his lips into a tight little line, and looked down at his plate before taking another gulp from his own wine glass.

Curious, I thought, and even while I participated in the mindless small talk I find so tedious yet effortless to keep up, I kept stealing glances at Sebastian, watching him and what he was doing. He seemed extremely uncomfortable, but since everyone else at the table was a stranger to him that wasn't surprising. He was a very beautiful young man. He looked like a teenager, maybe in his senior year of high school, but I fig ured if he was here with Jake he had to be in his early twenties. He had a rather large forehead, and short-cropped dark hair over gorgeous green eyes framed by long, curling dark lashes. Most of the time, his face was empty of expression, and he only spoke when he was directly addressed, flashing a nervous smile before giving a very short answer that ended rather than advanced the conversation. His skin was pale, but his cheeks were rosy with spots of color that looked almost feverish. I assumed he was Irish, given the combination of dark hair and green eyes and pale skin. He sat erect in his chair, but I also noticed he wasn't eating much of Lorita's food, just pushing it around on his plate with the wrong fork.

At one point he looked across the table at me. Our eyes met for the briefest moment before he averted his own.

Very curious indeed.

I'd known Jake Lamauthe for years, but wouldn't call him a friend. I'd never cared enough for him to want to get to know him better or to build a friendship. We often were at the same parties, as we knew most of the same people. We were always distantly friendly, the way people who barely know each other are at social gatherings, full of false bonhomie and cheer that didn't go particularly deep. He seemed to be in his late forties, and had established himself into polite New Orleans society through his exceptionally successful floral shop on Magazine Street. He'd cultivated the rich hostesses of the Garden Dis trict and Uptown, first to help his business grow – and then somehow managed to make the transition from hired help to invited guest. That took some doing in a city like New Orleans, where the lines of class were drawn before birth and rarely crossed. He was certainly never going to be asked to join Rex or Comus, of course, but he'd managed to charm his way into becoming a mainstay at parties and dinners hosted by the city's bluest bloods.

There was just something about Jake I didn't like, from the very first time we'd met, and nothing had ever warranted changing my opinion. He was an attractive enough man, if you liked that type. He'd always struck me as the kind of man who would have facelifts and color his hair – but then, he'd let it go gray and he looked better for it. But there was just something repellant about him. I could never put my finger on what ex actly it was about him I'd always found distasteful – but I'd never cared enough about it to figure it out. We were socially polite to each other, and I used his services on those rare oc casions I felt the need to host a gathering of some sort in my home. To give credit where it is due, he was a master when it came to floral décor. I myself was absolutely hopeless with flowers.

The dinner conversation continued to swirl around my head as a cater waiter cleared away plates and brought in des sert dishes of orange sorbet. His name was Luke, I think – he'd worked a dinner party at my house the previous month. I had chatted him up in that dreadful, nerve-wracking hour before my guests arrived, when I am always terrified no one will actu ally show up. Luke was a master's student at Tulane in Litera ture – he had actually heard of me and was familiar with my work. I smiled at him as I deflected a rather invasive question about my next book from Dolores Devlin, who was seated on my right – Dolores was always tactless when she drank gin, which was a regular occurrence, unfortunately. I turned away from Dolores and looked directly across the table.

Sebastian was watching me without expression and we looked directly into each other's eyes again. This time he didn't look away, but met my gaze fearlessly, as though daring me to speak to him. The pinkness of his cheeks in the candlelight made him look slightly feverish. Our eyes remained locked as Dolores chattered mindlessly away, not even aware that she'd lost my attention. I wondered which one of us would look away first, but then Lorita tossed out another one of her peculiar conversational gambits my way, and courtesy forced me to turn and address my answer to her.

After the dessert plates had been cleared and Lorita began ushering her guests into the drawing room for brandy, I excused myself and slipped out the French doors onto the terrace for a quick cigarette. As I lighted my cigarette, the streetcar clanged past on St. Charles Avenue. It was nice and peaceful out there. I sat down in a chair in the darkness, and stared up at the stars, wondering how much longer I had to wait before escaping this abysmal party without appearing rude. The French doors opened behind me. I turned my head, and watched young Sebastian come down the two steps.

He walked on the balls of his feet, which gave him an odd rolling gait that coupled with his immaculate posture gave him the appearance of being uncomfortable in his own body. His arms didn't swing as he walked, and his shoulders remained solidly in place. "Hello, Sebastian." I said, and blew a plume of smoke up to the sky.

He smiled at me, and even in the darkness I could not help but marvel at how truly extraordinary his beauty was. The smile – so rarely in evidence throughout the interminable dinner party – exposed remarkably white and even teeth, and dimples that deepened in the rose-shaded cheeks. "You're a writer." It wasn't a question. He sat down on the other side of the table from me and pulled out his own pack of cigarettes – Marlboro Reds. He tapped one on the edge of the table before lighting it.

I nodded. "Did Jake really hit you with his car, or was he trying to be clever?" I asked, stubbing my cigarette out against the sole of my shoe.

The smile disappeared, the expressionless mask slipping back into place. "Yes." He took another puff from his cigarette and didn't look at me. "Although he makes it sound like he ran me over. I was in my car. He pulled out in front of me."

"That's quite a story." I lit another cigarette. From inside the house I could hear a jazz recording I didn't care for – Lorita's musical taste was nearly as bad as her parties – so I was in no hurry to go inside and rejoin the other guests. I blew out smoke. "You don't like the story."

"It's how we met." He shook his head. "I just don't like the way he tells it to people. Sometimes, though, I wonder –" He cut his words off when we heard the sound of the doors opening again.

"There you are, darling." Jake put his hands down on Sebastian's shoulders proprietarily, and he stiffened almost imperceptibly in response. "You mustn't pester David, Sebastian – writers like their solitude, don't they, David?" Jake's eyes glittered, and he swayed a little bit.

I could smell the whiskey on his breath, and knew he was drunk.

"I'm sorry if I intruded." Sebastian replied, looking down submissively.

"Let's go inside, shall we, dear?" Jake gave me a malevolently triumphant smile of ownership as he guided Sebastian back up the brick steps and inside the house. But just before they went through the doors, Sebastian looked back at me over his shoulder.

It was a look of quiet desperation if I'd ever seen one. I lighted another cigarette, and by the time I'd finished it and rejoined the party, Jake and Sebastian had already made their apologies and left.

"I think Jake was a little drunk," Lorita slurred to me in what she thought was a whisper but could clearly be heard by everyone in the drawing room.

Sebastian's look haunted me over the next few days. I would be working on my book – I was in the corrections and revisions phase, which is always tedious – and when I'd stop to think for a moment, I'd see that look on his face again. I wasn't sure what it meant – and I replayed our interaction several times trying to figure it all out.

There was something about young Sebastian that had somehow lodged itself like a splinter into my psyche.

It was possible I'd misread the look and it had been some thing else entirely. Or nothing at all, for that matter. But the more I thought about it, the more I was certain he was appeal ing to me for help, which didn't really make much sense. Why me, and help from what? I cursed myself for not bothering to get to know Jake better in the past, or for at least not paying better attention. Several times I picked up the phone to call Lorita – she collected gossip the way some women collected shoes – but always stopped myself before I could dial. Lorita would naturally want to know why I was asking about Jake and Sebastian, and I didn't have an answer that would satisfy her curiosity. Once I'd hung up, she would start to wonder about why I was asking, what I was up to, as she poured herself yet another whiskey, and would eventually come up with her own explanation for why I was asking. By the next glass of whiskey she'd be convinced it was all true. And after refilling her glass a third time, she would be telling anyone who would take her call about my obsession with Jake Lamauthe's new lover.

And that was not something I cared to have spreading through the Garden District like bubonic plague.

Besides, even I myself didn't understand my curiosity about Sebastian.

It really came down to that haunting look he'd given me on the terrace.

I'd been alone two years – nearly two – since Robert had left. Certainly, Sebastian was a beautiful young man, but there were plenty of beautiful young men in New Orleans. If I wanted to see beautiful young men, all I had to do was drive down St. Charles Avenue in the late afternoon. The neutral ground between the streetcar tracks would be filled with beau tiful shirtless young men jogging, their muscular torsos gleam ing with sweat in the late afternoon sun. No, my fascination with Sebastian was a curiosity about the strange look on his face when Jake told the story of how they'd met, the way he'd stiffened ever so slightly when Jake touched him on the terrace, and that final, odd look he'd given me when they'd gone back inside.

I was thinking about that look as I climbed the stairs to my gym three days later, and wondering if I had crossed that thin line from curiosity to obsession when I ran into Sebastian coming out. His hair was wet with sweat, his soaked white tank top clinging to his muscled chest like another layer of skin. I could see his hard little nipples and every cut muscle in his stomach. He was wearing aviator sunglasses so I couldn't see his eyes as he brushed past me and mumbled a barely audible, "Excuse me." He either didn't recognize me, or didn't want to talk, so I just continued up the stairs.

I made it up another three stairs when he called my name. I stopped, and turned to look back at him.

He'd pushed the sunglasses up on top of his head and he was smiling, his dimples deepened in the rosy cheeks and the even white teeth gleaming in the late morning sun. Again I marveled at the difference in his face when he smiled. He started back up the steps toward me. "It's me, Sebastian." He held out his right hand. "I'm sorry, I was in a hurry and then I realized it was you."

I took his moist hand and shook it. "Nice to see you again, Sebastian." I smiled. "I didn't know you worked out here."

"I just started recently." The smile didn't falter in the least,. "I didn't know you worked out here, either. How often do you come in?"

"I try to get here at least three times a week." It was a lie – I hadn't been that regular since Robert left.

"Is this the time you usually come in?" He asked, frowning as he looked at his watch. I nodded, and he went on, "Well, maybe we could work out together? I have to run right now, but say Wednesday? At eleven?"

"Sure."

"Great." He turned and went down the stairs at a gallop, and I watched him go out the door before continuing on my way up to the second floor.

That was how Sebastian and I started working out togeth er. In the two days before we met, I kept telling myself, that he was just a nice kid who seemed like he needed a friend, that it would benefit me to have someone I met regularly at the gym so I could get rid of the spare tire stubbornly starting to form around my waist, and so on. That Wednesday morning, I couldn't focus on the pages I needed to revise, and kept pacing, looking at the clock and the slow creep of the hands around until it was finally time for me to get to the gym.

He was waiting for me, sitting at the counter reading the newspaper. He was wearing another white tank top like the one he'd worn the other day, with long baggy red basketball shorts that reached just past his knees. "I was afraid you wouldn't come," he said with a big grin.

"Why would you think that?" I replied, curious.

He shrugged. "I don't know – I really don't get out of the house much, and I don't really have any friends." He beamed at me again. "I hope we can be friends." He added shyly, not able to look me in the eyes.

I was touched, and felt sorry for him. It couldn't be easy being involved with Jake Lamauthe, I figured as we went through our workout. I'd never liked Jake, and he'd gone through any number of 'boyfriends' since I'd first met him. They were always younger, always rather pretty, if a little vapid, and they never stuck around long.

I found myself looking forward to meeting Sebastian at the gym – I didn't get out of the house myself often, other than errands and the gym. And while he was reticent at first, he eventually became more talkative. Not so much about Jake, of course, but more about himself. He was from Nebraska originally (*Of course*, I thought when he told me, *the corn fed good looks and the apple cheeks.*), but had left for New Orleans when he turned eighteen to make his way in the world. His parents were conservative, as was everyone else in the small town where he grew up, and he knew then he was different, not like the other boys he played football with or on the wrestling team. College wasn't an option, and after graduation, everyone expected him to go to work in the pork processing plant.

"The whole town smelled of stale blood," he said, making a face, "and I just wanted to get away. And New Orleans seemed like a magic place, you know? So I came here."

"And you met Jake, and now you live in a big house in the Garden District," I smiled, removing the forty-five pound weight plates off the bar we'd just finished using. His face darkened, but I pretended not to notice.

I also pretended not to notice other things – like the frequency of the ugly bruises or black eyes he would always try to explain away as nothing. "I tripped," or "I'm so clumsy," or "I'm always bumping into things" was the catechism I came to expect from him whenever he showed up trying to cover up another one. Jake was bigger than he was, of course – Sebastian was lean with no extra body fat on him anywhere. He couldn't have weighed more than one-hundred-and-fifty pounds dripping wet, while Jake was a big man, easily topping the scales at two-hundred-and-twenty pounds. I know Jake came to the gym in the evenings after he shut down the store, and he worked with one of the trainers – I used to see him when I'd come in to do the elliptical machine in the early evenings when I was stuck on whatever book I was writing; the mindless concentration of a cardio machine often helped me work through whatever problem I was having with my writing. I'd never heard that Jake was violent – but there was something about him I'd never cared for. Perhaps I'd always sensed there was violence just below the surface of his smiling and oh-so-friendly façade.

Many nights I would lie in my bed, staring at the ceiling, wondering if I should say something about them, or offer to help him get out of Jake's house. It was unusual. If Sebastian were a woman, there would be no question about it; I would say something, I would do whatever it took to get her away from her abuser. I would talk to her, sit her down and explain how the violence never stops, it never goes away no matter how much your man says it will, or how sorry he is. It only stops in death.

But he was a man involved with another man, and I didn't know if the bruising and the black eyes might be a part of some kind of kinky role play they both enjoyed. I didn't know if my intervention would be welcomed, or seen as an incredible intrusion and invasion of privacy. And I liked Sebastian, the workouts were the highlight of my week. Every Monday, Wednesday and Friday I would wake up and be excited, because

I was going to see him at the gym. I didn't want to do or say anything that would jeopardize that.

If he needed my help, I figured he would ask for it.

He was an adult, right?

The book was finally finished, and I printed out two cop ies and burned a CD, the way my publisher always wanted. I drove down to the Fedex office on Tchoupitoulas, and when the package was on its way to New York, I went into the PJ's next door to treat myself to an iced mocha as a reward for turning the book in only two months past deadline.

As I stood in the line, the guy working the register seemed vaguely familiar, and as I moved steadily closer to the counter as each person in front of me placed their order, I tried to re member where I knew him from. New Orleans is a small town, and this kind of thing happens all the time – you see someone in a different context than you're used to seeing them in and it drives you crazy until you remember. This guy, for example, may have used to work in a restaurant I frequent, or worked out at my gym for a while at the same time I did, or maybe was just one of my readers and had come to a signing. He could just be a fan who had become my friend on Facebook, and I was used to seeing his face on my newsfeed.

When I reached the counter, he smiled at me. "David! I haven't seen you in a while! How are you?"

"Good," I replied, trying to hide that I had no idea who he was. "And you?"

He smiled, and winked at me. He leaned over the counter a bit, and said, "I live in a roach-infested studio apartment and work here for next to nothing, but I am so much happier than I was!"

And in that instant, I knew immediately who he was – he was Sebastian's predecessor in Jake's life. "I'm glad," I replied, genuinely pleased for him, but with all kinds of questions rac ing through my head.

"I'm going to UNO for the next semester," he went on, oblivious to my fumbling for something to say. "Getting the hell away from Jake was the smartest thing I ever did."

"It was that bad?" I heard myself saying.

"You have no idea." He rolled his eyes. "What can I get for you?"

"Large iced mocha," I replied, and handed him a five dollar bill.

I'd planned on drinking it in the car on my way home, but instead I picked up a *Gambit Weekly* and sat down at a table. I pretended to read it while I watched him. *Here's your chance to find out about Jake and what goes on in that house,* a voice whispered inside my head, *and clearly he has no qualms about keeping Jake's secret.*

I watched as people came and went, drinking the mocha as slowly as I could, even as the ice melted and watered down the flavor. Each time I drummed up the nerve to go talk to him, someone would walk up to the counter to order, or the girl he was working with would start talking to him, or his cell phone would ring.

I finished the mocha and tossed it into the garbage. Figuring it wasn't meant to be, I started for the door to the parking lot when I heard him call my name. I turned and he came out from around the counter. In his hand was one of the store's business cards, and he pressed it into my hand. "Call me some time," he said with a big smile. "It would be nice to catch up."

I thanked him and asked, "Do you mind telling me what was so awful about being with Jake?"

"He was very controlling," he replied, his face darkening. He shrugged. "He didn't want me to work – didn't really want me to do anything besides go to the gym and be there in the house ready to do whatever he wanted me to."

"I see," I replied, trying to summon the nerve to ask the question I really wanted to ask. In my mind I could see the multiple bruises on Sebastian's arms and legs. *Did he hit you? Was he violent?* But I couldn't say the words.

"Call me," he reached out and touched my shoulder gently, a smile on his pretty face.

I nodded and he went back behind the counter. It wasn't until I looked at the little card when I was in my car that I realized that I'd forgotten his name in the first place.

Alone, in my house, I wondered what to do.

It was clear Jake wasn't right in the head, and I worried about Sebastian. The bruising could only mean one thing. I didn't believe for a minute he was that clumsy – watching him at the gym I could see he was graceful. Despite the awkward way he stood, his movements were always fluid. Besides, I nev er once saw him bump into anything at the gym.

Apparently, he was only clumsy in Jake's house.

Would my intrusion be welcome? I was his only friend – he had told me that often enough. There was no one else he could turn to, no one else he could trust.

But he could just walk out, I reminded myself. *No one is ever trapped anywhere, not in this day and time.*

He could always come to my house.

Tomorrow, I decided, *at the gym I will say something, offer him my house.*

But he didn't show up at the gym the next day, and he didn't answer when I called.

It was curious, I thought as I went through my own work out, lost in thought and not really paying attention to what I was doing. It wasn't like him. He never missed the gym – he'd often said it was one of the few times he could get out of the house. I worried and I wondered, and finally gave up on the workout as a lost cause and went home.

"Darling, have you heard?" Lorita breathed when I an swered my phone later that afternoon.

"Heard what?" I replied absently, thinking she was slurring her words already and it was only two in the afternoon.

"Darling, Jake went and shot that boy of his!" Her voice dripped with malice, and as the news went through me, I couldn't help but wonder how long she had hated Jake Lamauthe.

"Shot him?" I replied.

"Shot him dead," she said, not even bothering to hide her glee. "He claims it was self-defense, of course, that he caught the boy stealing from him and he attacked him, but apparently the police aren't buying his story."

"They aren't?"

"Supposedly they struggled over the gun, and it went off – at least that's what Jake is saying." Her voice sounded smug.

"But the police don't believe it for a moment. Apparently his cleaning woman told them Jake used to smack the boy around."

"How do you know all this?" I asked, playing with the pen on the table next to the phone. "And when did all this happen?"

"Last night, around two in the morning," I could hear ice clicking together as she took another drink. "His cleaning woman, you know, also cleans for Binky Claypool, and she told Binky everything this morning."

And now everyone in Uptown knows, I thought. "I have to go."

"But –"

I pushed the off button and put the phone back down.

Poor Sebastian, I thought as I filled a glass with gin. *Maybe – maybe I should have said something.*

I drank alone in the dark for the rest of the day, unable to forget that haunted look on his face.

The Story of My Unlife

by Laura Resnick

Laura Resnick is the author of the popular Esther Diamond urban fantasy series, whose recent releases include *Vamparazzi*, *Unsympathetic Magic*, and *Doppelgangster*. She has also written traditional fantasy novels such as *In Legend Born*, *The Destroyer Goddess*, and *The White Dragon*, which made the "Year's Best" lists of *Publishers Weekly* and *Voya*. An opinion columnist, frequent public speaker, and the Campbell Award-winning author of many short stories, she is on the Web at LauraResnick.com.

When I sat down to write this story, I had recently completed an urban fantasy novel called Vamparazzi, *for which I had done a ton of vampire research – which had proved to be a lot more interesting than I had expected. So I thought that writing a vampire story for this collection would be a good opportunity to use some more of that background material.*

As it turns out, I didn't use any of it. None! That's just what happens sometimes. Instead, once I started developing the heroine of this story, I soon found that her fate, rather than being ruled by the vampire lore I had researched, was largely determined by other people in the story maneuvering her into feeling uncomfortable about her singlehood – a state with which she's normally content. (As a single person myself, I've been there.) So I really enjoyed playing with that theme by pushing her into an impulsive (and fantastical) life-altering decision which this level-headed woman would never normally have made – and then seeing what happened next.

I realized I was going to have serious problems adjusting to being a vampire when I tried to bite someone in the jugular vein and discovered it's *much* harder to do than you might think.

Indeed, I was so stymied by the actual logistics of the pro cedure, now that I held a warm and blood-pulsing body in my arms ... that I let go of my prey and burst into tears. Which was not a promising start to my unlife.

I had a gloomy feeling that this whole thing had been a huge mistake on my part. I wondered if I could get it undone. Reverse the process. Become, er, un-undead.

It was not, after all, as if I had really thought this through before being turned. I had become a vampire on a night of over-indulgence in alcohol, casual sex, and morbid self-pity – none of which is ever a good basis for making major deci sions. In fact, it's fair to say that, when offered the prospect of being turned into a bloodsucking creature of the night, I was drunkenly intrigued but quite skeptical. I hadn't really believed, despite a pretty good sales pitch from he-who-became my sire, that I was getting into anything more serious than a risky and unconventional sexual practice with a total stranger. And the fact that I was willing to do *that* is clear evidence of how dys functional and unreliable my mental processes were that night.

My transformation had occurred at the wedding of an old college friend. And the stereotypical pathos of my behavior that night embarrasses me in retrospect.

Lucy was the only member of my old college gang with whom I was regularly still in touch, since I had moved to Chi cago a couple of years after we all graduated, whereas most of my college friends stayed in the New York area. I hadn't been back East for a visit in years, and I thought I would enjoy a trip there in autumn for the wedding. Plus, I wanted to be support ive of Lucy in her newfound happiness.

I also welcomed the chance that the wedding would offer me to see our old gang, many of whom would be there. There were some of them whom I hadn't seen since graduation day, fifteen years earlier. So when Lucy informed me she was get ting married ("Thank God! I was on the verge of becoming a spinster!" she burbled cheerfully at me by email), I had readily accepted her invitation to attend.

As the event approached, I thought briefly about trying to rustle up a date, but I had no idea whom I could invite to go with me. I hadn't had a regular boyfriend in several years; not since Todd had broken up with me. He had left behind some dirty underwear and the entire unpaid co-signed loan for his quickly wrecked sports car after he announced he was leaving me for a part-time calligrapher who, unlike me, really *appreciated* him and *understood* him... and was willing to co-sign his next car loan.

In fact, as I contemplated the unlikely prospect of finding someone to attend Lucy's wedding with me, I realized that – never mind not having a steady man in my life – I hadn't even been on a *date* in well over a year.

I shrugged off this depressing thought by concluding that the notion of bringing a date was silly, anyhow. I couldn't ex pect a friend or co-worker in Chicago to buy an airplane ticket just to keep me company at a wedding in New York. Besides, a date would undoubtedly feel bored or out of place there, since I'd be hanging out with my college friends and we'd be reminiscing about old times. So it obviously made sense for me to go alone.

Well ... that decision only seemed obvious until I got to the wedding – and discovered that every single one of my old gang had brought a date. Most of them, in fact, had brought spouses, domestic partners, or longtime companions. Another of my old friends, Mimi, was recently-divorced. She showed up with an infatuated new boyfriend who kept telling me how incredibly lucky he felt to have met such a wonderful woman as Mimi. My old study partner Calvin, who had come out of the closet after college, brought a man whom he covertly de scribed to me as, "Just a shag partner. We have absolutely noth ing in common, but the sex is stellar, so we meet a couple of nights per week for that. He's just here as a favor to me, since I didn't want to come *alone* to a *wedding*, of course."

"Uh-huh," I said.

Rather than reminiscing about old times, everyone in our group talked about the homes they were DIYing as a couple ("I could never do it on my *own*"), the fun they'd had together on exotic vacations ("but I wouldn't have wanted to go there *alone*"), their children and the challenges of parenthood ("I could never be a *single* parent"), or their fervent attempts to reproduce ("since time is running out for people our age, after all"). They all laughed over anecdotes about which partner in the relationship stole the covers at night, about fighting over the thermostat, and about hiding Christmas presents from each other.

I talked about my job and my cat.

None of them had seen me for years, and very few of them knew anything about my life for the past decade. So they were full of friendly questions and supportive comments.

Questions along the lines of, "So there's not anyone in your life these days? No one at *all?*" and comments such as, "Well, there's no shame in being single. I mean, in a way, I envy you" (this said while fervently clutching a spouse's hand).

It was one of those dark occasions when the single life with which you're normally content suddenly winds up feeling as if it's no life at all.

Thus, when Lucy's mother, who was circulating through out the reception hall, came over to our group to mingle and visit, I was immensely relieved by this opportunity to change the subject. She met everyone's spouses, partners, and dates, and she thanked us all for coming. She recounted some of the amusing and anxiety-provoking crises that had preceded the smoothly executed wedding, and she chatted nostalgical ly about our group's long-ago days as her daughter's college chums.

Then, without missing a beat, she turned to me and said with a sad smile, "You never married, did you?"

Caught off guard, I replied with a mixture of irritation and embarrassment, "There's still time. I'm not exactly in my grave."

Her eyes misted with compassionate admiration for my plucky spirit, and she patted my hand kindly. "No, of course you're not. *Plenty* of time, dear. Yes, yes, plenty of time. Don't you worry about it."

I *hadn't* worried about it until that evening. I also wanted to point out that, barely three hours ago, she had married off a daughter who was, in fact, four months *older* than I was. But surrounded by my old gang's awkward, pitying silence in the wake of her comment, I suspected this protest would sound pathetically defensive rather than calmly reasonable.

All things considered, I assert that it's both understandable and predictable that, as the evening wore on, I drank far too much and then flirted shamelessly with an attractive stranger who showed flattering interest in me. He, too, had come to the wedding without a date. He asked me to dance, kept me with him on the dance floor through several songs, and then started taking discreet physical liberties – which I (and the multiple Cosmopolitans I had by then consumed) readily encouraged. Eventually, with our bodies welded together as we swayed dizzily to the music, I told him that I was staying at this hotel and asked if he would like to see my room.

We were in the perfect state of inebriation for what followed – just drunk enough for the sex to be bold and uninhibited, rather than clumsy and incompetent. Unwisely, though, we subsequently raided the mini-bar and continued drinking. Thus I was so drunk that I listened with profound gravity when my partner (whose name, alas, I couldn't remember – if, indeed, I had ever known it) explained to me in a slurred but sultry monologue that he was a vampire and that he felt so close to me after two bouts of gloriously hot sex that he'd like to "turn" me – if I thought I would like that.

I vaguely recall that we talked about this a whole lot, but I have almost no recollection of what we said. And, well, a self-pitying, thoroughly drunk "spinster" at a wedding full of doting couples can be talked into almost anything by a man who is seductive enough – as this one was. Suffice it to say, he had his way with me, and I was blearily enthusiastic about it at the time.

When I woke up alone the next morning, I had a hangover of epic proportions and a horrified memory of having engaged in sexual blood play with a man whose name I didn't even know.

Oops.

I realized, with a combination of exasperated self-condemnation and anxious dread, that I'd need to get a blood test soon after I got home. Apart from that, though, I wasn't in any condition to think about anything besides my skull-splitting, stomach-churning hangover. I staggered around the room in a groggy daze, sloppily gathering and packing my things, then I made my way to the airport just in time for my flight. All things considered, I deeply regretted ever having agreed to attend the wedding, and I just wanted to go home and get back to my normal life.

I didn't know it then, but I would *never* return to my normal life. Though I did get back to Chicago in a timely and uneventful manner.

Of course, I experienced excruciating light sensitivity throughout my journey that day; but I attributed it to my hangover. If you're wondering how I survived that exposure to sunlight, it turns out (I have since learned) that vampires don't burst into flames or dissolve into ashes when exposed to the sun. We're just sun-intolerant; it's uncomfortable for us, but not terminal – not unless we overdo it. Since I'm half-Irish and half-Polish, this aspect of vampirism was the easiest one for me to adjust to, being very little different from my previous existence.

After I got home and unpacked, the thought of food didn't interest me, and I again attributed this to my hangover. It wasn't until the following day that I began to notice something strange about myself.

Feeling recovered from my weekend misadventure, I grabbed a muffin and some coffee on my way to work the next morning, as was my long-established habit. But I quickly discovered that the muffin tasted like sawdust and the coffee had no flavor at all. Moreover, within minutes, I was violently sick, bringing up everything I had just consumed. I thought maybe the food was off, or maybe I was still suffering the after-effects of my personal saturnalia. To be on the safe side, I avoided food and beverage for the rest of the day – and found that, despite the morning's messy episode and my continued light sensitivity, I otherwise felt fine.

In fact, better than fine. I felt *wonderful.* My sense of well-being that day was virtually unprecedented. I was energetic, alert, and full of stamina. I stayed late, working for thirteen hours, and wasn't even tired when I finally decided to call it a day and go home. My senses of hearing, sight, and smell were pleasurably heightened. And I was suddenly so strong that when I accidentally knocked an important file behind a massive photocopier, and I pushed against the machine in futile frustration, thinking the file was effectively gone forever now ... the machine moved as easily as if it were a shopping cart. I retrieved the file and then pushed the massive machine back into place with very little effort.

By nightfall, I was quite hungry. But I soon discovered that no matter what food I tried, it was all as flavorless as dust, and I also couldn't keep it down for more than a few minutes. Meanwhile, I went from hungry to ravenous. Yet nothing satisfied me or was safe for me to eat.

Despite all these obvious clues about my transformation, it was only when I logged on to my personal email account that night, confused and agitated by the strange experiences of the day, that I finally suspected the truth.

The eye-opening hint came in the form of an email from the hotel where I had stayed that weekend. They had revised my bill after I'd checked out, having discovered that I had virtually emptied the minibar in my room.

Then it alllll came flooding back to me.

Oh, shit.

Sometime after draining an uncertain number of little bottles of alcohol and before sinking into an unconscious stupor, I had offered my veins up to the naked stranger in my bed ... and I had greedily drunk from the artery he presented to me.

"Oh. My. *God.*"

I had not, as I had feared, contracted an STD as a result of that encounter. I had contracted *vampirism.*

I did what I believe almost anyone would do upon making such a discovery: I went to bed and hid under the covers.

In the morning, I called in sick at work. I stayed in bed, not answering my phone or door, and not collecting my mail or checking my email. For twenty-four hours, I dozed fitfully, hoping each time I awoke that I had dreamed the whole episode. Then I would test this theory by doing something like picking up my dresser (which weighs more than I do), and I'd realize with a mixture of horror, fear, and panic that, no, the nightmare was real and I had indeed become a supernatural being, a bloodsucking creature of the night, an undead *thing* ... And I hadn't the faintest idea of what to do about it.

Finally, around midnight that night, maddening hunger drove me out of my condo and into the streets in search of sustenance. I had watched enough vampire movies to have a vague idea of what I should do. I went to a singles' bar, encouraged a reasonably attractive but none-too-sober man to pick me up, and went home with him. Although I'd normally *never* do something that reckless (well, not unless I was a morbidly unhappy wedding guest), my supernatural strength gave me (perhaps misplaced) confidence in my ability to handle him if he turned out to be a violent psychopath.

I should make it clear that I had no intention of killing or harming him. Yes, I thirsted desperately for human blood, but I hadn't turned into a homicidal maniac, for goodness sake. I still retained my moral center. But since my sire had fed on me without harming me, I assumed I could do the same to someone else. And I was *starving* by now.

It was only once I was in bed with my prospective victim and I prepared to feast on the warm, luscious blood that I could smell through the heat of his skin and hear pounding alluringly through his veins and arteries ... It was only then that I realized I didn't know how to do this.

Yes, I remembered my sire sucking my blood. Mostly, though, I remembered the sensation being so erotic that it produced the most explosive orgasm of my life. That fiery shower of pleasure, combined with the large quantities of alcohol I had consumed, ensured that I was now extremely fuzzy on the logistical details of what had happened.

I recalled various vampire portrayals I had seen on TV and decided to imitate them and hope for the best. Under the guise of kisses and caresses, I got my mouth close to my partner's jugular vein, then I opened wide, preparing to feed – and expecting fangs to conveniently pop out of my mouth so I could pierce his flesh (*gently*, mind you) and drink.

My stomach rumbled hungrily, but nothing else happened. I removed my hand from my partner's body and raised it to my lips, exploring my teeth and then poking around in my mouth. Everything felt perfectly normal.

"Are you okay?" he breathed.

"Huh?"

"Did you bite your tongue or something?"

"Um, yeah."

Okay, I would just have to do this without fangs. I was by now hungry enough to eat the bed, let alone the man writhing temptingly in my arms. So I took a steadying breath, then I bit his neck.

He groaned with startled pleasure.

I bit a little harder. He grunted as his flesh squished be tween my teeth. I tasted sweat and cheap aftershave, but no blood. I pulled my head back and took a look; the skin of his neck was a little reddened, and I could see deep marks from my teeth, but it was obvious I had come nowhere near accessing his jugular.

I tried again, fiercely determined this time as I gnawed fe rociously on him.

"OW! Hey, that hurts!" He shoved at me. "*Stop.*"

I ceased biting my prey, let go of him, and rolled away from his body, realizing there was no way this was going to work. Seized by a combination of frustrated hunger, confused despair, and embarrassment, I burst into tears.

I'm not normally a weepy woman, but this moment was the culmination of several *very* trying days.

He initially tried to get his night back on track (i.e. get me back into the sack) with soothing words and caresses; but once he realized I was working my way up to a full flood of hyster ics, he encouraged me to get dressed and go home. Which I did.

After a long night of deep sleep induced by exhaustion and emotional trauma, I called in sick at work again the next day. Realizing that I would starve to death if I didn't find out how to feed myself as a vampire, I knew I had to track down the man who had done this to me. He was the only person of my acquaintance who could explain to me how vampirism worked in practical terms. Perhaps he could even tell me how to get this reversed.

I started by calling Lucy, then realized when I got her an swering machine that she was on her honeymoon in Hawaii. Presumably she had taken her cell phone with her, but I didn't know the number. I'd have to find someone who did know it. I searched my purse for the business cards and scribbled-on pieces of notepaper that some of my old college friends had handed me that weekend. I had found our reunion so demoral izing that I hadn't expected ever to use their contact informa tion, but now I was very glad that I hadn't thrown any of it away. At least one of them would surely have Lucy's cell num ber – or might even know who I had slept with that night and how I could contact him.

The first person I tried was Mimi.

"I'm so glad you called!" she cried. "No one had your phone number – well, Lucy, I suppose, but she was gone al ready – and we've all been *dying* to know what happened after you left the reception with that gorgeous hunk!"

"We slept together," I said shortly. "Do you have Lucy's cell phone number?"

"I knew it! Oh, my God! Did you even *know* him before that?"

"No." I asked hopefully, "Do you know him?"

"I knew it, I knew it! You're so brave!" Mimi enthused. "That is so exciting!"

"I don't suppose you happen to know his na –"

"I wish I could be like you and just *go* for it."

"I went for it because I was three sheets to the wind," I said. "Listen, I need to find –"

"Just tell me one thing," Mimi said. "Was the sex great? The way he looked on the dance floor, I had a feeling it would be *great*. Was it great?"

"Actually, yeah, it was great. But there was one little probl –"

"You are *so* much better at being single than I am. It's not that I want my jerk of a husband back – Jesus, no! – but I just feel so pathetic ever since my divorce."

I pointed out, "You're the one who showed up at the wed ding with an adoring new boyfriend, not me."

"Honey, he's gay."

I blinked. "Your boyfriend is gay?"

"He's not my boyfriend. He's my downstairs neighbor."

I sighed, realizing the truth. "You felt you couldn't show up at the wedding without a date?"

She made an affirmative noise. "But he's such a drama queen, he totally overdid it. All that doting, adoring talk about how wonderful I was and how lucky he was, blah blah blah. His act was so close to parody, I thought everyone there realized within a half hour that he was just my gay beard." She paused. "You really couldn't tell?"

She didn't have Lucy's cell number, but she thought that our friend Kathleen did. I wasn't enthused about contacting Kathleen, who had spent the entire reception talking about the joys of dual-parenting and the pleasure of spending time with her spouse by rehabbing their townhouse together. But my need was desperate, so I called her.

Initially, our conversation was repeatedly interrupted by her shrieking in foul-mouthed rage at her children (about whom she had crooned rapturously at the wedding). After she had locked them in the cellar (with my heightened senses, I could hear them pounding on the door and demanding release), she questioned me, as had Mimi, about that night.

"*God*, was the sex good?" she asked longingly. "*God*, I have not had good sex since at least two years before I wound up with Nathan."

"Nathan?"

"My husband. You met him."

Indeed, I had. Kathleen had clung to him like a burr all that evening. I asked, "Do you happen to have Lucy's –"

"When I watched you leave the ballroom with that guy, I swear, I wanted to beat you to death with my stiletto heels and take your place." Kathleen added, "Nothing personal."

She didn't have Lucy's cell number, but she did have the number of Lucy's parents. Feeling I was at least one step closer to my quarry, I dialed the number. Lucy's mother answered.

"Oh, hello, dear! How lovely to hear from you. Did you enjoy the wedding?" It was obvious from the sound of her voice that she was crying.

"Are you all right?" I asked.

"I'm fine," she sobbed. "It's nothing." She blew her nose.

"Please tell me what's wrong," I said in concern.

"Men are such *beasts.*"

I wondered if there had been some disastrous wedding-night revelation. "Is Lucy all right?"

"I'm not talking about Lucy!" she shrieked. "I'm talking about Harry!"

"Harry?"

"My husband."

"Oh."

"You might as well be the first to know," she said tearfully. "I'm leaving the bastard."

"*What?*"

"And I intend to get every penny I can! God knows I de serve something for the past forty hellacious, wasted years of my life!"

I sighed in weary exasperation. "You know, if all you peo ple hadn't been so goddamned phony at Lucy's wedding, my life would be working out *very* differently now."

She was too distracted by her own problems to pay any attention to what I had just said. Which was no doubt just as well. I got Lucy's contact number from her and ended the call.

I was surprised by how delighted Lucy was to pick up the phone to find me interrupting her honeymoon.

"God, I am so bored I could kill myself," she said.

That didn't really jibe with my image of honeymoons. "Really?"

"I should never – *never!* – have gotten married during foot ball season," said Lucy. "I haven't been able to peel him away from the TV since we got here. If he's not watching a game or a re-run of a game, then he's watching commentators *talking* about games. We're in Hawaii! This is my honeymoon! I *hate* him!"

"I love the life I had," I said wanly. "I *miss* the life I had."

"Huh?"

"Look, the night of your wedding, I left the reception with a guy –"

"Hey, I heard about that!" She added darkly, "I'll bet *he* didn't go into a trance in front of the TV as soon as you got him alone in a hotel room."

"I need to get in touch with him," I said. "He, um, you might say ... left something important in my room. I need to know what to do about it."

"Oh, you want his phone number?"

"Yes," I said with relief. "Also his name."

She burst into surprised laughter. "You didn't even know his name? Oh, my *God*, I wish I were you."

I also wished I was me – the pre-vampire me. "Do you know who he is?" I asked eagerly.

He'd been a guest on the groom's side. I heard Lucy asking her new husband for the guy's full name and contact information. It took her several tries to get his attention away from the TV. Then she had to search their suite for his cell phone, in which the correct phone number could be found.

My one-night stand was a business contact of Lucy's loathed spouse. Lucy relayed the information that the guy traveled a lot, so his cell was my best bet for reaching him.

I dialed the number.

"Oh, my God, it's *you*," he said, after I got him on the phone and explained who I was. "Are you okay? I mean ... how *are* you?"

"I'm a vampire now," I said without further preamble.

"Shit! So that part wasn't just a drunken delusion?"

"No," I said stonily. "Can it be undone?"

"Undone?" he repeated in obvious surprise. "No. It's a mystical transformation, not a tattoo." He added apologetically, "It's like circumcision. Once it's done, there's no going back."

"So I'm stuck being this way for the rest of my life?" I said shrilly. "I mean, my *un*life?"

"Christ, I'm sorry. I am *so* sorry." He sounded sincere. "I should never have done that while we were so drunk. Or on such short acquaintance. You had no way of knowing what you were getting into. What I did was wrong. I just got com pletely carried away. You were so sexy and hot, and so cuddly and funny, and I felt so ... But that's no excuse."

"If I was so *appealing*, why did you disappear without even saying goodbye?" This really wasn't the most important thing we needed to discuss, but suddenly I wanted an explanation.

"I *had* to go. I had an early flight to the West coast. I'm in Seattle on business right now," he explained. "I tried to wake you. I *really* tried. But you were dead to the world, and I didn't want to throw cold water on you or start slapping you awake. That seemed a little extreme."

"Well, I guess ..."

"So I wrote you a note and left my card."

"You did?" I said in surprise.

"Yes. On the dresser." Hearing my silence, he asked, "Didn't you see it?"

"No." Then again, I didn't think I had even looked at the dresser. I was so hung-over that I stumbled around the room in a hurried daze, throwing things into my weekend bag and then fleeing the hotel, afraid of missing my flight. "Damn."

"Well, anyhow, I'm glad you found me." After a pause he said, "You probably have a lot of questions."

"You bet I do! For one thing, I'm *starving*, and I don't know how to eat. I tried biting someone last night –"

"Oh, that never works," he said. "You don't want to do that."

"So I discovered," I said sourly.

"You didn't hurt anyone, did you?"

"No, of course not!"

"Just asking," he said soothingly. "Being turned is pretty overwhelming at first. Especially if your sire isn't around to help you and you don't have the manual."

"The manual?" I repeated.

"Yeah. *The Vampire's Guide To Unlife*."

"There's a *manual?*"

"Yes. Basic guidelines, policies and procedures, dos and don'ts, wisdom from the elders passed down through the generations. Stuff like that. It's really useful. *Essential*, in fact."

"There's a vampire manual," I said in bemusement. "Who knew?"

"If you give me your address, I'll have a copy overnighted to you."

"Okay. Thanks," I said. "But in the meantime, I am *so* hungry."

"Drink a lot of pomegranate juice. It'll tide you over until I get there."

"Pomegranate juice?" I blurted. "Will that even stay down? Nothing else I've tried –"

"It'll work. I know it sounds weird, but pomegranate juice soothes the hunger pangs and helps keep your energy up when you can't feed."

"Pomegranate juice. Go figure." Then I realized what else he had said. "You're coming here?"

"I need to bring you your pitchfork."

"You're bringing me a *pitchfork?*"

"That's what we call the tool we use to painlessly open a vein so we can feed," he explained. "Its formal name is in Greek, and I can never pronounce it right. It's a solid silver hand tool with two very sharp prongs."

Which presumably left a mark that looked like the victim was bitten by fangs.

"That sounds handy," I said. "Can you send it to me with the manual?"

"Sorry, that's not allowed – and I've already violated custom enough by turning you while you were drunk and barely knew me," he said. "I'm obligated to train you to use the pitchfork safely before I can give it to you, and then there's a whole ritual presentation we're supposed to go through. Vows and stuff like that. Don't worry, I'll walk you through it."

"Well, in that case ... when can you be in Chicago?"

"Uh ..." There was a pause while he checked his schedule. "I can get in Friday night and stay through the weekend."

"I'll be waiting." I added, "Hungrily."

"Pomegranate juice," he reminded me. Then he asked hesitantly, "Can you recommend a hotel near your place?"

I thought about the night we had spent together, which I was remembering a little more clearly now that I could hear his voice again. And I heard myself say, "Do you really want to stay in a hotel?"

"Well ..." I could hear a smile enter his voice. "The note you didn't find said that I really wanted to see you again."

I smiled, too. Then I said to my new vampire lover, "There's just one thing I want to get on the table and make clear before you start sleeping in my bed."

"Yes?"

"I'm definitely not interested in marriage."

Gift Horse

by Julie Compton

Julie Compton is a native of St. Louis, the setting for her debut legal thriller, *Tell No Lies*, which *Kirkus* gave a starred review and called "a taut, tense cautionary tale complete with courtroom drama and a surprise ending." Her second psychological thriller, *Rescuing Olivia*, was praised by *Kirkus* as "a pleasing hybrid of fairy tale and contemporary thriller" and by *Publisher's Weekly* as an "intense, entertaining second novel" with a "super-satisfying resolution." A lawyer by profession, Julie last worked as a trial attorney for the U.S. Trustee's Office, a little-known component of the Department of Justice. She left the practice of law in 2003 to write full-time, but still haunts the courthouse every now and then for her volunteer work as a guardian *ad litem* for abused and neglected children. She now lives near Orlando, Florida. Learn more at www.julie-compton.com.

I conceived the idea for this story after a discussion with an acquaintance about her difficulties finding a man. She had been divorced for a number of years, and although she had an active social life, she had only recently rejoined the dating scene, including online dating sites. In our conversation, it became clear to me that before she would even consider dating a particular guy, he had to meet certain requirements. Most were quite shallow, but the one that stuck with me the most was a height requirement, especially because this woman was petite. It wasn't just that the man had to be taller than her (which to me seemed odd enough, since I've been married almost twenty-five years to a man who is two inches shorter than me!); he had to be at least a minimum number of inches taller than her (I don't remember how many).

I remember thinking that she'd probably rejected so many great guys even before meeting them merely because she imposed this shallow litmus test.

Anna stopped by the pub on her lunch hour. She drove around the block several times before finding a spot near the entrance, all the while cursing under her breath the city's grand idea of adding cobblestones and parallel parking to create a small-town feel. Main Street had lost thirty percent of its parking spaces in the process.

The cool darkness of the pub was a welcome relief from both the blistering heat and the homeless woman on the sidewalk asking for change. It took a minute for her eyes to adjust before she could see Chris behind the bar. He worked the tap to fill a frosty mug with beer while he engaged in spirited conversation with a customer having lunch. A good-looking customer, Anna noticed.

When Chris saw her, he stepped out from behind the bar and enveloped her with a tight hug. She wondered, as she had so many times before, why the good ones were always taken.

"I hope that beer is for me." She winked at the man eating lunch and gave him a mischievous grin. He returned it, and with that first connection, she forgot her musings of Chris. *Just my type. Tall, dark and handsome.*

After introductions, during which she learned the stranger's name was Hank and that he was an infrequent customer of the pub (though frequent enough, Anna noted, that he and Chris seemed familiar with each other), she scooted onto a barstool next to him. She considered whether to bring up the purpose of her visit in front of Hank. Chris knew she'd come to pick up the box. After all, he'd been the matchmaker. (Well, at her urging). If she didn't mention it, he might, and then she'd have no control over the story. She didn't want to seem desperate, though sometimes, if she were honest with herself, she knew she came across that way.

Best to explain it herself, she decided, put her own spin on it. Hank might even find the reason behind her visit a bit intriguing.

"Do you have a minute to grab the box for me, Chris? I have to get back to work quickly today."

He nodded and slipped through a door to the backroom behind the bar. But before she could even initiate the beginnings of a real conversation with Hank, Chris returned. He placed the box on an empty barstool and said, "It's heavy. I wonder what he sent."

"Well, let's find out." Anna's commitment to return to her home office weakened as her curiosity grew. Hank's presence didn't hurt, either.

Hank produced a pocket knife and handed it to Anna.

"Thank you, sir," she said, and gave him a coquettish smile. She wondered if she should just forget about the contents of the box and pay more attention to this new man in front of her. Yet the memories of the emails and telephone calls with the man who sent the package compelled her to begin the surgery.

"I still don't get why you simply didn't have it delivered to your house," Chris said.

"I don't know the guy, and you really don't either, right? Not very well. I don't want him knowing where I live."

"So who's this gift from?" Hank asked. "A secret admirer?" Anna could feel his gaze as she sliced the tape and tugged at the cardboard flaps.

"I suppose you could say that."

She plunged her hand deep into the packing materials. Her fingers first touched glass. She grabbed hold and produced a bottle of wine. Chris whistled to show his bartender's respect for the vintage. "I guess you didn't mention to him that you were a beer drinker," he said.

"Guys prefer women who drink wine, don't you think?"

Anna set the wine on the bar and reached in again. She brushed against what felt like a small envelope, only smoother. She lifted it out – a seed packet. Forget-me-nots.

"Oh! I told him . . ." she began. She stopped, because it seemed too personal to share this information. In one of their many email exchanges, he'd asked what type of flowers she favored and she had told him Forget-me-nots. They weren't – she preferred tulips – but she'd thought the answer clever.

Once she'd unceremoniously discarded the seed packet next to the bottle on the bar, she dug back into the box. This time, she did find an envelope, except it was taped to something heavy.

"A book," she said. The sender had wrapped the package in glossy, robin's-egg blue paper and a white satin ribbon. "Hmm."

"Ah, your admirer is a reader," Hank said.

Anna tugged on the bow; the ribbon slipped to the floor when she moved on to the paper. Hank picked it up and set it next to the wine.

"It's a cookbook." She set it on the bar with a thud and a soft grunt. "I guess he expects me to cook for him."

"Maybe he plans to cook for *you*," Hank mused.

Anna stopped for a moment and looked at Hank. "You're right. Maybe he does. Now *that* would be nice."

She ripped open the envelope. A photograph fluttered to the ground. Hank retrieved it and held it for safe-keeping while she read the card.

> "Forget me not" until I can present you with the real thing.
>
> Dinner this Saturday? I've created a menu just for you.
>
> With much anticipation,
> Henry
>
> P.S. I know blind dates can be a bit scary, hence the picture.

She hated the name "Henry," but everything else about him thrilled her. *Would he finally be the one?*

Hank handed her the photo – a full-length snapshot of her mystery man standing casually in a doorway – and her heart collapsed like a fallen soufflé. *He's a troll.* No, he wasn't, not really. He wasn't handsome, but he wasn't ugly, either. But –

"He's . . . short," she said aloud, unable to hide her disappointment. She glanced at Chris and then at Hank, wishing now she *had* given him more of her attention. After all, Chris *knew* short was a deal killer.

~ ~ ~

Chris and Hank watched Anna step from the pub into the sunshine, lugging the box in her arms. Chris had given Hank ample warning about her, but still, he'd hoped this time would be different. The fake photo proved it hadn't been.

Hank tossed his credit card onto the bar. Chris pushed it away.

"My treat today, Henry."

When It's Wright

by Deb Stover

Once upon a time, Deb Stover wanted to be Lois Lane – until she discovered Clark Kent is a fraud and there is no Superman. Since publication of *Shades of Rose* in 1995, Stover has received dozens of awards for her cross-genre fiction. She has been active in many writers' organizations, and served at the national level on Romance Writers of America's Board of Directors. For more information, visit her website: www.debstover.com.

Kate McDonald discovers that "coming of age" is more than a cliché when her biological clock emits a strident alarm. To achieve her greatest wish, she must face her greatest fear – disorganization and her Great-Aunt Rachel – a serious manipulator disguised as Betty Crocker. "When It's Wright" addresses the contemporary issues of dating, marriage, coming of age at any age, and being careful what you wish for with the powerful one-two punch of love and laughter. Great-Aunt Rachel is a featherweight with world-class potential. Happy reading!

Great-Aunt Rachel was one part Mighty Mouse and two parts Betty Crocker. At least, with matters concerning her family's happiness.

And Kate McDonald had the awesome distinction of being that family. Extended, nuclear, whatever. She was it. As such, all the love, doting, and smothering attention Aunt Rachel could muster were reserved for her.

Kate's cup runneth over...and then some.

Here she was, home at last. After four years as a yuppie of the first order in Oklahoma City, Kate was back home in Boliver to stay. This move was the single greatest risk of her life, but it was now or never.

She finished her teeth and washed her face, then walked into the bedroom to join her aunt. Rachel McDonald was five feet nothing and couldn't possibly weigh a hundred pounds, yet the retired teacher had instilled many a graduating student with a healthy fear of failure. Small but mighty, Aunt Rachel commanded the respect of all who knew her.

Especially Kate. "You look gorgeous this morning," she said, planting a kiss on her aunt's soft cheek.

"Flattery will get you absolutely nowhere, but don't stop." Aunt Rachel smiled and sat on the edge of Kate's bed, her feet dangling just shy of the floor. "Did you sleep well, dear?"

"Yup. Like a rock." And she had. The fresh air and small-town peace and quiet had worked their magic. Then she noticed her aunt's dress. Since retirement, Aunt Rachel typically wore jeans, unless she had a good reason not to. "You going somewhere? It isn't Sunday."

"I forgot to mention it last night, but there's a wedding this morning." A sly smile tilted the corners of Aunt Rachel's mouth. "Mark Spencer's."

"Ah." Kate's face flamed and she bent to retrieve her running shoes from under the bed. "So old Mark is finally getting married."

"Yes, but it took him all this time to get over you."

Kate shrugged and chewed her lower lip, flopping into a chair to put on her shoes. "He dumped me. Remember?"

"Hmm. Well...whatever." Aunt Rachel fell silent until Kate looked up and met her gaze. "Would you like to go to the wedding, dear?" she asked.

"I wasn't invited." Elbows on knees, Kate propped her chin in her hands. "Besides, I don't want to go. Mark was a long time ago, and I'd be a reminder of things he shouldn't have to remember on his wedding day."

"Well, all right." Aunt Rachel slid off the bed and walked to the door, glancing back over her shoulder. "I'm still not sure why you decided to move back home, but I'm glad you did."

Kate drew a deep breath, not yet ready to tell her aunt about her master plan. The world wasn't ready for Aunt Rachel's reaction. "Planning advertising strategies just wasn't enough anymore." She shrugged. "Maybe it never was."

"Well, I can certainly understand that." She smiled. "I wonder, would you mind doing Fran a little favor this evening?" Aunt Rachel asked in what Kate recognized as a deceptively sweet tone.

She forced a smile and waited, suspecting her aunt was up to something, but Fran Ellsworth was Aunt Rachel's best friend. They'd known each other since childhood. "Uh, I suppose."

"Oh, good. Fran's grandson lives over in Tulsa." Aunt Rachel's faded hazel eyes twinkled. "He's coming all the way here this evening...just to meet you."

"Oh, no. Aunt Rachel, you didn't." Kate collapsed against the back of her chair. "Couldn't you at least let me unpack first?"

"Well, Fran arranged everything. He just moved from Chicago last month, and she worries about him meeting people his own age. When she heard you were coming home, well..." Aunt Rachel shrugged and flashed an innocent smile. "He's a doctor, you know, but if you'd rather not, I'll tell Fran to call him and –"

"No." Kate couldn't bear to disappoint her aunt. Unfortunately, the old woman knew it, too. Surrendering, she stood and crossed the room, taking her aunt's hands in hers. Besides, doctors were on her list. "You're a devil in disguise. You know that, don't you?"

"So I've been told." Aunt Rachel's smile could've lit the entire town. "Of course, I know you don't need a husband – "you're very capable and independent. I admire that."

Ah, if you only knew the truth....

"However, I won't be around forever, and –"

"You're not old, Aunt Rachel." Kate's heart vaulted into high gear. Her aunt looked extremely healthy for a seventy-two-year-old woman. Still, her age was cause for concern.

"Nevertheless, I won't be here forever, and everyone needs love and family." Her aunt lifted her chin a notch. "Even inde pendent women like you."

Kate released her aunt's hands and folded her arms across her midriff. "True." Kate drew a deep breath and released it very slowly. "Where am I supposed to meet Fran's grandson? Is he coming here? Her house?"

"No, it's our bowling night, so Fran and I won't be able to join you."

"Still bowling scratch?" Kate winked at her aunt.

"Is there any other way?" Aunt Rachel chuckled. "I can still out-strike and out-spare most young folks in the league."

"Okay, so where do I meet Dr. Ellsworth? Waitaminute. Haven't I met him before? Is he the one who spent the sum mer here with Fran when I was in junior high?"

"No, I don't think so. At least, Fran didn't mention it." Aunt Rachel plucked at a piece of lint on her sleeve. "Besides, I'm sure that incident with the snake was an accident."

"Hmm."

"At any rate, I believe that was his younger brother. Larry is a couple of years older than you."

Kate was stuck. So much for her vow to choose her own dates. Once Aunt Rachel heard about Kate's plan, it would be open season on blind dates. A lump lodged in her throat at the thought. *Scary.*

But this one was Fran's grandson – practically family. Be sides, she had to start somewhere. "All right, so where do I meet him?"

"In Rhonda Park at six o'clock."

"Okay." Kate gave her aunt a quick hug. "It's good to be home."

"Yes. And to celebrate, I'm going to bake your favorite chocolate chip cookies this afternoon, right after I take the Caddy over to Blackie's Garage."

"I can take the car in for you."

Aunt Rachel tapped her chin thoughtfully with her finger, then smiled as she reached into her pocket and withdrew the keys. "Fran is picking me up for the wedding, so I won't need the car until later. Thank you for offering."

"No biggie." Kate took the keys from her aunt. "I don't have anything planned this morning anyway."

"Please give this to Blackie for me." Aunt Rachel scribbled a note on a piece of paper and passed it to Kate, then she turned to grasp the doorknob. "By the way," she said without looking back, "since you're going downtown anyway, stop at Murphy's Drugstore for a soda. The new pharmacist is a real hunk."

Before she could recover from her aunt's maneuver, the door closed behind the older woman. So much for Aunt Rachel slowing down in her old age.

Kate pulled a jacket on over her T-shirt. Despite her resolve, she couldn't shake the familiar feeling that she'd been manipulated. Thoroughly.

Even though dating and finding Mr. Right were on her new agenda, Kate had very specific ideas about how to go about it. Boliver was close enough to Tulsa to allow her a wide selection of candidates until she found the right one.

Father of her future children.

"I've lost my mind." Sighing, she wondered again what her aunt's reaction would be to learning that Kate actually *wanted* to date and marry. That she wanted to have a baby...

She needed Aunt Rachel's help, but she had to impress upon the older woman the importance of research. Kate knew what kind of men met her qualifications, and she wasn't going to waste precious time dating just anyone.

This meant war. Stealth matchmaking called for nothing less than a guerilla counter-attack. She had to make Aunt

Rachel understand that even this aspect of Kate's life must be handled with common sense, logic, and – above all – good business sense.

Her stomach grumbled. She did say chocolate chip, didn't she?

~ ~ ~

After a morning jog around the old neighborhood, Kate showered and changed, then hopped into Aunt Rachel's be loved Cadillac. In mint condition, it ran on regular gas – plenty of it – and even had fins. Classic, sure, but still a barge.

"Why am I doing this?" she asked herself, navigating the *USS Caddy* into the church parking lot. "Because I'm nosey. What else?"

After parking in the shade, she retrieved her aunt's bird-watching binoculars from their usual place beneath the seat, and rolled down the window. Organ music drifted through the open doors of the church. It sounded as if the wedding was almost over. Good, then she could satisfy her curiosity and get out of here before anyone recognized her.

This was nuts, of course. It wasn't as if she'd been pining away for Mark Spencer all these years. Still, he was the only guy who'd ever dumped her. Of course, after six years the sting had dulled to a state of complete inertia.

A man came out the door and hurried down the steps, a camera slung over his shoulder and a tripod clutched in his fist. The photographer set up his equipment in a shady area adjoin ing the parking lot, obviously in preparation for the bride and groom's big exit. Kate adjusted the focus on the binoculars so she could get a good look when the time came.

But if anyone recognized her sitting out here with a pair of binoculars, she'd be mortified. Grimacing, she rolled the tinted window up partway, leaving just enough space for a clear view. But what good would that do? Her aunt's car was even more conspicuous than the binoculars.

Shame slithered through her, settling in her gut with all the pH balance of drain cleaner. "C'mon, Kate." She lowered the binoculars and chewed her lower lip, debating whether or not to drive away without getting a look at Mark's bride. "This is so lame."

Chuckling, she bumped the steering wheel with the binoculars and the horn emitted a low, ominous honk. A long, low, ominous honk. An unending, low, ominous honk.

"Oh, no." She smacked the steering wheel repeatedly, praying the racket would stop. The Cadillac sounded like a horny gander sending an all points mating call.

Kate reached for the ignition. She was acting like a jealous fool, even though she wasn't jealous. Mark had been a long time ago. Curiosity might've killed the cat, but the cat had been lucky compared to this.

Her fingers touched the key and perspiration popped out on her forehead. She felt like a kid sneaking a joy ride.

A pecking sound on the window sent a chill up her spine. Turning, she half-expected to find Mr. and Mrs. Mark Spencer standing hand-in-hand. Snickering.

Instead, she found a pair of piercing blue eyes beneath the brim of a policeman's cap. At least they weren't familiar blue eyes. With a sheepish grin, she said, "Hello."

"Hello. I'm Officer Wright. Having some trouble, ma'am?" His smile turned up at one corner, displaying a dimple in his cheek. "Pop the hood and let me have a look."

Her face flooded with heat as she fumbled around for the hood release, then she remembered that cars this old didn't have such amenities. "There isn't an inside release."

"Right, I forgot." He nodded, went to the front of the car and had the hood raised within a matter of seconds.

After a moment, the incessant noise mercifully ceased and Kate leaned her forehead against the steering wheel in relief. The hood dropped with a solid thud, and the officer reappeared at her window.

"I'm sorry for the commotion." She shrugged. "It's my aunt's car."

"Ah, you must be Miss McDonald's niece then." Muscles rippling, he braced his arms above the open window and leaned forward. "I disconnected the horn – it'll have to be fixed or the car won't pass inspection when her tags come due."

"I was on my way to the garage anyway." Kate retrieved her aunt's note from the passenger seat and unfolded it. "Well this explains a lot." She showed the note to her savior.

"Horn sticks," he read, then grinned again.

He was gorgeous. Kate knew everyone in Boliver, Oklahoma, and this guy was definitely a new addition. A tall, dark and handsome addition.

"Are you waiting for your aunt?" he asked, aiming his thumb over his shoulder. "Looks like folks are starting out now."

Everyone in town knew her aunt's car. Kate had to get out of here before someone recognized the driver, too. "Thank you again for the help, but I really need to get this horn fixed." She started the engine and he backed away.

"Drive carefully."

Another grin. Kate's chest tightened and warmth seeped through her veins. No contest – this man had the most devastating smile she'd ever seen. "Thanks." Too bad cops weren't on her list.

He stepped to one side and she saw a flurry of white lace on the church steps beyond him. Mark Spencer's bride. For a few seconds, she sat staring at the happy couple. They ran across the lane in front of the church to the grassy area where the photographer waited.

No longer caring about the bride's identity, Kate put the car in reverse, her face burning with shame. Thank goodness the policeman was someone who didn't know her personally.

She looked over her shoulder, then noticed young women gathering between her and the wedding couple, their backs toward the parking lot. The barrier between Kate and the groom was more than welcome.

The police officer stepped farther away and waved to her. Kate waggled her fingers in his direction just as something flew through the open window and hit her in the face.

Her mouth fell open and she hit the brake, gathering the sweet-smelling bridal bouquet in her hands. Everyone turned toward her.

Including the photographer and his camera.

~ ~ ~

Blind dates were designed for Masochists. *So what are you doing here?* Kate chided herself, as she approached the rendezvous point.

Simple. After eschewing all things matrimonial and maternal for many years, Kate McDonald, star account executive for Oklahoma City's most prestigious advertising agency, had been appalled that at the age of thirty, her biological clock emitted a strident alarm.

She never should have watched *Baby Boom.*

Ever the practical business executive, at first she thought she could schedule a baby very much like she controlled all other aspects of her corporate world: artificial insemination at ten AM, board meeting at eleven, pregnancy testing at noon, division reports at one, nanny interviews at two.

Yeah, right.

But she soon realized that balancing a baby with her demanding career would've been a superficial solution, barely skimming the surface of her powerful craving. She wanted much more. For the first time in her life, she wanted – no, *needed* – to embrace all things feminine.

So, not so simple. Who was she lying to? She wanted the kind of family life she'd never had. Both her parents died in a car crash when she was three, and Aunt Rachel opened her home, her heart, and her arms to her only niece. Kate really had no complaints. Her aunt had showered her with love and security.

A serious understatement...

Even so, Kate had always longed for the missing pieces that make a family. At school events, she'd felt awkward around the other children who had both parents while she had none, though her doting aunt tried too hard to make up the difference.

Remembering the time Aunt Rachel had insisted on attending the Father-Daughter Banquet, Kate had to smile. When Aunt Rachel set a goal, there was no stopping her.

Yes, Kate had enjoyed a secure, loving, happy childhood. She couldn't deny that. But was it wrong for her to want something more now? Something different for her own children? She had a hunch Aunt Rachel would approve.

Step number one – and Aunt Rachel definitely would like this one – Kate needed a husband. That was the logical way to launch this whole Mommy/Woman/Family thing. That didn't mean she would completely abandon her career, but there was nothing wrong with taking a sabbatical.

Her homework included compiling a list of qualifications for her prospective husband. Various personality types gravitated toward certain careers. No macho types for her – she wanted an intelligent, ambitious, beta kind of guy. Doctors, lawyers, accountants, and dentists made her list. Contractors, ranchers, professional athletes, and truck drivers did not.

After reading every book published on parenting and relationships, she decided on a back-to-basics approach, with a little good business sense thrown in for balance. Before she had a chance to change her mind, she'd requested a leave of absence from her employer, sold her uptown condo, donated all her business suits to charity, and sent her Great Aunt Rachel a quick note that simply said she was coming home.

"So here I am," she mumbled, the now-familiar anxiety rippling through her again. She had to make this work.

Maybe she should have told Aunt Rachel about her plan – and her list – before agreeing to a blind date. But even at thirty, she couldn't say no to this particular little old lady bearing chocolate chip cookies.

Warm chocolate chip cookies.

Besides, after this morning's embarrassment, she was willing to endure almost anything to keep Aunt Rachel off that subject. The sweet woman actually believed Kate had shown up at the church because she was jealous. Furthermore, this evening's date was with a doctor – safe, stable, respectable, and definitely on her list.

"You must be Kate McDonald." A tall blond man stopped in front of her and extended his hand.

Aunt Rachel had said tall and blond. Of course, it would be just Kate's luck if he turned out to be a weirdo stalking stupid, trusting women in the park. *So much for not talking to strangers.* "Yes, I'm Kate." She shook his hand, though her gaze zoomed in on the huge Old English Sheepdog at his side, re strained by a worn leather leash.

"I'm Larry Ellsworth," the man said. "My grandmother told me all about you."

Before she could respond, the hairy monster placed a huge paw on Kate's thigh, capturing her silk broomstick skirt with a set of razor-like toenails. She reached down to release the expensive fabric just as the beast decided to return his paw to the ground where it belonged. Unfortunately, her skirt and the dog failed to part company along the way.

"My skirt!"

The animal danced around trying to free himself, pull ing Kate's skirt halfway down her hips before she managed to catch the drawstring to avert involuntary – and very public – flashing.

"Do you mind?" Kate drew a deep breath and tried to smile. "Could you, uh...?" She pointed down to where the dog still stood on the ruined silk.

Her date stared at her with a confused expression, then finally looked down at the drooling mutt. "Oh." Larry's face reddened as he stooped to free the destructive toenail. "Care ful, Hugo. You could have hurt yourself."

"What?" Surely Kate hadn't heard correctly. He stood up right as she tugged her skirt back up to her waist.

"Sorry," he said, giving her a nervous grin.

Gee, thanks. Kate shrugged, wondering what kind of night mare she'd stepped into this time. Blind dates always ended in disaster for her, and this one seemed destined to follow tradi tion. She should have known.

Just when she thought she was safe, the pooch ducked be hind her and shoved its snout between her legs. "Hey, I've had about –"

Larry pulled on the leash until the animal reluctantly aban doned his investigation, seeming satisfied that Kate was a friend. *Ha! Friend, my fanny.* Of course, her fanny was exactly what he was after.

"I hope you don't mind me bringing Hugo along." Larry inclined his head toward the dog. "He's been low on self-con fidence since the move, so I couldn't leave him home alone."

"Self...confidence?" Kate bit the inside of her cheek, struggling to prevent a smartass comment. "A dog? Oh, I get it. This is a joke. Right?"

Scowling, Larry reached down and covered both the dog's floppy ears with his hands. "Shh. He'll hear you."

"And that's a problem?"

"Dogs understand a lot more than most people give them credit for." Larry gave Hugo a pat on the head, then stood to face Kate again. "Some have even been known to commit suicide because of low self-esteem."

"What...*kind* of doctor are you, Larry?"

"Didn't your aunt tell you?"

"Uh, no." She gave him a strained smile as her suspicions exploded. "Aunt Rachel left out that teensy weensy detail."

"I'm a veterinary psychiatrist, specializing in canine counseling." He shook his head with a low chuckle. "I just don't understand cats, so I refer them to another doctor."

Aunt Rachel, I'll get you for this. Kate managed another smile, though she knew it probably resembled a grimace. Veterinary psychiatrists were definitely *not* on her list. "How interesting. And there's actually a demand for your...specialty in Tulsa?"

"My practice is starting out slow, but word will get around."

"Oh, I'm sure." Kate struggled against the urge to tell Larry just what she thought of his specialty. Instead, she gestured toward the dog. "So is this one of your patients?"

"Hugo's my own. He's like a brother to me."

"Ah, somehow, that doesn't surprise me." She sighed and looked beyond Larry and his canine brother at other couples and families walking through the park. Just her luck. She aimed for "Father Knows Best" and ended up with *The Shaggy Dog*. "So I guess dinner is out." Once the urge to roll her eyes passed, she met his gaze again.

Larry shrugged and flashed her a boyish grin. He was really quite attractive in a nerdy sort of way. Straight blond hair, blue eyes, thick glasses...

"Actually," he pointed to a pizza stand across the street, "I took the liberty of ordering a pizza. I'll just run over and pick it up, then we can picnic here in the park." He patted the dog again. "That way we'll all enjoy the evening."

"Woof," Hugo said.

"Sure, that sounds fine," Kate lied.

"One vegetarian deluxe coming up."

"No pepperoni?"

Larry looked at Kate as if he found her insane. "Of course not. Even Hugo's a vegetarian. Don't tell me you aren't?"

"Uh, well...no, I'm not." Kate gave a nervous laugh. "I'm a carnivore at heart. Strange, I've never heard of a vegetarian dog before."

"It's one of my theories." Larry's expression grew solemn and he rubbed his chin with his thumb. "See, Hugo knows meat comes from other animals, so it's bound to lower his opinion of himself when he realizes he's eating flesh."

She swallowed hard. "Flesh?"

"What do you think meat is, Kate?"

"Never mind." She'd never see a hamburger in quite the same light after this. How sad. The human soul required both chocolate and hamburgers for survival in this dog eat dog –

She groaned. "Vegetarian pizza sounds fine." *Anything.*

Larry started toward the crosswalk, then stopped and turned to face her again. "I'll need both hands for the pizza." He extended the leash to her.

Kate stared in horror at the leather handle attached to a hairy canine that surely outweighed her. "You want me to...to keep Hugo?" Her throat went dry. She wasn't exactly afraid of dogs, but she hadn't spent much time with them either. "I don't know, it might be easier if I just go after the pizza myself."

"No, I want to check the order. Sometimes they try to slip in some meat byproducts or MSG when customers don't pay attention, especially in these small towns." He held the leash toward her. "It'll only take a minute." He smiled again.

With a sigh, Kate accepted the proffered leash. "All right. Hugo and I will wait right here."

"Why don't you two walk over to the picnic area and find us a table? I'll meet you there."

Kate looked down at the animal, with its tongue lolling out the side of its mouth, leaving a puddle of drool on the side walk, dangerously near her new beige pumps. As she looked up, Larry turned and rushed to the corner stoplight.

"Why do I let Aunt Rachel talk me into these things?" Kate muttered, then turned toward the pond and picnic area.

Hugo had other ideas.

She tugged on the leash. The dog didn't budge.

"Oh, what now?" She stared at the huge dog, fighting against the powerful urge to picture him as a rug. *Not nice, Kate.*

"C'mon, Hugo."

Nothing.

"I'll even let you make a pit stop at the fire hydrant. Please?" Much to her amazement, he rose. "Okay, now what?" With a shrug, she started to walk and Hugo loped alongside. She could handle this.

As they neared the shaded area where picnic tables bordered the banks of a duck pond, Hugo picked up speed. The leash pulled tighter and tighter as he tugged and lurched toward the water, burning her hand where the leather cut into it.

"Hugo, stop," she shouted, but he lunged again, snapping the leash in two.

Kate stared in horror as Hugo ran between a couple sitting on a blanket beside the pond, then splashed into the water, sending ducks quacking and fluttering from his path of destruction.

"Hugo!" Kate stomped her foot and ran down the bank after the animal, arms wind-milling in a desperate effort to keep her balance, Monty Python-esque. "Come back here or I won't let you have any pizza."

The animal ran along the bank, splashing muddy water up at parents and children who'd obviously come to feed the ducks. Screaming children and angry parents scrambled out of Hugo's way as he wove in and out of the water, wreaking havoc in his wake.

As she neared the pond, her foot slipped and she slid the rest of the way down the bank on her rear, landing at the water's edge, minus one beige pump, with her skirt bunched up around her hips. Hugo lumbered by, flinging water down the front of her silk blouse and skirt.

So much for "Dry Clean Only."

"Why me?" Tears stung her eyes, but with a surge of determination, she overcame the urge to cry. "This is ridiculous."

After all, wasn't her self-esteem every bit as important as Hugo's? Pushing to her feet, Kate looked across the pond, where Hugo happily terrorized the animals in the petting zoo.

"That your dog, lady?"

The male voice sliced right through her. Kate swallowed with difficulty, then turned slowly to face a pair of familiar blue eyes. The same police officer who'd rescued her at the church now stood staring at her with a stern expression on his drop-dead gorgeous face.

What were the odds? In a town the size of Boliver, pretty darned good.

"There's a leash law in this town," Officer Wright continued, shaking his head as he scribbled something on a piece of paper, tore it off his clipboard and handed it to her. "You'd better catch the dog before someone gets hurt, or I'll have to call Animal Control."

"Oh, yes. *Please* call Animal Control. Please, please, please, please?" Kate reached for the paper. "What's this?"

"A citation for violating the leash law."

Frowning, she scanned the paper. "Listen, Officer Wright, he's really not mine." Exhaustion and defeat pressed down on her. "Really. C'mon, I don't even own a dog. Just ask my aunt."

"Even if you don't own him, you have the leash in your hand, and you were calling him by name. That makes you responsible."

"But –"

"Look, Ms. McDonald, I'd rather not have to do this, but the city's cracking down on strays. A little boy was badly hurt last month just a few blocks from here."

"I see. I'm sorry about that." Kate looked down and sighed. "This has been one helluva day."

"Yeah, you've been kinda busy," he said quietly, his voice surprisingly gentle.

Kate looked up again, finding his crooked grin had returned. Who was this guy? He looked better suited for Hollywood or New York. And what was he doing in a town like Boliver?

Besides writing her a ticket?

"He's really not my dog." Kate pulled a tight smile. "But I'll make sure to give this citation to his real owner," she added. "We'll see what that does to *his* self-esteem."

"Self-esteem?" He arched a brow and his eyes twinkled. "By the way, I don't think we've officially met. I'm Jack Wright."

"Kate McDonald." She shook his hand, savoring the warm, rough feel of his skin. A shiver skittered down her spine. "It's a pleasure." *Even if I'm a mess and cops aren't on my list.*

"Where's the owner?" Jack asked, continuing to hold her gaze after he'd released her hand.

"Where's Hugo?" an anxious voice intruded.

They turned in unison to face the blond man. "Hugo?" Jack echoed.

"My dog. Kate, where is he?"

"Hold on there," Jack interrupted, as Larry started to walk away. "Hugo – the big sheepdog or whatever – is yours?"

"Of course." Larry handed Jack the pizza box, then turned to face Kate again. "Where's my dog? I told you how fragile his ego is right now."

Kate rolled her eyes. "Your precious mutt broke the leash." She handed him the broken leather handle. "He took off around the pond. I'd say *his* self-esteem is just dandy now."

"Well, I guess this belongs to you then." Jack balanced the pizza box in one hand, reached out and took the citation from Kate, then held his pen poised above it. "Just let me fill your name in here, then we can all be on our way while you catch your dog."

"Dr. Larry Ellsworth."

"Doctor?" Jack shot Kate a questioning glance.

"Don't ask." Kate grinned. "Trust me on this."

"You two *know* each other?" Larry demanded, glancing from one to the other. "What's going on here?"

"Oh, nothing." Kate laughed with a toss of her head. "I was just disturbing the peace a little earlier today."

"You're a...a criminal?" Larry took a step away from Kate, taking the broken leash with him.

"Does that scare you?" she continued, her voice growing louder with each syllable. She should be ashamed of herself, drowning in guilt. *Later.* "I can be real dangerous. You know, I even eat meat – *red* meat – on occasion."

"I think we'd better cancel our date." Larry turned to look toward the pond. "Hugo, there you are."

The furry beast plodded toward them, dropped Kate's missing pump at her feet, and delivered a sloppy kiss to his master's smiling face.

"Oh, that's really gross," Kate said, gingerly sliding her foot into the soggy shoe. With her foot encased in the chewed leather, she couldn't resist one more dig. "Even if you are brothers."

Jack scratched his head. "Brothers?"

"Officer, arrest that dog." A large, bald man rushed toward them, huffing and puffing and waving an accusing finger at Hugo.

"Arrest the *dog*? Why would I want to arrest the dog?"

"It stole my steak. Snatched it right from my hand as I was laying it across the grill." The man waved a huge meat fork in the air. "Arrest it before I barbecue the dog instead."

Larry covered Hugo's ears with both hands. "Shh. He'll hear you."

"Oh, I've had enough of this." Kate released a ragged sigh. "Hugo is a *dog*, Larry. He isn't human. He stole this man's din ner, because he wants to eat and be treated like a *dog*. I think the least you can do is pay this man for his loss."

"But Hugo is a vegetarian."

"Maybe he thought it was *beet* steak."

Jack made a snorting sound then cleared his throat, obvi ously trying to maintain a professional demeanor. "Okay. Will you two work it out as gentleman?"

They looked at him, then at each other and nodded.

Jack started to laugh and Kate joined him. While the men argued about the pilfered steak and Hugo's alleged guilt or in nocence, they walked away.

"Will they be all right?" Kate asked, hoping the men wouldn't come to blows over a hunk of meat. Her gaze swept the length of the man at her side, bringing a flash of heat to her face. The word "beefcake" mentally followed "hunk of meat."

He shrugged. "There's nothing more to do unless the guy wants to press charges. I have a hunch he'll find me if he does." His sexy smile returned.

Now why can't Aunt Rachel find me a nice doctor who's more like this cop?

In comfortable silence, they walked halfway around the park before Jack paused. "Well, I'm on duty."

She looked at him expectantly, not really certain why. *So much for lists, McDonald.* "Ah, I guess you have to get back to work then."

"Yeah, duty calls." He stared at her for several minutes – the tension between them grew palpable.

I'm definitely editing that list.

"I'm off duty in an hour. Are you free for dinner? Steaks?" He winked.

"Sounds good." Kate smiled and relaxed for the first time since her big plan launched.

"Pick you up at your aunt's house?"

"Perfect." And it was. For now...

Suddenly, he chuckled and looked down at the white box in his hands. "Uh-oh. I think I stole Hugo's pizza."

Kate laughed, too. "It's all right. I think he already ate."

Killing Time

by Marianna Jameson

New York Times bestselling author Marianna Jameson writes women's fiction and high-tech eco-political thrillers. After spending twenty years in the software, aerospace, and defense industries, she's enjoying new adventures in the corporate security and intelligence worlds. For more information about Marianna and her books, visit her website at www.MarianaJameson.com.

Small-town beauty queen Merrilee Chastain is the feminine equivalent of the South's most beloved treat, Ambrosia; she's timelessly beautiful and unfailingly sweet, has a light, airy way about her that's full of delightful surprises, including a few nutty ones here and there, and she's quintessentially Southern. Everyone who knows her knows that Merrilee wouldn't even hurt a flea on a rabid dog, much less anyone's feelings. It's why she's been voted Miss Congeniality in every single beauty contest she's ever been in, and that's a lot. But Merrilee's never shared her deepest secret with anyone because they'd get the wrong idea. The truth is she really just doesn't like people, but she learned early that being nice to everyone gets better results than being honest does. It's when some people, the bothersome ones, try to demand honesty from her that she gets a bit put out. And then she has to deal with them. Being the perfectionist she is, Merrilee doesn't believe in do-overs or second chances. She deals with the bothersome ones once, and makes sure they never bother her again. Ever.

Merrilee is a glorious and deadly flower, a lovely dream gone wrong, and I've been living with her in my head for a few years now, until, in her own charming way, she politely refused to be sidelined again. Just like the character, her story needs its time in the spotlight. Here it is. I hope you enjoy it.

Mid-1980s, Athens, Georgia

“Oh, honey.” The mixture of sympathy and amusement in Susanna’s voice was cruel, just plain cruel.

“I’m fine.” Merrilee pressed the thin slices of cucumber more tightly to her burning eyes and held her breath, hoping she could suppress another sob. She’d been doing well for the last half hour. None of her roommates had so much as checked up on her while they were getting ready for school.

She felt her cousin’s hand alight on her shoulder and, a moment later, give it a little squeeze. It was the squeeze that did it. A soft sob hiccupped through Merrilee’s iron-clad beauty-queen composure, and then she felt tears begin to slip from beneath the cucumbers. She crossed her arms on the battered old table and slumped forward to rest her face on them, not caring about the cool, wet, green disks that fell to her lap. Her cheeks crumpled as a fresh wave of tears threatened to consume her.

”Are you going to be all right, Merrilee?”

Taking a deep breath and forcing a smile, Merrilee lifted her carefully pouffed and sprayed head and nodded, giving a dainty sniff.

”I’ll be fine, thank you, Susanna,” she said softly, sitting back to dab at her brimming eyes with the lace-edged handkerchief she pulled from the pocket of her quilted silk bathrobe.

Susanna patted her shoulder and said with a tease in her voice, “You’re the only person I’ve ever met who knows how to accessorize properly for a crying jag.”

Merrilee managed not only to keep the smile on her face, but to keep her dislike from showing.

“Honey, please try to feel better about it. It’s just a rhinestone tiara and a satin sash, not life and death,” Susanna said, setting her book bag on the floor so she could more safely pop the top on her SlimFast shake. “I’d love to stay and take you to lunch, but I have to get to class.”

"Thank you. I'll be fine," Merrilee repeated more firmly.

Susanna bent down to give her cousin an awkward hug. Merrilee tilted away ever so slightly so as not to let the gesture disturb her carefully tousled hair.

"I'm done with classes at four, precious. Let's go out to Tweeter's for happy hour."

"Thank you, Susanna, but I have to work," Merrilee said with another delicate sniffle and pulled the lapel of her bath robe down so Susanna could see the crisp pink neckline of her candy-striper uniform. "I'll be there until eight, and then Dr. Todd is taking me out for a drink."

Susanna lifted her eyebrows. They needed a waxing. "You're going on a date with Dr. Todd? T-O-D-D, as in Dr. To-Only-Double-Die-for Todd? When did that happen?"

A warm curl of satisfaction momentarily eased Merrilee's grief. "Oh. I didn't tell you? Well, he was just so nice my first day back after the pageant and all. Everybody was. Well, ex cept that awful Anne Crenshaw, bless her heart. She's that Yan kee nurse who hates me." She managed a shaky smile as she dabbed gently under one eye and then the other so as not to tug the delicate tissue. "Well, everybody was just so sweet when I came on the floor. The patients gave me a round of applause and the nurses bought me flowers. And then Dr. Todd came on duty and handed me a little teddy bear with a sash that said 'You're Peachy', and asked me out for tonight. It's the only night he's not on duty all month. Isn't that just *sweet*?" She let her impeccably manicured hands drop to her lap as she blinked back fresh tears.

"The man has no idea what he's in for. You'll be engaged inside of a week if he doesn't watch out," Susanna laughed. "You'll have to tell me all about it in the morning."

"Oh, I sure will."

"You look better already."

"Thank you. I feel better," Merrilee lied. "Well, right now I have to get these brownies made and cooled before I leave."

Susanna picked up her backpack from the floor. "More brownies? No wonder all those old folks love you, Merrilee. You give them a free sugar buzz every time you walk in the door."

Merrilee stood up, knowing and not caring that her sunny, pageant-perfect smile was at odds with her red-rimmed eyes and disastrously puffy face. "Of course they love me, Susanna. Everyone loves me," she said calmly. "Well, except for that Nurse Crenshaw."

The cousins hugged once more and then Susanna left, and Merrilee was alone. She closed her eyes and counted to ten.

Just a rhinestone tiara and a satin sash? How could she have said that to my face?

Merrilee knew that her cousin – Susanna had always been the smart one, the one who was going to "go places" – thought that she was just an airhead, a blue-eyed, Barbie-doll blonde with no ambitions beyond paddling in the warm, safe shallows of life. But she was wrong. Pageants weren't the shallows; they held dangerous riptides below their pretty, glittering surface. It was a life as cut-throat as the law career Susanna was aiming for. The blue-light smiles and porcelain complexions were a beauty queen's version of body armor, and just as necessary. A pageant was war; the combatants had perfect manners, is all. Outsiders just didn't realize it. Any of it.

And the sparkling tiara and embroidered sash that should have been hanging in her closet right now were more than symbols, they were life-long goals and, though no one would ever hear it from her lips, they were no less than her birthright. Losing the Miss Georgia title five days ago had been such a blow that Merrilee had thought she would die right then on stage, and even now wasn't sure she might ever recover. Be ing named first runner-up and Miss Congeniality didn't make up for it. Not one bit. Merrilee's mother, grandmother, and great-aunt had all been Miss Congeniality *and* they'd won the title. Merrilee – and her mother, grandmother, and great-aunt – would never consider what she'd done to be an achievement; all the four of them would ever see was her failure.

She went into the tiny bathroom of the drab student flat she shared with Susanna and two other girls from their home town of tiny Resurrection Island and stared into the mirror for a long minute. The fresh cucumbers hadn't done a blessed thing except get her skin sticky. Her homemade cucumber-mint gel would best fix her face after all that crying, she decided, and reached for the small, smoked-glass jar high on the cluttered second shelf of the over-the-sink cabinet.

The living situation had been a little awkward at first, with Merrilee being the only one of the four who wasn't actually enrolled at the University of Georgia. Or any other school for that matter. But no amount of her tears or her mother's silence had been able to persuade her ordinarily tractable daddy to let her enroll. He thought it was a foolish waste of good money to send his only daughter to nursing school when all she wanted to do was marry a doctor. So, instead, he was paying for her to just live in Athens with her friends on campus. In an apartment near the medical school.

Instead of going to classes, lectures, and the library with the other girls, Merrilee divided her time between volunteering as a candy-striper at the nearest nursing home and working part time at the ward desk in Pediatrics at the university hospital. It was all part of her plan; of course she wanted to marry a doctor, but not just any old doctor. He had to be young enough, good-looking enough, wealthy, and from a good family, naturally. But he also had to be a compassionate and gentle man who wouldn't be short-tempered with her or get cross easily, and someone who was kind to children and the elderly. There were always plenty of young and old around when her family came together. She was Southern, after all, and family was family was family, no matter how distant the connection. So she needed whoever she married to fit in.

Merrilee didn't particularly like being around old sick people, or even young sick people, for that matter. Not that she ever let it show. She considered her work at the nursing home as a necessary evil. She worked there because that's where a lot of the residents filtered through with the real doctors on their rounds. Even though she would have preferred a full-fledged doctor, most of them were already married. Besides, on her tally, catching a resident counted. And Dr. Todd was a resident.

He was tall, handsome, and charming despite being a Yankee, and Merrilee had decided the day she met him that enchanting Dr. E. Pennington Todd – she'd been invited right away to call him Penn but hadn't, preferring to maintain a charming, flirtatious distance – was worth whatever she might have to do to get him, even volunteering at Hillside Manor.

The nursing home smelled bad and so did a lot of the patients, but just in the few months since she'd started working there, things had changed. Not those things. Everything still smelled like pee, or dust, disinfectant or old cooking grease depending on where in the building you went, but the atmosphere had changed. Now, when she smiled, people smiled back. They were genuinely happy to see her, if not when she arrived, then by the time she was into her shift. And it wasn't just she who had noticed the difference. Everybody there noticed what a positive effect she had on the patients. One day a shift supervisor had even made a point of telling her that she brightened the staff's day just by walking through the door.

Of course, just like gliding across a stage in an evening gown, there was more to it than what you saw on the surface, but if people wanted to believe that it was her smile and charm, and her pageant-learned friendliness that had changed the feeling at the nursing home, Merrilee wasn't going to raise any objection. Besides, it wouldn't be polite to point out to people that they were wrong, and she was always polite.

Finished patting the cool green gel on the tear-induced puffiness below her eyes, Merrilee went back into the kitchen to finish making the brownies. The gooey treat was the only thing she could cook with any degree of success, and everyone loved them so much that she had to be careful that no one had more than one per batch. That wouldn't be fair to the others, and she wouldn't want to cause any trouble, anyway.

Merrilee returned to the flour-sugar mixture she'd been measuring half an hour ago before she had started thinking about the pageant, and carefully broke the eggs and oil into it. She mixed it by hand, then poured in the chocolate that she had melted and cooled. Then, in went the chocolate chips, mini-marshmallows, and broken pecans from her granddaddy's farm. She smoothed the lumpy batter into the two pans she'd already greased and dusted with cocoa, making sure every nut and marshmallow was submerged in the chocolate goo.

Satisfied that the bumpy, glossy mixture was ready to go into the oven, Merrilee reached into her bathrobe pocket for the small plastic bag of marijuana she'd gotten just that morning from the no-account Atlanta boy who lived downstairs. She took an empty iced tea glass from the cabinet and rolled it over the bag a few times to grind the dried buds into powder. With a practiced hand, she dipped her fingers into the bag and sprinkled exactly enough across the top of the batter to ensure that everyone would get enough to feel good but not enough to get obviously stoned. Then she dusted the batter with sugar to give the surface a light, crackly shine that would hide the herb dust, and slipped the pans into the oven. She set the timer, taking in a deep, satisfied breath. It was a good thing she did, bringing her special brownies to all those poor old people. They'd been so miserable the first time she'd seen them, what with all their chemotherapy treatments and bed sores and nasty diseases that made them shake and tremble and drool and wet themselves and what all, and made their families prefer to let people like her take care of them. Her brownies brightened their days and eased their troubles and gave them something to look forward to. She had no doubt at all that what she was doing was a good thing.

She was their angel of mercy.

Twirling on one pedicured foot, she went into the bathroom to see if the gel had worked its miracle. It was time to put on her makeup and happy face and go to work.

~ ~ ~

"Merrilee."

Merrilee stopped walking down the hall, took a deep breath, and did a graceful turn-around, presenting a smiling face to Anne Crenshaw, RN, who was only a few years older than she but was her supervisor today and a pain in the neck most of the time. "Yes, Ms. Crenshaw?"

"Are you going on your dinner break now?"

The woman came to a stop a few inches away, close enough for Merrilee to identify the soft, lingering fragrance of Nina Ricci's *L'Air du Temps* beneath the odor of old age and stale air that clung to everything in the building.

"Yes, ma'am, I am. Is there something you'd rather I do?" Merrilee asked, bracing herself for Nurse Crenshaw's usual request that she do a round of bedpan emptying right before supper.

Anne smiled, and Merrilee wondered if it hurt, it was such an unusual expression for her. "No. I'm taking my break now, too, and I thought we might have dinner together. I have my new car. You're the only one who hasn't asked to drive it, so I thought I'd offer."

"Well, bless your heart, aren't you just the sweetest thing?" Merrilee said to cover her surprise while she tried to determine what lay behind the invitation. Anne had always made it clear that she didn't like Merrilee, especially when it came to her interaction with the medical staff, and Penn Todd in particular.

"Is that a yes?" the nurse asked, glancing at her watch. "We only have half an hour."

"Why, yes, ma'am," Merrilee said, widening her smile against the smart retort that was tempting her. "Let me just get my handbag. I'll meet you out back directly."

Merrilee's smile froze and she about died when she saw the car. It was a brand new, fire-engine red Corvette convertible with a white interior, white-wall tires, and little flames custom-painted along the side panels. It fairly screamed *tacky*, but it wouldn't be right to back out, so she slid into the passenger seat hoping her sunglasses were big enough to hide most of her face.

Anne drove the car along the quick route out of town, but it was quitting time and the streets were full of people. And nearly every one of them looked over – some appreciatively, some not so – at the two blondes in the ragtop 'Vette with the top down and Heart's latest hit blaring from the speakers. Merrilee kept her smile sunny and her eyes straight ahead at every stoplight, wishing she had something to put over her hair. It was going to be a mess by the time they got back. She knew that was by design. She had no doubt that Anne Crenshaw knew about her date with Penn. The only sort of woman who would suggest to another woman that they drive anywhere in a convertible with the top down was a jealous one.

It wasn't until they were well outside of town and cruising along a real country road, a long, slope-shouldered straight away through freshly plowed fields, that Anne pulled onto the skinny strip of packed gravel bordering the asphalt and tossed the keys to Merrilee with a grin that stopped a good bit shy of friendly. "Here you go. Ever driven one of these before?"

Merrilee smoothed a hand over her irretrievably tangled hair. "Why, no, Ms. Crenshaw, I haven't ever been *in* a Corvette before. It's just the cutest thing. It's awfully nice of you to let me drive it, but I really don't think I should. Thank you just the same." *You bitch* was added silently. Merrilee had never used bad language and wouldn't start now, however much she might be tempted. Or justified.

"Go on. I insist."

"All right, then, I guess I will. Thank you."

Merrilee, who had also never had the slightest inclination to drive a sports car, masked her nervousness as she took the keys from her boss, picked her way around the front of the car, and slid behind the wheel.

It was an awful sensation. The car was so low to the ground, she felt like her behind would be bumping along the pavement. Her legs were straight out in front of her and she had to set the seat all the way forward to reach the pedals, and then the steering wheel seemed too close to her chest.

Gritting her teeth behind her smile, Merrilee tried to see the bright side. At least the woman had the sense to drive into the country. It would have been mortifying for Merrilee to have to explain to any of her friends who might have seen her driving around town just what she was doing behind the wheel of a car like this one.

Anne sat in the passenger seat, arms folded across her wide, flat chest, looking entirely too pleased with herself.

"It's got a reputation for being a man's car, but I don't care. I like it because it's sleek and fast. Driving it takes a little getting used to. There are a lot of horses under the hood, so take it slow. I figured you can't do much damage on this road. There's only fence posts to distract you. Nothing sparkly."

Merrilee ignored the comment as she brought the engine to life and pressed the accelerator to an easy speed. They drove in silence for a few minutes, until Merrilee became comfort able enough to relax her white-knuckled grip on the wheel and dutifully compliment Anne on the car.

"Thanks," she replied dismissively, and leaned forward to turn off the music. "Actually, Merrilee, I didn't bring you out here just to let you drive my car. You probably couldn't care less about the car."

The jumpiness that erupted in Merrilee's tummy was the same kind that happened when it was just her and Miss Forsyth County remaining on the center of the stage last week. And just as she had under the spotlights and in front of the tele vision cameras in that awful moment, Merrilee kept her face serene and her mouth shut. She was a Davis descended from Jefferson Davis on her mother's side and a Lee, as in Robert E., on her father's. She could handle whatever Yankee ugli ness Anne Crenshaw was about to dish out, and she'd do it Southern-style, with grace and a smile.

"You're not going to take the bait, are you?" Anne laughed, but it wasn't a nice laugh. "Okay, princess, I'll just cut to the chase. I know about the brownies."

The breath Merrilee had been holding eased out from her constricted chest.

At least it's not about my date with Penn.

Her relief was fleeting.

"I said 'the brownies', Merrilee," Anne repeated in a sharp, patronizing tone. "You know, the *pot* brownies you've been feeding to the patients and staff for the last few months. The brownies that could get you fired *and* thrown in jail. Distribut ing is a felony, pumpkin. So is elder abuse."

A quick glance at the speedometer showed she was doing seventy miles per hour. Merrilee realized she'd been accelerat ing as her panic rose. The fence posts were flying by.

"Hey. Slow down," Anne snapped.

"What are you going to do?" Merrilee asked as she eased her foot off the gas pedal. Her voice was shaking, but she knew the noise of the engine covered it.

"As soon as we get back, I'm going to call the director and tell him all about you. And just in case he doesn't believe me, I have a few brownies saved, all wrapped nice and tight in my locker. I'll give those to the cops." She paused. "And then I'm going to tell Penn Todd when he arrives. I would imagine he'll break his date with you at the very least. Crazy as he might be about you, he's too smart to get involved with a drug pusher." She paused, looking smug, and let a silence build. "So now that that's out of the way, pull over and give me the keys."

She's going to tell Penn.

The car rolled to a stop. Anne unfastened her seatbelt and held out a hand. Her other hand was already on the latch to open her door.

Merilee looked away to stare straight ahead, though she saw nothing. She dropped her hands to her lap, already twisting the ring she always wore on her right hand. It was her great-grandmother's wedding ring, a dainty, pear-cut ruby. "I'm not a drug pusher, Ms. Crenshaw," she whispered hoarsely. "Don't call me that."

Anne snorted. "Sure you are. You're a pusher. Now, get out of the car and let me drive."

Do not cry. Do. Not. Cry. "Stop saying that word. I'm not anything of the sort. I'm not."

"You don't take money, so I can't figure out what's in it for you, but –" Anne continued. Her flat, stiff-jawed voice was starting to grate on Merrilee, and she blinked, tuning out the nasty nasal drone.

The director won't understand, but Penn will. He knows me. When I tell him –

"I'm doing good. Those people feel better because of me. They like me. I do more for them than you ever have with your pills and sponge baths and scolding, Ms. Crenshaw." The words burst out of Merrilee and, as if to punctuate her state ment, she stomped her foot on the gas pedal.

She hadn't taken the car out of gear and it shot forward, careening wildly onto the road.

Merrilee's slack hands came up too late. Anne, panicking as she slammed sideways into the dashboard, was already reach ing across the open cockpit. Her upper arm pinned Merrilee into the driver's seat as she grabbed the wheel.

Instinctively, Merrilee fought the crushing pressure of Anne's arm, which was forcing itself against her sternum, mak ing it hard to breathe. Pushing back against Anne's bulk, Mer rilee sought stability where she could find it and braced her foot against the gas pedal.

The car surged forward again, the tires spitting gravel as the car swerved onto the opposite shoulder, the gearbox screaming even louder than Anne. Fence posts whizzed by perilously close as the car refused to provide Anne even a split-second opportunity to straighten the wheel and get the vehicle fully onto the asphalt.

That's when the answer to Merrilee's troubles presented itself.

Anne, bigger, stronger than Merrilee, was stretched awkwardly across her lap as they both fought to control the steering wheel. In that position, Anne's solar plexus was unguarded.

She was so vulnerable. So close.

Using force she never knew she possessed, Merrilee wedged her elbow into the space and gave one hard, sharp jab. Anne reared up, her hands clutching her stomach now instead of the steering wheel, her eyes wide with the certainty of death as she tumbled backward onto the passenger seat retching and gasping for air.

Merrilee gripped the steering wheel with both hands at the top and twitched it slightly, aiming the car straight into one of the fence posts rushing toward them. Then she closed her eyes and jammed the accelerator to the floor.

Every cell in her body felt the bone-shattering blow of the car hitting the pole. The momentum slammed her face onto the backs of her hands, which still clutched the wheel. A fraction of a second later, the blunt force of the impact threw her back against the car seat with a violence that drove all the air from her lungs. She heard something crack inside her neck as her head hit the headrest, but felt nothing because everything went dark and still.

Maybe seconds, maybe minutes later, Merrilee's eyes fluttered open weakly. Every part of her hurt, and she was glad for it. It was proof she was alive and not paralyzed. She twitched her feet, then her hands. They were covered with sharp crumbles of glass that scratched as she lifted them up. The ruby was darker, and it took her a minute to realize it was covered in blood. She raised her fingertips to her face; they came away red and she stared at the blood, still bright, still thin and runny. She was too disoriented to panic at the sight of it. Instead, she wondered if she'd scar.

It wasn't until she became aware of the sweet, familiar scent of sun-baked wood, so close that she could almost feel its heat, that she realized she was alone in the car. She turned toward the smell. The movement sent hot, blinding pain stabbing through her neck, into her head. When her vision cleared, the spiked, jagged bottom of the fractured fence post swam into view. Its vicious, shard-like points aimed skyward, resting precariously against the deeply Vee'd edge of the windshield's frame. Everything was eerily blurred by the fringes of acrid steam billowing from beneath the crumpled hood. Then she noticed the flat top of the post was embedded at a sickening angle into the broken, gaping maw that had been the backrest of the passenger seat.

A smothering, surreal fog of delayed shock engulfed her then, and she fought for a breath, just one good breath that wouldn't hurt. Looking past the post that was too, too close to her, Merrilee's gaze drifted toward a crumpled heap of white, blood-stained nylon and blond hair that lay in the field a short distance from the car.

Anne.

Relief washed through her, soft and comforting. Anne Crenshaw was dead. She had to be. There were no moans, no cries, no sounds coming from her direction at all, even with her legs and arms resting at impossible angles, splayed stiffly, obscenely across several freshly plowed furrows. Calm now, too tired to move her gaze, Merrilee watched the body for a while, hoping she wouldn't see any movement. And she didn't until her attention was captured by a thick strand of Anne's hair caught by a playful breeze. Long and blond, it swayed gracefully in the early evening air, like a happy, friendly stalk of young wheat. Or a banner, a banner waving in surrender. Or triumph.

Anne's dead. She can't tell Penn about the brownies. I'm safe.

The pain that wracked her chest with every breath was getting worse. Even blinking was becoming difficult. Her smile, though, was serene as she closed her eyes and gently rested her head against the seat. She heard voices then, from a distance, shouting, and what sounded like people running, and then the first faint whine of sirens seemed to float toward her across the hot, darkening field.

I'm safe.

A Dream of Flight

by Victoria Strauss

Victoria Strauss is the author of eight fantasy novels for adults and young adults, including *The Stone Duology* and *Passion Blue*, a YA historical fantasy coming from Marshall Cavendish in 2012. She has written hundreds of book reviews for magazines and e-zines, including SF Site, and her articles on writing have appeared in *Writer's Digest* and elsewhere. In 2006, she served as a judge for the World Fantasy Awards.

An active member of the Science Fiction and Fantasy Writers of America, Victoria is co-founder, with Ann Crispin, of Writer Beware, a publishing industry watchdog group that provides information and warnings on the many scams and schemes that target writers. She maintains the popular Writer Beware website (www.writerbeware.org) and blog (www.accrispin.blogspot.com). She received the Service to SFWA Award in 2009 for her work with Writer Beware.

Learn more about Victoria at www.victoriastrauss.com.

The protagonist of this story, the master, is loosely (very loosely – I don't make any claims to historical accuracy) based on Leonardo da Vinci. I've always been fascinated by Renaissance art and invention, and the idea for the story came to me as I was watching a documentary about a man who created a modern replica of Leonardo's wings. I wondered what would have happened if Leonardo himself had built the wings. What did they mean to him? Would he actually have used them? Would he have flown, or fallen?

The story is also very personal, as I wrote it following a period of serious uncertainty and self-doubt about my writing career. The master embodies the feelings of burnout and stagnation that I was struggling with then, and his ultimate realization – that failure for an artist isn't getting it wrong, but not trying – is something I remind myself of as often as I can.

Toward midnight, the master took advantage of the pause between an exiting troupe of acrobats and an entering quartet of madrigalists to escape the banquet. He half-feared his patron might insist he remain, but the patron simply waved dismissal, as if the master were no more than a servant. Which, in a certain sense, was true.

The master had come on foot, and headed home the same way. He kept to the shadows, his soft boots all but silent, as if he were one of the footpads his brother often reminded him he ought to fear. Yet he felt at home in the darkness, at the edges and in corners – perhaps because he too was a thief. He stole the images the night gave him, the sleeping beggars, the gangs of drunken youths, the prostitutes and their customers, the scurrying vermin and slinking cats, snatches of other people's lives glimpsed through unshuttered casements. Like a man at a high window, he observed the world – always engaged, rarely touched, a distance deliberately cultivated over the years of his career, for he believed that an artist must not judge, but simply *see*.

On this night as on others, he reached his estate without incident, and unlocked the postern door beside the gates to let himself in. His villa lay directly across the open courtyard, its windows dark. To the left was the great workroom where he taught his apprentices and directed his journeymen. To the right stood the stables, and, tucked between the stables and the outer wall, the freestanding structure that was the master's private studio, where he pursued his personal projects.

The studio's huge double doors were barred from within; a smaller door was cut into them, locked with a padlock whose key the master kept around his neck even when he slept. Entering, he lit a lamp and carried it over to his desk. The room was too large for the lamplight to reach very far; it illuminated the surface of the desk, with its mess of papers and drawing materials, touched portions of the drafting table and the easel, suggested the presence of shelves and workbenches and projects in various stages of completion: an improved printing press, devices to hoist weights, unusual tools, scale models of bridges and buildings. The recesses of the ceiling were lost in shadow, though at the room's far end a deeper blackness seemed to stir.

The master leaned back in his chair. His notebook lay nearby, but he made no move to open it. More and more often lately, when he turned out the pockets of his memory, the images he had stored up like treasure seemed tawdry, derivative, not worth setting down. Tonight, also, he was distracted by thoughts of the banquet. His patron, displeased with the slowness of the master's progress on the massive painting the patron had commissioned to commemorate his victory at the Battle of Six Hills, had seated the master near the table's head, making sure the master would hear every word of his discourse on the interesting new painter he had just heard of, recently arrived in the city and seeking to establish a workshop. Should one not support new talent and the progress of the arts? Of course, one did then have the dilemma of *choosing*, for in the matter of patronage, resources could only be stretched so far. The master's anger had made him lightheaded, but he controlled his emotion as he always did, by retreating inside his head and observing the gathering as if he were not part of it.

Ah, the master thought, sighing, *what chains bind us, here upon the earth!*

Abandoning the reproach of the unopened notebook, he took up the lamp and crossed to the place where a greater mass of shadows clotted the darkness at the ceiling. A rope stretched down, taut with the weight of what it supported, secured to a cleat set into the wall. The master placed the lamp on the floor. Freeing the rope, he let it out, leaning against the pull of what descended, whispering, from the heights: a shape cut out of night, a pair of wings.

From end to end, they stretched four times the height of a man, and were as deep as a man is tall. Wood and bone formed their supporting framework, built to resemble the wing-structure of birds and bats. Their forward edges curved in a smooth arc; at the rear, they ran to points along each strut. Oiled silk, bat-black, clothed this skeleton – lighter than the kid leather the master had used for his initial constructions, stronger and more flexible than the parchment he had tried later. A complex arrangement of springs and pulleys enabled the wings to move at the will of the operator, who would hang from a leather har ness, with a pair of loops into which his feet could be tucked in flight.

The master felt the tightness in his chest that always came at the sight of them – his wings, his most daring experiment and most beautiful artwork, a perfect synthesis of all his skills. They were the fruit of years of study and observation, innu merable trials and countless errors. Through them, he would break the bonds that fixed human beings to the earth – the first outside of myth to do so. He would *see,* at last, not just things, but everything – cities, landscapes, entire continents, laid out below him like a painting. What a treasure for the artist-thief who lived behind his eyes! What bliss, to abandon the leaden earth, to shake off the things of the world, and fly.

And these wings *would* fly. Earlier designs had been wrong in theory or inadequate in execution, but these...when the time was right, they would bear him into the sky.

The master tied off the rope. He stood a moment, simply gazing, then moved so that he stood beneath the wings, the harness against his shoulders. He gripped the levers that con trolled the pulleys, as he would when he flew at last. He closed his eyes. Almost, he could feel the wind.

There was a creaking, a soft thud. Startled, the master dropped his arms and stepped forward, nearly kicking over the lamp. "Who's there?"

"It's only me."

"Mouse," the master said. The intrusion would have been unwelcome at any time, but the sense of being caught in a private moment lent his voice an extra edge. "What are you doing here?"

"I thought you might be thirsty." A boy emerged from shadow: the youngest of the master's six apprentices, a dark-haired youth of fourteen with wide-set eyes and a pale face that sloped away from a long nose. All the apprentices had nicknames; Mouse's pointed, twitchy features had given him his. In his hands he held a steaming mug. “I brought you mulled wine.”

“You should be in bed, not mucking about in the kitchens.” The boy looked stricken, and the master sighed. “Come, give me the cup.”

Mouse obeyed. Unlike the other apprentices, who were the sons of men well-to-do enough to pay a sizeable apprentice fee, he was a child of the streets. He had presented himself at the master’s door four years ago, demanding to be taught. Intrigued by his irrational self-confidence, the master had given him charcoal and paper, and discovered that the confidence was not, after all, misplaced.

For the sake of that surprising talent, the master had apprenticed the boy free of charge. He had since come to regret it. Mouse worshiped him with a violent and excessive love, something that the master, who disliked strong emotions in others as much as he detested them in himself, found deeply distasteful. Worse, Mouse’s talent was in thrall to his devotion. The master strove to awaken the individual artist in his apprentices, rather than simply training them to copy his own style, as many of his colleagues did; but Mouse aspired to do no more than make himself an imitation of the master. In the past year, the master had begun to think seriously about finding Mouse a different place – for the boy’s sake, he told himself. Apprenticed to an artist he did not adore so much, perhaps Mouse would fulfill the promise the master had first seen in him.

“Your wings, master.” Mouse’s voice, which retained only a trace of his original rough street accent, was reverent. “I love to see your wings. When will you fly them?”

“Soon.” The master was aware of the wings at his back, swaying in the air currents of the room. *Now,* they seemed to breathe. *Fly us now, this moment!*

“Master, could I...” The words trailed off.

“Could you what?”

Mouse drew a breath. “Could *I* fly them? Please?”

The master looked at the boy, surprised. “You want to fly my wings?”

“Yes! I want it more than anything. To rise above the earth, to reach the clouds – it would be like touching heaven!”

"The wings can only be flown by someone who understands the principles of their making, Mouse. Besides, they are made for a grown man. They would be too heavy for you."

"I could do it," the boy insisted. "I know I could. Oh, master, they've been here so long, and you say they're ready but you never fly them, and I just thought...I just thought how sad it would be, if they hung here forever and never felt the wind –"

"Enough!" The master set the untouched mug of wine down hard on a nearby workbench.

"But Master –"

"No. These wings are not for you. Now get to bed, where you should have been long ago."

Mouse's face crumpled. He turned and fled into the darkness. After a moment came the thump of the closing door.

The master stood a moment, drawing deep breaths, willing himself back to his preferred state of disconnected calm. But he could not banish his anger, or rid himself of the image of Mouse, little Mouse with his pale face and twitching nose, harnessed to the wings. The effrontery of it! The presumption! Wherever he turned, lately, there Mouse always seemed to be. It was like having a second shadow. It was like being haunted.

Behind him, the wings moved softly, whispering of perfection. But the master's mood was ruined. He hauled them back to their place at the ceiling, then left and locked the studio. The darkness that most often dwelled there returned. Dust stirred by the wings' ascent settled again on the shrouded easel, the unfinished machines, the abandoned models, the unused tools and untouched supplies.

~ ~ ~

The next morning, while the master sat looking at the correspondence he had not the energy to answer, his brother came to say that there was trouble among the apprentices. Mouse had accused the Saracen of stealing his brushes, which the Saracen of course denied. The younger boy had rushed to the apprentices' quarters and flung open the Saracen's clothing chest; the Saracen had pursued him and knocked him down. The brushes were indeed hidden in the chest; the apprentice master found them after he broke up the fight.

"The Saracen has been punished?" the master asked.

"He has been thrashed and sent to the kitchens for the day."

"Why do we have an apprentice master, if he cannot con trol the apprentices?"

"You know the problem, brother. Mouse is a charity case. It might not be so bad if the other boys did not envy his talent, or if they did not see him as a sycophant for the way he dotes on you."

"I suppose you want me to do something."

"I want you to speak to the boys." The master's brother was a small man, thin as a wire, with incurving shoulders and a forehead permanently folded into a frown. He resembled the master, who was tall and robust, with a springing mane of iron-gray hair, not at all. The master trusted him above any man on earth. "Tell them that such behavior will not be toler ated. It will have more weight if you say it."

"I have in mind something else." The master was not aware that he had made a decision; the decision was simply there, fully formed. "I've been thinking for some time that it would be best for Mouse to leave us. His talent is too much in service to imitation. He needs a master who can teach him bet ter – why are you shaking your head? Do you disagree?"

"Not with your assessment, brother. He makes so much difficulty among the boys, I would not be sorry to see him go. But I don't think you'll be able to persuade another painter to take him on charity."

"I'll sponsor him, then."

The master's brother sighed. "You can't afford it."

"What do you mean, I can't afford it?"

"Ah, brother, how many times have we spoken of this? The workshop is lucrative and the patron has been generous, but it is *your* work that supports us. It is *your* reputation that sustains us. More and more, you turn down commissions – or you accept them and then abandon them. I have let servants go, I've dismissed journeymen. I economize in everything. And each day I wake in fear that you will cease even the pretense of work –"

"Enough!" The master turned his face away. For a mo ment there was silence.

"You could manage it if you took on two new appren tices," the master's brother said. "One to fill Mouse's place and offset the fee to get him a different master, and one to support our household."

It was the master's turn to sigh. An extra apprentice, an other link in the chain of burdens that bound him to the earth. But at least he would be rid of Mouse.

"Very well," he said. "You may see to it. They must have talent, though. I will not take on talentless boys for the sake of their fathers' purses."

The master's brother nodded. "When will you tell Mouse?"

"I had thought...perhaps you..."

"No, brother. You are his teacher. That is your task."

The master opened his mouth to protest, but his brother's steady regard stilled the words before he could speak them. He let out his breath in another sigh. "Where is he?"

"In the dormitory." The master's brother got to his feet. "Break it to him kindly. He is young, and he loves you very much."

~ ~ ~

The dormitory was at the back of the workshop. It smelled of smoke, oil, wood shavings, gypsum dust, and unwashed boys. Mouse lay on his bed, sprawled on his stomach, his pil low pulled over his head.

"Mouse."

The boy's entire body convulsed. He flung himself to a sit ting position, the pillow flying to the floor. His eyes were wild; a bruise darkened one cheek. "Master," he gasped, "Master, I didn't start it –"

"I know that, Mouse. I know about the brushes."

Tears overspilled the boy's eyes. "Please don't punish me."

"Calm yourself. I have something to say to you."

Mouse gulped, wiped his nose on his sleeve, dug the heels of his hands into his eyes and rubbed his hands on his hose. The master turned away, repelled, looking instead at the pat terns of light the morning sun laid upon the floor. He wished, not for the first time, that he could transition from the present moment to a chosen moment in the future, avoiding all the moments in between.

"A student," the master began, "must be a crucible for his master's teaching. The master's wisdom and the student's gift must combine, combust, and out of that must come transformation, so that the student may become the artist he is meant to be. A student cannot be merely a vessel, pouring out again what is poured in. Do you understand me, Mouse?"

"Yes, master," the boy said. "You've told us many times."

"You have talent. Yet you will not...be a crucible. What you bring out of yourself is only a shadow, an imitation of me. I have tried to help you, but there has been no improvement, and I've come to believe there never will be, not as long as you remain with me. You are not well served here. Another master could teach you better."

"Oh, no, sir! No one could teach me better! I know you haven't been happy with my work, but I'm trying, I really am, in fact I have a new painting all finished, I've been meaning to show you –"

"Mouse, I have made up my mind. As soon as I find another place for you, you must go. I know this is...a surprise, but you will be better off, I promise."

There. It was done. The master braced himself for the outcry that would surely follow. When he heard nothing, he turned. The boy sat motionless amid his disordered sheets. His mouth hung open. His face was as blank as fresh canvas.

"Mouse, did you understand what I said?"

Mouse sucked in a breath. "You don't mean it."

"I'm afraid I do."

"But you're my teacher. You have to teach me. No one else can teach me."

"You'll soon realize that isn't true." The master forced himself to speak gently.

"I'll change, master." The boy was crying again, his nose running, tears dripping off his chin. "Whatever I'm doing wrong, I'll change, I swear, only don't send me away! I'll die if you make me go!"

"I doubt that, Mouse."

Mouse's voice broke. "But I thought you loved me."

"It is not love that makes an artist. Training makes an artist. And I cannot train you any longer. It's for the best. You'll see."

The master began to turn away. There was a scrabbling, a thump. Mouse leaped off the bed and flung his arms around the master's waist, with such violence that the master staggered.

"Master, oh Master, don't send me away, oh please don't send me away! I'll do anything, anything!"

Mouse's body shook; the master could feel his unnatural heat. The horror of being touched that way – of being seized, of being *restrained* – was visceral. Without a thought, he pushed the boy away and clouted him across the face with full force of his open hand. Mouse fell back onto the bed.

"I will not tolerate...such displays." The master was breathless. Mouse stared up, not crying now, his face white with shock. "I simply will not."

Unsteadily the master left the room. He could still feel the blow, throbbing dully in his palm.

Behind him, there was silence.

~ ~ ~

In the afternoon, the master packed his brushes, summoned two journeymen and an apprentice, and went to the patron's palace. It galled him to do it, after the insult of last night. But the encounter with Mouse had disturbed him more than he wanted to admit, and the distraction of work – even the detested painting – was welcome.

The initial stages of the project had absorbed and even energized the master. As conventional as the subject matter was, it afforded him the opportunity to realistically depict the carnage of battle. There had also been problems to solve and techniques to adapt, for in his vanity the patron had demanded a truly enormous work, and the fabrication of the wood panels, as well as the transfer of the design to the prepared surface, had presented many challenges.

All this had been accomplished in an intense burst of creative energy and with remarkable speed. Once the actual painting began, however, the master had been overcome by the familiar reluctance. Often he was so burdened by disgust and boredom that he could not paint a stroke; and dread of this feeling, as much as the feeling itself, created a powerful aversion that kept him away from the painting for days or even weeks at a time. Nearly three years along, the background was almost complete, but the battle, which the patron insisted must be entirely by the master's hand, was not even half-finished.

The master set the apprentice to unpacking supplies, and ordered the journeymen up onto the scaffold to work on the wooded hills and stormy sky that filled the painting's upper third. He himself returned to work on the battle scene, dominated by the patron on his great chestnut charger, surrounded by his lieutenants, pages, trumpeters, and standard bearers.

After perhaps an hour of dreary effort, the sound of footsteps and voices announced the patron's approach. The master put down his palette. The patron was accompanied by his usual entourage of aides and hangers-on, and also several of the noblemen who had been his guests last night and had witnessed his insult to the master. The master felt something within him tighten. He bowed, holding the position for a moment before straightening.

"How pleasant to see the artist at his labor." The patron smiled an acid smile. "Perhaps you might speak a little about your great work, for the benefit of my guests."

The master began the short speech he had given many times before. The entourage listened with varying degrees of interest or boredom. The patron's cold blue eyes never moved from the master's face.

"From words to work is a surprisingly long journey," he observed, when the master had finished. "As you may see by the fact that my battle is yet more charcoal than paint."

"But the colors," said the nobleman who had shown the keenest interest. "Exquisite. And the faces, each different from the next. Though it may take long to complete, what a masterpiece you'll have when it is finished!"

"A masterpiece won't much benefit me if I die before it's done," the patron replied. Yet he seemed pleased by the praise, and did not protest when the nobleman stepped forward to inspect the painting more closely.

The patron rounded up his people at last and led them away. The master returned to his palette and brushes, which lay on the floor where he had left them. The thought of taking them up, of going back to work, was suddenly sickening. The completed figures seemed flat, unutterably dull. The unfinished portions of the painting – the expanses of white gesso, the charcoal tangle of the under-drawing – loomed before him; his hands hung at the end of his arms like lead weights. In this one unfinished painting, he saw all his unfinished paintings. In the obligation to complete it, he saw all the obligations of his identity as an artist, a monstrous outgrowth of his talent, as if a pearl had grown a shell and not the other way around.

Abruptly, something in him shifted. An image bloomed in his mind, an irresistible impulse. He seized his tools and began to mix new colors from the supplies laid out by the ap prentice. "Pack up," he told the boy when he was done. "We're finished for the day." Ascending the scaffold, he gave a similar order to the journeymen. As they clambered down, he set to work on a portion of the sky where painted clouds separated to let painted sunlight stream through. Even before his present troubles, he had not been a swift worker – but when inspira tion gripped him he could be very fast indeed. It took him only a few moments to finish.

He stepped back to the limit of the scaffold boards and regarded what he had done. High above the bloody turmoil of the battle, a man strapped into bat-black wings flew toward the parting of the clouds, his arms stretched in longing or sup plication to the sunlight and blue sky beyond.

Heaven, a voice seemed to whisper inside the master's mind.

~ ~ ~

"Brother. Wake up."

Roused from tangled dreams, the master opened his eyes. He had sat up late in his studio the night before, paging through his notebooks. He could not say what had spurred him to do this; perhaps the pure flare of inspiration that had driven him on the scaffold, reminding him of how long it had been since he had felt anything similar. He knew that he was not sketching as much as in the past, but he had not truly realized how sparse his entries had become, or how many drawings he abandoned after only a few lines. In his early years, ideas had spilled from him as fast as his hand could move; he had filled pages in a single night, cramming them so full the paper hardly showed – the booty of the artist-thief, a treasure trove that held the seeds of the great paintings that had made his name. At last he could no longer bear it, and returned the notebooks to their shelves and went to bed, seeking refuge in uneasy sleep.

"What is it?" he asked.

"There has been a burglary."

"A burglary?" The master pushed himself up in bed.

"Sometime during the night. One of the maids came into the courtyard before dawn and found the outer gates standing open. We are searching now to see what may have been taken, but brother, the great doors of your studio were open also, and the lock on the small door was forced."

"*What?*" The master's hand went to his chest, where the key to his studio lay beneath his nightclothes. "Has anything been stolen?"

"I cannot tell. Only you know what is in there. You must come see for yourself."

Beneath the brightening sky of dawn, the courtyard was still gripped by night. The gates had been closed and re-barred, but the studio doors had been left as they were, yawning onto blackness. The master's brother went off to supervise the search; alone, the master forced himself to approach. Stepping inside, he raised the lamp he carried, but could see no obvious disturbance. He turned where he stood, a slow circle, finding nothing out of order. Last of all he raised his eyes to the ceil ing, where shadows gathered like wadded silk.

Thus it was that he discovered that his wings, his floating, whispering wings, were gone.

For a moment he stood motionless. Understanding ran through him like red-hot wire.

"Brother." The master's brother appeared in the doorway. "The apprentices have been roused, and we cannot find –"

"Mouse." The master saw Mouse's stunned face, turned up at him from the bed yesterday. He saw Mouse's eyes, shining in the lamplight the night before. He heard Mouse's voice: *You say they're ready, but you never fly them...*

"The boys say he was there at bedtime. None of them will admit to waking when he left, or that they know where he has gone."

"He has stolen my wings."

"Your wings? But –"

"He means to fly them." The master set down the lamp on the nearest surface and started for the door. "I must stop him."

By the time he reached the courtyard, he was running. Behind him, he heard his brother shouting his name; then the sound fell away and he was in the street, thick with early morning traffic. He had not run like this in years, but he barely felt the strain. A terrible emotion pressed him forward, a mix of dread and rage unlike anything he had ever experienced.

The city was built on high ground. Beyond the eastern walls, a cliff fell precipitously to the river plain below. It was here, where hawks rode the wind, that the master had intended to test his wings. Mouse knew this, for there was a time when the master had indulged his apprentice's fascination with his work. The cliff, he knew, was where Mouse would go.

Panting, the master raced through the city gates. A small crowd was gathered at the cliff-edge, but the master saw no boy, no familiar sweep of silk and struts. To the east, the simmering ember of the sun had only just cleared the horizon. The master reached the watchers, pushed through them to the edge of the drop. With a sense of absolute recognition, as if he were looking not upon a fresh tragedy but a painting whose every line he knew, he saw below, on the still-shadowed flatness of the plain, the crumpled wreckage of the wings and the boy trapped within them. The sight transfixed both his selves – the artist who strove only to *see* and not to judge, and the feeling, judging, fallible man the artist denied. It pinned the two together, and for a moment made them one.

"I must go down," he said, or thought he said.

A stairway cut into the stone of the cliff led down to the plain. The climb from the heights was a nightmare the master did not clearly remember later. It seemed to take an eternity to descend, to cross to the place where Mouse had fallen.

"Stand aside," the master gasped when he reached the crowd that had gathered around the wings. "Let me through."

One lovely curve survived, the long spar of the wings' windward edge. The rest was destruction, a mess of splintered struts and torn silk. Mouse had been unstrapped from the harness, lifted free and laid on the grass. Blood marked his mouth and nose. Nearby, a group of men was plundering the wreckage for materials to improvise a stretcher.

The master knelt beside his apprentice. Mouse's face amid the tawny grass was as white as gesso, his mouth sloping open, his eyes closed. The master reached to touch his throat – a reflex gesture only, for who could survive such a fall? To his astonishment, he felt the beat of blood, faint but unmistakable.

"Mouse," he said. There was no response. He turned to the watchers. "Did any of you see?" he demanded. "Did any of you see what happened?"

"I did," said a man who wore the insignia of the city watch.

"Tell me."

"I was walking my rounds. I saw them going through the gates with that contraption, this boy and another. Strangest thing I ever seen. I followed them to the cliff. The other one helped this one with the straps and such. There was a bit of a crowd by that time, with this one shouting like a madman that he was going to fly, fly like a bird all the way to the sun. Didn't think he'd be able to stand up under the weight, but he managed it. The other one run off then, and this one jumped. Jumped right off the edge." The watchman shook his head. "Never seen anything like it."

"Master."

It was as faint as a breath, but the master heard. He looked down. Mouse's eyes were open.

"Master...am I dying?"

"Hush," the master said. "Help is coming."

In the grass Mouse's hand moved, lifting, groping at the air. The master caught it in his own. Mouse sighed, closed his fingers around the master's. "Don't...be angry..." he whispered.

The master quelled a rush of bitter emotion. "Why, Mouse? Why did you do it?"

"You said...I had to leave. Wanted...to fly. Was...last chance."

"But I told you you couldn't work the wings. You foolish boy, why didn't you heed me?"

Mouse's gaze shifted, so that he looked not into the master's face but beyond it, as if at something only he could see. The corners of his mouth curved – a smile of such remembered joy, such secret understanding, that the master felt his heart turn over inside his breast. Then the smile faded. Mouse's eyes fell closed.

The master knelt motionless. He was aware of the warmth of the sun on his back, the springy grass beneath his knees, the boy's fingers still gripping his own. He reached down and peeled them away, and rose, shakily, to his feet.

"We can take him now, sir."

The stretcher-makers had brought their makeshift contraption and laid it beside the boy.

"Tell me," the master said to the man who had spoken. "Did you see it? Did he fly?"

"Yes, sir." The man's brow creased. "I wouldn't have believed it if I hadn't seen with my own eyes. Out over the river he went, and back. It was the second time he turned that he fell."

"Ah," the master said.

"He must have been mad, to try such a thing."

The master looked down at Mouse, broken in the grass's embrace. "He was a thief," he said.

They lifted Mouse onto the stretcher. He cried out when they touched him, whimpered as they carried him to the cliff. It took a long time to hoist the stretcher up the angles and switchbacks of the stairs, a long time to bear it through the streets. By the time they reached the master's house, Mouse was dead.

~ ~ ~

They never learned the identity of the boy who had helped Mouse steal the wings. The apprentices all denied involvement. A street child, perhaps, the master thought, a connection from Mouse's former life.

The master's brother saw to Mouse's burial. He parceled out Mouse's possessions among the other boys, and gave

Mouse's bed to the new apprentice, who, with the master's permission, he took on the week after Mouse's death. The ap prentices, who had despised Mouse while he lived, turned him in death into a kind of legend, passing the tale of his exploit back and forth and embroidering it as they did.

The master could not bring himself to enter his studio, unable to bear the thought of the empty space where his wings had hung. He kept to his chamber during the day and walked out alone at night, mourning his wings, his masterwork, wrecked by the desperate act of a rejected boy. He knew it should be Mouse he mourned; the wings could be re-made, but Mouse was gone forever. Yet he had loved his wings, and he had not loved the boy. Mouse had done what no artist could forgive: he had appropriated another artist's work, and then destroyed it. Even if the master built the wings anew, even if he stepped out upon the air and soared like Icarus toward the sun, he would only be following in his apprentice's footsteps. He would be free, but he would not be first.

He had not known that mattered to him, until now.

There was one other remnant of Mouse: a sheaf of sketches and several small wood panels that were his personal work. The master had instructed his brother to burn them, but his brother refused, and for a week they sat on the master's desk, awaiting disposition. One day, returning to his room after lunch, the master was seized with rage to see them there. He scooped them up, intending to burn them himself.

Halfway to the door, something stopped him – a spasm of curiosity, or perhaps of conscience. He returned to his desk and began to sort through the sketches. As he expected, they were well-wrought and uninspired. The panels were the same: technically fine, but dull.

The final panel, unlike the others, was wrapped in canvas and tied with a cord. The master cut the cord and folded back the cloth.

It was a self-portrait. Mouse had painted himself from the waist up, against a background of deep shadow from which he only partially emerged, his skin glowing gold as if with the last light of the sun. No harness crossed his bare chest, but an arc of wings sprang from behind his shoulders, only a little blacker than the shadow with which they merged, their shape defined by subtle highlights. Mouse's right hand was raised, the forefinger pointing upward – toward the sky. His head was tilted to the side, as though in question; his dark eyes met the viewer's, and on his mouth was the smile he had smiled just before he died: faint, enigmatic, full of secrets.

The master was stunned. The other panels he had seen in various stages of completion, for he saw and criticized all his apprentices' practice works – but not this one. Here, at last, was the promise he had glimpsed in the street child who brazened his way into an apprenticeship. His own influence was apparent in the shadows, the warm skin tones, the silky brushwork – but in subject and composition, the painting was utterly original. He heard Mouse's voice, the day the boy had learned he would be sent away: *I have a new painting all finished, I've been meaning to show you.* This must be what he had meant.

Mouse's painted eyes held the master's. In them the master saw the dream of flight, his own dream mirrored back at him. He heard again what Mouse had whispered as he lay bleeding in the yellow grass: *Wanted to fly...was last chance...*But now it seemed to him that Mouse had not been speaking of himself, but of the wings. It was they that had wanted to fly. Had they not breathed their desire to him the night before he cast Mouse off? Had they not breathed it on many other nights in the three years since he built them? Why had he never answered?

And now the master *saw*, as an artist should see, not the world outside but the one within, to which he so rarely turned his attention. He saw that he would never have strapped on the wings, not because he was afraid to fall, but because he was afraid to fail. The wings unflown, the sketches unmade, the paintings unfinished – they spared him the agony of completion, the moment in which idea, irrevocably consigned to form or function, became less, fell short. The moment in which the artist, dreaming of perfection, learned anew that perfection was a dream.

Mouse had not feared completion. He had put on the wings, and he had flown. For the first time, in the thought of his apprentice, the master found the ache of sadness.

After a little while the master wrapped up the panel in its cloth and carried it downstairs. In the courtyard, sunlight poured from an eggshell sky; the master paused and lifted his face, relishing the warmth. With the key that hung around his neck – a new key, for a new padlock – he unlocked the door to his studio and stepped inside. He laid Mouse's painting on his desk, then went to open the shutters, raising clouds of dust that made him cough. Cool northern light flooded the room, illuminating the abandoned projects, the discarded artworks, the litter on the workbenches and tables. It had been ages since he had looked upon his studio in daylight. He was appalled at the neglect.

His eyes rose to the empty ceiling, where the rope that had supported the wings still hung from its winch. But they did not linger there for long.

Crossing to the shelves, the master rummaged until he found a stand on which he could prop Mouse's painting. He set the painting in the stand and placed the stand on his desk, where he would be able to see it. Then he returned to the courtyard and headed for the workshop, to commandeer an apprentice to help him sweep the dust away.

I Brake for Biker Witches

by Angie Fox

Angie Fox is the *New York Times* bestselling author of several mysteries featuring vampires, werewolves, and things that go bump in the night. She claims that researching her stories can be just as much fun as writing them. In the name of fact-finding, Angie has ridden with Harley biker gangs, explored the tunnels underneath Hoover Dam, and found an interesting recipe for Mamma Coalpot's Southern Skunk Surprise (she's still trying to get her courage up to try it).

Angie worked in television news and then in advertising before beginning her career as an author. Visit Angie at www.angiefox.com.

When my biker witches aren't hurling spell jars, they're on the road with Lizzie the demon slayer, keeping the world's nasties at bay. The gang of mostly sixty and seventy-something seniors started out as a peaceful coven, but decades ago, when they were attacked by a demon, they hit the road and never looked back. Now it's hard to imagine life without Harleys, glittering skull do-rags and enchanted hideouts. Just watch out for the Frozen Underwear spells. These witches know that life can be short, and they're not going to waste a minute of it.

Author's Note: The events in this story take place after the mayhem that transpired in *The Last of the Demon Slayers*. However, there's no need to read any *Accidental Demon Slayer* books in order to understand it. In fact, your house will probably be a lot cleaner if you don't invite the biker witches inside. I'm still finding spell jars behind the curtains and half eaten cookies under the couch.

Chapter One

It was a dark and lonely night. No, seriously – it was. You wouldn't believe the pitch black you get in the middle of the desert in California. No lights. No people. Nothing. We hadn't even seen another vehicle in almost an hour.

I gunned my Harley and heard the answering roar of two dozen biker witches on my tail.

We were one-hundred-and-fifty miles into the Mojave des ert, on our way back from Las Vegas to L.A. Some overzealous jerk had reported a demon infestation in Sin City, but when we'd gotten there, we'd only found a half-succubus running a pampered pet salon.

We let her be. I couldn't smite a dog person, especially after she had my Jack Russell Terrier smelling like Paws-4-Patchouli. Besides, the girl with the demonic bent was more good than bad. My demon slayer powers had told me that much.

The headset inside my silver helmet buzzed with static and then clicked. "Where the hell are we?"

My biker witch grandma's voice tickled my ear. "Zzyzx."

I didn't quite catch that. "You cut out."

"Zzyzx." Grandma said, "It's the name of the town."

Frankly, I didn't see anything but a straight dark road and acres of scrub. Still, there was something here that wasn't quite right. I'd felt it at the back of my neck for the last fifty miles, the prickling unease that signaled trouble.

It had gotten worse in the last minute. Way worse. "Does anyone else feel that?"

"You mean like low in my stomach?" Ant Eater asked.

"Yes." And tingling up my spine. It wasn't necessarily demonic – I knew exactly what that felt like. But it was something *else*. Something I'd never felt before.

The radio crackled. "Maybe we need to stop and get some snacks," my Jack Russell terrier suggested.

"No," everyone said at once.

In his defense, Pirate was a dog with a one-track mind, usually trained on food. Because of our powers, we could hear him talk, and talk … and talk. We should never have given him a headset.

At least the sweet-smelling troublemaker was riding shotgun with Bob. I didn't want Pirate up here with me if we ran into trouble.

Our headlights reflected off a lone green highway sign up ahead. "Well would you look at that," I said under my breath. In big, white letters it read: Zzyzx.

Pirate gave a yip. "I just won the alphabet game."

"Wait." Ant Eater's voice sharpened. She was the scariest biker I knew. That's why she always rode shotgun. "You see that? Dead ahead."

"I see it." My pulse thrummed with anticipation. A figure of a man stood under the sign. We wouldn't have seen him so far out, except he was glowing.

Jesus, Mary, Joseph and the mule. We couldn't even take one ride through the desert without trouble.

I could almost hear the witches going for their spell jars.

We slowed as we approached, our headlights trained on a bald man with a thick, braided beard. I strained for a better look as recognition wound through me. I knew him from somewhere.

"Holy hell," Frieda whispered.

Then it hit me. I remembered where I'd seen him before. Frieda had been carrying his picture for as long as I'd known her. She'd post it over her bed, clip it on her spell books, have it handy wherever we happened to be. She'd rub him on the forehead and hum the same tune every time.

This was Mister Love in an Elevator.

He'd been dead for as long as I'd known her.

I ground my bike to a halt about ten feet back from him. Close enough to talk, far enough to throw a switch star if it came to that.

Frieda would tan my hide. I said a silent prayer for Mister Love in an Elevator to behave.

One by one, the Red Skull witches cut their engines. I took my helmet off and hung it over a handle bar.

Frieda had already scrambled out from behind one of the bikers toward the front. She approached the phantom slowly, all the while holding a spell jar behind her back. It swirled with a brackish, blue and gold liquid.

Grandma stood next to me as I dismounted, one hand on my weapons belt. I tilted my head toward her. "What's she got?"

"Ghost zapper," she said, her voice gritty from years of hard riding and semi-truck exhaust. "It blasts their energy field. Damned thing better not be expired."

Good point. We didn't get too many ghosts.

This one wore leather chaps, a black leather jacket and a Texas bikers T-shirt.

I pulled a switch star from my belt, just in case. It was flat and round. Five blades curled around the edge.

The white from Frieda's zebra print leather pants glowed in our headlights as she tottered forward on four-inch, red wedge sandals. "Carl? Is that you, baby?"

Sweat tickled the back of my neck. Frieda was a sitting duck if this didn't work.

Amusement sparked from the ghost's heavy lidded eyes. "Well don't you look pretty?"

She stopped a few feet in front of him, her red dice ear rings swaying as she shook. "Are you … alive?"

He wound his thumbs under his black leather belt. "Aw, now you know I'da come back for you if I was." He glanced past Frieda, his bottomless blue eyes locking on me. "I wouldn't be here now. Except we need your help."

Dread pooled in my stomach. This couldn't be good. "Who's *we*?"

The ghost eyed me. "We got a new gang going, for those of us who have passed on."

Oh lordy.

"Shouldn't you be in heaven or something?" Frieda asked.

"Not yet, baby." He touched her fluffy blonde hair. It ruffled slightly as his fingers moved straight through it. "You still need us, whether you realize it or not. But we've gotten into a little trouble in the meantime."

He had to be kidding. I was a demon slayer, not a ghost whisperer. I couldn't babysit a bunch of undead bikers. "What exactly do you want me to do?"

He turned his back on us as a chrome and black Harley appeared on the side of the road. Neat trick.

"Come on," he said, heading for his bike, "I'll show you."

Chapter Two

"Oh sure," I muttered as we trailed after him through the darkness, sharp rocks sounding like fireworks under our tires. "Go off road. Follow an undead biker through the middle of the Mojave desert." I could feel the dirt in my eyes. I could taste it in my mouth. Our Harleys weren't built for this.

"No worries, demon slayer," Ant Eater's voice sounded behind my ear, "I know where we are."

My bike was vibrating so bad my arms were going numb. "What? With magic?"

"GPS."

Okay. Well there was that.

Ant Eater chuckled low in her throat.

We'd been following the former Carl for at least twenty miles. I stared out into the night sky, the stars impossibly bright now that we were truly in the middle of nowhere. And about due for a breakdown.

We gunned our engines up and over a small rise.

I stopped so hard my bike skidded sideways.

"What the hell is that?" Grandma choked.

Lights shone from a building below. Only it wasn't a build ing exactly. It was a shell of a foundation, half buried in the dirt. Phantom walls surrounded it and I could see glowing fig ures moving inside.

The structure shimmered and, in that moment, I could make out a distinct, two-story Wild West tavern. Cracked paint announced the Tanglefoot Saloon. The rough wood front looked gray from the weather and age. At the horse hitch out side, I saw a line of ghostly gray horses. And motorcycles.

The image shifted into the faint outline of a two-story stuc co building with neon bar signs in the window. Then it shifted back to the saloon. Iron Maiden's *Twilight Zone* thumped out into the parking lot, mixed with the faint tinkling of a piano.

What the –? I glanced at Grandma, who just shook her head.

We pulled closer. Weeds sprouted around the front of the saloon and a prickly pear cactus grew straight through the sign for the Paradise Bar and Grill.

Our tires nudged the edge of a cracked parking lot. The desert stretched for miles in every direction.

"It's not real," I said, almost convinced.

"Damn straight," Ant Eater said, agreeing with me for once.

We could deny it until gypsies grew wings, but there it was, as if it had sprung from the desert floor itself.

"I smell pickled eggs," Pirate said, scrambling through the maze of Red Skull bikers, heading for the front door.

"Wait." I scooped him up. I was detecting something else.

"Demonic?" Grandma asked.

I opened my senses. "Maybe."

There was a raw energy to this place, like nothing I'd ever felt before. There was also a wrongness that I couldn't quite put my finger on. I tucked my dog under my arm. "Stick close, buddy," I said, not giving him a choice.

"Aw now, Lizzie. Why don't you let me have any fun?" His legs dangled as he tried to push off me and jump down. "I'll be careful."

Like a bulldozer.

Grandma studied the phantom bar. "Okay," she said, rub bing at her mouth. "I want half of you to stay outside and make a perimeter," she said to the witches. "Get your spells out and be ready to use them." She eyed Carl, who had already walked up to the front door and stood beckoning us. She raised her voice. "The rest of us will follow Carl."

Ant Eater leaned in close as she pried off her leather riding gloves. "You sure that's a good plan?"

"Best one we got," Grandma muttered.

I was with Ant Eater on this one. A demon could take many forms. Of course, I wasn't naïve enough to think we were safe outside, or anywhere for that matter. "I'll go first," I said, setting my dog down on the ground. "You," I said, point ing at him, "are on backup patrol." Maybe I could at least keep him out of trouble.

"Now that's just crazy," he said, circling before he sat. "Who ever heard of a watchdog going last?"

I gave him a quick rub on the head before Grandma, Ant Eater and I led the way across the parking lot.

The ghost paused at a shimmering wooden door. Clusters of cinnamon sticks wrapped in sage faded in and out of the wood and a rusty red substance streamed down the frame.

It was all too familiar – and stinky. Okay, so maybe I was starting to believe that Carl really was the ghost of a Red Skull biker witch.

He opened the door and music poured out, along with a great deal of bar noise.

I stepped inside and nearly fell sideways.

The Tanglefoot/Paradise looked like a saloon straight out of a Wild West movie. The large, high-ceiling room featured a scattering of rounded tables under gaslit chandeliers. The walls were rough wood. A long carved bar stretched the entire length of the back, with a mirror behind it. Along one side, a piano hunkered next to a modern sound system.

Biker witches crowded the tables, playing poker with outlaws and cowhands. Saloon girls wove between the tables. Cheers erupted over a minor fistfight next to some kind of big, round gambling wheel.

Sadly, this wasn't the strangest thing I'd ever seen.

And then I laid eyes them.

"There's Hog Wild Harriet," I gasped, "dealing poker." And cheating from the look of the cards stuffed in her bra. I could see them every time she faded out.

And there was Easy Edna, Lucinda the Lush and a half dozen other dead witches. They'd been killed helping us, sacrificing for us.

Grandma drew up short. "Son of a bitch."

"Heyyy!" Betty Two Sticks staggered up to us, her Woody Allen glasses slipping down her nose, a bottle of 1800 whiskey in hand. "This stuff is good. Now I'm seeing demon slayers." She poked me with a finger, only it went straight through. "Damn it all, it is a demon slayer. I was hoping you'd make it."

I turned to Grandma. "She's smashing drunk."

Betty screwed up her face like she had to think about that one. "I know you are, but what am I?"

"They're all here," Grandma muttered. "I know every goddamned one of them."

Unbelievable. I stared at the drunkard next to me, from her tie-dyed bandana to her steel-toed boots. "What is this place?"

Betty stuck her face inches from mine. She smelled like the inside of a Jack Daniels bottle. "Hey," she tried to whisper, only she was on full volume, "you gotta meet this guy. He shot seven people. He's the fastest gun in…" She turned around. "What are you the fastest gun in?" she yelled to a table of outlaws behind her.

This was too much. "Where's Carl?" I leaned to see past Betty. "Oh. Great." He was over by the jukebox, trying to make out with Frieda. That was a big help.

The bar flashed to modern and then back West again. And Betty had clearly forgotten the meaning of personal space. I took a step back. "Why are you here?"

She pondered me, like it was a tough question, not even flinching as one ghostly cowboy clocked another over the head with a whiskey bottle. "I'm socializing," she concluded. "Had my eye on a few of them hotties from the Lazy K Ranch."

Oh geez. "No, I meant –" How could I explain?

It was like reasoning with Pirate, only way worse. I didn't want to think of these dead bikers stuck here. They deserved to be in a better place.

"You can move on, Betty," I said, ducking as a chair flew past my head. It didn't matter. The chair crashed straight through Grandma and skittered across the hardwood floor. "Why didn't you go to the light?"

I wasn't sure how one went to the light, or got out of this place for that matter, but I hoped somebody around here could give her a few hints. Then again, it could be a spiritually sticky place. Clearly this Wild West show had been playing for awhile.

She clutched the neck of her whiskey bottle, eyeing me intently. "Scarlet went to the light."

At least that was one.

"She was a real pussy about it too. The rest of us are wait ing," she said proudly.

My head was starting to hurt. "For what?"

She flipped her long grey braid behind her back. "For you."

Okay that was creepy. My heart thudded in my chest. This had better not be a trap.

"You see this?" Grandma clapped a hand on my shoulder. "Rubber Neck Reba, Easy Edna," she said as the ghosts of biker witches ambled up behind her.

I gave a half wave, not getting this at all. Grandma merely grinned, watching as the biker witches, live and dead re-united. Some tried hugs, but their arms went straight through their friends, so they'd settled on clinking whiskey glasses and gathering around the rough, wooden tables and along dusty barstools.

"Damn, it's good to see everyone. I wouldn't mind spend ing a century or two holed up here," Grandma said, her gaze traveling over the bar. "Except for that," she added, fixing on a rickety wooden staircase near the back bar. A thick, yellow fog tumbled down it. I could feel malice at the top of those stairs.

I focused my demon slayer senses and saw it like a dot in the back of my mind – latent evil waiting to strike.

And then I saw someone else and my heart instantly light ened. "Uncle Phil!"

I'd lost my fairy godfather almost a year before. He'd died saving me.

Leave it to Phil – he wasn't partying or goofing around. He was busy working some kind of a spell at the foot of the stairs. Well, at least that was the only thing I could figure from the way he waved his short, thick arms.

He stood in a cloud of silver sparkles, his bushy eyebrows fixed in concentration and his bulbous nose as red as it had ever been. I could almost smell his familiar bubblegum scent.

"Watch my back," I said to Grandma as I made a path straight for him.

Phil didn't see me until I was almost up on him. When he did, his mouth broke into a wide grin. "Lizzie! I knew you'd come. I just knew it." His voice shot through me like sunshine. "I'd hug you, but I'd go right through you."

Didn't I know it. "What are you doing here?"

Fairy dust settled over his pointy ears, which looked like they'd been crammed on as an afterthought. "I told you I'd always watch out for you."

Sure, but, "Here?"

A frigid wind whipped from the top of the stairs, startling us both.

"Just a second," Phil said, replacing pennies that had tum bled down. It was then I noticed the coins littering the stairs.

"What are you doing?"

"Basic fairy protection," he said, hurrying. "We use coins for good wishes, but their positive energy can also work against evil spirits, or any basic malicious entity. So far, I've got eighty seven dollars and thirty two cents." He scowled at the mounds of mostly nickels and pennies. "I'd like at least a hundred dollars."

Another dose of cold power blasted the stairs and more change scattered down the steps.

"Cripes. We're down seven cents," he said, lobbing a nickel and two pennies back up. He glanced over his shoulder. "You wouldn't happen to have any extra change, would you?"

I hitched my switch star and began digging in my pockets. "Two quarters and a dime."

His eyes lit up. "Oh yes. That's good. We like the big spenders."

I'd never been accused of that. "What is this?"

"It's related to wish magic," he said, carefully arranging the coins on the bottom steps. "Only this is a lot more power ful than what you humans do when you throw pennies in the fountain at the park."

No kidding. "Is that where we got it?"

"Of course. Now aim for the top. As you throw it, ask for the darkness to fade. I want to get as many up there as I can."

"Okay," I said, stepping onto the bottom stair.

"Wait. No!" He grabbed for my arm and his fingers went straight through. "You'll be incinerated!"

"How?" I froze, one foot on the stairway, scattering change as I drew switch star.

Phil's eyes had gone wide with shock. They darted to me, then down to my foot, then back up at me. "By stepping on the stair," he said slowly.

He gawked at me like I was the crazy part of this equation.

"Yes, well I suppose that's one advantage of being a de mon slayer," I said, suddenly embarrassed. Of course there were a whole lot of disadvantages as well, one being whatever was waiting for me on the second floor.

"Keep up the magic down here," I said, double check ing my switch stars, "I'm going to go see what's eating your pennies."

Phil's nostrils flared. I could see he was torn. "I can't pro tect you, Lizzie. Not up there."

"I know," I said, my hand hovering above his arm, wish ing I could give him a little reassurance. "Maybe I can protect you."

Chapter Three

I took one step at a time, trying not to disturb the change, more for Phil's sake than my own. If I failed up here, he'd need the protection.

The coins were slick under my feet as I made my way up.

The evil at the top of the stairs pulsed with energy. It called to me as the air temperature plummeted.

I blew out a breath and watched it cloud. Ice meant evil.

My fingers tightened in the handle of my switch star.

Focus.

This wasn't about me. It was about what needed to be done up here. I braced myself on the second to the last step.

It was pitch black beyond the doorway. I could almost feel whatever-it-was breathing in the darkness. Adrenaline slammed through my veins.

I reached into the front left pocket of my weapons belt and drew out a Lamp Spell, a little something special Grandma had brewed up for me. It skittered across the floor and light burst from the broken gaslamps along the walls of the second floor hallway.

It illuminated the narrow space and a portal unlike any I'd ever seen before. *H e double hockey sticks.* It was as large as two people and glowed with an unearthly blue fire. Sparks scattered from it, charring the walls and floor. It thrummed, as if it were trying to grow.

My mouth went dry. I gripped the entry way as it slowly began to advance on me.

Could I switch star a portal?

I didn't know.

Portals thrived on energy. For all I knew, my switch star would be like hitting it with a power boost.

Hell.

"Grandma?" I called down the stairs. There was no re sponse. Either she couldn't hear me or she couldn't get close. I wasn't about to turn my back on this thing to find out.

"Oh frick." I didn't have much of a choice here. I drew back, ready to fire.

"Wait!" A redheaded witch stepped from behind the puls ing blue mass.

Recognition hit me like a rock to the stomach. "Scarlet?"

She was supposed to have gone to the light. I wanted that for her, needed it. She'd died saving me. She deserved some peace.

But there she stood, in black leather pants and an emerald bustier. She flipped her long red hair behind her shoulder as she gathered her composure. I think she was as surprised to see me as I was to see her.

"They told me you'd moved on."

"Not yet," she said, worry creasing her brow. "I can't leave everyone else here. They refuse to go," she added, as if she couldn't quite believe it.

"They need to leave," I said, thinking of the trashed Betty. "But you can't make that decision for them."

"Oh so you want me to abandon them here forever?" She crossed her arms over her chest. "Typical, coming from you. Always the individual. You never thought about the group."

I flinched as the portal spat a blue spark way too close to my arm. "Whatever you're working on here has gone bad." Be sides, "I don't think our friends want to go." At least, not yet.

"Doesn't matter," she said, as if it were fact. "I'm going to save them whether they like it or not." She smiled, a sweet turn of the lips laced with venom. "So kindly keep your switch stars away from my portal."

"You're messing with free will, Scarlet." No wonder evil had seeped in. "This is a portal to a bad realm."

"Impossible," she said, her eyes widening as I drew back to fire. She rushed to stand in front of the pulsing blue mass, blocking me.

"Move aside," I ordered.

"No." She was frantic now. "It will go to the light. I'll make sure it does."

The portal was growing behind her. "You can't choose that for anyone but yourself, Scarlet." My fingers whitened on the handles of the switch star. "Now back away." I didn't want to take a chance on her getting hit, but I wasn't about to let this thing get any more out of hand than it was.

"Don't fuck this up, Lizzie. You can't fuck this up," she hollered, shaking, tears in her eyes as she scurried to the edge of the hissing portal. "I'm not going to leave them behind."

"Scarlet, no!" I drew back and fired as she shoved it straight for me.

Chapter Four

I dove to the floor as my switch star slammed into the por tal. Energy shot out, singeing my arms and numbing my teeth.

The brightness blinded me for a moment. I lay clutching the floor, blinking against the dots. Horrified, I saw the portal zoom straight over me and down the stairs.

"Son of a –" I took off after it, with Scarlet right behind.

She hit me with a blast of power as we dashed headlong for the runaway gateway to God-knew-where. I felt it like an electric punch to the back. Coins popped underfoot. I grabbed for the railing as she tried to throw me down the stairs.

"Duck!" I screamed at Phil, who hit the deck as it zoomed past him.

"Red Skulls! Defensive positions." Grandma hollered from behind him, her voice clear above the fray.

Witches took cover under tables and behind the bar as the portal swooped low, zapping two outlaws, the stereo system and a cowboy strumming a guitar.

Phil was still on the floor. I dropped to my knees next to him. "What do we do?"

He swung a fist straight through me and into Scarlet. She went down in a heap. He sat up, breathing hard, grey hair wild. "I'd never hit a lady, but she was about to hex you."

"She's not a lady," I said, urging him behind the nearest overturned table. "I don't know what she is anymore."

The portal zipped over the bar, shattering glasses and ex ploding the long gold mirror. A ghostly piano player plopped down on the bench and began playing the Wabash Cannonball as cowboys and outlaws went after the portal, guns blazing.

"Fire in the hole!" Grandma hollered as a wave of spell jars blasted the portal. It shimmered, turning purple and then back to blue.

Our biker witch reinforcements poured into the bar, led by Pirate.

"Let 'er rip!" Grandma hollered. This time, the portal shook under the onslaught.

Grandma ducked behind our table. "Lizzie, we need one last blast of juice," she said, digging a jar out of her pack as the piano banged and witches scrambled to reload.

"You ready?" she asked as I drew a switch star and focused all my energy, all my love, all my desire on blasting that deadly gate to hell where it belonged.

"Ready."

She gripped my shoulder. "Hold back until I tell you," she said, standing up. "And … fire!" She threw the jar like Roberto Clemente.

The portal shot sparks as each spell slammed into it.

"Go, Lizzie!" I threw and as the portal turned purple, my switch star tore a hole straight through it.

The biker witches and the outlaws cheered as it folded in on itself, sparking and hissing. It collapsed in on its own energy until it disappeared with a loud crack, sucked back to wherever it came.

I knelt on the floor, sweating as Phil and I stared at each other wide-eyed.

"I'd say we did it," he said, in the understatement of the year.

I forgot and tried to embrace him. Naturally, I went straight through him. "Damn it." The air was warm and smelled like bubblegum, which made me smile.

"Don't curse," he said, grinning as widely as I was.

"Did we lose any?" Grandma asked, finger jabbing the air as she counted the witches. She exhaled. "We didn't lose anybody."

Just a few outlaws and the blackjack dealer. I clapped her on the shoulder, as relieved as she was. We always seemed to lose somebody.

The biker witches were dusting off, hugging, sharing whis key bottles and greeting the reinforcements. It was a reunion all over again.

"Wait." I scanned the bar. "Where's Scarlet?"

She stood at the bottom of the stairs, a death spell in each hand.

I approached her slowly, one hand on my switch stars. But much of the fight had already gone out of her.

She was unfocused, bewildered. "What happened to me?" she asked, almost to herself. "What did I do?"

"It's okay," I said, stopping a few feet away. "You're back with us now." I imagined a shimmering white tunnel above her head. I could feel it, open and ready.

"But …" She stared at the path above her, torn.

"Go, Scarlet." She deserved warmth. She deserved peace. "Go to the light."

Fear glanced across her features, replaced with a firm re solve. She nodded to me, accepting at last. "Thanks, Lizzie."

"I'll never forget what you did for me," I said.

She smiled faintly and then tilted her face toward the light.

Scarlet rose up, becoming one with it, and at that moment, I too felt peaceful.

The bar had gone quiet as the biker witches, both alive and dead, stood watching.

"You should go too," I said to the rest of the ghosts.

They murmured among themselves, not moving. Carl shook his head slowly. He walked up to me, the steel chains of his biker boots clinking with every step.

"So nice of you to make it over here," I said, thinking of his earlier defection with Frieda.

The corner of his mouth tipped up. "You did just fine on your own." He grew serious. "I wasn't lying when I said you needed us, Lizzie." He stopped, studying me. "There's a revo lution brewing in hell."

"I know." I was going to have to face it. "But it's not your war."

He seemed surprised. "Of course it is. When each of us died, we were given a choice. Go to the light or wait to make a difference."

I stood, not sure what to say, as I looked out on the bar full of ghostly biker witches.

"We're your last line of defense," Carl continued, "and I don't mind saying, I think you're going to need our help."

"From ghost bikers?" I was still trying to wrap my head around it.

Grandma chuckled. "Is there any better kind?"

"What about them?" I asked, as a table full of cowboys broke out into an off-key rendition of The Yellow Rose of Texas.

One who could definitely use a shower and a shave guf fawed. "Peace and light ain't what we're after."

Obviously. "Then what are the rest of you waiting for?"

"A good fight," said his buddy. The men at the table cheered and stomped their boots against the dusty wood floor.

Yeah, well I could probably arrange that.

A tussle broke out between the outlaws at the bar. "We'll just have a little fun here until you need us." Carl grinned as Betty handed him a shot.

"How will I know how to find you?" I looked out at the motley crew of outlaws and bikers. It wasn't like we'd be fight ing demons in the middle of the desert.

"You'll find us," he said, toasting me before downing his whiskey.

"I'm glad," I said, and heaven help me – I was.

A Pearl Island Wedding

by Julie Ortolon

I'm late bloomer when it comes to reading – and writing. Because of my dyslexia, I didn't discover either joy until my mid-twenties when I discovered romance novels were worth the effort. Now, I'm totally addicted to both. My biggest joy is exploring the things that excite me through my characters. Since travel is one of those passions, I set all my stories in places I've actually been. Sometimes those real places morph into fictional places – like the setting for the Pearl Island series, my imaginary spin on Galveston, Texas.

Secondary characters add flavor to a story the way side dishes compliment a gourmet meal. Being in this anthology allowed me to serve up one of my favorite secondary characters in a story of her own. Chloe Davis first appeared as twelve-year-old tomboy who'd just run away from home in Lead Me On, book two of my Pearl Island trilogy. In that story, I could see glimpses of the woman she would become and I wanted to meet that woman. The only way to do that is through the writing process.

I've had the pleasure of revisiting Chloe several times now, through the bonus chapters I added to the original Pearl Island trilogy, and in the Masters of Seduction anthology where Chloe and Luc meet and fall in love. Here, at last, I get to give Chloe the happy ending she so richly deserves in "A Pearl Island Wedding."

She had to stop the wedding. Panic clutched Chloe's chest as she stared with horror at the phone in her hand. How could all her happiness come crashing down around her with one phone call?

Sitting alone in the gift shop, she glanced frantically about, wondering what to do. Her gaze skipped over porcelain tea sets, dolls in antebellum dresses, models of pirate ships, and other souvenirs related to Pearl Island's colorful past. Manag ing the gift shop at a bed and breakfast might seem an unlikely choice for a former tomboy who happened to come from one of the wealthiest families in New Orleans, but it had been a dream job for Chloe. It had made her part of the family who owned and ran Pearl Island.

And now her mere presence at the inn was about to bring disaster to the small, private island.

She had no choice. She had to stop the wedding!

Heart pounding, she hurried out of the gift shop into the mansion's central hall, which was wide enough to serve as a lobby. Afternoon light filtered in from the exterior rooms, glowing off the wood floors and dark paneling. More light poured through the soaring stained-glass window over the landing of the grand stairs. Guests frequently enjoyed the sit ting area before the hall's ornate fireplace, filled with flowers more often than flames in deference to the Texas heat, but now the Victorian wingback chairs stood empty.

Where was everyone?

The absence of guests didn't surprise her, since they'd closed the inn to anyone not in the wedding party. The grooms men who'd arrived that morning had elected to stay in the bun galows scattered about the island, no doubt to have privacy for the bachelor party. Luc's parents and grandmother weren't due to arrive until just before the rehearsal that evening. As for Chloe's mother, Diane had thankfully opted to stay at their family beach house on nearby Galveston Island, greatly reducing Chloe's stress during the last few days.

But where were Aurora, Allison, and Adrian, the two sisters and brother who owned Pearl Island? Where were Luc and her uncle, Scott, who'd married Allison twelve years ago? That was the year Chloe had visited the island for the first time, when she'd come looking for her uncle after running away from home.

She'd found more than her uncle. She'd found the stable, loving home she'd always craved.

Hearing laughter coming from the music room to the left of the grand stairs, she wove her way past the seating area, then drew up short in the doorway to stare in awe. Allison and Aurora had transformed the room into an exotic garden, exploding with tropical flowers. Pearl Island had hosted many weddings, but none of them had been this dramatic.

When Allison and the others had asked Chloe what she'd wanted, she'd told them nothing too girly. She'd wondered how they'd pull that off in a room that boasted frescos of cupids on the ceiling, gilded Rococo molding, gold silk draperies, and an ornately painted baby grand piano. What she saw now looked like the inside of a Fabergé egg. Fanciful, but bold.

What could be better for her and Luc? Her fiancé might look like a buff but clumsy computer nerd, but as the owner of a gaming software company, he had a streak of warrior and a dash of pirate.

Climbing a stepladder, Allison fussed with the greenery and flowers that covered the wedding arbor. A petite brunette with a love for all those tea sets and dolls she ordered for the gift shop, Allison would have done the whole room up in white tulle and pink roses if given free rein. That she'd put her personal taste aside had Chloe blinking back tears.

With her back to Chloe, Allison tipped her head to the side, studying the arbor. "I think it needs something. Rory?" she called to her sister. "See if you can find the white turtledoves."

"Alli, are you sure?" Aurora frowned. Her height and long riot of reddish-gold curls made her Allison's opposite physically as well as in personality. Even as the youngest of the St.

Claire siblings, Aurora's effervescent energy served as the driv ing force behind the inn. "Chloe said no froufrou."

"Turtledoves are not froufrou." Allison plopped her hands to her hips.

"Okay." Aurora sounded leery, but searched through one of the storage bins that held Allison's stash of decorations. "Here you go."

Taking the pair of white doves, Allison nestled them into the flowers at the very top of the arch, then leaned back to admire her work. "There, see? It's the perfect touch."

And it was. Seeing it, Chloe lost the battle with her tears.

"Okay, what next?" Allison asked. "Tying bows to the chairs?"

"No. Stop." A lump rose in Chloe's throat. "Don't do any thing else."

Allison and Aurora turned with puzzled frowns.

Chloe took a deep breath to force the words out. "I'm canceling the wedding."

"What!" the sisters gasped in unison.

"Chloe, what is it?" Allison started down ladder. "What's happened?"

"I –" Her mind raced for where to begin. "I need to find Luc. But just – just stop. Don't decorate anything else."

Shaking, she went back into the hall. "Luc! Where are you?"

Remembering he'd offered to help Adrian, the chef of the family, get ready for the rehearsal dinner, she crossed to the dining room on the opposite side of the grand stairs. In con trast to the whimsical frescoes in the music room, here King Neptune ruled the ceiling, stabbing his trident toward anyone sitting at the long wooden table.

"Luc!" She called when she found the room empty. Decid ing to try the kitchen, she headed toward the door to the but ler's pantry. The door swung open just as she reached it, and she stumbled back to avoid a broken nose.

"Whoa!" Luc grabbed her upper arm. "You okay?"

"Actually, no." Her voice caught at the sight of him look ing slightly rumpled but utterly sexy. He'd remembered to have his shaggy blond hair trimmed for the wedding, but he'd apparently forgotten to comb it that morning. The short-sleeved plaid shirt screamed geek, but the toned body inside came from hours at the gym. He frequently laughed that a complete lack of athletic ability didn't mean he couldn't lift weights.

"Did I hit you?" Concern drew his brows together over green eyes.

"No, it's not that." Her throat closed. "I don't know how to tell you this."

"What?" He frowned, clearly alarmed. "What is it?"

"I – I'm calling off the wedding." Her vision blurred with tears.

"W-what?" Luc's stomach dropped to the floor.

"I can't marry you tomorrow," she cried. "I'm so sorry!"

"Oh my God." The room spun as all the blood drained from his head.

"Grab him!" Someone shouted. Chloe's Aunt Allison, he thought. He felt hands on his arms, guiding him into a chair. Another hand shoved him forward. "Head down. Between your knees. Rory, find Scott!"

"On it!"

Luc focused on breathing as he stared at the hardwood floor between his feet. Chloe's watery hiccups came to him as if from the far end of a tunnel, along with her aunt's comfort ing coos. He wanted to sit up, but feared he'd pass out.

One thought rang through his brain: Chloe had changed her mind about marrying him.

He knew the endless decisions had frazzled her nerves these last few days, but she'd never hinted about having second thoughts. Just that morning, she'd been obsessing over the fit of her gown, because she'd lost five pounds since the fitting, and he'd told her she could show up for their wedding naked for all he cared, just as long as she showed up.

She'd wrapped her arms about his neck, laughing as she said, "Just try to stop me."

Couldn't she have said, "Hmm, about that, maybe we should talk about this whole marriage thing"? Had she said that? No. Instead, she'd kissed him in a way that had his body revved and ready for the wedding night – which now, apparently, wasn't going to happen. Because she'd changed her mind about marrying him!

Holy crap!

"What's going on?" a deep voice demanded. Chloe's uncle, Scott.

"Chloe's having a panic attack," Allison said. "She's talking nonsense about calling off the wedding."

"It's not nonsense!" Chloe insisted. "I have to cancel it!"

"Okay, everybody calm down," Scott said in his no-non sense manner. "Chloe sit."

Luc saw a pair of well-worn deck shoes appear beside his own white running shoes, then felt a hand rest on his back. "You okay to sit up?"

He sucked in a few deep breaths, let them out slowly, and straightened. The room took another spin, but settled. Scott's deceptively sinister-looking face came into focus.

Chloe sat in a chair a few feet away, her face buried against Allison's stomach while her aunt stroked her long, brown hair. The thought of her never letting him run his hands through the silky strands again constricted his chest.

"He doesn't look so good," someone said.

He turned and saw Adrian standing in the doorway to the butler's pantry. The first time he'd met the renowned chef, host of the cooking show *Caribbean Spice*, he'd felt a stab of jealousy knowing that Chloe, at age twelve, had had a crush on him. What female with a pulse wouldn't have crush on a man who exuded sex appeal from every pore? Wearing his black hair in a ponytail only emphasized a face that had female viewers all but swooning.

Luc's jealousy had died a quick death when he realized Adrian had a nurturing streak toward his younger sisters, and even Chloe, that made him a genuinely nice guy.

"Move." Adrian's wife, Jackie, poked him in the ribs from behind. Adrian stepped aside, allowing his spitfire of a wife to step into the room. Wavy dark hair surrounded her exotically intriguing face. The captain of a fully restored pirate ship that served as both her charter business and the couple's home, she stood with her feet braced slightly apart as if standing on a quarter deck. "You're right. He doesn't look good."

Great, Luc thought, rubbing a hand over his face. Just what he needed. An audience to watch Chloe ditch him.

"What's going on?" Aurora's husband, Chance, asked as he entered from the hall, looking every inch the tall, thin banker with his conservative blond hair and wire-rimmed glasses.

"Luc nearly fainted," Aurora told him.

Better and better, Luc nearly groaned. At least all the kids were playing in the private apartment in the basement.

"You're not going to pass out, are you?" Scott asked.

"No, I'm cool." A huge lie.

"Good." Scott slapped him on the shoulder before turning to his niece. "Okay, what gives?"

"DeeDee just called me," Chloe said, referring to her grandmother.

Okay, that explained a lot, Luc thought as she struggled to pull herself together. Any contact with her family, other than her uncle, sent Chloe into a tailspin. The fact that Chloe called her grandparents by their first names, John and DeeDee, struck him as odd, but he had yet to meet them. Maybe the lack of affection suited them. He may have known Chloe back in high school, since they both grew up in the French Quarter, but they'd lived in different worlds. His mother waited tables while his father played in a jazz band. His grandmother told fortunes in one of the voodoo shops. Her grandfather, on the other hand, owned LeRoche Shipping, a multi-billion-dollar com pany, while her grandmother reigned like a queen over New Orleans high society. How had someone as down-to-earth as Chloe come from that background?

"The worst thing in the world that could possibly happen has happened," Chloe announced.

Breath held, he watched her take in the circle of expectant faces with tear-filled hazel eyes while he tried to imagine the "worst thing that could possibly happen." Pestilence, plague, a force five hurricane, the complete collapse of the grid, the end of the world as currently known?

"John found out about the wedding," she cried. "He's de cided to come!" She slapped a hand over her mouth as if to call back the horror of her words.

That's it? Luc stared, dumbfounded.

Allison swung to her husband, eyes blazing. "Your *father* is coming to Pearl Island?"

"Hey." Scott's hands flew up as if she'd pulled a gun on him. "It's the first I've heard of it."

"Over my dead body!" Aurora looked like an Amazon ready for battle.

Luc listened in amazement as angry indignation erupted all around him. Even Chance, Aurora's normally calm husband, added his voice to the clamor of objections.

Finally, Luc let out a shrill whistle. The sound pierced the noise and silence fell.

"If I could get a word in..." He shifted toward Chloe. "Let me get this straight. You're calling off the wedding because your grandparents plan to crash it?"

"Not both of them. Only John. DeeDee is much too busy and very annoyed that I didn't give her ample warning." Chloe's voice took on the snooty tone she always used to mimic her grandmother. "How gauche of me to not give her a month, at least, to find a suitable dress. Whatever would the women of Galveston think if she showed up wearing last year's fashion?"

"Wait a second. She's not coming because she doesn't have time to buy a new dress?" He gaped, trying to imagine any thing less than a trip to the hospital keeping his grandmother away from tomorrow's ceremony. "Are you serious?"

"Yes, I'm serious!" Chloe sprang to her feet. Her trim body vibrated with tension as she paced, her waist-length hair swinging about her. "I don't *care* about DeeDee. I'm glad she's not coming! But John is!" She covered her forehead with both hands as if her brain might explode. "This is a disaster!"

"No, it's not." Allison pulled Chloe into her arms. "We won't let him ruin your wedding."

"We'll get a restraining order!" Aurora decreed.

"In less than" – Chance checked his watch – "eighteen hours?"

"We could always raid our stash of pirate costumes for pistols and swords," Adrian suggested dryly, but the gleam in his eyes told Luc he was only half kidding.

"I like the way you think." Jackie wiggled her brows at her husband.

"Oh God, *see*?" Chloe flung an arm toward Adrian and his wife. "I have to cancel the wedding."

"Not cancel." Allison cupped Chloe's face. "Postpone. When John gets here, we'll tell him he's mistaken, that there is no wedding, and wait for him to leave Galveston. Then we'll have the wedding."

"Wait a second." Luc held up a hand. "Can we talk about this? I understand all of you have reasons to dislike John Le Roche. I know this feud goes back generations. But come on. He's Chloe's grandfather. Don't you think he has a right to come to her wedding if he wants?"

"No!" Everyone shouted in unison.

"Okay." Luc raised his other hand. "It's just that I kind of have my heart set on getting married tomorrow."

"So did I." Chloe looked at him with heartbreak filling her eyes.

Luc scowled at their audience in frustration, then stood and faced Chloe. "Can I have a moment alone with you?"

Before Chloe could answer, Luc took her hand and started walking. She stumbled after him, out of the dinning room, across the hall, and into the music room. He didn't stop un til they stood before the arbor where they were supposed to exchange vows tomorrow. Turning to her, he took both her hands in his, and looked her hard in the eyes. "Do you mean that? That you want to marry me?"

"I do."

Relief washed over his face as he touched his forehead to hers. "I like the sound of those words."

Realizing he'd misunderstood the source of her panic, she wrapped her arms about his neck. "Oh Luc, I love you. That hasn't changed."

"Thank God." His mouth met hers in a kiss filled with the need for reassurance. Rising on her toes, she kissed him back, giving and needing the same. Passion flared quickly, intensified by fear of outside forces tearing them apart. Her body molded eagerly to his as he trailed desperate kisses over her cheek, her neck. His arms tightened as he held her hard against him, his cheek pressed against her hair. "Then let's get married. Tomor row. With or without your grandfather here."

"I can't!" She pulled back, forcing his arms to loosen. "Not after everything the St. Claires have done for me. They are my family. Not because we're distant cousins several times removed. If anything, that blood tie gives them reason to hate me, the way they hate my grandfather. Instead, they accepted me and gave me a home."

"And here I am, taking you away from this, back to New Orleans." He tucked a stray strand of her hair behind her ear. "Home of all your bad childhood memories."

"They weren't all bad. I had my Uncle Scott. Even so…" She managed a little smile. "I don't suppose you'd reconsider moving the headquarters for your company to Galveston."

"Someday, maybe."

"Never mind." With a sigh, she stroked his cheek. "New Orleans is your home, where your family lives, and you have wonderful childhood memories. Plus, you promised we'd visit Pearl Island a lot."

"We will. And we'll make new memories for you in New Orleans." He laid his hand over hers. "Before we can do that, though, we sort of need to get married. I'd like to do that tomorrow, as planned."

"No." She stepped away, breaking the embrace. "I can't repay everything these people have given me by bringing John LeRoche into their home. This may be a bed and breakfast, but it *is* their home. More than that, it's their heritage. I told you the story, Luc, about how my side of the family inherited Pearl Island generations back, then basically neglected it until the St. Claires, the rightful heirs, managed to buy it out from under my grandfather. They turned a dilapidated mansion into this." She turned in a circle, her arms held out. "John, however, has never, and will never fully give up. He wants –" She bit her lips, then lowered her voice to a whisper. "He wants the Pearl back."

His eyes widened, telling her he understood. She didn't mean the mansion, the island, or even an actual pearl. She meant the ghost inside the house.

Chloe knew that Luc, with a fortuneteller for a grandmother, had little trouble accepting the Legend of Pearl Island. A legend that dated back to before the Civil War.

"The story I told you, though, isn't the one I was told growing up." She let her gaze drift about the room, imagining all that had happened inside the house. "My side of the family described Henri LeRoche, founder of LeRoche Shipping, as a powerful man blinded by his love for a beautiful opera singer people toasted as the Pearl of New Orleans. The story painted Marguerite as a mercenary gold-digger who refused to settle for being a mere mistress."

"What?" Luc scowled in indignation.

"I know." Chloe smiled weakly, glad to see he'd taken Pearl Island – with *all* her inhabitants – into his heart. "A complete pack of lies, but it's important for you to hear this version, to understand just how greatly my family wronged Marguerite and all of her descendants. Until very recent years, this is the story most people in Galveston believed. Aurora, Allison, and Adrian managed to turn that around after they bought Pearl Island, but they grew up having everyone believe the worst of their great-great-great-grandmother."

She moved to the piano, seeing the room how it must have looked a hundred and fifty years ago, a room befitting an opera singer from New Orleans. "People believed Henri purchased this island and named it Pearl Island in her honor, then built this grand mansion as a wedding gift. Those two things are true, but from there, Henri convinced people he was the victim, a man tricked into marrying a faithless wife. He claimed that on the night Marguerite died, she was trying to run away with one of her numerous lovers."

"Captain Jack Kingsley," Luc filled in.

Chloe nodded, continuing her circuit of the room. "Henri claimed he tried to stop her on the stairs, implying that despite her infidelities, he loved her too much to let her go." She moved to the doorway, where she could see the stairs. "We think it happened on the landing. There, before the stained glass. The two struggled, and, according to him, she accidentally tripped and broke her neck as she tumbled down."

Glancing over her shoulder, she saw Luc raise a brow as if to say, *People actually believed that?*

"Then, crazed with grief, Henri raced to the ballroom on the third floor and the cannon on the balcony." Chloe faced him. "I ask you, what sort of man mounts a cannon on the top floor of his house?"

Luc frowned. "Hadn't the Civil War just broken out when all this happened?"

"Oh, I assure you, that cannon was already there. And I'll tell you what kind of man does that. The kind of man who hires pirates to transport goods for his shipping company. Doesn't exactly speak too well about my illustrious ancestors, does it?"

"Some people enjoy claiming pirates in their family." He smiled.

"Actually, Henri wasn't a pirate himself. He wasn't even a captain. He just did a lot of questionable business with unscrupulous men." When she thought about Henri LeRoche, she always pictured him being as handsome and heartless as her grandfather, John. Gazing upward, she pictured that storm-ravaged night so long ago. "He fired that cannon on Captain Kingsley's ship, the *Freedom*, without a qualm, knowing Jack would never fire back, not with Marguerite inside the house. Jack had no way of knowing she was already dead. Henri sent Captain Kingsley and several members of the crew to a watery grave along with the ship."

She lowered her gaze to Luc. "Have you ever wondered why Henri never faced charges of murder?"

"I assumed because he was a wealthy man with a lot of clout. That, and people in Galveston were a bit preoccupied with a Yankee blockade sitting in their harbor."

"He wasn't charged because he convinced people Captain Jack Kingsley, one of the few privateers brave enough to run that blockade, was a Yankee spy. That Marguerite, as his lover, had been passing him secrets." Her voice tightened with anger. "Galveston heralded Henri LeRoche as a hero and condemned Marguerite and Jack Kingsley as traitors to the South. His crowning sin, though – the thing I find the most unforgivable – is he disowned his own daughter, claiming she'd been fathered by one of Marguerite's 'numerous lovers.'" The tears threatened to return, so she blinked them back. "He left everything – his fortune, the shipping company, and Pearl Island

– to a male relative back in New Orleans, which is why my side of the family held it for generations."

"Don't tell me you feel guilty about that." He crossed the room to take her hands in his. "You had nothing to do with it."

"But my family perpetuated the lies. Some of them still do." When a tear slipped past her lashes, Luc brushed it from her cheek. "Marguerite couldn't have had all those affairs if she'd wanted to. This house, this 'wedding gift' was nothing but a trick to get Marguerite to marry a man who didn't love her at all. He wanted to own her. So he built a mansion on a private island as a gilded cage to lock her inside. This house was her prison."

"All because of a voodoo blessing at her birth." Luc pulled her into his arms.

"All because of a voodoo blessing." Resting her cheek on Luc's chest, she thought about the true story that started the night Marguerite was born.

The old voodoo woman who served as midwife at her birth discovered the mother, a New Orleans prostitute, planned to send the baby to an orphanage. Deciding anything was better than that fate, the voodoo woman blessed the child in a way that turned the baby into a good luck charm. Naturally, the mother decided to keep the child to see if the blessing worked. Which it did. The mother went from a prostitute in a brothel to the pampered mistress of a wealthy man.

As Marguerite grew into a woman, numerous people ben efited from association with her, having their fortunes grow as if by magic. Hearing this, the unscrupulous Henri LeRoche methodically set out to seduce her, not out of love, but out of greed.

"He beat her on their wedding night," Chloe said, tighten ing her arms about Luc's waist. "Did you know that?"

"No." Luc stroked her hair. "I knew she suffered a lot of physical and emotional abuse, but no, I didn't know that."

"The only affaire she ever had was with Captain Jack, and that was toward the end of her nightmare of a marriage. I've read her diaries. God…" Chloe shook her head. "She and Jack secretly loved each other for years. It's heartbreaking." Lifting her head, she looked up at him. "Can you imagine the torture of repeatedly being in the same room with someone you love so much it hurts, to look into their eyes, and see they feel the same, but not be able to say the words aloud?"

"I don't want to imagine it."

"Once they confessed how they felt, though, and Jack realized the hell Marguerite endured, he begged her to run away with him. She refused, putting her daughter before herself. She should have gone, Luc. She should have scooped up her daughter and escaped with the one man who loved her more than life itself."

"Hindsight's easy." He cupped her cheek.

Closing her eyes, Chloe nodded. No doubt if Marguerite had known what the future held, she would have fled. When Henri learned about his wife's infidelity, he beat her savagely and locked her away. She managed to get word to Jack. He'd been sailing to her rescue the night Henri murdered her by shoving her down the stairs.

The lovers had been so desperate to reach each other, their spirits refused to give up. Marguerite's ghost remained trapped in the house with Jack's ghost trapped amid the wreckage of his ship, the two of them searching for a way to reunite.

Opening her eyes, she willed Luc to understand. "Letting John come here would be like having Henri come back from the dead. John isn't physically abusive, but he is a greedy user, just like Henri. He doesn't care about my wedding. He just wants an excuse to get inside this house."

"To what gain?" Luc asked with an edge of impatience.

"To be near Marguerite." She stared at him, wondering how a man as genius-smart as Luc couldn't see that. "To steal some of her good luck."

"Okay –" Pulling away, Luc pressed fingertips to his forehead. "So, John spends a couple hours in the house, soaking up some of Marguerite's good luck. It's not like he can hurt her. I hate to point this out, because I know all of you accept Marguerite as simply part of the family, but, um, well – she's dead."

"*Lu uc.*" Chloe glanced about before lowering her voice. "We know that."

"What's your grandfather going to do? Try to steal her? He can't. She's a ghost."

A crashing sound came from the hall, like glass shattering on the floor.

Luc and Chloe stared at each other then dashed toward the sound. The rest of the family came running from the dinning room. Everyone turned about, looking for the source of the sound.

"Oh my God," Chloe gasped when she saw the mirror over the fireplace. Jagged cracks splintered the pieces that remained in the frame, while glistening shards littered the mantle and hearth.

A few heartbeats of silence passed as everyone stared.

"Okay, I concede," Luc finally said in a deceptively calm voice, his heart pounding in his chest. "Apparently Marguerite's not too happy about having John LeRoche in the house either."

"That wasn't Marguerite." Allison slowly shook her head, staring at the mirror. "She's never done anything like that."

"I agree," Scott said. "If she did things like that, all kinds of freaky things would have been happening when our side of the family owned this house."

"Then what happened?" Luc asked.

Several glances were exchanged before Aurora answered. "Captain Jack."

"I agree," Adrian said with a meaningful look at his wife. As a direct descendant of Captain Jack Kingsley, she'd provided the missing information that had convinced the state of Texas to do an underwater excavation of the shipwreck. In doing so, they had freed Captain Kingsley's ghost from the ship, allowing the ill-fated lovers to finally reunite.

For a while, the family thought the two spirits had moved on, but apparently Marguerite didn't want to leave now that her descendants occupied the house. On many occasions, when one of them needed help, Marguerite showed up, but never as anything more than a cold spot sometimes followed by a premonition. With her spirit hanging around, however, the family and guests frequently had amazing strokes of good luck.

As for Jack Kingsley, they'd had a few guests claim they'd glimpsed a dashing man wearing jackboots and a captain's coat wandering about, but he'd never done anything.

Adrian let out a breath. "Something tells me Captain Jack isn't going to take too kindly to having John LeRoche any where near Marguerite."

"What do you mean?" Luc felt a jolt of alarm. "Are we talking slamming doors? Pictures flying off the walls? Food platters crashing to the floor?"

"Maybe." Allison's eyes shifted back and forth, as if look ing for just such an occurrence. "We've never had to deal with Captain Jack."

"This is terrible." Chloe framed her face with her hands. "See? I told you. We have to call off the wedding."

"No." Luc slashed a hand through the air. "Absolutely not. We are getting married tomorrow, right here." He took Chloe's hands. "I love you, and I'm not going to let your grandfather or the temperamental ghost of a pirate –"

"Privateer," several voices chimed.

"Whatever!" Luc rolled his eyes. "I'm not going to let them postpone our wedding."

"There is an alternative," a husky female voice offered.

Luc turned to see Jackie smiling. "Don't change the date," she said with a bold gleam in her eyes. "Change the location."

"To where?" Chloe asked. "We'd never find a place to seat fifty people on such short notice?"

"Sure you will. The *Pirate's Pleasure.*"

~ ~ ~

Sitting in the captain's cabin of the fully restored ship, Chloe felt the vessel sway gently and heard the soothing creak of wood. She'd been aboard the majestic *Pirate's Pleasure* many times, but it never failed to make her heart swell with awe. To think she'd be getting married on the ship in less than an hour had terror and joy playing tug of war in her stomach.

Terror at the enormity of marriage. Joy at the thought of spending her life with Luc Renard.

Pressing a hand over the butterflies, she tried to let the quiet space soothe her jangled nerves. The hectic frenzy of moving the wedding and reception from the inn to the ship had ended for her, at least, when Allison pulled her down to the captain's cabin to help her dress. She imagined others still scurrying about, dealing with flowers, food, setting up chairs.

Here, though, the calmness settled about her as she sat in her wedding dress at a wooden table while Allison brushed her hair. The cabin served as the main living quarters for Adrian and Jackie. A bed piled with pillows was recessed into one wall, with curtains to close it off from the rest of the room. The ta ble in the middle served alternately as a desk and private dining area, while custom wood cabinets, shelves, and cubbies made good use of wall space. The wall sconces and the wrought iron light hanging from the beams added to the nostalgia and romance, while mullioned windows filled the aft wall, offer ing an unobstructed view to the mouth of the cove. Sunlight sparkled off the gentle azure waves as palm trees swayed in the afternoon breeze.

The day couldn't be more perfect for a wedding.

"I can't thank you enough, Alli," she said, holding her head still while her aunt ran a brush through the full length of her hair. "I feel as if you didn't just give me one amazing wedding. You've given me two."

"You might want to wait until we've actually had a wedding to say that." Allison reached for the veil lying on the table and settled the headband into place. "I just hope Rory managed to finish everything before the guests started arriving."

"When has Rory ever failed once she set her mind to something?"

"True." Allison laughed.

"I don't know how you managed to pull this off, though. Not only moving all the decorations, but calling all the guests and telling them to come an hour early."

"Well, it helped that all the guests from out-of-town stayed at the inn last night."

"The invited guests, anyway." Chloe's stomach churned. "Has there been any sign of him?"

"Not yet." Allison secured the veil with a few bobby pins.

"Do you think we'll cast off before he gets here?"

"We're good to go the minute Adrian loads the last of the food."

"God, I've been so much trouble for you."

"Stop that, Chloe." Allison kissed the top of her head. "This has been a joy for all of us. Don't you know how much we love you?"

Twisting in the chair, Chloe smiled up at her. "Thank you." Realizing her aunt had finished with the veil, she rose and enveloped her in a hug. "I love you so much. All of you, but you especially." Emotions swelled, hot and sweet. "I wish you were my mom."

"I *am* your mom." Allison's arms tightened about her.

"Speaking of, is she still angry about having to get up so early to help?"

"Don't worry about Diane." Allison fussed with the veil. "Scott knows how to handle his sister."

"That he does." Chloe laughed, then sobered. "You two have done so much for me. If I hadn't had you ... I don't know what I would have done."

"Stop it, you'll make me cry." Alli shook a finger at her. "And don't you dare cry. You'll mess up your makeup."

"Is it done?" Chloe nearly danced in place.

"Almost." Allison grabbed a brush and dusted on a bit more blush. "There. Now close your eyes and step right over here, in front of the mirror."

Chloe let her aunt guide her.

"Ready?" Allison asked close to her ear.

"More than." Her nerves tangled.

"Open you eyes," Allison whispered.

Chloe let her eyelids lift slowly. In the full-length mirror before her she saw a stunning woman dressed in a simple V-necked, cream gown that draped without fuss along her curves to the tops of her slippers before it fanned out into a small train. In a concession to the warm coastal weather, a lighter-weight, but not-quite-sheer fabric made up the shoulders, long sleeves, and upper back. The veil, as quiet as a whisper, would float to her waist all the way around when the front was lowered into place. For now, it only trailed down her back. Her sable hair fell thick and straight past her shoulders to curl gently at her waist.

The image staring back at her looked timelessly regal.

"Oh, Alli!" She raised a hand and touched the mirror. Since leaving behind her tomboy days, she'd learned a fair number of feminine skills, but she'd never looked this elegant. "Is that re ally me?"

"That's you." Allison stood behind her, dressed in a com plementing gown of peach to coordinate with the tropical flowers. They made a pretty pair, with Chloe a couple of inch es taller, but both of them dark-haired and beaming. Allison grinned. "Luc is going to swallow his tongue."

"I hope so." Chloe laughed. "I've kind of put him through a lot these last few weeks. I'd hate for him to take one look at me and change his mind."

"Not a chance. Besides, I have this theory that all the stress leading up to the wedding is a good test for a couple. It can make what comes after seem like a breeze."

"Nice theory. Too bad it doesn't work out that way for all couples. My mom's had four weddings, and look at how they've worked out."

Allison turned her around so they stood face-to-face. "You are not your mother."

"I hope not." Chloe searched her aunt's eyes. "I want what you have with Uncle Scott. If you have any words of wisdom..."

Allison hesitated, then sighed. "Okay, if I have one bit of advice, it's this: Be nice."

Chloe frowned.

Allison took one of her hands. "Respect and common courtesy are every bit as important in a marriage as love. I see people treat those they love desperately, madly, passionately with less patience than they'd show the clerk in a convenience store. They act as if being married gives them a free pass to say awful, hurtful things because of course they'll be forgiven. It's not okay. Ever."

"I think you just described my family." Chloe bowed her head.

"Then never vent your frustrations with life by snapping at the people you love. It's not nice." Allison lifted Chloe's chin. "Be nice to Luc. He's a good man who comes from a very close and loving family. I have a feeling he's going to be very nice to you."

"I hope so." As they hugged again, the engines roared suddenly to life beneath their feet. Chloe pulled back with a gasp. "Are we casting off?"

"Sounds like it."

"Is it time?" She glanced at a clock. "We're leaving early. Why are we leaving early?"

Fearing she knew the answer, Chloe hurried to the aft windows. Staring through the mullioned glass, she saw only water and beach since the ship had been docked with the bow toward the island. Slowly, though, the ship turned, making a wide arch. She knew Jackie's crew planned to run on engine power until they cleared the cove, then they'd cut the engines and unfurl just enough sails to provide a quiet, gentle ride during the ceremony.

As the bow swung toward the mouth of the cove, more of the island came into view. The land rose, covered with a tangle of oaks and palms, until she saw the Pearl Island Inn perched atop the highest point. Built of native Texas pink granite, it seemed to challenge God and nature to try and wear it down. Fanciful gargoyles snarled down from corners of the multiple angles of the roof while a steep spire stabbed upward from the turret.

And there, striding down the trail that led from the mansion to the pier, was John LeRoche, a tall, formidable figure of a man in an impeccable dark suit.

With a gasp, she pulled back, as if he could somehow reach out across the water, into the ship, and snatch her back.

Glancing over, she found Allison frozen, her face pale.

"Are you okay?" Chloe reach sideways and took her aunt's hand.

"Yes, it's just ... I've never seen him in person." Allison's gaze remained riveted on John LeRoche. "Isn't that odd? He's my father-in-law, my children's grandfather, and I've never even met him."

"I know." Chloe squeezed her aunt's hand. After Scott and Allison became engaged, Scott patched things up a little bit with DeeDee, but John still wouldn't have anything to do with the son who had disowned him.

"All I've ever seen are pictures," Allison said.

"Not quite the same, is it?" Chloe watched her grandfather stride out onto the dock. John always looked so handsome and charming in photos. In person, however, he frequently exuded exactly the energy he did now, that of a man who did not take kindly to being challenged. He came to stand at the end of the pier, fists on hips as he watched the *Pirate's Pleasure* slip away. She wrapped her arms about herself.

"Don't worry." Allison moved closer to drape an arm about Chloe's waist. "He can't hurt you or any of us. Scott won't let him. As for the inn, we hired a security guard to tell anyone who shows up today that we we're closed. He won't get inside."

"I know. It's just ..." Chloe felt a chill go through her. She knew it couldn't be a ghostly cold spot, they were too far away from the inn for that. "I just realized something. This is what Marguerite wanted. To get away from the man who caused her so much pain, to sail away from it all and be with the man she loved. She never got to do that."

"No." Allison's head rested on her shoulder. "But you do."

"Yes." A smile started deep inside Chloe, slowly warming her, as she watched her grandfather grow smaller and smaller. The smile finally blossomed over her with a sense of victory. "Yes, I do."

An Hour Later

Luc couldn't believe he'd just been married on a pirate ship. The ceremony had passed in such a blur, he half wondered if it had happened at all. They'd decided to have the wedding in the ship's dining room, to be out of the wind. Somehow Allison and Aurora had worked their magic to give the rough-hewn space the feel of a cozy chapel, with rows of chairs where rug ged trestle tables normally sat.

He remembered standing before an arbor with his grooms men beside him along with Chloe's cousins Derrick and Rafe, the ten-year-old identical twins serving as ring bearers. He'd had a bank of flowers behind him and a crowd of people before him, making him feel uncomfortably on display.

He remembered smiling at his parents and his grandmother as they'd been ushered down the aisle to their seats. They'd all toned down their normal Bohemian attire a tad, but not enough to erase their irrepressible, and irresistible, personalities. His grandmother, grinning impishly, had given him a little finger wave, which he'd returned as subtly as possible.

He remembered an usher showing Chloe's mother, a very striking and stylish woman, to her seat. She bore a startling resemblance to Chloe with nearly identical features, all ruined by her sour expressions and impatient body language.

He remembered little Nicole, Scott and Allison's daughter and the youngest of the children, coming down the aisle with a basket of flower petals. She'd looked adorable in ruffles and ribbons, her brow dimpled in concentration as she dropped one petal at a time.

He remembered the bridesmaids including Aurora and Allison.

Then the music swelled.

Everyone stood and turned.

And Chloe appeared on her uncle's arm.

That's where all memory stopped. Along with his heart. She stole his breath away. Her face lit with a devastating smile when she saw him standing at the altar in a tux – looking presentably neat he hoped. Happiness like nothing he'd ever felt before washed over him. He hadn't stopped smiling since, except for the brief moment after the minister had said, "You may now kiss the bride." Actually, a flicker of memory told him he'd been smiling – and laughing – as his lips met Chloe's. But then, he sort of recalled her laughing too.

He looked down now and found her smiling still as they reached the top of the hatch stairs and stepped out onto the sun-washed deck of the ship. He wanted to scoop her into his arms, but heard the wedding party clamoring up the steps behind him. All the guests followed, pouring up through the hatch until they filled the main deck between the quarterdeck and forecastle.

"We did it!" Chloe cheered and threw her arms around his neck.

"We did!" He twirled her about, then set her on her feet. "Now, it's time to party."

"That it is, sir." She tapped him on the chin with a sassy grin, finally the Chloe he knew: the bold, vivacious woman he'd fallen in love with, not the stressed-out worrier who'd had him off-balance the last few days.

He looked about for what to do and where to go first. In the bar area, a protected spot up against the forecastle, Adrian had set up a buffet. A masterpiece of a wedding cake, with tropical flowers cascading down the multiple tiers, com manded center stage on a table. The ship's well-trained crew, dressed in pirate garb, passed through the crowd with trays of champagne. The dichotomy of pirates and champagne made Luc laugh.

"Happy?" Chloe asked him, as people surrounded them offering congratulations.

"Oh, yeah." His face felt permanently frozen in a wide grin. Between handshakes and hugs, he managed to smile back at his new bride. "You?"

"Ecstatic. Except ..." Her brow dimpled unexpectedly. "I think we're supposed to go back down to take photos, then back up here to cut the cake."

"I have a better idea." He looked around at the crowd of people still waiting to offer congratulations, thought about the last few days in which he'd barely had a second alone with Chloe, and grabbed her hand. "Come with me," he said and pulled her toward the steps to the forecastle.

"Luc! What are you doing?" Laughing, she followed him, not even trying to resist. "We need to do photos."

"We will." He continued up the steps and gave thanks when he found the small forward deck free of people. With Chloe's hand in his, he walked to the bow pulpit before he stopped and turned to face the ship. "I just need a chance to take it all in."

Admiration joined his elation at the sight before him. Fine ly carved red and yellow rails edged all three decks of the black-hulled vessel, with blue water all around. On the quarterdeck across from him, he saw a muscular, bald-headed black man grinning as he gripped the wheel. Luc wondered if they'd let him take the helm for a few minutes later, after the photos and cake-cutting. Lifting his gaze, he admired the masts. With so few sails open, they rose like bare crosses against the blue sky. "It must be quite a sight to see her under full sail."

Watching Luc's face, Chloe smiled at his boyish glee. "Would you like that?"

"Oh yeah." He lowered his gaze to smile at her. "Someday. Maybe on one of our visits back."

"Hang on." Pulling away, she stepped to the rail overlooking the main deck and cupped her hands to her mouth. "Ahoy, Ti."

"Ahoy?" the dark-skinned man called back.

"What are you doing?" Luc chuckled as he came to stand beside her.

"You'll see." She gave him a sideways wink before calling back to the quarterdeck. "What say you to unfurling more canvas?"

Down on the main deck, faces turned back and forth, like fans at a tennis match, their excitement palatable.

"I think it a splendid day to feel some wind in our sails," Ti shouted back in his heavy Caribbean accent. He always enjoyed playing things up for the passengers. "If ya be up for a bit of speed."

"I'm always up for that." Chloe search the crowd until she spotted Jackie standing with Adrian and the rest of the family. "Well, captain?"

A grin split Jackie's face. A moment of perfect understanding passed between them before Jackie nodded. Jackie more than anyone knew how much this moment must mean to Luc, a man who had only sailed the seas virtually on his computer. As successful as Luc might be with his computer gaming company, nothing beat the real thing.

Jackie raised a hand. "I declare Luc Renard captain for the day."

"Seriously?" Luc's eyes danced with excitement as he looked at Chloe.

She smiled up at him, loving him more than ever for his childish exuberance coupled with that quick brain of his. He saw the world as no one else did, filled with a myriad of op portunities and adventures.

"Seriously," she told him.

"All right." Busting with enthusiasm, he cupped his hands and called out orders to Ti, the first mate. Chloe could only marvel. The man may have never captained a ship in real life, but he'd written enough pirate gaming scenarios to know his sails. Since Jackie had installed remote controls, the canvas be gan to unfurl in proper sequence, filling with wind. The ship dug in and plowed through the waves.

Pressing her hand to top of her head to hold the veil in place, Chloe laughed. "Is that what you wanted?"

Luc pulled his eyes away from the billowing sails to smile at her. "Next to marrying you? Oh, yeah."

"After all I've put you through, it's the least I could do."

He cupped her face so he could stare deep into her eyes. "You are worth every bit of it."

"One last treat." Grinning, she pulled him back to the bow pulpit. "Stand and enjoy."

"Wow," he said with the wind full in his face, the water rushing beneath him. "Just wow."

"Eloquently put." Chloe laughed.

When she tried to step away to give him room, he caught her about the waist. "Not so fast. Come here, you."

He pulled her to stand in front of him so they both faced the wind, his arms wrapped about her waist.

Chloe smiled, breathing the moment in. "The first time Jackie took me sailing, I stood right here and understood com pletely why Captain Jack called his ship the *Freedom*. That's how it feels, isn't it? Like pure freedom."

"It is." Luc settled her more snuggle against him. The rhythm of the ship reverberated deep in her belly, making her deliciously aware of the hard male body behind her.

"We're so lucky, Luc." Tipping her head, she smiled up at him. "To have the freedom to be together."

"Thinking about Marguerite and Jack?" He kissed her forehead.

"Quite a bit today."

"Then let's do something for them, make one more vow."

"What?"

"From this day forward, let's make the most of every mo ment we're given."

"I love you, Luc." She reached up to cup his face. "Or should I say, Captain Renard."

"I love you too." He smile as well. "Mrs. Renard."

"Oh my goodness. That's me."

"That's you. Finally." With the wind whipping about them, the ship pounding beneath them, he lowered his head and sealed their vow with a kiss.

Down Under

by Karen Tintori

Karen Tintori is an internationally bestselling author of fiction and nonfiction whose novels have been translated into more than twenty-five languages. Her books cover genres from historical narrative nonfiction to mystical thrillers. She earned her B.A. in journalism from Wayne State University, lives in Michigan, and holds dual U.S.-Italian citizenship.

Elizabeth Simms: Carole was quite the clever one, handing me May Sarton's At Seventy – *"a lovely little journal by a woman nearly as crazy about gardening as you are." Sarton is indeed a splendid writer, sharing so much more than the life cycle of her white peonies or of her aging, seventies and then eighties self. How I savor her wisdom on this growing old business. She and I could have been fine friends. I tucked her poem,* A Thought, *into the frame of my bureau mirror. Here's how it ends: "Brute power/ Is not superior/To a flower."*

Peter's hand dove for his pocket as his nostrils contorted in an explosive sneeze. The small reception area reeked of wet umbrellas, peonies and over-cooked coffee, although it was barely eight in the morning. He frowned at the bright pink flowers, no doubt snipped by some middle-aged secretary. He bet she hummed as she harvested them. Like Elizabeth used to back when he'd found it charming. Back when he'd first moved into her house. Back in Adelaide.

"Mr. Simms?"

Peter jerked his gaze from the jar of peonies to the man charging toward him, hand outstretched, projecting the energy of at least one full pot of coffee. His face was tanned and weathered and dominated by startling green eyes and a fleshy nose.

"Matthew Brighton." His handshake was pleasantly painful. "Please, come inside."

Matthew Brighton was the only attorney Peter had considered to handle his divorce. Brighton didn't advertise. He didn't need to. Everyone in Detroit knew his name.

A fresh legal pad was slanted across the center of Brighton's desk; an expensive black fountain pen set atop that, cap removed. Brighton sat back into his chair, flipping through the pages of the preconference questionnaire Peter had mailed back to him last week. The upper left corners were creased below the staple, the papers softly rumpled, clearly reviewed. Peter took a deep breath, convinced he'd made a wise choice.

"I see you and your wife were married in 1976." Brighton glanced up. "No minor children."

"None, no." Peter slowly exhaled. "Elizabeth has a daughter from her first marriage. But she was already away at university when we first met."

"So no child support…" The nib of Brighton's pen scritched across the lined yellow pad as he began jotting notes. "How do you make your living, Mr. Simms?"

"I'm a retired engineer. Thirty-three years at Ford, then took the buyout. I do a bit of mentoring down at Wayne State."

"And your wife – also retired?"

"You could say that. Last time she worked outside the house was –" He cocked his head to study the wide window to his left, as if the raindrops splattering the glass held the answer. "I'd say a good twenty years ago. Maybe more."

Brighton studied the questionnaire, found Elizabeth Simms's age. His pupils narrowed as he calculated the two-de cade-plus span in this May-December divorce. Elizabeth was the December.

"And what type of work did your wife do?"

"She worked in a florist's shop."

"I gather she's been drawing Social Security for a few years now?"

"Oh, Lord, no." Peter gave a small snort and picked at the crease pressed down the front of his suit pants. "She didn't accumulate enough work credits. Never did much of anything very productive at home, either." His lips flattened in a straight line that curved downward at each end. "No, I take that back. She did garden."

Brighton looked up. "You haven't listed any car loans or leases – nor credit cards. Do you or your wife owe any out standing debts?"

Peter shook his head. "Not a dime. I never believed in it. Pay the credit card bill the day it hits my mailbox. Paid cash for every car I've ever owned, from the first. Even with the A Plan from Ford. Only loan I ever took was the mortgage on my house, and that's been free and clear since 1987. Put extra against the principle most months and got that one paid off early."

"No debts." Brighton's pen pressed noisily across the pa per as he continued. "Now as to marital assets, you've listed a house in Troy, several banks accounts, a car, your pension…"

"All of which will be going into my name." Peter sat for ward, as if to supervise his attorney's notations. "We've already come to terms on the property and bank accounts. The division is fair. I've made certain my wife has everything she needs."

Brighton studied his client for a moment and Peter held his gaze. “In that case, with regards to the marital home, we’ll prepare a quit claim deed for your wife to sign, or you can file a copy of the divorce judgment with the register of deeds to have her name removed.”

Brighton flipped over the filled page and poised his pen at the first line of a fresh yellow sheet. “Mr. Simms, what is the reason for the divorce?”

Peter shifted in his chair. “For some time now, Elizabeth has entertained plans to return to Australia. To spend her waning years with her daughter and grandson. To return to her – our – roots.” Peter lifted his chin. “I don’t share those dreams.”

As his attorney regarded him with an expression of neutral attention, Peter Simms began recounting the progressive breakdown of a long and loving marriage, the amicable parting of ways, the noncontentious resolution of the sort of irreconcilable differences that inevitably blossom in a May-December marriage when the wife reaches eighty-one, beset by falls and fractures and frailties, while the husband is still a robust racquetball player of fifty-seven with unchanged drives and urges and needs. He recounted the restraints on a shared social life when the wife gets wobbly and wields a rubber-footed walker to steady her gait while the husband runs six miles a day at the club on a treadmill set to maximum incline and holds season tickets to the Tigers and Red Wings.

As he recounted the limits on their physical intimacy, Peter turned toward the insistent thwack of the rain now slapping the window and found himself swamped by the sudden memory of the first time he and Elizabeth had made love, back when Elizabeth’s eyes were clear and blue and her hair was sun-kissed and so long that it skimmed the dimples punctuating the curve right above the swell of her buttocks. Peter was an engineering student who had answered an ad for a room with kitchen privileges and then talked the new widow into halving his rent in exchange for yard work and the sort of odd jobs around a house that a husband might do. Some two years later, he had run in from the hardware shop and straight to the bathroom, unwrapping a new rubber flapper to silence the toilet that kept hissing all night, only to shock the hell out of himself, and more so Elizabeth, who had just pushed open the frosted glass shower door to reach for her towel.

She screamed, he screamed, and the towel fell from her grasp as the rubber stopper went flying, packaging and all, and then the two of them fell to the floor in a heap of giggles. The nervous laughter gave way to hilarity as they held on to one another, gasping for breath, trying to get to their feet only to slip to their knees in hysterics once again until they found themselves prostrate on the narrow bathroom floor, their laughter trickling to soft moans and hard kisses.

They'd thumbed their noses at convention and especially at Elizabeth's disapproving daughter, Grace, and one year later they'd danced a little jig up the aisle to "Mrs. Robinson," the cheeky recessional for their garden wedding. Elizabeth read through the classics, took up flower arranging, and toiled in her gardens, and Peter landed a choice position in vehicle operations at Holden Motors. In the evenings, he tinkered with a plan for improving upon General Motor's new catalytic converter, an idea that sparked the attention of Henry Ford II and a lucrative offer to join the automotive giant in Michigan as part of the team developing a small car proposed by Lee Iaccoca to replace the Pinto.

"Has your wife retained counsel?"

Startled from his reverie, Peter redirected his focus, pressing the small of his back against his chair to sit straighter in his seat.

"As you can see –" He gestured toward Brighton's legal pad. "We've settled it all neatly, so no, there's no need." He leaned forward. "Is there?"

"No. As long as she isn't contesting, we can prepare and file all the papers."

"How long would you project this entire process will take?" Peter cleared his throat. "Now that we've sorted everything out, my wife is anxious to get situated with her family in Australia."

Brighton leaned back in his chair, tossing the chunky pen onto the legal pad. "At least sixty days, but not much more." His dark brows drew together, estimating. "The hearing could be set as soon as early September. You'd appear in court and then could finalize everything that same day."

Sixty days. September. Perhaps before Elizabeth's birthday...

"Theoretically," Brighton continued, checking his watch, "if we get the papers drafted today, we could file them and have your wife served as soon as tomorrow."

Peter's fingers felt stiff with cold as he took Brighton's proffered pen and signed the retainer agreement. *Tomorrow, then.* He looked quizzically at the white paper, the black ink, and blinked. His name staring up at him seemed as strange as a misspelled word.

"I am sorry about your circumstances, Mr. Simms. As an attorney *and* counselor – and I do take my role as a counselor quite seriously – I will usually advise my divorce clients to con sider working at saving their marriages, but in this case…"

Peter raised his shoulders in a shrug of resignation. "If this tells you anything, Mr. Brighton, we've been here in the States now for more than thirty-six years and my wife still flies the Commonwealth Blue Ensign out front beneath the Stars and Stripes. I'm afraid Elizabeth is a transplant that never took."

Exiting Brighton's office suite, animated now by a young male receptionist and several clients perched expectantly on the leather sofas, Peter made a beeline for the men's room he had spotted earlier at the far end of the hall. He opened the hot water faucet full bore and welcomed the rush of pum meling heat into his chilled fingers. Avoiding his image in the mirror above the sink, he soaped his hands and scrubbed them together, raising a thick lather as he sang the "Happy Birthday" song to himself – Dr. Oz touted it as the requisite length for a thorough hand washing.

~ ~ ~

The rain had tapered now to a steady drizzle, and the squeaky slap of the windshield wipers served as a metronome as he drove, regulating the rhythm of Peter's heart beats, mea suring his breaths, marking off the miles home.

Can I get rid of it by September? He pictured the failed parade of realtors' signs peppering his front lawn this past spring, pic tured Carole throwing her hands in the air when yet another week ended without a nibble. "Put in a French drain already, divert the rainwater from the side of the house and maybe you'll keep the basement and storm cellar dry long enough to sell." When he flat out refused to rent a back hoe and trample Elizabeth's peony gardens so he could hack out a six- by six- by six-foot drainage pit at the back of the yard and fill it with peb bles, Carole quietly watched *Dancing With the Stars* with Eliza beth, bathed her charge and tucked her into bed, loaded up little "Coop" and drove off to Arizona that night without him.

"No, no, Carole will be back soon," he told the neighbors, to convince them as much as himself that Elizabeth's caretaker had gone out west only for a short family emergency.

Yet, here he was again, for the third time in his life – for the second time with this second set of neighbors – imagining himself the object of curious smiles and salacious whispers. Once Carole began staying the night, he knew their eyebrows raised at exactly what kind of care the comely blond caretaker might be giving to whom. If they drove past as he carted the trash to the curb, or collected the mail from the mailbox stand across the road, they'd wave their hellos or stop to inquire after Elizabeth. But he knew they wondered, as they walked their dogs past his house each morning and after they tucked in their children each night, why the caretaker's yellow Mini Cooper never moved from the center of his driveway. Just as he knew they were gossiping now about all the reasons Carole's car was long gone.

Peter shook his head, dismissing the neighbors. He had more worrisome problems to mull at the moment than the halogen searchlight of public attention. He'd heard not a peep from Carole, not even after he'd left her two messages last week that the back garden looked like a tornado had uprooted most of it, but the damned French drain was in the ground and pumping like a charm, all forty feet of buried plastic PVC pipe running circles around the gazebo and discharging sump water, just like she said, into the pebbled pit.

Much more pressing, as early as tomorrow, a process serv er would be ringing his front doorbell looking for Elizabeth.

But Elizabeth was already gone.

~ ~ ~

Peter drew a thick red X across the date on the kitchen wall calendar. Sixty days. Two months. Eight weeks. He had no choice but to get through them one by one, crossing off a square each night the same as if a European vacation waited at the end of the parade of hatch marks marching toward Labor Day. All it took now was time. But time was making his mind snap.

"Now close your eyes and keep them tight and tomorrow will be here before you know it," his father would say, retucking the duvet around him when he couldn't fall to sleep before a big test or his birthday or a holiday. "Time has a mind of its own, just like you do." He would tap Peter on the forehead to drive home his point. "It stretches and it twists and it snaps back and it springs forward very much like the big fat blue rubber strop on your slingshot. It is a mysterious thing that goes slow when you want it to go quickly, and quickly when you'd much rather it go slow. And you can't change a thing about that, no matter how many times a night you peek at your bedside clock."

Though his days were occupied with packing up and sorting out and keeping the house in tip-top shape in anticipation of the realtor's call, July and all of August trickled by. Peter's only company was CNN and the soft and steady click of his digital bedside clock as it ticked off the minutes until the divorce hearing.

Many nights he woke to nature's call, startled anew that Carole's side of the bed was cold, sheets smooth. Most mornings, from decades' habit, he would start up a kettle for Elizabeth's tea before he remembered. And each time his phone rang he jumped, holding his breath as he squinted anxiously at the caller display.

In the few weeks since the latest FOR SALE sign went up and he confided to the neighbors that Elizabeth had gone to Australia to live with Grace and that he had decided to downsize to a condo somewhere warm, he'd finally experienced the community embrace he had always craved. He fielded more dinner invitations and had more genuine conversations with the folks at his end of the sprawling block than in all his years on Greentree. Life was one big irony. Now that he was leaving, he almost wished he could stay.

Carole would never stay. And now he couldn't either.

His cell phone trilled, once again triggering an adrenaline burst through his gut. He grabbed for it. Squinted. *Suzanne.*

"You're not answering my texts!" she scolded. "And I've got possible good news. The young pregnant couple wants to bring the three sets of parents tonight –"

What the... His heart was pumping so fiercely his eardrums throbbed. He squinted at the notifications panel on his phone. *Why in blazes hadn't he heard the texts come in?* He thumbed past Suzanne's messages. What if Carole had texted him and he'd missed those, too?

"Sorry. I haven't a clue why I didn't hear them." *No. Nothing from Carole.* "So." He rubbed his eyes. "When would you like me to be absent?"

He'd head out this very second, stay gone as long as she told him. Hell, he'd even turn cartwheels across his roof in the rain if Suzanne asked him to. That lovely lady had already earned her sales commission and then some, simply sitting in his backyard gazebo behind her oversized sunglasses, filling out the sales listing paperwork on the very afternoon that Brighton had advised him the process server might make his first attempt. Kismet, it was. Peter smiled, mentally replaying how effortlessly everything had panned out.

"Let me run inside for a minute while you get started and I'll brew up some iced tea," he said to Suzanne, rising from his vantage spot overlooking the side driveway. Halfway to the sliding glass door at the kitchen, he turned back. "Oh, Suzanne –" Then he drew his eyebrows together as if something had just occurred to him. "If that messenger I'm expecting should show up with that envelope while I'm inside, you can take it for me. Just tell him you're my wife."

When he returned, he made a show of his thirst, downing two tall glasses of tea as Suzanne scribbled away. And the split second he caught the glint of a car nosing onto his driveway he jumped up –" Would you excuse me a minute?" Turned on an apologetic smile –" Too much tea." Then ducked inside, and stalled just long enough for Suzanne to pretend to be his wife.

And now she had an interested buyer. He should be elated, but how could he? He'd done everything Carole had asked of him and more, and she was killing him by inches with her pro tracted silence.

His cell phone trilled again. *BRIGHTON LAW.* Peter sucked down a bracing breath.

"Mr. Simms. It's Matthew Brighton. Just wanted to let you know that your divorce hearing is docketed for next Thursday, September seventh at 8:30 a.m. You'll be receiving notice from the court, likely in today's mail, but I also like to call and con firm that you and your wife still consent to proceed."

Docketed. Peter closed his eyes, calculating that there were but nine more boxes to cross from his calendar. *An end date to the end game.*

He found his voice. "Yes. Absolutely. 8:30 a.m., September seventh. And you did say that my wife does not have to ap pear? With her mobility issues and all –"

"That's correct. She's been served with the papers and we've entered her default. You and I will appear before Judge O'Brien and have this wrapped up before noon."

"One more thing. Out of curiosity, Mr. Brighton." Peter cocked his right shoulder, winching the phone against his ear as he flipped the calendar and circled September seventh with his red marker. "In Michigan, how soon after a divorce can someone apply for a marriage license?"

"The same day. The two Clerks' offices are steps away from each other." Peter could hear his attorney rustling papers. "There's a three-day waiting period to marry after applying for the license. But the Clerk has the discretion to waive that time frame for good reason."

"Very well." Peter began opening the blinds on all the win dows facing out onto the back gardens. "I'll be there on the seventh before 8:30."

He made a quick visual of the kitchen and living room, checking that he had left nothing out of place, and then flipped a switch to fire up the tiny fairy lights he'd hung like lace across the gazebo. Couldn't hurt, especially if the young couple and the parents were still here as the sun set. Elizabeth truly had fashioned an enchanting, peaceful space back there, hadn't she?

Backing out of the garage, Peter decided he would shoot downtown to Motor City Casino to kill a few hours. He punched speed dial and willed Carole to finally answer.

~ ~ ~

Carole circled onto the block, her slender fingers so completely curled around the steering wheel at the ten o'clock and two o'clock posts that her peridot-polished nails disappeared into the pads of her palms. Her stomach cramped as the Mini Cooper ate up the road toward the Simms's house, even though she knew Peter was at the club and would be for at least another hour. That she could stake her life on. But the stake she'd come to see for herself was the one he had sworn was in the ground, big, white and made of wood, with a realtor's FOR SALE sign hanging from it.

Near his end of the block she slowed to circumvent the gaping maw of the recycling truck angling across the road. She glared at the attendant slinging two emptied bins pell-mell onto opposing driveways and pressed hard on her horn. *Jerk.* Same guy who cracked Peter's bin this winter, slamming it at the icy driveway like that.

Peter. Last night was the first she had spoken to him in nearly three months, though she had pounced on every message within seconds of his call. No matter how tensely her gut twisted to respond with silence, no matter how many weeks he languished, she had to be certain they had any chance at a future. Peter had to come around to her way of thinking. Her way of thinking was sound, sensible and fair to all of them. The only plan that would work.

So she had let him stew, let him believe she was two thousand miles away in Arizona when she was actually holed up at Rory's place in Ann Arbor, barely an hour away, waiting for the voicemail message she needed to hear.

But now…

She was dumbfounded. Elizabeth had up and left? Asked Peter for a divorce, took her share and flew off to live with her daughter in Australia? she thought as the recycling truck passed her. My God, the woman depleted her strength getting in and out of the car for a trip to the doctor. Carole shook her head. It made no sense. Yet Peter vowed it was God's truth. The divorce was all but final. The house was all but sold.

And Elizabeth is gone*? He didn't even give me a chance to say goodbye.*

From three houses out she spotted the sign, partially ob scured by the recycling truck now idling at Peter's driveway. The Jerk began his attack on the jumble of bags, boxes and a broken lawn chair huddled at the curb. Carole turned to glare at The Jerk as she slid past, and in that instant caught the glint of something with metal legs sailing into the truck.

She braked at the corner, pausing longer than she normally would at the stop sign. *No.* She shook her head and the thought with it and made her right turn. *No way The Jerk had just trashed Elizabeth's walker.*

~ ~ ~

Simms v. Simms was the third divorce up that morning. The hearing lasted less than five minutes. By ten o'clock, Peter and Carole had signed their marriage license application. Four days later, they stood before the same judge and pledged that only death would part them.

Anxious they might lose their dream house to a higher bid der, the young couple offered Peter five thousand more than his asking price, and told him to expedite the title work. His kind of people. They were paying cash.

They closed on the twenty-eighth of September, giddy with first-time homeownership as Peter handed over the keys plus six days' rent money to remain in the house until the mov ing trucks pulled up on October third.

The days flew by in a flurry of packing and tossing and five-hour sleeps. "You don't mind waiting until November for a honeymoon?" Peter asked, tucking long-stemmed crystal into the slots of a wine carton.

"I mind waiting another hour for dinner," Carole coun tered, taping shut a box brimful with bathroom necessities. "What do you want from Pei Wei?"

She returned a half hour later to a ringing phone and Peter out near the drainage pit, pacing through the rebuilt peony bed with the watering hose. She dropped her purse and the carry out on the kitchen table, but the answering machine beat her to the call.

"Mum! Ian and Jason and I called to sing, but I fancy you and Peter are out celebrating. "

Carole froze, ice and confusion competing for her brain. Her vision narrowed as the chill flowed now to her stomach, and from very far away she could still hear the voice in the answering machine, singing now, with other voices, deeper voices, singing, "Happy Birthday."

And then she knew. With a clarity so chilling it was frost bite to her heart. *The French drain.* She forced herself to the doorway, out into the yard where she realized Elizabeth was buried, gaining momentum as she flew at Peter with both fists flailing at his back.

"How could you? Oh my God, how could you? You stupid fool. Didn't I tell you I wasn't in any hurry? That I would take care of Elizabeth – I didn't care how long?"

Peter spun toward her, dropping the hose in a grab for Carole's wrists. "It's not what you think."

She pulled free, stumbling backwards toward the gazebo. "We could have started fresh in Arizona, the three of us," she shouted. "Nobody knows us there. We would have blended right in."

"Carole." He took a step toward her. "Carole, please. Lis ten to me."

"No. You listen to me." She took a step back, retreating from Peter and the frenzied whipping of the garden hose. "We could have lived openly as husband and wife, if you'd only listened to me. Who would have ever guessed that Elizabeth wasn't your mother? Who? You have the same last name, the same accent. This could have worked out so perfectly."

His face was a blank. "Just calm down. No one can hear us. We can still make this work."

Instinctively, she reached for the thatch rake propped against the gazebo, blinking water from her eyes, keeping them trained on Peter. The spitting nozzle blasted his shirt, then his pants, then flooded the floor of the gazebo as the hose danced and twisted. "Work? Work with you? A monster, a murderer?"

"It was an accident." He started toward her, sliding in the wet muck, spitting water with each word. "You have to believe me."

"I'm calling the police." She slashed out with the rake, clipping Peter's ear with the heavy curved tines. Then she ran.

Stunned, he staggered sideways in the muddy flower bed and tripped over the flailing hose, pitching headfirst into the gazebo steps.

Carole whirled toward the sickening thwack. Peter lay motionless, his head twisted impossibly toward the crazed, dancing spray.

She ran to him and checked hopelessly for a pulse. *Nothing.*

Terror gnawed through Carole's gut with such ferocious heat she barely made it into the bathroom. Her legs quivered, buckling more than once as she struggled to her feet, to the sink, to scrub her hands. Rocking rhythmically, forward and back, forward and back, Carole filled her cupped hands with icy water and threw it at her face. "I'm sorry. I'm sorry. Oh God, I'm so sorry." She gripped onto the front lip of the sink, convulsing in sobs. "Oh Elizabeth, I am so sorry! I never meant to fall in love with him. I loved you, too. You know that, Elizabeth. You have to know that."

She wobbled to the living room and pulled the plastic tarp from the sofa, dragged it outside, dragged Peter's body almost effortlessly across the wet grass to the storm cellar and shoved. She shuddered at the rolling thunder of flesh on wood.

Gulping down great gasps of air, Carole grabbed for the granite countertop to stop the kitchen from swaying, but her grip was flimsy. She looked at her fingers, all of them tingling and going numb. Oh God, she couldn't afford to hyperventilate to unconsciousness.

"Stop!" She startled at the voice and swiveled toward the door before recognizing the command as her own. "Stop… right…now!" She had to force down the panic and concentrate, make a plan. *Breathe in, now breathe out, slowly, deliberately.* She rummaged under the sink and fished out a plastic food bag she had used to marinate chicken. *Slowly…deliberately…*

Covering her nose and mouth, she sucked down the sour smell of vinegar and garlic.

Leaning against the cupboard, she slid to the floor. At least she wouldn't break anything if she toppled. Her breathing was coming ragged now, minute by minute flowing more rhythmic. She had to think.

Carole glanced around the kitchen, fighting to clear the static swarming through her brain. Water. She needed water. God, she'd never been so thirsty.

Cautiously, she pulled herself to her feet and took a tentative step toward the cupboard. Then another. Shoving her glass against the ice dispenser on the refrigerator door, Carole suddenly zoomed in on the business card slanted behind a daisy magnet. She filled her water glass and took the card to the kitchen table. Her head was clearer now. Her breathing much more calm. She thumbed the number into her phone and concentrated on the dial tone. She knew clearly what she had to do. The only thing she could do.

"Yes. This is Carole Simms. I'd like to set up an appointment with Mr. Zazian," she droned in a disembodied voice. "My husband… Peter… We…. I… I really need Mr. Zazian's help. I've made a horrible mistake."

She drew a shuddering breath and stared at the raised lettering shimmering on the parchment business card. "How quickly can I get an appointment? I need to see him about a divorce."

The Thief-Taker: a story of Mirlacca

by Ashley McConnell

Ashley McConnell is the author of the *Desolada* horror novels set in Nevada and New Mexico, the *Mirlacca* fantasy series, and numerous short stories and media tie-in novels. Her current projects include a new *Mirlacca* novel and a mystery series involving cats, Morgan horses, white shepherds, and a dead body or two.

Kian is a character I've had in mind for many years. As an adult, he serves the Emperor of Miralat as an investigator, a spy, and if needed, as an assassin. One day I decided to work out exactly where he came from and how he developed the skills he needed to survive not only in the Emperor's Court but in the dark alleys of the capital city, and the first question was, "Where did Kian come from?" I saw him as a beggar boy, but how does a beggar boy become a part of the Court? The answer was through contact with a favorite character from the original fantasy trilogy, Adri-nes of the House of Derlai vn'Sai Khor. This story takes place several years after the original trilogy, and magic in Miralat is changing. And it's not just magic that's evolving – Kian doesn't know it, but this Emperor's birthday celebration is going to change his whole life.

It had been a long, unprofitable afternoon, and Kian was hungry. Kian was always hungry. Radeke said it was because he was growing. Kian hoped he was wrong. It was harder to cut purses when you got bigger.

He slid through the crowds gathered to celebrate the Emperor's Birthday in Mirlacca's Great Square. Being small, slight, nondescript helped a lot when it came to avoiding the guardsmen. Radeke had said there would be a lot of guardsmen – not to prevent honest thieves from earning a living but to prevent some fool from calling the Emperor ill names. Kian didn't care what they called the Emperor, as long as they didn't catch him in the process. Thief-takers, Radeke called them. They wouldn't take *him*. He was too little to be worth anything – at least so far – but anything he'd stolen, well, they'd steal it from him, and then it would be theirs, not his. Not his, he corrected the thought hastily, Radeke's, really.

He probably should have dressed better, he realized. His regular dirty tunic and leggings would have been fine on any regular market day; he'd fit right in with the farmers and tinkers and traders and fortunetellers. Today, though, people were more interested in dressing up and celebrating, and more than one fine townsman saw him coming and put a hand protectively over his pouch. He couldn't seem to convince them, today, that he was just another harmless waif. He stood out too much. He wished there was some spell that would make him invisible, without costing him a cup of blood or somesuch to pay the balance for it.

He paused briefly by a cookstall to snatch a stuffed roll while the proprietor was busy flirting with a young lady who'd gotten away from her chaperone, and crammed it into his mouth while he considered his options. All right, maybe being small had disadvantages, too – he couldn't see anything but masses of bodies all around him, clad in fine light cloth in reds and blues and even the occasional yellow. That didn't help him identify a mark. He couldn't see them clearly enough, focus enough. If he focused, he could convince them, he thought.

But he knew the Square as he would have known his own bed, if he'd owned such a thing; and the best place to see the whole Square at once was from the roof of the Cattlemen's, on the opposite side from the Palace. He finished the roll, rubbed greasy hands on his tunic, and turned his back on the mass of humanity in front of him to find the back alleys that led to the Stink Street, that would take him in turn to the series of broken walls, niches, and ladders that would allow him to climb to his chosen vantage point.

The walls of the Palace rose up at the far end of the Great Square, with two eight-sided towers flanking the Great Gate and the smaller ironbound door beside it. Kian had watched once as the Guilds had processed through the Great Gate, ten abreast, and debated with himself whether he should sneak in among them – it would have been easy to blend in, say, with the Herdsmens Guild. He decided against it; he had no idea what lay on the other side of the Gate, and didn't fancy finding himself without an escape route.

Well, that wasn't quite true. He had climbed one of the back walls once, and found himself in a small garden. He'd stolen figs from one of the trees. Radeke would never have believed where they'd come from, so he'd eaten them himself. The Emperor's figs should have tasted of gold or something marvelous, he thought, but instead they tasted like figs. Very good figs, but still, he'd stolen the like from gardens all over the city. Maybe that was why he didn't care about the magnificence of the Birthday celebration; if the Emperor was so special, why weren't his figs better than anyone else's? The only difference Kian could see was that he lived in a bigger house.

Now, the Gate stood ajar to allow five horsemen to pass through, shoving their way into the crowds. They weren't knights or lords, even Kian could tell that much, but maybe they served the Emperor himself; he could tell from across the Square that their clothes were best quality, their jewels very fine. Their horses were big, more like warhorses than the quick light couriers, but tacked out with fancy breast plates and cruppers, more for show than battle. But even those great horses had trouble finding a way to the circle of fountains that marked the center of the Square.

Usually a line of guardsmen stood before both the larger Gate and the smaller door, but not today. Maybe they'd lost the perfection of their line in the swirling mass of humanity surging and ebbing like the waters of Mirlacca's bay. Kian grinned at the thought of the polished guardsmen bobbing helplessly like fishing boats, torn from their appointed moorings.

The perimeter of the Square and the borders of the fountains were edged with the little temporary sheds that the craftspeople and tinkers and vendors of all kinds of meats and drink would put up for fair days. Every fair day – and today was no different – some of the flimsy little shelters would collapse under the weight of humanity and animals pushing into them. They would sag into their owners' goods, the waxed-cloth roofs entangling whoever was unlucky enough to be caught beneath. Regular fair days were very good for the quick and the fearless; Kian could read how the crowd moved and predict which merchants were most likely to be in the path of disaster, and position himself just right to snatch whatever was available when the supports began swaying and the owners began their frantic, futile lunges to try to keep them upright.

Today, though, wouldn't be a good time to try a shed grab. Too many people, too hard to make an escape. If five armed, mounted men had difficulty forcing their way through, it was too likely he'd be collared or trapped. He hoped he could convince Radeke of that, anyway.

Purse-cutting and a light snatch had been today's plan, and his targets should be near the edges of the Square, near the alleys and thoroughfares that relieved the pressure of so many people. But he could not shake the feeling that this would not work, not today. Kian wondered whether the Palace itself could even hold as many people as he could see below him.

The horsemen were edging around the margins of the square, being forced by the mass of people into the shed rows. Kian winced as he saw one of the animals, a warhorse taller at the shoulder than he was, lash out with a hind leg at someone.

He could hear the screams even over the ongoing rumble of crowd noise.

It had not been a fortunate day for the one who was kicked, he thought, but perhaps not for the horsemen either, because the tone of the crowd around them had changed, be come more shrill. For a moment he was very glad to be safely above it all, but then he became too interested in what was happening to be nervous.

The irritable horse kicked again, bringing down a shed support this time, and now there were screams of anger along with the agony. Now, instead of giving way to the horsemen, some of the crowd pressed even closer. The riders were close enough now that Kian could see the whites of the horses' eyes as they tossed their heads, unable to spin and bolt away from the tangle of cloth coming down on them. The riders them selves were shouting, at the crowd and at each other. Hands were clutching at the horses' caparison, snatching at the jewels in the harness, striking at the horses' sides, the legs of the riders. In Kian's considered judgment, they had been idiots to venture out into the Square to begin with; he wondered who they were and what they had thought they were going to accomplish.

Now the crowd was trying to unhorse at least one of the riders, and from his vantage point Kian could see the guards men trying to drive a wedge through the crowd to help. They were using clubs, not edged weapons, but the hum of rage around them grew as blows fell and more and more people became aware of what was going on.

The smaller door to the Palace was opening now, and more guardsmen were coming out. Kian looked up across the roofli nes and saw even more appear – bowmen now. Those riders must be important – important enough, at least, to call out the Emperor's own to come to their aid, and cut down the hon est citizens who had only gather in his imperial honor. Kian's opinion of his majesty slipped yet another notch. Didn't he know that people all together had no brains at all?

Either the horsemen were unarmed – more proof of their stupidity – or they were trying not to strike at their attackers, using the weight of the horses themselves to force their way out of the vendor's rows and over to the only reasonably clear space against a wall – which happened to be the face of the Cattlemen's Guild. Some of the crowd had turned to pillage the sheds; some had fallen under their fellows' feet. It had at least relieved a little of the human pressure against the horses, for whatever that was worth. It spoke well of the riders, Kian supposed, that they'd managed to make it across the Square at all, but there was nowhere to go from here, and the smell of slaughtered beasts was doing nothing to sooth the ever-more-frantic horses. They had been making for the Northern Gate, he supposed. He wondered if they knew that there was access through the slaughterhouse livestock alley. Perhaps that was what they were aiming for, but if so, they didn't look like they knew where to go next.

Now they were directly beneath him, pushed almost against the wall of the Cattlemen's, close enough that he could almost reach down and snatch off the jeweled and feathered cap from one of the rider's heads. Silvery grey it was, with a red stone winking in the middle of the clear ones. Radeke would let him off beatings for a year for a brooch like that!

That cap was just too tempting. He licked his lips, took a deep breath, hooked a foot on the overhang, and snatched, just as the rider's horse did another half-rear, and the cap was his.

He had not reckoned on the rider's reflexes. The man managed to not only sit the levade, but spin the horse as well, almost forcing it into the wall, and its head slammed against Kian's arm as he flailed for balance. The rider's arm shot out and grabbed, and Kian found himself dragged off his perch and dangling far too close to the threshing hooves.

"Damned little thief," the rider gritted, and even though it felt as if his arm was going to be pulled entirely out of its socket, Kian laughed. The laughter was swallowed by a yelp as the horse spun again and he was nearly flung out into the angry crowd, or worse, under the horse's steel-shod feet. "Tell me why I shouldn't just drop you!"

And he was preparing to do just that, Kian could tell. The man stank of anger and desperation, but not fear. All the fear Kian could smell, suddenly, was his own. "My lord," he gasped, feeling the man's grip begin to loosen, "I will show you the way out!"

His captor gave him a quick, searching stare, and for a moment he thought someone walked in his mind, turned it inside out and examined all the seams as if looking for tears. He couldn't talk, but he could lift his other hand and point to the arched, split door a few feet away.

Locked?

The question was as clear in his mind as if spoken aloud, so naturally his mind answered it. *Barred inside.* It was as close to coherence as he could come.

The man nodded sharply, as if he could hear the words, and snapped out commands to the other four men. Three of them swung their horses' hindquarters until they were nearly touching the Cattlemen's door, and on another spoken command the three horses shifted, bunched, and six hind legs lashed out.

Perhaps the Great Gate could have withstood that; the Cattlemen's certainly could not. Even the crowd gave way, awed. The command was repeated, and both sides of the door caved. One hung drunkenly on its hinges; the other simply fell inward, raising dust.

The horsemen bolted inside, and Kian, dangling helplessly by one arm, came with them, will he or no. By and large, he thought dazedly as he swung, trying to avoid being smashed into the stalls that lined the alley inside the building, he would rather the no.

The Cattlemen's Guild city headquarters' ground floor was a combination of holding pen and abattoir. It stank of blood and fear and shit and urine from half a dozen species, not just bovine. The pride of the Guild was their ability to provide fresh meat to the Palace, straight from the hooks to the Emperor's own kitchens. To do that, they had to be able to bring in kine of all descriptions from the farmers and herdsmen outside the City, and they did it by way of the Stink Road that led from the Guild building all the way to the Farmer's Gate on the south end of Mirlacca. It was one of the straightest roads in the city, to accommodate the herdsmen. The five riders and their unwilling guide burst out of the Guild building into the holding yard, milled around, and found the Stink Road gate.

By now Kian wanted nothing more than to get down and find out if he still had a working arm. His captor didn't seem to be paying him the slightest attention, but he was still a prisoner, and by this time a prisoner in considerable pain. His yells made no impression, so he tried what had worked before. He spoke without opening his mouth.

Let me down!

He found himself somewhere else – a place with wall hangings embroidered in gold thread, clean rushes on the floors, a bed heaped high with pillows, occupied by an old man with rheumy eyes and long fingers that plucked restlessly at the coverlet. Someone looked on that old man and felt awe, as if he represented something much more than drool and old man smell.

The chestnut horse jolted to a stop so fast Kian screamed again, and the other four riders were two lengths ahead before they realized what had happened. His scream was for the agony in his arm, and the wall that pushed him out of that room and, abruptly, back in the place that smelled of blood and hurt as he had never hurt in his life.

"Adri, what are you doing? Let's get out of here while we still can!"

"They're not following us," the man holding Kian said, and lowered him gently to the ground. Kian would have appreciated the gentleness more if he'd been capable of noticing. The sudden lack of pressure allowed blood to flow back into the joint, and it hurt even more. It *hurt.*

"They're not following us," Adri repeated, staring down at Kian, who was curled up on the filthy floor, moaning, wanting to touch his shoulder and not able to. "Who'd want to follow us into a slaughterhouse?"

Certainly the horses weren't happy about it. Two of the riders were having distinct problems controlling their animals, who wanted to get away from the close quarters, the low ceiling, the smells of blood and cattle and pigs and wet steel.

"Go ahead," Adri said. "There's something I need to take care of before I go."

"Oh, Lady bless," the other man said. "We'll wait for you outside the city walls. Don't be all day about it." The four allowed their mounts to lunge for the open gate. Adri kept his chestnut from following with some difficulty. Kian wished he'd just go. He needed to crawl off somewhere and put his arm back – he'd heard that could be done, even that arms worked afterward. He didn't want to be a cripple, make a living beg ging. Radeke had no use for beggars.

Adri had dismounted, dropped his reins. The chestnut horse stood as if he was tied to the floor, and not happy about it, but nonetheless he stood, head high and ears pinned. Kian hoped he wouldn't decide to spin around and kick again; on the others hand it might just put him out of his misery.

"What did you do?" Adri asked, crouching beside him, grabbing his chin and forcing Kian to look him in the eyes.

"I don't know," Kian whimpered. He should have let the crowd pull them down, damned rich men, good for nothing, fat pigs, ducks for downing. . .

"You bespoke me, you little street rat." Adri jerked Kian's chin slightly, forcing him to look into the man's eyes. "How did you do that?"

"I don't know! I don't know what it was, I just wanted you to *put me down!*" Kian's voice rose in a scream as his shoulder jolted. "You've pulled my arm off!"

Adri's hands gripped Kian's jaw and head, forcing his mouth shut, even as his one good hand scrabbled against them. "Tell me again, little street rat. Tell me what you want."

He couldn't twist away, he couldn't open his mouth, how was he supposed to –

Pig, fat lordling –

Demonspawn palace trash –

With a snort of disgust, the man shoved Kian away, back into the dirt. "I thought so. Either it was a fluke or I imagined it. What could gutter scrapings like you know?" He turned away to mount the horse, grabbing the dropped reins and breaking whatever spell he had used to keep the beast in place. Kian cringed away as the horse bolted toward the back entry, and glared after it in helpless rage.

I hope it throws you and tramples you in the pig shit, lordling! As the words formed in his mind, he caught a glimpse: a boy, clinging for dear life to the mane of a red horse far too big for him as it refused to jump, spinning and dropping him into a creek.

The chestnut horse dropped its back end and skidded to a halt just outside the entry. Adri swung himself off and ran back. "You *did* do it. Lady's Hands, you really did."

He lifted Kian to his feet, not roughly this time. Kian couldn't see the man's expression, because his companions were crowded in the entryway, blocking the light. They were calling for him, impatient, wanting to be on their way on whatever mysterious errand the Palace had sent them.

Once again the image of the old man in the bed rose before Kian's eyes, only to be brushed aside, impatiently, and replaced by Radeke.

Radeke holding a cup of cold gruel to his lips. That was his very first memory, that and how hungry he had been.

Radeke wielding a lash on the legs of one of the other boys – Mika had kept back some pins – the blood had sprung out in red lines on Mika's calves, and he had screamed for hours after. Kian could feel, even through the memory, a brief pressure on his own leg, checking for those scars.

And Radeke again, cuffing him until his head rang and shoving him into a cold corner of the fisherman's shed, flinging a scrap of filthy wool over him – but there had been no gruel that day nor bread, either. That was the day he'd gone into the Emperor's garden, and bragged of it, but he hadn't brought any of the figs back with him.

And the day he'd awakened to see the dim boy shivering beside him, whimpering – Dimmy couldn't talk – and had reached out to him, maybe to comfort, maybe to take his shirt – and found himself wandering in a vague, foggy place, looking up at someone he knew was himself and knowing he had to get back to himself before all the vague fading light around him went away –

Adri cursed, and Kian flinched.

"No, damn you –" Adri took a deep breath. "Damn *me*. I can't take you with me, I have to go –"

And I wouldn't go with you anyway, Kian thought, and then froze, wondering if somehow the man could hear those thoughts too.

"Look," Adri said, "You have to come with me, but I must *go*. You have a gift, boy – what's your name? Who do you belong to?"

"Serris," Kian lied automatically. "I belong to myself!" 'Gift,' he thought angrily. Liar.

Adri lifted an eyebrow. "Serris? Really?" The image of Radeke flashed in his mind. Kian could see it there. "Never mind. Do you know where the Inn of the Three Courts is, in the Gem Quarter? Be there on the sixth night after next Lady day, when the moon rises, and ask the proprietor for Adri-nes. There will be – food in it for you, boy. A good blanket, a whole one. Just for you. You won't regret it."

Kian clenched his jaw. As if he would be anywhere near the Gem Quarter that night, or any other, at the command of this ungrateful son of a – he wasn't sure what would be bad enough. Hadn't he saved the man's life, him and his friends too? And the thanks he got was a shoulder on fire, crippled for life.

Adri blinked, reached out one hand so that it hovered over the injury, and Kian yelped and tried to back away.

Hold still echoed in his mind, and he held still despite all his effort to run.

Heat poured from Adri's open palm, almost visible, and wrapped itself around Kian's shoulder, sinking through his tattered shirt and soaking into the pain, absorbing it. He watched, amazed, as the man's face went white, his eyebrows like charcoal smudges against his face as the heat continued.

Adri staggered, almost falling into Kian as one of his companions, tired of waiting, came back for him and then caught him, exclaiming. The touch released whatever it was that held Kian in place, and he ran, heading for the side halls where they couldn't see him. He spun to star at the silhouette of the bareheaded man standing framed in the far doorway of the slaughter alley.

"Remember!" Adri's voice, hoarse and strained, echoed after him. "Sixth night! The Three Courts!"

It still got a snort of disbelief in response. Radeke, he thought.

But then, there was the blanket. That man, Adri, he had meant it about the blanket. And the food. Kian could tell.

"And you can keep the cap!"

Kian's fingers clutched into the soft wool of the cap, still held tight in the hand of his once-injured arm. He could go back to the fisherman's shed. He could give the cap and its jeweled brooch to Radeke, and it would be Radeke's. As he was Radeke's. If you held it, it was yours. If someone took it away, it wasn't yours any more.

Or he could keep the cap. And have food. And a blanket.

Kian smiled crookedly, and wondered if this is what the figs had felt like when they were stolen.

Vanished

by Diane Whiteside

Arriving third in four generations of published authors, Diane Whiteside has more than a dozen novels, four novellas, and a collection of short stories under her belt. Creator of the Irish Devil and Texas vampire series, she has written fantasy and historical novels for both print and e-publishers, traditional and independent publishers. For more about her books or to contact her, please visit her website at www.DianeWhiteside.com.

I adore the strong, silent men of Appalachia. They do what's necessary to provide for their families – and that usually means dirty, difficult, dangerous work with long absences from home. My foster father went to work in the coal mines at age thirteen, his brother-in-law was a long-haul trucker, his two younger brothers served in the 82nd Airborne for decades, and a nephew followed them into the Marine Corps. They don't talk about their jobs, especially not the pain and the loneliness. But they do throw wonderful parties with lots of music when they come home to their womenfolk.

They're the inspiration for Richard, the hero of "Vanished." As one of them said, "What are you going to do, when you've got family to look after? You do what you must."

The clock struck nine P.M., the note sharp as a bugle call before it disappeared into the West Virginia mountains. I glanced around, distracted from climbing stairs in stilettos rather than my beloved clogs.

The tower still stretched toward the starlit sky above the hotel's stone bulk. The lake rippled silently over the ancient slag pit, where a century's coal mining refuse was buried with my hometown's lost dreams.

But more condos hid among the trees along the hillsides than had been here ten years ago. Broderick, the hotel owner, could always find new ways to pad his wallet.

Slimy lizard.

I moved on toward the banquet hall, my precious necklace hidden safely against my heart.

In and out and make it fast, that was my plan. Visit my high school's ten-year reunion just long enough for one dance with somebody, anybody other than Richard. Then leave, having wiped out all memories of that one perfect night at senior prom.

Yeah, right.

The clock struck again, more urgently. I craned my neck for one last glimpse – and nearly fell sideways.

It was an old-fashioned tower clock, perfect for a hotel resembling a medieval castle. A king and his warriors paraded in a circle, while his drummer marked time on the bell. I'd blown kisses to that gallant monarch a million times while growing up.

So why was there a queen on his arm now, looking as if she'd always been there? I reached the banquet hall's mezzanine, still trying to remember all the clock's figures. Here, a gaudy disco ball's sparkling reflections slipped away into the shadows.

"Looking for another dishwashing job, Cindy?"

I drew myself up to face down Abner Little's arrogant smirk. He guarded the reunion's reception table, perched on its edge like a hungry vulture.

"Hah! You can't afford a CIA-trained chef. I came for the ten year reunion."

He glowered. "Reservation?"

"Don't need one. Remember? Members of the graduating class just need to show up." My foot reached for the first step down to the boisterous ballroom.

"What about your date? You need a ticket for your boyfriend."

I hesitated, trapped by too many memories of the last man anybody had called that.

Abner, damn him, saw my weakness and pounced. "Or did you lose this one, too? Went off to the big city but couldn't hang on to a man." He brayed in satisfaction.

Memories slammed into me and I flinched.

"The young lady is welcome here at any time." A large hand grabbed Abner's shoulder and wrenched him away. My old nemesis stumbled into place at his master's heels, transformed from an unpredictable menace to a lurking shadow.

"Good evening, sir." I bowed formally, wary as an apprentice in a butcher shop. Clad in his usual pristine tuxedo, the hotel owner's angular frame dominated the narrow stone balcony. His deep-set eyes caught more secrets than any surveillance camera and his long, crooked nose proclaimed victories in brutal fights.

"Will you be staying with us after the dance?" Broderick's voice was more polite than his roar the last time we'd met.

"Sorry, but I have to be back at work." My face softened into a smile. An untraceable car plus two Mafia hit men to guard my back... Best payment ever for catering a wedding, even if I had to leave at midnight to return the car.

"Pity. The hotel provides a free bed for every graduate."

The way it had paid for my father's grave?

"No, thanks." I flung my head back and glared at him. My necklace slipped free from my neckline and fell forward, flashing crimson and gold.

Broderick's eyes blazed. Suddenly a great paw, edged by long, sharp claws, lunged toward my throat. I choked and tried to pull away but couldn't move.

A man yanked me into his arms. I staggered and clung to him, my only stability. The clean scent of woodlands, long gone yet all too familiar, teased my senses.

"Leave her alone, Broderick. Your quarrel is with me."

That voice…

My head snapped around and I stared at a stranger. Or was he?

"Richard?" *The* name ripped my throat like forgotten dreams. "But he's gone forever."

"You know better than that, love. So does our host."

Love? Calling someone honey or sugar meant little in these mountains. But love? That was special.

Broderick snorted a harsh laugh. "Wondered when you'd come crawling back, boy."

I found my feet but still gripped my rescuer's arm. Hard muscles – and how many weapons? – hid under his well-cut, black suit. A sword hilt nudged my hip.

"I don't need to crawl, innkeeper – not when I've been invited to the ball." The newcomer suddenly held aloft a ticket to the reunion.

Broderick's face flushed scarlet and his hands clenched.

I eased my fingers toward my phone, tucked inside my purse which was slung across my body. If Broderick caused trouble – get me arrested – my Mafioso chauffeurs would raise hell. It'd only take a moment to unlock the phone and call them.

"Back off, Broderick. I'm protected by the laws of hospi tality." My escort's voice was lethally sharp, more dangerous than any command barked on a small town football field years ago. His face was sun-kissed and his hair raven black. Yet bit ter experience threaded silver through his hair and crows' feet around his eyes. His mouth hadn't relaxed in laughter for far too long.

It had been a decade since Richard had taken me to the high school prom, then vanished with his mother never to be seen again. Surely this wasn't the same man, no matter how often I'd seen him and Broderick fight.

"Only while you have the ticket and keep the peace," Broderick snapped.

"True. But as long as I do, your own castle will fight to protect me."

"Harrumph. We'll see who's polite longest, you hot-tempered brat. For now, I'll leave you two alone." The hotel proprietor shot another searing glare at my face. "May she ruin your plans faster than she did mine."

He walked off, whistling, Abner in his shadow. The staring, polyester-clad throng fell away from him like pigeons before a hawk. The DJ hastily booted the latest country hit into play and my former classmates began dancing the Texas two-step.

I shook out my red tango dress before I dared to glance upward.

The not-quite stranger studied me, hopeless longing lurking behind his blue eyes. He bowed, as Mrs. Broderick had taught us all, and offered me a corsage. A pair of red and white roses in full bloom wrapped with white ribbons, exactly like the one I'd worn to my senior prom.

Sparks floated around it, prettier than any fireflies.

Sparks? Maybe a reflection from the iron chandeliers?

My jaw dropped open and I cooed, "thank you."

I instinctively reached for it, although I had no idea where it had come from. Live flowers would have bruised under his suit's linen and no other hiding place was nearby.

"Darling Cindy." His fingers lingered when he pinned it to my thin dress's only shoulder. "May I have this dance?"

"Of course." Take the floor with whoever this was, as compared to Broderick or Abner? Why not? Besides, I needed answers. And maybe the chance to kick somebody in the teeth for having Richard walk out on me way back then.

My partner led me down the stairs and into the banquet hall, now a glittering ballroom. I was more graceful now, probably because my balance didn't depend solely on the damn high heels. We stepped onto the dance floor's edge to join the former football team, still tanned and fit, but sporting military insignia and combat veterans' watchfulness.

The music caught us and we came alive, turning, kicking and shuffling to the same line dance choreography. Richard's teammates and their cheerleaders took up position around us, and we moved fluidly together.

It was like the good old days, when Mrs. Broderick – the old bastard's wife and my boyfriend's mother – tricked us kids into loving dancing.

Even the big ballroom still looked the same. Local colleges' colorful emblems blazed from shields hung high above the fireplace, under the wrought iron chandeliers and sconces. Massive stone pillars framed the lake view like ribs, while a breeze drifted in from the terrace doors. People ate and gossiped at tables scattered around the edges.

As for me – I was too comfortable with my partner. How else could he have moved us from the outer track, with the line dancers, to the inner rail, with the slower couples?

"Who are you – really?" I asked, in-between twirls.

He shot me a quick glance then pulled up his trouser leg.

I stumbled. I recognized those perfectly fitting, ostrich skin cowboy boots. They were custom-made from my design for Richard, after he had led our team to the state football championship. The stitching on the shafts even spelled our initials.

He caught me before I knocked anybody over.

"It is you!" My heart pounded against my throat.

"Hush!" Richard released me.

The tune sank to a halt and our classmates stretched.

"Why the hell did you vanish?" I lowered my voice. He owed me an explanation for disappearing without a word after the best night of my life, then letting me answer all the angry questions.

His mouth tightened, and I grabbed his hand. "Tell me!"

He jerked his head toward the carving stations. Behind them, Broderick leaned against the wall and studied us like a butcher calculating his first strike. Abner sharpened the longest carving knife I'd ever seen – ostensibly to slice a gigantic turkey.

A shiver ran through me. What could Richard do against those two?

The DJ announced the next song with a flourish and a pop ballad flowed from the speakers. I tugged Richard more fully back onto the dance floor, my heart beating a little too fast.

Broderick's thin lips twisted in a smirk, as he watched my flustered face. He leaned over to speak to Abner and both their smiles deepened. But he couldn't stop the wave of our classmates filling the enormous ballroom to dance cheek-to-cheek with their partners. Surely there'd be safety in a crowd, right?

Richard snorted and pulled me into his arms. Even my fancy manicure couldn't make my callused, scarred hands look graceful on his shoulders.

"Where have you been?" I asked, eager for some answers I could understand. "And why the hell did you never call?"

"For crying out loud, Cindy…" Any excuses he might have made withered under my glare. He twirled me to a quieter corner of the dance floor. "It's too dangerous to tell you."

"Broderick nearly pounded down our front door the morning after senior prom, demanding to know where you were."

"What?"

"Father didn't want to wake me up, but who could sleep through that much noise? Everybody who lived along the river flats came out to watch the excitement."

I stopped, remembering how my stepmother had tried to make the town's richest man's arrival into a social triumph, only to be ruthlessly ignored. "Father and I helped search for you in the mountains later on, of course."

"I'm sorry. But you must believe you were better off not knowing anything." His clipped tones hinted at agony too great to be revealed.

I nearly slapped him for spouting that nonsense. We'd always shared everything, good and bad.

"You should be sorry. All those weeks afterward, Broderick insisted I knew where you and your mother were. He even harassed Dad to make me talk."

"No way!"

"He ruined Dad's diner and drove him into bankruptcy. My stepmother and stepsisters left town."

"Oh hell, Cindy, your father loved thinking up new chicken specials for that little joint."

I blinked back tears. "Even then, Dad and I couldn't con vince Broderick I didn't know anything. Broderick swore that since you and I had been inseparable since tickling trout in kindergarten, we'd have worked together to help you vanish."

Richard's hand tightened on mine.

"That's when Dad and I agreed we were glad your mama was free of that S.O.B. A day later, Broderick sent Dad to his grave in one final shouting match."

Richard broke stride, as if he'd been hit, and his eyes turned barren, emptier than a pantry raped by a mob.

"If I could have saved him, I would have, Cindy." His voice resonated through my bones and he tucked me closer, his cheek against my neatly pinned up hair.

I choked back old grief against his pleated white shirt. I'd decorated Mom and Dad's graves tonight before I'd come here. I'd shared a private laugh with them at my stepmother who'd lost Dad's insurance money when she bolted – and thus funded my culinary education. Ten years was long enough to ease some pain.

I was grateful for the DJ's change to a slow Latin number. The sensual music made it easier to cling and whisper to a partner.

"So, Richard – where have you been and why the hell didn't you tell me beforehand?" I asked the harsh-featured man who held me so carefully. Why couldn't anybody else have felt this perfect?

"We left because it was the only way to save Mother's life." Richard's gaze met mine, crystalline as the purest lake. "You know how he treated her."

I shut my mouth, reminded of years when I'd winced at her stiffness. I couldn't stop her bruises but I'd tried to salve them by bringing her wildflower bouquets.

"Your mother's a wonderful woman," I acknowledged and circled back to my true problem. "But Broderick is filthy rich. He could find anyone, anywhere on Earth. Why was he so sure he could only find you through me?"

"You're joking." Richard shook his head. "It's been twenty years; you should have had a good life without me by now."

"What rock have you been under?" I gaped at him. "Does that banner say twenty to you?"

His gaze snapped around and around, again and again, every movement tracking another sign welcoming our graduating class's ten year reunion.

"Blessed goddess, all I could see was you when I came through the portal." His fingers clenched on his sword hilt. "It's been that long for me."

"That's crazy." It didn't seem insane when I saw the certainty in his hard face, though. "Tell me the truth."

"My mother is queen of the Gentry and I'm their prince."

My mouth dropped open wide enough to swallow an entire ox. The legendary Gentry, who could make sorcerers cower and witches flee? Not possible.

"Have I ever lied to you before?"

"Not since the day we met and I shoved you into the river for saying fish could fly."

"So trust this story, too."

"Ohhkaaay." If the truly scary stuff was worse than him being a Gentry prince, maybe I wanted to go back to my original plan: Find somebody other than Richard to party with then live a simple life.

Maybe.

"Broderick is an enemy dragon."

I opened my mouth to object, but closed it when I remembered the gigantic claw trying to grab my necklace.

"Still with me?"

I nodded. Maybe the next chapter would be simpler, just to make my stomach happier.

"He kidnapped me when I was a baby. Mother tried to stop him, but she too was captured. As heir to the throne, I –"

Richard would be the *king*?

"I was guarded by protection spells, but those would expire when I turned eighteen. Mother poured her own magic into supplementing them."

That sounded scary.

"Broderick took us here to Earth where he built a fortress" – Richard's strong fingers indicated the stone castle around us – "and we posed as a family."

"You must have hated that."

"If I fought him, Broderick beat her." His even tones stuttered for the first time, then steadied.

"Why, that sadistic –"

"He planned to take me home and kill me on my father's frontiers when my guardian magic faded."

"Your eighteenth birthday."

"The day after our senior prom." Agony flickered through his eyes. "But I couldn't leave without one last night with you."

I gulped. "That's why you worked so hard to make it into the perfect date."

He nodded. His mouth was closed against any betraying word, but his eyes caressed every inch of me.

Oh, how I wanted to believe him. But where could I find proof?

The music ended on a low, wailing note and we stopped obediently, still holding hands. The DJ disappeared and his station went dark.

"My dear girl." Broderick bared his teeth in a fake smile. He was backed by Abner and our high school wrestling team, all of them still big, fat and meaner than meat grinders. "I have a job for you."

My feet immediately moved me closer to Richard's warmth.

"I'm sorry, but the young lady and I are still dancing. You'll have to wait." Richard sounded viciously pleased.

"The DJ has left." Broderick's smile stretched to a well-honed sneer.

"Really? I don't think so." Richard's voice deepened to a purr.

A soft, sweet tune stole into the ballroom and my heart lifted at Richard's mother's favorite song.

"Another time perhaps." I kept my expression politely bored, as if I'd declined a supplier's bribe to buy illicit produce.

The tune started to fade.

The older man's face darkened to crimson. "She'll stay here as payment for how your people killed mine." He reached for me and the dance squad applauded.

"Never with one of your kind." I'd never heard such venom come from Richard. "Your family turned our land into a slagheap, so they could mine gold."

"Useless gelding." Broderick surged closer, bringing the stench of filthy, ancient chimneys. "Your parents married to unite their magic. But you're so pitiful, you can't even hurl a sword. My people are strong and shall hunt treasure any way they want – with claws or cyanide."

"Cyanide?" My family had mined West Virginia's mountains for generations. Even a little bit of cyanide murdered plants and animals – and people, too – for generations.

I charged toward my old enemy, anger blinding me, but Richard caught me by the waist. Broderick's eyes lit with pure satisfaction, glittering like freshly sharpened knives.

The Gentry prince whistled his mother's song like a bugler summoning reinforcements. An instant later, all of the DJ's speakers amplified his call into a full-throated orchestral demand. The DJ's lights shifted to an insistent, seductive glow.

I caught my breath. Would anyone help us?

Our friends from the football team streamed past Broderick onto the dance floor. Within moments, a dozen dancers blocked him from us.

My would-be abductor hissed angrily but stepped back, his angry gaze vowing retribution on the crowd. We were safe – for now.

Richard swept me into the old-fashioned waltz. "Too easy," he muttered. "Never been able to summon an orchestra by myself before."

The DJ was back at his station when we swung past. He was humming along to the old folksong no trendy DJ should know.

My stomach lurched when I looked at him.

"Richard, honey, how did you get the DJ back here and spinning tunes so fast? Especially your mother's favorite song?"

"Magic."

"Same magic that powers dragons and the Gentry?"

"Yes."

I couldn't quite believe him. "If I asked him to play a medley of Elvis's Gospel hits, you're telling me he'd do it – and nobody would blink."

Richard snapped his fingers. I begged for a halt after the fourth tune filled the air. As he promised, nobody had noticed – except Broderick, whose glare was hot enough to fuel bonfires.

"Okay, I believe you!" I leaned my forehead against Richard's shoulder. "Magic. Heaven help me."

"It's easier to do it when you're near me." His voice was ragged.

"Everything's easier when you're close and harder when you're away." I was too dazed not to tell him the full story. "The night Dad and Broderick had their last fight, I nearly called you on my cell phone the way that creature demanded."

"Why didn't you call before then? Like the night I disappeared?" Richard's voice was elaborately calm.

"Broderick pushed too hard, until his arguments sounded fishy."

Richard's silence told me I'd been right, and Dad too for agreeing with me. "Why did I have to do it, not Broderick?"

"Because I'd only answer a call from you. That would have completed the spell and allowed him to track and kill me. If he'd called from his phone, the anti-dragon spells protecting my home would have sent any attack straight back at him." Richard's thumb lightly rubbed my hand, as if he needed to reassure himself I was there.

I stared up into his face and finally read all of the truth in his eyes. "You'd have risked dying to help me."

"Of course." He kissed my fingers.

"You shouldn't be here, not if a phone call could kill you. Why did you come back?"

"To fetch my heart." His voice was so ragged, I almost couldn't understand him.

"Your heart?"

"The necklace I gave you."

I instinctively clasped the ruby pendant, big as my thumbnail and wrapped in a golden web.

Richard's lips curved slightly. "I poured all of my love into it, hoping it would protect you."

"You said it was a token of your eternal love."

"It is – and it also holds my magic."

"You're the Gentry's heir – and a warrior. If there are more beasts like Broderick out there" – His scars confirmed that guess – "you need all the help you can get."

"I can't work magic without it." Agreeing probably hurt more than his wounds had.

"You can't help your people against Broderick's filthy kin folk." All the nights I'd clutched that necklace and whispered my loneliness to it… But that filthy creature had to be stopped. "I'll give it to you."

"If I take it back, the bond between us will disappear."

Ouch. My reignited teenage dreams vanished. "We only have tonight."

"Yes. My mother's spell sent me back the first night you returned here. When my heart is whole again, I can return to my people."

"If Broderick doesn't kill you first."

Richard glared at me, and I glared back, willing him to be cautious for once.

"Or I slaughter him," he snapped.

"Your sword doesn't look big enough to take on a dragon." I chewed my lower lip. "Not with their armored hide."

"I know how to do it." Richard's frosty blue eyes warned me not to question him.

I gave him my best fake smile, last used when he dived off Rainbow Arch the summer before our senior year, and rested my forehead against his shoulder. We still had a little time to gether before our high school reunion ended, if Broderick be haved himself.

Good luck to us on that.

Richard and I danced in silence, locked in each other's arms. We circled the floor like migrating birds, linked to each other's rhythm and unable to stop lest we crumple. His hands supported me, his scent filled my lungs, and his legs set my dress's silk swirling. I could have stayed with him forever.

The music faded into a long, drawn-out chord. The chandeliers and wall sconces' light warmed to a soft glow.

Richard laughed and spun me away, his expression transformed into the young champion I'd adored.

I threw my head back and laughed with him. Then I sank into a curtsy, the way his mother had taught.

Richard bowed to me. Perfectly, of course.

I came to my feet, ready for another dance. One stiletto heel rolled under me.

I tumbled sideways, away from Richard – and Broderick lunged for me. He ripped my hem, but I came up on the far side of the dance floor, with him between me and Richard.

Somebody squeaked and our classmates turned back to stare.

Abner leered from the carving station, where he guarded the staff exit. Wrestling team members blocked the doors to the terrace, ready to take down any foes.

Richard's hand dropped to his sword's hilt.

"Let her go, Broderick. Your quarrel's with me, not her." He sounded appallingly calm.

"After you're dead and I've sucked her bones dry. I'll enjoy my revenge on both of you, young fool."

Broderick's dry tones sent shivers through my skin.

Richard drew his sword and held it high. The blade lit up the immense ballroom brighter than the grand chandeliers or the DJ's fancy electronics.

Broderick rumbled deep in his throat. He coiled himself into a towering spiral, yet his hungry gaze never left Richard. He spun round and round, growing bigger and bigger, until finally even his eyes disappeared into the whirlwind.

People backed toward the ballroom's corners.

My skin was colder than a blast freezer's innards. This fight was not something cops could solve.

A gigantic red dragon, big enough to fill the dance floor and with claws like butcher knives, burst out of the cloud and charged Richard.

Guests screamed and tried to hide behind curtains.

Richard shoved me toward the dessert buffet's miniscule safety. Then he leaped for the fireplace mantel and grabbed the giant West Virginia shield above it.

Broderick blew a fiery gust at Richard but he blocked it with the blue-and-gold shield.

Somehow I fumbled my necklace over my head and began to spin it like a slingshot. If I threw the jewel to Richard, surely he could use its magic.

The ruby flashed out at the arc's end – and met a mighty burst of flame from Broderick.

I yelped and yanked Richard's precious gift back to me. A few quick twists wrapped it safely around my wrist. But what could I do for him now?

Broderick roared with fury and lashed out with his spiked tail. Richard leaped aside, like a dancer, but the DJ's station shattered into kindling. Shards flew across the room.

As if inspired by the dangerous dance, Richard's old foot ball teammates whooped and tackled Abner's wrestling team mates, while the cheerleaders laid into the dance squad. The re maining guests stampeded toward the stairs to the mezzanine, and the parking lot beyond.

Broderick roared again and a table dumped chocolate sauce onto the floor next to me. I dived sideways, desperate to escape the angry dragon.

My eyes met my love's terrified gaze for a moment before his expression shifted. My heart stopped at the desperation I saw there.

"Afraid to fight a knight, you dried-up bag of skin? Or do you think you can only defeat unarmed girls?" Richard taunted our enemy.

Broderick whirled to face him, his talons ready to shred the soft-skinned human.

Richard raced away from me, through the doors to the terrace.

Broderick bellowed again and followed, his tail pulverizing tables like breadcrumbs.

No way would I let my love fight alone, not again.

I vaulted over the carving station, the way I'd learned as a line chef. I rammed my elbow into Abner's ribs and slammed him with a hip check, a move perfected in far too many testosterone-fueled kitchens.

He collapsed onto the floor and wheezed. The turkey's slimy carcass fell into his lap.

I snatched up his huge carving knife. The staff door wobbled and faces peeked around the edge. I hastily hurled my shoes at them and the heels' sharp edges barely missed their eyes. The door slammed shut, but I didn't have time to celebrate.

I needed to save Richard so I could feel whole again.

Broderick had Richard pinned in one corner of the terrace. Richard's shield was singed around the edges but the blue-and-gold chevrons still blazed valiantly in the middle.

Richard raised his sword and charged Broderick's scarlet throat. His enemy bugled a battle cry and counter-attacked. Silvery blade and brazen dragon fire thrust and parried in a deadly, whirling dance, backed by moonlight's pitiless gleam.

I growled deep in my throat and sprang forward to help. I wasn't a warrior but I had mastered the CIA's exotic game class. After all, many of those beasts were built just like a chicken.

Uh-huh. Keep telling that to the heartbeat pounding in my throat.

I ducked underneath Broderick's belly into shadows reeking of sulfur. I'd have to find my mark by instinct, not sight.

The two opponents paused to hurl more curses at each other. Broderick was luridly specific about his plans for roasting and seasoning Richard.

I snarled. No way I'd let him do that to my love.

I stretched and thrust high into the dragon's thigh, where his skin was most fragile. The long knife slid home and I twisted it, then pulled it free. Exactly like Dad had taught me to carve.

Broderick bellowed angrily, and I retreated to the castle wall below the tower.

Richard dropped his shield and swung onto his enemy's shoulder.

I shoved my tumbling hair out of my eyes and watched for an opening to help him.

The great lizard reared up onto his hind legs and the motion slung Richard onto its bony spine.

Broderick's wounded leg folded under him until he couldn't run. Yet his head whipped around to send flames at his mortal enemy.

Richard, please take care…

He clawed his way up the knife-edged scales. I bit my lip so I couldn't scream and distract him.

Finally he knelt below the crimson horns. Teetering precariously on the thrashing dragon, he slammed the blade into the base of Broderick's skull. The reptile reared and screamed in agony. It thrashed wildly until it knocked its attacker free. Richard dropped onto the pavement beside me, bloody sword in hand.

Broderick keened again and hurled himself into the air.

"We can't let him go far, Cindy," Richard muttered. He put one foot down, hissed, then left his weight on the other foot. "If Broderick flies between worlds, his magic will heal him."

We had to bring our enemy back? Yuck.

Perhaps the ruby would help. I slid that hand toward our escaping enemy, half-hoping, half-fearing the consequences.

The dragon dived at us, in a torrent of dragon-fire that eclipsed the moonlight.

I leaped to block it from Richard – and he thrust me behind him and his raised sword. I clutched his waist to strengthen us both.

Broderick came closer and closer, the wind through his wings humming an ode to death.

Richard grunted in effort.

Broderick's flames brushed the sword, halted and fell back. His dive tightened into a fiery arc as his crest's spines and talons exploded. He screamed again and dropped into the silent black lake.

Beads of water flew high and danced with the moon to become jewels. They washed the terrace clean and erased Broderick's stench. One by one, the football team and cheerleaders slipped onto the terrace.

Richard wrapped his arms around me. I closed my eyes and wished time would stop so we could stay together.

The tower clock whirred into life and sent out the king's trumpeter, the court's final figure, who only appeared at noon and midnight.

"You must leave." I stepped away from my own true love and tried not to cry. That was not how I wanted him to remember me.

"No, I'll stay this time." Agony drove the words out through lips tight set in a harsh face.

I stared at him, horrified. Richard had to return and destroy the rest of Broderick's kin, even if separation meant eternal loneliness for us.

"You can't stay, honey. Just take the necklace and go." I shoved the pendant at him.

He caught me by the wrists, love and despair in his beautiful eyes. The glowing ruby swung between us like my heart's bittersweet hopes.

The clock struck midnight's first note.

"Richard, my son."

Both of us stared up at the queen in the tower. It looked like… Surely it couldn't be?

"Mother?" Richard croaked.

"Yes, dear."

My head spun. What was she doing here – and as a figure in a mechanical clock? But I didn't have time to worry about that.

"The veil is thinnest between our worlds tonight at midnight."

He nodded impatiently and drew me closer. "Yes, of course. But –"

"Hush! We have very little time."

He tapped his foot but stayed silent.

"Together, you two have all of Richard's magic."

He jerked and stared down at me, wild hope running through his gaze.

I blinked at him, confused.

"If you kiss her *now* – while the clock is *still striking twelve* – then you can bring her across with you."

"Cindy, will you leave all of your friends and everything familiar, to come with me?" Richard's hands tightened on mine.

I took a deep breath. Dad always said sometimes you had to bet everything on your instincts.

"Yes – oh yes, my forever love!"

Richard kissed me. I could have danced, I could have flown, I could have locked myself closer to him for hours longer. *Oh Richard…*

Behind my eyelids, the ruby flared around us and the clock's chimes became a cascade of joy, not a demanding stomp.

When Richard lifted his head, a pink and gold dawn brightened the sky overhead. The sweet tang of springtime forests filled the air and birds chirped happily.

My love wore peacock clothing now, not a warrior's black gear. His white tunic and royal blue trousers were perfect dancing attire above his ostrich-skin boots. Even better, no silver streaked his hair and only joy creased his face, not anxiety.

I reached up on ache-free feet and pushed a raven-black lock out of his eyes.

Whose hands were those?

I hesitated, then waggled my fingers. My slender, unscarred, callus-free hands. My hair hung loose to my waist, confined only by a slender band around my temples. My red dress was gone, replaced by a white lace and crystals gown, fit for a Gentry princess.

My necklace was now a golden bracelet and Richard wore its mate, each set with a single ruby.

Both of us had been reborn.

The clock's warriors and courtiers cheered from around us. They were led by Richard's mother and the king, who looked remarkably like my darling.

The Gentry, indeed. Good heavens.

"I always dreamed you'd join me here one day." Richard pulled me close until our hearts pressed together. "Welcome home, my love."

His mouth came down on mine and I eagerly lost myself in his kiss, the first of my glorious future.

Autumn Treasures

by Catherine Anderson

Catherine Anderson is a *New York Times*-bestselling author of more than thirty novels, which have been published all over the world. She resides in the Pacific Northwest with her husband.

Sam Jones is a character who sprang from my imagination when I asked myself the question, "What if?" I married my childhood sweetheart right after he joined the Marine Corps, and over the course of our long and happy marriage, we've often said we were destined to be together. But what if something had happened to keep us apart? Both of us believe that our paths would have crossed again. Sam, a purely fictional person who bears no intentional resemblance to any real individual, took shape in my mind, and his story, a tribute to true love, is one that could happen to any of us.

Sam Jones pulled his BMW sports car onto the shoulder of the unpaved road, so lost in memories that he didn't worry about the encroaching bushes on the country lane scratching the brand new paint. Sunlight lanced through the glass into his eyes. Even with all the windows up and the air conditioner running, he could smell the red-clay dust so reminiscent of his youth. Before cutting the engine, he hit the control to roll back the convertible roof, sighing as the openness surrounded him. He sat there, drinking in the never-forgotten smells and sounds of this place, sacred in his mind for over forty years now. A breeze, redolent with the scents of laurel, myrtle wood, myriad wildflowers, and moistness from the nearby creek, ca ressed his face. When he closed his eyes and listened to the whispering tree leaves and grasses, he was swept back in time and felt twenty years old again.

Only he wasn't – and knew he wasn't. His arthritic joints and recently replaced right knee would harshly remind him of his actual age the moment he opened the door and struggled to his feet. Why the hell had he bought a sports car so low to the ground? He'd heard of men having mid-life crises and act ing like kids again, but Sam was beyond that stage. He'd turned sixty-three last spring. When he saw a sexy young woman, his imagination kicked into gear but was unaccompanied by any action below his belt.

Maybe he was entering his second childhood. Why else was he here on a hot July afternoon, following up on a promise made forty-three years ago? *Don't forget me, Sam. Swear to me you won't. I'll be eighteen soon. My parents won't have any say. Meet me here next July 8th. I'll be here waiting, I promise.*

Sam had sworn never to forget Sherry Bradford, but he'd been unable to agree to the rest of her request. He's just been drafted into the Marines and was scheduled to start boot camp training at the San Diego MCRD in less than three weeks. A guy didn't tell Uncle Sam to shove it up his ass, not even for love. And oh, how he'd loved his golden-haired, amber-eyed Sherry – with his whole heart, body, and soul. He'd settled for swearing he'd return to their special meeting place on July 8th as soon as he was free to do so, and Sherry had tearfully ac cepted that, with a stipulation. If anything went wrong, they'd each come back here on that date every single year until Fate brought them together again.

Fate proved to be a heartless and fickle bitch. Sam had been assigned a thirteen-month tour of duty in Viet Nam, and once there, he'd ended up having to stay for a second hitch. At first, he and Sherry had written long, passionate letters to each other, filled with avowals of love, desire, and fidelity. She'd come from a wealthy family, her father a surgeon, her mother a physical therapist, and she had been expected to attend uni versity, preferably to become a physician. Over time, Sam had begun to sense tension in her missives to him, and then he'd received a tear-streaked plea for swift rescue. *My parents want me to marry him, Sam. His name is Raymond Whitaker. He's a cardiotho racic surgeon just like Daddy and a lot older than me. Daddy won't take no for an answer. I don't love him, Sam, I swear, but Mama has already ordered the gown and is planning the wedding. I don't know what to do! Come, home, Sam. Please? Get emergency leave somehow. We can run away. Once we're married, what can Daddy do but accept it?*

Going home wasn't an option. He'd been stuck in a tropi cal jungle doing field maneuvers, crawling on his belly half the time to avoid sniper fire and praying he wouldn't wander into a minefield. Well, he'd been lucky – sort of, anyway. But his best buddy hadn't been, and the resultant explosion had landed Sam in a medevac helicopter with shrapnel in both thighs and his chest. He'd damned near lost his right leg from the knee down. He'd been on crutches for a year, had to use a walker for six months after that, and at only a little over twenty-two years of age, had been thoroughly convinced that he would be a cripple the rest of his life, only half a man.

What did he have left to offer a girl like Sherry who lived in a fancy house and had parents with letters behind their names? Hell, even Sam's name was generic. His millworker dad hit the bottle every night. His mom worked as a nurse's aide and held things together with a huge capacity for love and an overabundance of patience. She'd seemed content to live in a shabby rental, follow a stringent budget, and pour her husband another drink whenever he snapped his fingers. Sam, with his pins shot out from under him, had faced some hard facts. Sherry Bradford had been born to a lifestyle he could never provide. He was a nobody from the wrong side of the tracks and destined to remain there. He'd written back to Sherry, try ing his damnedest to keep all the "poor me" shit out of it, saying simply that as much as he loved her and as much as she might love him, they just couldn't make it work. By enlisting the help of a friend, he'd posted the missive to Sherry from his former duty station so she wouldn't know he was hurt or be able to track him down.

Her response had gone to Viet Nam and then boomer anged back to him at the stateside military hospital. In that letter, she'd sworn never to marry Whitaker and said she would go to their secret meeting place once a year on July 8th for the rest of her life. Sam, older, wiser, and far more disillusioned than he'd been at twenty, had saved the letter but never wrote back to her. A year later, his mom had sent him the newspaper clipping of Sherry's marriage to Raymond Whitaker.

End of story. It had hurt like hell, but after another year passed, he'd married Eva Miller, a nurse he'd met during his stateside hospitalization, and they'd built a life together. After months of physical therapy, Sam had gotten a loan to attend college and become a mechanical engineer. Eva had borne him three sons, Michael, Richard, and Isaac. Leukemia had taken Richard from them when he was twelve. A year later, Eva lost both her parents in a small plane crash. A man couldn't go through grim trials like that with a woman and not come to love her.

Now, two years after losing Eva to the same disease that claimed their son, Sam was alone with his best years behind him. He was fresh out of career aspirations, feeling that he'd reached his pinnacle and faced the downhill slide. Michael and Isaac were both happily married with families of their own, far too busy to spare much time for dear old Dad. There was nothing left for Sam to look forward to anymore. Maybe that explained his impulsive purchase of a snazzy sports car. He'd hoped it might add some zest to his life. Only it hadn't.

So here he sat on a dusty old road, lost in the past, his heart still leashed to a girl who had long since become little more than a sweet memory. He listened to the cooling engine tick. He wondered if he'd lost his mind. Coming back here was undeniably insane. And yet he'd felt compelled to make the long drive for reasons he couldn't begin to understand and sure as hell couldn't have explained to his sons. Not that either of them would give a shit. *Live a little, Dad. These are your golden years. Mom didn't want you to be alone. You promised her. Remember?* Both boys were successful – Michael the owner of a grocery store chain, Isaac doing well with his dental practice. It wasn't as if they were worried about their father tying up with a gold digger and blowing their inheritance. Sam was free to do anything he liked, and Eva, God rest her dear soul, had given him her blessing.

Only there was nothing he really wanted to do. What was so golden about being his age and having rusty hinges for body joints? What was so golden about going on a cruise or eating out alone? He missed Eva. There was nobody to mess up the newspaper before he got a chance to read it. No knee-hi support stockings hanging over the edge of the Jacuzzi whirlpool tub to dry. No cereal bowl left in the sink to get crusty. No shoes kicked off in the bedroom for him to trip over. He didn't even have a dog.

Sam sighed and looked up the hill he'd have to climb to reach the cave where he'd once met secretly with Sherry. *Shit.* Unlike the gradual slope he remembered, the barely visible trail appeared to go straight up. He saw boulders and patches of loose rock. Would his knee implant hold up if he tried to make the ascent? And, hello, why should he bother? No feet had touched that weed-choked path in years. Sherry was happily married to a successful cardiothoracic surgeon and probably living in a metropolitan area. How old was she now, sixty or sixty-one? If she'd had kids, she was probably a doting grandmother. And if she ever thought of Sam, it was undoubtedly only in passing.

Sam almost cranked the ignition and put the roof back up to keep the billowing dust out of his new car. But as his fingers touched the key, his hand fell back to his knee, an old hand with enlarged knuckles and liver spots. He was nuts, but even so he crawled out of the BMW and started up the damned hill. After going fifty feet, he had to stop and grab for breath. As he stood there with his hands on his hips, blowing like an overworked racehorse, he measured the remaining distance, judged it to be a hundred yards of vertical impossibility, and nearly turned back. How would he explain to his sons if he fell and broke a hip on that slide of slate above him? Worse yet, he could get bitten by a rattlesnake, prevalent in this area of southern Oregon. He might wave away a broken bone by saying he'd fallen getting out of the tub, but a snakebite would be a bit more problematic.

Once a Marine, always a Marine. As a young man, he'd run up this hill, so eager to hold Sherry in his arms that he'd never even felt winded when he reached the top. He'd be a pickled onion if he let this incline whip him now. So up he went, one painful push at a time until he finally reached the cave.

Only it wasn't a cave. More like a crack in the sheer crag of rock. For an instant, he thought he'd come to the wrong place, but as he limped closer he saw it – initials etched in the stone, encircled by a lopsided heart. A smile touched Sam's lips. Memories swamped him – such wonderful, precious memories. He sat in the opening, which was far narrower and shallower than he recalled. How in the hell had he passionately embraced a girl in here? The ground was rocky. He guessed they must have cleared away the stones to create a smoother surface. And he and Sherry had never "gone all the way," the teenage expression back then for actually doing the dirty. They'd only kissed and petted, yet another expression that was undoubtedly familiar only to old fogies. What did kids call it now, groping each other?

Sam closed his eyes for a moment. God, he was pathetic, a lonely old coot, clinging to the past. He needed to drive home to Portland and get a dog, damn it. A golden retriever, maybe. They were friendly. Bad for shedding, though, and his daughter-in-law, Kristen, was allergic – not that she'd darkened his doorstep since Christmas. He might be better off to get one of those new-fangled canines he'd read about, a mix between a Labrador and poodle. Supposedly they were hypoallergenic and didn't shed. But, no, he wanted a golden. With that snazzy car, he needed a blonde sitting in the passenger seat, and if she made Kristen sneeze, tough shit.

He chuckled to himself and was about to get up when he caught a flash of brightness from the corner of his eye. He turned and saw a quart jar resting in a crack of the cave wall. Puzzled, he plucked it out. The label read *Kraft Mayonnaise.* In side the container was an envelope. He unscrewed the lid but couldn't fit his hand in the mouth of the jar. He ended up fish ing and scissoring with his middle and index finger to get the letter out. It was addressed simply, *To Sam.* His heart jerked and picked up speed. This had to be from Sherry . . . but it wasn't her handwriting.

Trembling, Sam broke the seal. Inside he found two folded letters, one thick, the other a single page. He opened the short one first.

Hi, Sam.

You don't know me, but I know a lot about you. Mom kept you a secret for years, but after I turned thirty, she finally came clean. Imagine my surprise when I learned I was named after a man I didn't know existed. Ah, well, off subject. After Mom divorced my dad – he was unfaithful to her from the start, and she finally got fed up – she made the annual pilgrimage to this place every single year on July 8th. She always hoped you might be here sometime, waiting for her. She knew you were happily married and she was glad for you, but she still hoped you might meet her here one day, just as friends and for old time's sake.

Now that she can never come again, I took it upon myself to make the pilgrimage for her this one last time. I wanted you to know that my mother never stopped loving you. This jar will probably sit here forever, and her letter and mine might never be read unless kids happen upon the cave. But on the off chance that you one day decide to return here, maybe you'll find it. I hope so. It would be great if you could read her letter and at least know she never forgot you.

All best, Samantha Whitaker Ames

Tears filled Sam's eyes. *Sherry*. He gazed out over the rough terrain, his heart panging at the thought of her faithfully trudg ing up that steep slope year after year to meet a man who'd never appeared. He assumed from Samantha's letter that her mother had passed away. The thought pained him. *Sherry, so in love with life and with him*. How could she possibly be dead? But then, for Sam, life had been a harsh teacher. He'd held his twelve-year-old son in his arms as the life had seeped from his body, and years later, he'd also embraced Eva as she left this world. Everyone had an expiration date.

With shaking hands, he opened the letter from Sherry. He had to blink to clear his vision and read.

My darling Sam:

I know you were happily married to a won derful woman named Eva. You can find people nowadays on the Internet and learn almost any thing. My sincere condolences. You must miss her dreadfully, and I am so sorry you lost her. For years, I went to the cave, even when I knew you were tied to someone else, not so much because I hoped to rekindle an old flame and in terfere with your marriage, but because though

> you and I were lovers, we were also friends, and I never stopped missing you. I adored the sound of your laugh and the way your eyes always warmed before you smiled. I could never really turn loose of you. Until I heard Eva passed on, I just visited the cave and then left, leaving no sign that I'd been there. But now, knowing she's gone, I no longer feel it is wrong to let you know I've never forgotten you. On the off chance that you might one day start reminiscing about a foolish young girl you once loved and visit the cave, I want you to find this letter. I've had a hip replacement and should no longer make the climb, so my daughter is going in my stead. Anyway, foolish old woman that I am, I'm including my contact information. No obligation on your part, but if you read this someday – before I'm shuffled off to a retirement home – and would like to call, I'd love to hear your voice. Or, better yet, just show up unannounced on my doorstep. I'll make a pot of coffee or tea and serve it with whatever cookies I have on hand. We can reminisce about the good old days.
>
> Love always, Sherry

Sam reread the letter three times. *Damn.* She lived in Grants Pass, only a thirty-minute drive away. A glance at his watch told him it was half past one. Was mid-afternoon an appropriate time for a lover from the past to knock on a woman's door? Hell, as far as that went, was any time appropriate for such a harebrained act? He'd feel ridiculous. No matter.

He managed to get down the slope, and punched Sherry's address into his navigation system. As he turned the car around, he recalled an adage that he'd heard since early childhood. *There's no fool like an old fool.*

~ ~ ~

Heat rolled from the oven when Sherry opened the door to check on the roast. Samantha was coming for dinner, and her favorite meal was a slowly baked rump roast with potatoes, carrots, and onions accompanied by a salad and a nice red wine. And homemade chocolate chip cookies for dessert, of course. It would be a simple, no-frills meal, but that was fine. Eric, Samantha's husband, was away with their son, Jamie, for a week-long Boy Scout camping trip along the McKenzie River, so it would be a girls-only night, suggested by Samantha, Sherry felt sure, because it was July 8th. Samantha was bringing *Fried Green Tomatoes*, Sherry's favorite flick, to watch after they ate just in case they ran out of things to talk about.

As if, Sherry thought with a smile. Samantha was a chatterbox. When she wasn't going on about Eric, *the* most wonderful man on earth, or her son, *the* cutest kid who'd ever walked, she spoke enthusiastically of her fashion-consultant business, which Sherry had passed on to her after retiring, telling amusing stories about her clients. And when she ran out of tales about eccentric customers, she gave updates on the latest news about mutual acquaintances, mostly Samantha's childhood friends and their parents – people around Sherry's age, many on their second or third marriages.

With a sigh, Sherry closed the oven, checked a cooling cookie to be sure it would be chewy, and then headed back to her office, where she'd been working since early morning on a wedding gown design she felt certain would be eye-popping gorgeous. Another Sherry Whitaker original would soon become some young bride's dream come true. It was what Sherry loved most about retirement, being able to design and create. Her income wasn't as steady, but she still did well annually, and for the first time in her life, she could let her imagination run wild.

The doorbell rang just as she perched on the stool in front of her easel. *Sigh*. If it was Paula Marks from next door again, Sherry would be tempted to put salt in her coffee instead of sugar. The woman had too much time on her hands now that she no longer worked, and she seemed to think Sherry's sole mission in life was to provide her with entertainment during the lull time between her two favorite afternoon soap operas.

Not! Paula was nice, but on an everyday basis, her conversation grew stale. Sherry began rehearsing lines about a headache as she started for the door.

It wasn't Paula. An older man stood on the porch. Not a salesman. He was dressed too casually for that in tan Dockers and a pale blue Polo shirt. She glanced past him at the fancy sil ver Beamer parked in her driveway. A Realtor, maybe? Houses in her neighborhood didn't often go on the market, and it was a coveted area. Sometimes agents went door-to-door, asking homeowners if they were interested in selling, which Sherry definitely was not.

She was about to give the guy a brush off when she finally looked at his face – really *looked*, that is. Recognition came with a jolt.

Sam.

Though silver now streaked his dark hair and the years had etched a road map on his face, every line and plane of those rugged, chiseled features were engraved on her heart – that square jaw, the firm yet full mouth, and the blade-like nose that still sported a bump along the bridge. He'd changed, of course. *Drastically*. But not those blue eyes.

His lips tipped into that crooked grin she remembered so well, and he held up a glass quart jar. "I brought along the evi dence. You *did* extend me a standing invitation to knock at your door unannounced. I decided to take you up on it."

Sherry didn't take time to analyze her response. "It took you long enough to come," she cried. And then, somehow, without making the decision, she'd launched herself into his arms. He caught her close, his embrace just as strong and hard as she remembered. Dimly she heard the jar hit the pavers and shatter, but she was so overcome with feelings that she could focus only on Sam. *Sam*. She'd dreamed of seeing him again, *prayed* to see him again. And now, at long last, he was finally here.

"Sherry," he whispered, his face pressed against her hair. "Ah, sweetheart."

Tears streamed down her cheeks. She realized she was plastered against him and knew she should let go, but her arms seemed to have a will of their own. Sam didn't seem to mind.

He tightened his hold, swaying from side to side, taking deep breaths as if the scent of her hair was addictive.

Finally, when they both regained their composure, they moved from the porch into the house. Sherry clung to his hand. "I'm afraid to turn you loose for fear you'll disappear."

He laughed – that deep, rich laugh that had echoed so many times in her memories. "Now that I'm here, wild horses couldn't drag me away. You look –" He broke off to study her face. "I expected to see an old lady with a cane. Instead, you're even more beautiful than you were at eighteen."

She waved away the compliment but was pleased all the same. Leading him to the kitchen, she directed him to a bar stool and forced herself into hostess mode. For a few seconds, silence descended – an uncomfortable silence. But then, as she put on a pot of coffee, Sam said, "Remember my old black Ford, and that time the cop caught us necking up at the gravel pit?"

That was all it took; the ice was broken, and the years that had passed since they'd been together seemed to fall away. They spent at least an hour reminiscing and laughing so hard at times that their sides ached. Then they moved out onto her patio to sit at the table, side by side, elbow to elbow, to talk even more. Sam told her about his war injuries, his resultant feelings of inadequacy, and why he'd opted out when her marriage to Whitaker had been imminent. Then he spoke reverently of Eva, their life together, and how difficult the last two years had been without her.

"Last year on July 8th, I thought about going to the cave," he confessed, "but I wasn't ready yet. This morning –" He shrugged his broad shoulders and smiled. "Well, I felt like an old fool for going, but now I'm really glad I did."

Sherry squeezed his hand. "I'm glad you did, too."

He'd told her about his life, so she reciprocated, giving him a brief recap of her miserable marriage, the nasty divorce, and how she'd picked up the pieces of her shattered existence to finally chase her own dreams as a fashion designer and consultant. "Raymond never really loved me," she admitted. "To him, I was merely an opportunity. He hoped to speed-launch his career as a surgeon by riding on Daddy's shirttails, and he did.

He was having his first affair with another woman less than two months after our wedding."

"Ah, Sherry, I'm sorry. You deserved so much more than that."

Sherry no longer felt even a pang of hurt when she thought of Raymond. "You're absolutely right. I did. And eventually I left the bastard and grabbed hold of the brass ring!"

Sam chuckled. "In fashion? I thought your dad was dead set on you going into the medical field."

"He settled for getting a surgeon as son-in-law. I became the little suburban wife, expected to have two point five children, drive a minivan, and support my husband in his career. I didn't go to college until after the divorce, and even then, I went on my own dime. Dad refused to fork out a single penny on tuition. My goals were, in his opinion, idiotic."

"But you proved him wrong," Sam said. No question rang in his voice. "Is he still alive?"

Sherry sighed. "No. He passed away four years ago, my mother a year later." She fell silent, searching Sam's sky-blue eyes. A lump formed in her throat, and she dreaded hearing his answer, but she had to ask the question. "So, Sam, where do we go from here? Are you going to thank me for the coffee in a few more minutes and drive home to Portland?" Sherry sat back on her chair to put some distance between them before she could continue. "This may seem bold, but I'm too old to play games. Am I ever going to see you again?"

His gaze remained steady on hers. "We were only kids forty-three years ago. Deeply in love, I'll admit, but still just kids. Could we have made it work back then? Do we have enough in common to make it work now? I don't think either of us can answer that question yet."

Some of the tension eased from her body. "I'm well aware that we'd be crazy to make rash decisions and take up where we left off, Sam. That isn't what I asked."

He trailed a forefinger, gnarly now with a bit of arthritis, along her cheekbone. "Of course, you'll see me again. I think we owe it to ourselves to explore the possibilities. You've mentioned that you have plans for tonight with your daughter, but if I stay over at a motel, will you be free tomorrow?"

Sherry laughed and caught hold of his wrist. "Free as a bird. What are we going to do?"

He turned his hand to clasp hers. "We'll follow our noses, spend the day together, see where it takes us. It's so good to see you again. It may take a crowbar to pry me away from you until tomorrow morning. I keep thinking this can't be happening, that I'm dreaming and will wake up. But it's real. You're real."

"I misplaced my crowbar. Stay for dinner. Samantha would love to meet you, Sam, and I have two spare bedrooms. I won't hear of your staying at a motel."

"And neither will I."

Both Sherry and Sam jumped. They turned to find Sherry's daughter standing in the open doorway that led onto the patio. Still sweaty from a tennis match with her friend Olivia, Samantha looked wilted in her shorts and damp T-shirt. Her short, dark hair clung in curls to her forehead.

"You must be the legendary Sam," she said with a saucy grin. "I saw the broken mayonnaise jar on the porch and used my exemplary deductive reasoning to draw that conclusion."

"And you must be Samantha." Sam stood to shake hands. "It's good to meet you." He cocked his head to survey her face. "You have your mother's beautiful whiskey-colored eyes. And her smile."

"Thanks. The rest of me is all Whitaker, except for my character. In that department, I also took after my mom." Samantha waggled a finger under Sam's nose. "Don't you dare even *think* about getting a room tonight. Mom's got guest accommodations, and I want to get to know you."

Sam chuckled. "I'd love to stay for dinner."

Samantha led the way back into the house, Sam and Sherry following in her wake. Sherry thought that Samantha, tall, dark, and sturdy of build, looked enough like Sam to be his daughter, and when she glanced up into his twinkling blue eyes, she knew he was thinking the exact same thing. They exchanged a secret smile – the kind of smile only lovers can share, communicating without saying a word. Sherry knew then, with deep certainty, that Sam Jones wasn't going to suddenly disappear again.

The autumn of their lives lay before them, full of delightful possibilities. For far too many years, they'd gone their separate ways, but now they'd come full circle. It felt right. So beauti fully, incredibly *right.* Sam squeezed her hand and grinned.

And though he was too honorable a man to voice it yet, she saw a promise in his eyes. Crazy as it was, they were go ing to do precisely what he'd said they shouldn't; pick up right where they'd left off and learn where their love for each other might take them.

Tunnel Vision

by C.J. Lyons

As a pediatric ER doctor, *New York Times* bestseller C.J. Lyons has lived the life she writes about in her cutting edge Thrillers with Heart.

C.J. has been called a "master within the genre" (*Pittsburgh* magazine), and her work has been praised as "breathtakingly fast-paced" and "riveting" (*Publishers Weekly*) with "characters with beating hearts and three dimensions" (*Newsday*).

Learn more about C.J.'s Thrillers with Heart at www.cjlyons.net.

The stalker's drive to possess another person has fascinated me ever since I was in college and stalked by an older man. Twenty-five years later, the memory of feeling helpless, that any decision I made would only make things worse once he twisted my actions through his warped lens of obsession, still leaves me breathless with anxiety.

In "Tunnel Vision," I decided to turn the tables on a stalker, asking myself: What if a stalker was being manipulated to fulfill someone else's twisted needs? What if the person he'd tied his fate to, the person he "loved" so very much that he devoted his life to analyzing her every waking moment, what if that person used the stalker's obsession against him?

From those questions two characters emerged along with their twisted tale of obsession, possession, and desire.

If you don't love me, it does not matter, anyway
I can love for both of us.

~Stendhal

Everything I did, I did for us.

She smiled and I knew. Not her normal, painted on for the world smile. No, this smile was her secret smile, aimed only at me.

Then she mentioned attending the Van Gogh opening at the art museum and did her patented twisty finger wave with her right hand, freshly manicured and painted with the OPI color she chose especially for me: Keys to my Karma red.

Bright and sparkly as Dorothy's ruby slippers – just like our love.

I knew what she wanted me to do. Finally. Tonight was the night.

Rewinding the newscast, I watched over and over, concen trating on every detail, etching it into my brain, making certain I hadn't missed any part of her message. Details. They're vitally important. So many people are too busy, too distracted, to fo cus on what really matters.

Not my Janice. She knows the importance of details. Which earrings to wear – the small freshwater pearls in the gold filigree setting instead of the gaudy Swarovski crystals her husband had given her for their anniversary. How to part her hair. On the right, the side I prefer, instead of pulling it straight back or doing that crazy diagonal part she'd played around with for awhile.

Even down to her shoes. I was probably the only person of the half a million who watched her broadcast who saw that while her dress was a navy blue and white polka dot silk – and I knew for a fact that she had the matching navy Giuseppe

Zanotti sling backs sitting on the third row of her shoe cubby--she wore a pair of dowdy brown suede pumps.

Fashion mishap, anyone else might have assumed. Not me. I knew better. They were a message. For me. And me alone. Then she made a mistake in her newscast – Janice never makes mistakes. Never.

She said the event began at seven pm tonight – wrong. The opening was tomorrow. At eight.

Yes. Tonight was the night.

~ ~ ~

Everyday I bring her flowers. Not just any flowers. Leda damask roses. Fragrant white roses edged in crimson, her favorite. Today when I arrived at her office at the TV station, she gave me her usual smile as she signed my clipboard. Academy Award material. I don't know how she did it; stay calm and cool like that. Me? I was jittery and flustered and sweaty and tingly as a schoolboy on his first date.

I barely escaped without confessing everything to her. Tonight. I had to wait until tonight.

Watching the clock, I filled the time tinkering with my latest design. An elegant fountain pen, the kind rich executives carry. I like to think it's my flair for aesthetics that sets me apart from the others in my line of work. You have to be able to blend in anywhere – whether it's a deliveryman carrying a clipboard and flowers or a corporate officer attending a confidential meeting.

Like I said, it's all in the details.

Finally it was time to get into position. I timed my approach perfectly – her gated community had a shift change that corresponded to peak dinner-delivery time. Using one of Janice's neighbor's names, I called the guardhouse and told them to be expecting a delivery from Travanti's, a swanky Italian place. As usual, they waved me in as soon as they smelled the aroma of tomato sauce and basil wafting from my van.

I stashed the van behind the maintenance shed on the golf course before crossing through the woods to Janice's house. Burrowing into a pile of dead leaves at the edge of the trees, my khaki trousers and brown jacket blending in perfectly, I watched the back of her house through my Brunton Echo zoom monocular. Her house – bought and paid for by her husband, Stan, the stockbroker – was 4200 square feet of glass and timber, styled to look like one of those mountain vacation homes you see in glossy travel magazines.

I hated that house. We'd find a real cabin to live in, no faux rustic ambiance for me and Janice, only the real thing. I was thinking up north, in the mountains. But all those windows – it was as if Janice knew they'd come in handy. From my vantage point, I could easily see movement throughout the house ex cept for the dining room and den at the front.

Of course, I wasn't counting on using only the windows for surveillance. I swapped the monocular for my phone, called up the video app. *He* was home. Stan. Arguing with Janice in the den. She fixed him a cocktail and he raised his hand like he was going to hit her. I wished I had a sniper rifle, could take care of things right then and there.

No. I had to stick to my plan. Up close and personal. So Janice could see how much I really cared, that we're meant to be together. Forever.

She spun away from him, pressing her palms against the window as if trying to escape.

I'm coming, I called out in my mind. She looked up and smiled. Right at me. We're that much in synch.

Pocketing the phone, I slid through the bushes in the back yard, skirted the pool, and hopscotched my way through the security cameras' blind spots to the basement window with the broken latch. Then I was in.

~ ~ ~

The first time I'd come here, to Janice's house, I'd spent most of one rainy day mesmerized by her basement. The soft rain gave the air a pleasantly musty scent, like the perfume of a rare bookstore. Fitting, since Janice was such a rare find. So beautiful, so intelligent, yet so vulnerable.

She needed me. I hadn't had that in a long time. It made me feel powerful. Strong. I would do anything for her.

I wanted to know her. Everything. Where she'd come from, who she was. That day in the basement, surrounded by carefully packed and stacked cartons of her past, that's exactly what I discovered.

It was obvious she hadn't opened many of these boxes in decades, although she still kept them with her, diligently mov ing them each time she relocated. I hit the treasure trove when I found a box that had stickers from six different moving com panies – the oldest in the archive.

Inside I found diaries with tattered fabric covers, edges frayed, revealing the cardboard beneath. Yellowed pages filled with a schoolgirl's scrawl – sometimes in pink, how charming was that? – I's dotted with hearts or stars or big, empty O's of amazement. She double-crossed her capital T's, making them look somehow exotic.

I held the diary to my chest, inhaling her dreams in the perfume of paper and ink. How I understood her – like no one else could. We shared the same hopes and dreams. But both our lives had taken detours. I'd been betrayed by the men I served under, my so-called superior officers. She'd wanted to travel, experience life – not be trapped in a sterile, glass-walled cage with a jailor for a husband.

Her high school yearbooks were filled with inscriptions from friends. Most personalized; there weren't many of the stock "have a great summer." She was popular, well-liked. From the tone of the inscriptions and her smiling, alpha-girl appearance in the group shots, it was obvious she was a leader.

Of course she was. My Janice would never take a backseat to anyone. Which was why I needed to help her escape from Stan. How the hell she'd ever ended up ensnarled in his web of treachery, I'd never understand. Except even the strongest of us can have our weakness, I guess.

Lord knew, Janice was mine. I would die for her. I would kill for her.

That day in the basement, I began planning. You don't let someone you love stay trapped in a relationship that is slowly strangling the life from them. They may not even realize they need help. That's okay. I knew what needed to be done.

~ ~ ~

I waited in the basement, listening, breathing in the house and its occupants. Janice was expecting me – heck, I could have maybe just walked up to the front door – but I couldn't take any chances. Any mistake I made, she'd pay the price.

Water gurgled through the pipes. My eyes adjusted to the darkness. Nothing had been moved since my last visit. My footsteps were silent as I crossed the floor and went up the stairs to the kitchen.

The kitchen was a white tile and gleaming chrome monstrosity that didn't go with the house or Janice. She was so much more the tea in a thick mug, cuddle in her robe type. Her kitchen would smell of cinnamon and cloves, a waft of cayenne to spice things up. She'd use a French press to make coffee (I'd found one in her boxes from the last house) and splash the beans with a hint of pure vanilla.

Warm colors, golds and reds, would embrace her as we cooked side by side, our hips nudging, fingers brushing. I could see it all, down to the spark from the polished copper pots and pans. Me and Janice. Every detail would be perfect.

This kitchen, cold and barren, had an island the size of a pool table sitting in the center, two ovens, three stove tops, two refrigerators, a sink you could bathe a flounder in, another double sink, two dishwashers, two bar stools, and a set of open steps heading up to the bedrooms on the second floor.

The hallway behind me led to the front of the house. Beside me was a long prep counter, its surface empty except for a knife block. There was one missing: a Wusthof Dreizackwerk eight-inch chef's knife. The hole it left behind was a black slit in the flesh-colored maple. Maybe it'd been forgotten in one of the dishwashers or sinks. Still, that little detail made my skin prickle in warning. I drew my weapon, a Beretta nine millimeter, holding it at my side.

Footsteps from the staircase yanked my attention away from the counter. And there she was, bathed in the fading sun streaming through the wide windows, wearing a pink silk dressing gown, hair wet, feet bare, face naked.

She glided down the steps, her gaze locked on mine. One hand slid along the polished oak banister, caressing it the way she wanted to caress my skin. My breath caught at the thought and I stood straighter. Her other hand was behind her back as if she held a surprise.

She reached the bottom of the steps, stood only four feet away. The closest I'd ever come to her without other people around.

I raised my Beretta. She raised her knife – the eight-inch Wusthof Dreizackwerk I'd noticed missing.

The Beretta wasn't for her. But who was the knife for? The sun slipped below the tree line, leaving us cloaked in shadows. "Janice. It's okay."

Her gaze darted from the gun to my face and back again. The gun frightened her – the opposite effect than what I'd wanted. I re-holstered it. There'd be plenty of time to draw it again once I got upstairs to where her husband was.

"What do you want?" Fear made her voice tremble and I hated that I'd put it there.

I held my hands up, palms out to her, offering her every thing. "To take care of you. To love you. To save you from him."

Both our eyes went to the top of the stairs. She heaved in a breath, let it out in a motion that deflated her, made her turn from fashionable TV news star to frightened little girl in less time than it took to pull a trigger. Head angled low, she edged her gaze up, meeting mine. Uncertain. Hopeful.

Then she stepped towards me, holding the knife out by the handle. I took it. It was sticky with her sweat – she must have been terrified. I pulled her to me in a quick hug, her body pressing against mine like a prayer answered.

She pushed away. I chided myself: too much, too fast.

She clicked on the lights – a row of tiny halogen bulbs set in trendy cobalt blue glass votives hanging upside down from the ceiling. "Who are you?"

Now she was teasing – or testing me. "You know who I am."

She circled around the back of the island, placing it be tween us. I hid my disappointment. She was traumatized; I had to take things slowly.

"Johnny Boy?" she asked. "The guy who keeps sending those nasty pictures of himself?"

My surprise cracked into laughter. Then I saw she was serious. What was wrong with her? I frowned. "No."

"Janicelover334@hotmail.com? Is that you?"

Anger broiled the back of my eyes, my vision narrowing to a bright sharp spotlight focused on her. "Janice, stop kidding around. It's me, Richard. We see each other every day."

She frowned, then smiled. I relaxed. Her sense of humor – wicked. "Of course, the flower delivery guy. Never thought it would be you. I thought for sure it would be one of the others."

"Others?" For the first time that night I felt uncertain.

She fluttered her fingers, the OPI Keys to my Karma sparkling in the halogen lights like wet blood. "My stalkers. You wouldn't believe how many there are. I've been sending invites all week, knew one of you guys would be coming – wasn't expecting the delivery boy."

I didn't like this side of her. She'd have to learn that her sense of humor could be cruel if she carried a joke too far. "I'm not a delivery boy. I own AstroLite Tech –"

"You really don't get it, do you? Look down at the knife."

It took all my willpower to tear my gaze away from her and look down. The knife in my hand wasn't covered with sweat – it was covered with blood.

My insides hollowed out, a cold like February taking up residence. My eyes kept staring at the blood, my brain noticing every detail: the orange Trident insignia turned brown with blood, the three steel rivets, the way the well-constructed grip contained the blood without becoming slippery, the wickedly edged tip of the broken blade.

Despite all the sensory information, I still didn't comprehend. Didn't want to comprehend. Tunnel vision of the psyche. "What –"

"Not what. Who. My dear husband. Dead upstairs in the shower. Just like you'll be soon." The sound of the front door opening punctuated her words. "Here comes Sebastian, another of my fans. He set up a hidden camera at the basement window – that's how I knew it was safe to go ahead and take care of Stan. We have it planned down to the last detail."

I couldn't help myself. I had to be certain. I looked at her first. Before spinning around to confront the steroid-freak in the security guard uniform advancing on me, gun drawn. I never had a chance to reach for my Beretta. My hearing collapsed, all I could hear was my blood pounding as three bright lights flashed before me.

Getting shot isn't like in the movies. You don't fly off your feet or spin across the room. It's like being sucker punched. Then comes the burning. You drop anything you're holding, double over, slide to the floor. The pain isn't so much pain as it is a wave swallowing you whole, swamping you in a rush of blood and confusion and terror.

I would've done it for her. If only she had asked me.

Then everything went black.

~ ~ ~

Janice Sampson took the cup of coffee the detective offered and gripped it with both hands. She was trembling so badly she ended up sloshing most of it onto the table in the interview room. "I'm sorry –"

"No problem," he said graciously. "Here, let me get that." He grabbed a few tissues from the box sitting between them and wiped up the mess. "You've had a rough night of it."

She nodded.

"We'll try to make this fast."

"T-thank you."

"So, this Richard Lindeman, you knew him?"

"No. Not really. I saw him when he delivered flowers – I didn't even know his name."

The detective leaned back in his chair. "You know he doesn't work for a florist, right?"

She shook her head. "He doesn't?"

"No. He's former military intelligence. Records are sealed so we don't know much except that after leaving the Army he created his own tech company. They specialize in audiovisual surveillance."

Her hands flew to her throat. She covered by smoothing out her robe, cinching it tighter. "Surveillance?"

"Yep. He had your whole house wired for video. The lab boys are looking at the footage from his computer now."

"He was – watching me? Everywhere?"

The detective nodded. "Everywhere. We even found a camera in the bathroom fan. Above the shower stall where your husband was killed."

She raised the cup of coffee to her lips but didn't drink. The detective took advantage of the pause and slid a pen from his pocket, placing it on the table between them. It was an el egant fountain pen, black onyx finish sparkling as he twirled it.

"Of course those were only videos. Thanks to this," he tapped the pen, "we have both audio and visual of everything that went on in the kitchen tonight."

She leaned forward, her face mere inches from the table top, staring at the pen.

"Nice work isn't it?" The detective asked. "Such attention to detail."

Goldfarb's Red Scarf

by Steven Womack

Steven Womack is the Edgar and Shamus-Award winning author of ten novels, including his latest, *By Blood Written.* A scriptwriter as well, he wrote the scripts for the ABC Television-movie, *Volcano: Fire On The Mountain*, and the CableAce Award-nominated *Proudheart.* A native of Nashville, Tennessee, Womack has been, at various times: a factory machine operator; a reporter for United Press International; a stringer for the Clayton, Missouri *Citizen;* a skip chaser; a paste-up person and typesetter; and a few things he now confesses he can't even remember. In addition to writing, he has for the past sixteen years been on faculty at the Watkins College of Art, Design & Film in Nashville, where he is currently and thankfully in his last year as Chair of the Film School.

I confess: this is the most autobiographical piece of writing I've ever done. It's barely fiction, and it's about as far away from my usual work in suspense and crime fiction as possible. I did graduate from an all-boy's boarding school and I was a terrible athlete. In my three years of running track and cross-country at Western Reserve Academy, I won precisely one race, and it, too, was intramural. So while Nathan Goldfarb's not completely me, he's pretty close. And there was a cross-country and track coach at the boarding school I attended whose nickname was "Stretch." The only difference is the real-life Stretch was always very kind to me and everyone else. He was a much more supportive and patient man than Stretch Wharton in the short story. So I took some liberties with that character.

There was no visible, obvious reason why Nathan Goldfarb should be the worst runner – and perhaps the worst athlete – in Academy history.

On first appearance, it made no sense. His body was lean, lanky, with long legs and the outline of ribs showing through the skin of his abdomen. There was nothing superfluous about him. He was neither fat, nor clumsy, nor even that slow. In practice, he ran respectably if not spectacularly. At worst, he should have been a mediocre runner, an uninspired runner, or to use a phrase common at the Academy, an "underachiever."

But no, Nathan Goldfarb was a *terrible* runner. He was the kind of runner who during cross-country season would stagger across the finish line not only dead last, but so far dead last that the stands would be empty, the opposing team on its way to the bus after clearing out of the locker room.

Goldfarb's problem was the voice in his head. A continuous mental monologue punctuated every painful stride, every stitch in his side, every agonizing gulp of air, until finally he was sandbagged by the relentless voice. All he heard was how much it hurt, how little chance he had. And as he fell farther and farther behind, the voice would begin to berate and hound him.

Barely six weeks into Goldfarb's freshman year, cross-country coach Lou Wharton – whose lifelong nickname was "Stretch" – realized what he was up against and tried to palm him off on the soccer coach. By then, word had gotten around and it was too late. Athletics were compulsory at the Academy – always had been, always would be. And cross-country, with its inherent assumption that running involved no particular skill beyond putting one foot in front of the other at a rapid pace, was the dumping ground for the boys who had little or no athletic talent. Stretch Wharton was stuck with Goldfarb, and probably would be for the next four years.

Midway through the season, after one particularly disastrous performance in which Goldfarb had come within seconds of posting the worst time in freshman cross-country history, Stretch summoned Goldfarb to his office in the back of the gymnasium. The tiny office was a converted storage room, with a desk, one four-drawer filing cabinet, and one metal folding chair for visitors.

Goldfarb timidly knocked on the door. "In!" Stretch yelled, his gravelly voice echoing off the painted cinderblocks.

Goldfarb opened the door and peeked in, his face paler than usual. Stretch swiveled in his tattered office chair.

"Goldfarb, sit down!"

Goldfarb entered, book bag over his shoulder, his rumpled khakis looking as if he'd slept in them, his food-stained school tie pulled down to the second button of his white shirt. Stretch motioned to the metal chair, then leaned back and extended his long legs across the desk, crossed them at the ankles, and intertwined his fingers behind his head.

"Goldfarb," he began. "I want to talk to you. Tell me, son, are you happy here?"

Goldfarb sat stiffly and lowered his book bag to the floor. He shuffled in the seat as if trying to find a comfortable place. He looked across the desk at the tall, gray-haired man who stared at him through rheumy, bloodshot eyes.

"Well, son?"

"I –" Goldfarb stammered. "I don't know, I never really gave –"

"How did you wind up here, Goldfarb? What made you decide to come to the Academy?"

Goldfarb looked down at his shoes. "Well, my father and my grandfather, they both –"

"Ah!" Stretch shouted throwing his head back. "So you're Ben Goldfarb's boy?"

Goldfarb's brow wrinkled. His father had been captain of the track team in 1974, his senior year. His grandfather had been student body president and winner of the Headmaster's Trophy in 1945, the year he graduated.

Now that Goldfarb was at the Academy, he didn't like to think about all that.

"Yes sir," he answered.

Stretch gazed at Goldfarb for a few seconds, the silence between them like the edge of a freshly stropped razor. Goldfarb tried to meet the older man's stare, but couldn't. He looked down at the floor again and tapped his right foot.

"Have you got a nickname yet, son?" Stretch demanded.

Goldfarb blushed. Everyone at the Academy was given a nickname sooner or later, and the weaker the boy, the more cruel the nickname.

"Yes sir," Goldfarb whispered, glaring at the concrete floor as if trying to make it give way so he could dive into the earth and pull the dirt in after him.

"Well?"

Goldfarb looked up. "It's Goldfart."

Stretch's laugh bounced off the walls. "Goldfart! I love it."

Goldfarb stared. He didn't.

"Son, you can be a decent runner," Stretch growled. "It's in you. It's in there somewhere. All you have to do is dig until you find it."

Goldfarb's nose itched, but he was afraid to scratch. "Okay, Stretch, I –"

"Good, son, I'm glad we understand each other! Now get out there and make us proud!"

Goldfarb stood a bit too quickly, relieved that he was getting off this easily. He grabbed his book bag, turned, and stumbled out the door.

Stretch watched the kid struggle to leave his office, then sighed as the door shut and he was once again alone. He had seen this before and he knew what the problem was.

Goldfarb, he knew, had no heart for this sort of thing.

~ ~ ~

The years and the seasons went by: cross-country in the autumn, winter basketball, track and field in the spring. Goldfarb went through the motions, quietly and steadily proving himself to be one of the worst athletes in memory. Goldfarb managed to survive, however, even fitting in with a certain category of boys who came and went for their four years at the Academy without ever making much of an impression on anyone.

It was Academy tradition that any boy who persevered even when he lacked the skill, talent, speed, or agility to make the Varsity team would be allowed to run up enough points his senior year to earn a school letter. There were always easy competitions somewhere during the season where the lesser-equipped boys could be thrown into the breach without causing too much risk to the season record.

The year Goldfarb turned senior, the first cross-country meet of the season was against the local public high school. The public schools put most of their efforts into football, and as a result their cross-country teams were generally much weaker than those of the private schools, one of the few instances in which this was true.

As the boys filed out of the locker rooms in their thick cotton warm-ups, a steep chill was already settling in. Even though it was early September, the leaves had started to turn and the first frost had been recorded. It was four o'clock on a Saturday afternoon, and even now the sky was darkening.

Stretch Wharton stood at the starting line with his clipboard in hand, scanning the list of boys and planning his strategy. His assistant coach, Leo Ripley, who also served as both a Spanish teacher and housemaster for the largest dormitory, approached him.

"What's it look like, Stretch?" he asked.

Stretch looked up at the sky. "Snow, damn it," he muttered. "Early this year."

Ripley smiled. "No, I mean for the line-up."

Stretch took the pencil from behind his right ear and quickly checked off twelve names, then handed the clipboard to Ripley. Ripley stared at it a moment.

"No," he finally said. "You can't –"

"Got to," Stretch said. "He's a senior."

Stretch reached into his sweater and pulled out a whistle on a lanyard. He blew into it, hard, and the shrill warble echoed across the field. The boys jumped up from the grass where they'd been stretching and ran across the cinders to the starting line in front of the bleachers, which were slowly filling with spectators.

"Here we go," Stretch barked. "Today's starters. Adams, Benchley, Dortman, Dubus, Goldfarb –"

Time seemed to stop as the boys collectively gasped. They all turned, stared at Goldfarb, and as they did, a smile spread across the thin, tall boy's face.

Stretch rattled off the names of the rest of the starters, then walked away for a quick confab with the opposing team's coach. A few moments later, he looked at his watch, walked back to the starting line and blew hard on the whistle again.

"Two minutes," he commanded. "Line 'em up!"

Then he turned just as Leo Ripley walked up to him. Some thing caught his eye and he stopped cold on the cinder track, his brow curling into rolls of flesh and his eyes bulging.

"What?" Ripley asked. "What is it?"

Stretch nodded and Ripley turned his head. "Jesus," he muttered.

The crowd of runners was off the track, shucking their warm-ups, adjusting jock straps, shaking off the last minute nervousness. At the edge of the crowd, Nathan Goldfarb had just neatly folded his warm-up and placed it on the ground. As he stood up and turned, the other boys saw what Stretch Wharton and Lou Ripley had already seen.

Nathan Goldfarb wore a long, shiny red silk scarf around his neck. He'd tied it loosely at the throat and thrown it jauntily over his left shoulder, where it hung limply almost to his waist.

"What the hell?" Stretch whispered.

Ripley shook his head. "I've never seen anything like it."

"What do we do?" Ripley said after a moment.

"I don't know," Stretch answered.

"We've got to do something," Ripley said.

Stretch's eyes narrowed. "Get me Weezer."

George "Weezer" Wilson, the captain of the cross-country team in the fall, the swim team in the winter, and the track team in the spring, was one of only about six twelve-letter men in Academy history. The son of a senator, Wilson was a brilliant student, exceptional athlete, had a winning personality in pub lic, and had barely missed being elected student body president the previous year. Already into Harvard on early admission,

Wilson was astonishingly arrogant even for someone with his qualifications.

"Yeah, Stretch," Wilson said as he trotted to the coach. He brushed his straight blond hair back over his head and squared his broad shoulders.

"Weezer, step into my office," Stretch said, and the two walked a few yards down the track out of earshot.

"What's with the scarf?" Stretch asked.

Wilson shrugged. "I don't know. I've never seen it before."

"We've got to do something about it," Stretch said. "If I do it, it'll look like I'm trying to stifle his individuality, or some such bull crap. Besides, he's a senior. But if you do it…"

Wilson smiled. "Consider it done." With that, he turned and trotted off toward the group of boys, who were doing calf stretches in a circle on the grass a few yards from the starting line.

Weezer Wilson walked up to the circle, leaned down, and tapped Goldfarb on the shoulder.

"Hey, Goldfart," he said. "C'mere."

Goldfarb stood and followed Wilson over to the side of the bleachers.

"Look, Goldfart, the guys and me got together and, well, we had a little talk."

Goldfarb gazed at Wilson. This was perhaps the fourth or fifth time in their four years at the Academy that Wilson had even acknowledged his existence, and the only time the two had ever had a private conversation.

"Yeah," Goldfarb said hesitantly.

"It's the scarf, Goldfart. It's got to go."

"Wait a minute," Goldfarb said.

"No, it's embarrassing. You're embarrassing all of us."

Goldfarb's shoulders sagged, as if someone had let the air out of him. "It's the first time I've ever been a starter. I was just having a little fun," he said weakly.

Weezer Wilson gave him that award-winning smile, that smile that had already gotten him more sex than any other senior in the history of the school, and threw his arm around Goldfarb's shoulder.

"Hey, Goldfart, it's no big deal. It'd be different, you know, if you were like… any good or anything."

"Okay," Goldfarb muttered, shaking his head. He reached up to untie the scarf. As he did, a cold drizzle began falling.

The timekeeper blew his whistle and the runners gathered at the starting line, the Academy boys in their clean, pressed uniforms and the public high school kids in their ratty, unmatched shorts and T-shirts. Most of the Academy boys wore expensive track shoes – Pumas, Adidas, Sauconys – while the public school boys all wore cheap tennis shoes.

The timekeeper raised his starter's pistol in the air and fired. In a blur, the mass of boys stampeded down the track past the stands.

The three-mile-long cross-country course began on the track, continued around the hockey pond, then along a line of trees on the other side of the track, through a long field, then out of sight of the stands. For the next fifteen minutes or so, the boys ran down a long incline that tempted many of them to speed up as the running was easy. It was all a set-up, though, as the experienced boys knew. For right after the downward incline, they would round a turn and face Cross Country Hill, a long slope that became ever steeper for almost a straight mile. More than one young, overconfident boy had found himself on his knees halfway up Cross Country Hill losing his high-carb, pre-race lunch.

Stretch and Ripley stared hard as the boys left the track, rounded the hockey pond, then started down the tree line. By then, the pack was breaking up as the faster boys gradually worked their way forward, leaving the slower ones back.

Just before the fragmented line of boys began to disappear for the course's long second act, Stretch could make out through the rain, even with his presbyopic eyes, Nathan Goldfarb dropping farther and farther behind.

Stretch turned to Ripley, shaking his head. "Jesus," he muttered.

Goldfarb didn't even finish the race. He left the course with a cramp in his side before the crest of Cross Country Hill and cut back to the football field just as the public school boys were gathering up the last of their gear. A chorus of hoots and catcalls swelled as Goldfarb crossed the empty football field, his uniform soaked with a freezing mixture of sweat and rain. He ignored the insults and the jeers, walked over to the stands, picked up his warm-up suit, and with his head down, walked slowly to the showers.

~ ~ ~

The long season went on, with winter arriving early that year. Goldfarb ran in a few more races, but not once did he ever finish in the money. Not a single point did he accumulate toward a letter, and at the end of fall semester, his name was conspicuously off the awards list.

The last week of the semester, right before finals, the Green & White games began. The Academy colors were green and white, and each boy who attended school was labeled – in a process so secret that no one even knew how it came about – as either Green or White. It was a label each boy would wear all his life. The only exceptions were the legacies; they alone knew what they would be. Goldfarb's grandfather was Green, as was his father.

The Green & White Games were intramural; only the boys who had not lettered in a school sport were allowed to com pete. It was a chance for the younger, less talented boys to win a little glory for themselves. The games were historically a rau cous time, with lots of pranks the week of the games. Greens and Whites would compete to see who could pull off the most outrageous stunt.

The Green & White cross-country race was the last event and the highlight of the games. As the week progressed, the weather worsened. A storm blew in from the Canadian plains, across the Great Lakes, and down through the Midwest like a juggernaut. As the boys filed out of the gymnasium on the blustery, frigid last day of the games, snow had already begun to fall in stinging torrents. The crowd of runners shivered at the starting line, jumping around to stay loose, eager to begin the race if for no other reason than to get it over with.

"Are we waiting for anyone?" Stretch yelled above the howling wind. As he did, he turned toward the gym and saw a lone figure crossing the parking lot, headed toward the stands. He squinted, then turned to Ripley.

"I don't believe it," he said.

"What the –? Can we let him?" Ripley asked.

"I don't think we can stop him."

"But he's a senior," Ripley snapped. "Seniors never run the Green and –"

"He's never lettered," Stretch answered. "We can't stop him."

The younger boys lined up at the starting line as Nathan Goldfarb trotted up to the stands, unzipped his warm-up pants, turned and dropped them. Then he stood, grabbed each sleeve with its opposite hand, and with one smooth, quick mo tion, pulled his jersey over his head.

Hanging from his neck, draped loosely over his left shoul der, was the red scarf.

"*Jee zus*," Ripley whispered. "He's at it again."

Goldfarb loped over to the starting line and joined the mob of boys standing in the cold. The snow was beginning to accumulate now, obscuring the black cinders of the track and the grass on either side. The wind blew the snow so hard that no one could see beyond the 100-yard lane. Two hundred yards away, the hockey pond was covered in a thick mist.

Goldfarb stood next to Brad "Be-Rad" Hamilton, a soph omore who had missed making the Varsity team by only six seconds. He'd captained the J.V. team and was on track to be about an eight-letter man by the time he left school.

Hamilton glared at Goldfarb, then reached out and flicked the red scarf. "Where the hell you think you're going, Gold fart? I'm gonna kick your ass."

Goldfarb looked down at the boy, who was more solid but about four inches shorter. "Be-Rad, just shut up and run."

"Let's get this over with!" Stretch yelled just beyond the starting line. "It's cold out here." He raised his arm in the air and fired the pistol.

Goldfarb almost tripped as the crowd of boys surged around him. He got his footing, finally, and began the run in a relaxed canter, his arms pumping, his head up, running directly into the sharp, stinging snow as it blew straight down the track.

At the end of the 100-yard dash lanes, he hung in with the pack as it left the track and turned toward the hockey pond. His lungs were beginning to burn as he took in the frosty air, but for some reason he couldn't fathom, it didn't hurt. In fact, it felt good. Nathan Goldfarb had never felt good running before.

As the herd of runners rounded the hockey pond, Be-Rad Hamilton pulled solidly into the lead. The boys ran into the mist that floated above the water, and for a moment Goldfarb lost sight of the leaders. He concentrated on keeping his footing and working on a rhythm and then something began to happen, something he'd never experienced before.

He stopped thinking.

This had never happened before. In every other race he'd ever run over the past four years, Nathan Goldfarb had never stopped thinking, never stopped listening to the voice.

But now the voice was still. Now there was only silence, both in his head and around him. As the ever-lengthening string of runners crossed the embankment after the hockey pond and began the long run down the tree line, even the sounds of footsteps and breathing all around him began to lessen. The silence deepened and soon Nathan Goldfarb could only hear the sound of his own easy, relaxed rhythmic breathing.

He picked up the pace, and as the run continued, Nathan Goldfarb began to pass people. The first few were the small boys, the weaker ones who couldn't keep up even in an intramural race. But then he began to pass a few of the older boys, the boys who were solid Junior Varsity performers, the boys with athletic futures. The group reached the end of the tree line and turned left into the field that would take them out of sight of the stands, and for the first time in his life, there were more boys behind Nathan Goldfarb than in front of him.

He passed one runner who turned as he went by and gave him a look of surprise. The group exited the field and began the run down the long downhill incline. This was where the voice in his head would tell him, over and over again, to pace himself, to hold back, that Cross Country Hill was just in front of them and that it would *kill him* if he hit it with nothing left.

This time the voice was quiet. Nathan relaxed and let the wind and gravity pull him onward. He ran faster, his stride lengthening, his arms flying loosely out to the side. It had never felt like this before. He was running fast enough now that the scarf was flying behind him, pulling on his neck, tightening around his throat. He reached up with his right hand, hooked his index finger through it, and tugged the scarf to loosen it.

He was nearly at the bottom of the incline now, his legs and arms flying. He passed one boy as the spray of sleet and snow lessened enough to see ahead of him, just beginning the long run up Cross Country Hill, the panting body of Brad Hamilton.

Nathan felt pressure on his legs and lungs now as he began the steep run up the Hill maybe twenty yards behind Hamilton. There was nothing but the rustling of the wind in his ears. He was not even aware of his own breathing; he was, in fact, aware of nothing but the run – only the run, and the fluid, almost Zen-like trance that had begun to settle over him.

Nathan could see Hamilton's legs, the normally smooth rhythm broken now by the strain of the Hill. There was an obvious weightiness, a clumsiness, to the younger boy's stride. Nathan sensed instinctively that Hamilton was tiring.

They were three-quarters of the way up the hill now, Na than a scant few yards behind Be-Rad. Be-Rad turned, saw who was right behind him, almost crowding him now, and snorted.

"Goldfart, what are you doing?" he gasped. "Get the hell out of here before I kick your ass."

"Screw you, bucko," Nathan said between breaths. He pumped his arms harder and two strides later, found himself beside the younger boy.

"I mean it, Goldfart," Hamilton warned, his voice break ing. "Back off."

Nathan flapped his wrists at the end of each swing to loos en them up, then pushed even harder as they approached the crest of the hill.

"Damn it," Hamilton yelled, then threw out his right arm in a wide arc, connecting with Nathan's chest, clotheslining him.

Nathan started down, his feet slipping, and as he felt himself sliding, his feet tangled with Hamilton's and they both went down in the snow.

Hamilton went down chest first, the impact knocking the breath out of him, but Nathan rolled as he fell. As he hit the ground, his momentum carried him over Hamilton's splayed body, mashing him even harder into the ground. He banana-rolled past him and came back up onto his feet. As his feet churned and caught the ground, Nathan was off again with barely a missed stride.

The crest of Cross Country Hill was just in front of him. Nathan glanced back. Hamilton was still down, face-first in the snow, just beginning to pull himself up.

As he topped the Hill and started the downward side, Nathan Goldfarb was alone.

He stayed alone, his legs spinning, his pace actually picking up as he bottomed the hill, turned, ran past the right side of the hockey pond, and back onto the track. Across the football field, the few spectators left in the stands stared, astonished, at the red scarf flapping behind Goldfarb in the stiff winter wind.

Goldfarb rounded turn three of the track, sprinted around the curve into turn four, then down the straightaway toward the finish line. The boys in the stands began cheering and yelling, then standing on the wooden bleachers and stomping their feet. A cheer arose from the throng: *Goldfart! Goldfart! Goldfart!*

Tears ran from Goldfarb's eyes, in horizontal streaks from his eyes to his ears, turning to ice almost instantly. There was ice in his hair now, the sweat in his jersey already beginning to crystallize. He was aware of the wetness, a moisture on his face that was different from the normal sweat. There was a fierce burn in his lungs, as if his chest were about to burst.

Goldfart! Goldfart! Goldfart!

Goldfarb grinned broadly as he approached the finish line. Out of the corner of his left eye, he saw the first of the other runners climbing the embankment and coming onto the track. He wasn't certain, but he was pretty sure the closest guy behind him – nearly a quarter-mile back – was not Be-Rad Hamilton.

For the first time in his life, to the cheers of perhaps two dozen of his classmates who had braved the snowstorm to watch, Nathan Goldfarb broke the tape at a finish line.

He ran on a few steps past, then stopped, leaned over and let his head hang down, his hands on his knees, his chest heaving. He was already starting to tighten up in the cold, but he didn't care. Over his shoulders, the boys cheered on.

He straightened, stared up at the gray, heavy sky for a moment, then turned and watched the stands. The red scarf hung down off the left side of his neck, wet and heavy. He grabbed it with his right hand and threw it recklessly over his left shoulder. The boys cheered even louder.

Decades later, he would remember this as the finest moment of his life.

At the finish line, Stretch held the stopwatch up, straining to read it through the blowing snow. Ripley walked up to him.

"How'd he do?"

Stretch held the stopwatch out in front of his assistant. "Kid took fourteen seconds off the school record."

Ripley grinned. "Unbelievable. Maybe we should've let him wear the bloody scarf all along."

Ripley's smile was not returned. Stretch glared first at him, then turned toward Nathan Goldfarb as he stood there silent and still in front of the stands.

"Bull," Stretch snapped. "Kid's a loser. If he could do it today, he could've done it before. What good's it do now?" Stretch raised his clipboard to note the time, then turned and walked away.

Behind him, Nathan Goldfarb stood in the snow, gazing up at the crowd, as the cheers went on.

Tell Them Herbert Sent You

by Katie MacAlister

For as long as she can remember, Katie MacAlister has loved reading. Growing up in a family where a weekly visit to the library was a given, Katie spent much of her time with her nose buried in a book. Two years after she started writing novels, Katie sold her first romance. More than thirty books later, her novels have been translated into numerous languages, been recorded as audiobooks, received several awards, and are regulars on the *New York Times*, *USA Today*, and *Publishers Weekly* bestseller lists. She lives in the Pacific Northwest, and can often be found lurking around online.

Way back in 2003 I was asked to launch a line of Young Adult books, and despite never having written in that genre, I agreed. How hard could it be to channel my inner sixteen-year-old, I thought? As it turns out, the five books I wrote around a young woman named Emily were not only easy to write, but a blast to boot.

Emily was the girl I always wanted to be – confident, smart, with a penchant for getting into crazy situations, and a deep love of quirky things and people. And when I sat down to write the short story for this anthology, I knew I had to bring her back as an adult. I was thrilled to see she was just as prone to getting into trouble, just as wacky, and just as crazy wild about the love of her life, Fang.

Subject: I'm getting married in the morning…
From: Emmanator@yanksabroad.com
To: Dru@druandfelixforever.com
Date: 4.14pm 24 September 2012

Well, not *this* morning, but tomorrow morning. Assuming my family doesn't drive me insane first, that is. I tell you, Dru, when Brother said he and Mom were going to spend a month here in England, I thought it was a good thing – Brother missed England as much as I did, only, of course, I came back here two years ago when Fang finished his degree, while Brother had to stay in Seattle and teach medieval history. Anyway, when he said that they were going to be in England for a month, I was all yay. But after just one day I caught him saying to Mom, "Chris, I think we should move back here. Emily and Francis clearly need our help."

"His name is Fang, Brother, which you well know," I told the old one, assuming that he had forgotten *yet again* that Fang dislikes his real first name, which, since Brother is exactly the same way, shouldn't escape him, and yet it obviously does. I wonder if Alzheimer's has set in already? I'll have to ask Mom what she thinks. Where was I? Oh, yes. "And we don't need you. At least, not in the way you mean. We have most of the house restored, and Dr. Benner is thinking about retiring, which means Fang would be the senior vet, and my job is going along splendidly, not that you asked about it."

I may have given him a gimlet look at that point, but I'm not exactly sure what a gimlet look is, except it sounds like it would have been perfectly appropriate for Brother.

"You're young and foolish," Brother said, waving a dismissive hand as he struck up a contemplative pose and gazed out of the window to the south pasture. "I commend the decision to cease living in sin with Fang – unlike your sister, who evidently believes cohabitation is perfectly fine and not going to result in my early death – but it's obvious to me that you could do with the benefit of our advice."

I rolled my eyes at his dramatic speech (honestly, is there anyone more drama queen than Brother?), and was about to tell him that we were just fine as we were, but then I caught sight of Fang walking over the field from the town, and I had to shove Brother out of the way in order to plaster myself against the window so I could watch.

I know it's just too, too gushy to say this, but you're my oldest friend in the world, and Dru, just the sight of Fang still makes me go all wobbly inside. It's not his nummy puppy-dog brown eyes, or the way his hair curls, or even the manly stubble – did I tell you he's going through a manly stubble phase? I so love it! I just want to rip off all his clothes and pounce on him when he's stubbly – where was I again? Man, maybe Brother's Alzheimer's is wearing off on me. Anyway, there was Fang walking to the house looking so gorgeous I just wanted to have my womanly way with him right there in the field, only I couldn't of course, not only because it had just been seeded with barley seed, but also because hello, sex in dirt? Not comfy in the least.

So the entire way from Bourton (which really is the cutest village ever; I can't wait for you to visit us so you can see it) to Melrose, which is in the Scottish Borders, Brother went on and on and on about how we needed his advice, etc. By the time we got to the hotel, even Mom was ignoring him. I think he would have continued to make his non-existent case for them moving here, but luckily, the first people we saw in the lobby were my Aunt Timandra and her dishy Scottish husband, Alec. Do you remember me telling you about them? They have a sheep farm that I worked on that year when we lived in England while Brother was doing the scholar exchange thing.

"Brother!" Aunt Tim said, yanking on Alec's arm and hauling him over to where we were dumping our luggage next to the reception desk. "Chris, you look wonderful. And there's the blushing bride and groom. Let me hug you, Fang. And Emily, my dear, I love the new haircut. You look so happy and you're not even married yet!"

"That's what illicit sex will do for you," I told her, giggling when Brother looked outraged.

"Are Bess and Monk not here yet?" Mom asked, looking around the lobby.

"Haven't seen them. Are they coming to the wedding after all?"

"Bess said she was going to put off some big animal rescue campaign to be here, but only because Monk felt it was impor tant to support family," I told her as Mom, Aunt Tim, and I wandered over to the elevator while the men did manly things like check us in. "Even though he's not technically part of it, but that's fine, because I like him, and he did help me get my fabulous new job. Did I tell you about it?"

Aunt Tim shot my mother a wary look. "Something to do with computers, I think?"

"That was my old job. I was the process engineer respon sible for creating organic semiconductor devices using flexible substrates. Now I work in holography with a fabulous firm that puts oodles of money into research. It's great fun. I get to make large format cylindrical shims."

"Putting that physics degree to good use, eh?" Aunt Tim said, smiling and patting my arm. "We're very proud of your shims, you know, Emily. And proud of Fang's practice, as well. There's the man himself. Fang, did Alec ask you about this new sheep disease we've heard of from New Zealand?"

I won't bore you with the general talk that went on after that, mostly because it concerns sheep, which Fang specializes in, but also because Brother kept trying to get Aunt T to admit that he and Mom should move to England.

Then we split up to go to our rooms so we could get ready for the stag party/bachelorette party thing, which, yes, was late in the day (so to speak), but we held off having them earlier because Mom said Brother really wanted to be there for Fang's stag party.

Why? I have no idea. Fang said he'd wait to have his party so Brother could be a part of it, and of course, I couldn't have mine without Holly, and she was off in Nepal doing Bud dhist nun stuff, and didn't get back until last week, so it just happened that both parties are going to be tonight, on Wedding Eve. Oy.

More later, once the parties are over. Hugs to Felix. Hope your cold is better.

~ ~ ~

Subject: Re: I'm so excited for you!
From: Emmanator@yanksabroad.com
To: Dru@druandfelixforever.com
Date: 10.27pm 24 September 2012

> just wish I could be there for your special day, but the doctor says that I'm not supposed to be doing > anything that could make Felix, Jr. come early, so it's bed rest and nothing but bed rest for me. Tell me

> everything that happens at your party!

Party was fine. Nothing exciting, just Mom and Aunt Tim and Holly and me in a corner of the hotel's dining room, because the private dining room that Aunt Tim had tried to get was booked with some group called Spirited Lives (ghost hunters) that is staying at the hotel. Evidently there are lots of haunted places around here. Brother is crazy wild to see them all, but that's Mom's problem, not mine. She's the one who married the medieval scholar; *she* can put up with being dragged around to every castle and historic bump in the ground.

A weird thing happened when we left the dining room, though. Mom and Aunt Tim hit the ladies' room, so Holly and I were standing by the elevator when we heard this odd scratchy noise.

"What on earth?" I asked Holly, looking around.

Her eyes got really big. Since she shaved her head (I guess that's the latest fashion for Buddhist nuns), her eyes look huge, but even so, they were like saucers. "What's that noise?" she asked at the same time.

I was about to answer, but a man's voice drifted out to us.

"Everyone is in place, sir," he said in a soft voice like he was whispering, but not quite, if you know what I mean. "There's only a small wedding party and the group at the hotel. No one will get in or out without us knowing."

Holly grabbed my arm.

I pointed to the small passage leading off on the far side of the elevator, leaning in to whisper in her ear, "It's the cops!"

"What are they doing here?" she whispered back.

"Dunno. Maybe the ghost people have done something wrong."

The elevator – which was ancient by the way, since the whole hotel was as old as the hills – creaked to a stop next to us. We hurried in to it and went up to my room, keeping our eyes peeled. Sure enough, there was a woman standing around at the end of the hall on the third floor. She didn't look like a cop, but she gave us a thorough once-over.

"Don't look now," I said to Holly as I pretended to admire a painting of a badger. "But that policewoman is staring at us."

Holly opened her mouth to say something, stopped, then slapped her hand over her mouth and nudged me with her elbow.

"What?" I asked, glancing down the hall at the cop. She was still there, frowning at us.

"Your tiara! You're still wearing it!"

"Oh. I suppose a beaded penis bachelorette tiara would make some people stare, yes," I said with much dignity, and removed the tiara that one of Bess's crafty friends made for me. We went into my room, and had a good long discussion about Holly's new life as a Buddhist, and why the police would be skulking around a hotel filled with ghosty folk, and all sorts of other stuff that I'll tell you about when I get back home and we can Skype again.

Mom and Aunt Tim came up after that, and they sat around and did the "You're getting married!" thing where they talk about when they got married, and how happy I'll be (like I'm not wildly in love with Fang now, and happy as we could be in our own little house with four dogs, three cats, and the neighbor's deranged rooster who is in love with our ducks), and that sort of stuff. After a while, though, they toddled off, and I was left all by my lonesome, since Brother insisted I not be allowed to have steamy monkey lovin' with Fang the night before we were married.

Honestly, fathers!

Anyway, I was in my jim-jams and about to text Fang to see how his party was going, and whether or not Brother was boring him senseless, when there was this odd sort of tapping sound on my window. At first, I thought it was a ghost or something, but no ghost would hang around a second floor window. At least I don't think one would. So I went to look out the window, and what do I see but Bess hanging out of the tree that's next to my window, with a black cloth bag dangling from her mouth.

"What the hell, Bess?" I said, opening the window. "Have you completely lost your mind?"

"Not quite, although if you had taken any longer to come to the window, I might have. Here, take him."

She reached across the space between the tree and window, shoving the bag at me.

"Him who? Is this a wedding present? What are you doing in the tree? If you think you're going to ruin my wedding with your weirdness –"

"The only thing I'm ruining is a heinous and horrible venture that should be utterly destroyed. And I'm in the tree because your hotel is crawling with police."

"I know. Holly and I think the ghost people are smuggling drugs. Or into white slavery. One or the other."

I swear Bess rolled her eyes, but it was hard to be sure because she started climbing down out of the tree. "Trust me, it's not ghosts the police are after."

"Then what are they doing here?"

"They're after a horrible group of pigeon fighters that are based in an abandoned abbey right outside of town."

"They're *what*?"

"Pigeon fighters. You know, like cock fights except with pigeons." She nodded toward the bag that I now held. "Just keep him safe. His name is Herbert. He's a very valuable racer, and since you're marrying a vet, he'll be safe with you. Say hi to Mom and Brother for me. Oh, and have a nice wedding tomorrow. Sorry Monk and I won't be there after all, but we're going to have to disappear for a few months."

"Why?" I asked, watching in amazement as she started to climb down the tree.

"The pigeon fighting consortium is after us. They're ruth less, utterly ruthless. Our lives aren't worth a plugged nickel. And the police are looking for us, too, but that's only for break ing into the pigeon compound."

The bag lurched in my hands, almost causing me to drop it. "What on earth have you gotten yourself involved with now – Bess? Bess!"

She slid away into the darkness, Dru, just like a ninja or something equally stealthy. I stared into the darkness for a few seconds in total and complete incomprehension of everything that was my older sister, but the bag moved again and I figured I'd better find out what she had foisted on Fang and me.

I set the bag on the little round hotel table and opened the drawstrings. A plump bird in a cowboy costume marched out of the bag, shook his feathers, cocked his head and gave me a good long look, then lifted his tail and pooped on the bag.

"A pigeon?" I asked him. "A prizefighting racing pigeon?"

He blinked at me.

"One wearing a cowboy hat, vest, gun belt, and little spurs? What the…*Bess*!"

It did no good running out of the hotel to look for her, of course, especially as I was in my boy shorts and tank-top paja mas, and barefoot to boot, but as I stood on the hotel's grassy lawn, swearing at nothing, I knew that my sister had once again lost her mind. "Why did she have to pick my wedding to do it at, that's what I want to know?" I asked no one in particular as I marched back into the hotel, ignoring the people lounging casually around the lobby. They were either ghost hunters or cops, and at that moment, I didn't care who they were, I just wanted to find my sister so I could strangle her. With Herbert the racing pigeon's tiny little lasso.

BRB, someone's at the door.

~ ~ ~

Me: Police searching hotel! They prbly know abt hummus!

Today, 10.52pm

Dru: Hummus? What are you doing with hummus?

Today, 10.53pm

Me: Herbert, not hummus. Stupid automobile.

Today, 10.57pm

Me: AUTOCORRECT! GRR!

Today, 10.57pm

Dru: The police are chasing you because you have hummus in a car? Is it some Scottish thing?

Today, 11.01pm

Me: Why are you texting me silly questions when I'm on the run for my life?

Today, 11.05pm

Dru: Look, you're being arrested for having ve hicular hummus, not me. Don't get naked with me.

Today, 11.06pm

Me: Hope that was sup. to be snarky & not naked, or else you've lost your marbles. More later. Must find Fang & demand he hide Herbs & me from police.

Today, 11.09pm

~ ~ ~

Subject: Re: WTF?
From: Emmanator@yanksabroad.com
To: Dru@druandfelixforever.com
Date: 9.24pm 25 September 2012

> tell me why you thought the police were after you for having hummus in a car in the first place.

For the last time, they weren't after me for hummus, that was my phone's autocorrect error. They were after me for Her bert, the expensive racing pigeon who has his own set of sil ver spurs, and the cutest little bandolier and matching guns. I couldn't figure out why they'd dress up a racing pigeon; you'd think the cowboy hat would make it difficult for him to steer properly when he's flying.

So. Let me fill you in with what happened. It's all so very strange, and really, I have Bess to blame for everything.

I didn't find Fang last night after I was done texting you. He was still out at his stag party, although I texted him once I got settled in Holly's room (it took a bit of explaining to get her to understand how I came by Herbert, but in the end, she was totally on my side), and he said they were all sitting around listening to Brother and his Uncle Hugo talk about the good old days of stag parties, when there were cakes filled with women in bikinis, and lots and lots of booze. I told him to call me, and when he did, I explained that the police were after me, and he said, in that way he has where he's kind of sighing when he talks, "What have you done now, Em?"

"Nothing! It's all Bess's fault. She shoved Herbert at me and didn't tell me he was a hot bird. Holly and I thought the cops were here for the ghost people, but obviously, they're af ter Herbert. And maybe Bess and Monk. Which is why I'm hiding out in Holly's room right now – because they'd never suspect a Buddhist nun of being in on a heist, right?"

"Emily," Fang said with yet another one of those sighs, "I may not have had a lot to drink tonight, but I've had enough to leave me at a state where you're not making the least bit of sense. Who's Herbert, why are the police after your sister, and what does the ghost hunters' group have to do with anything?"

"Your uncle didn't bring a cake, did he?" I asked, suddenly suspicious about just what was going on at that stag party.

"There's no cake, and since I know you're going to ask, no women here, either. Just Devon, your father, my uncle, and two of my cousins who are presently passed out face down in a plate of cold spaghetti. How was your party?"

"OK. Mom and Aunt Tim got tipsy. I went back to my room to show Holly my dress and have girl-talk time, and then Bess showed up with Herbert. He's a pigeon. Bess says you should look at him because he's valuable."

I could have sworn I heard him mutter, "Not another ani mal," under his breath, but all he said to me was, "Bring him to my room first thing in the morning, and I'll look him over."

"But Fang, he could be hurt or something –"

"Have to go, love. Your father is insisting we go to some pub that Hugo was telling him about. I'm the only sober one, so I'll have to drive. See you tomorrow morning."

"But –"

He clicked off, and after seething for a few minutes at the idea of my father dragging Fang off to a pub where there were who knew how many women who would fling themselves on him, I put Herbert in the bathroom and closed the door, rounded up Holly, and marched downstairs to the reception desk.

"I'd like the key to room 306, please," I told the clerk.

He consulted a laptop. "That room appears to belong to Dr. Francis Baxter, DVM. You do not look like Dr. Francis Baxter, DVM."

"I'm not, but that is my fiancé, and we're getting married in the morning, and I want to go to his room now. To…er… leave him something."

"What sort of something?" the clerk asked, all suspicious-like.

"A present," Holly said, smiling at him. He looked startled.

"She's a nun," I said, gesturing toward Holly. "She wouldn't lie."

"We don't lie," Holly agreed. "It's against our precepts."

"I didn't say you did, but regardless of that point, I am forbidden by law to allow an unauthorized person into someone's room. If your fiancé would like to authorize you, then I will be happy to give you a key."

"He's out having his stag party," I protested. "He has to drive his drunken cousins and my father and his trouble-making uncle around."

"Then I'm afraid you will have to wait until he can authorize you. Yes, madam?" He leaned to the side to speak around me to the people behind us.

"I'm so going to be writing your corporate headquarters about this," I grumbled as I turned and moved aside. The two people – a man and woman in black pants, and matching leather jackets – looked seriously out of place in the pretty little hotel lobby. They looked…tough. I could just see them swaggering around beating up old people. I glanced back at them as we walked to the elevator, and saw the man slip the clerk some money. "Did you see that?" I asked Holly as the elevator lurched upward.

"See what?"

"That man gave the clerk a tenner. They look like serious criminals. I just bet you that they are part of that ghost hunting group that the cops are here for."

"I thought you said the cops were after Bess and her boyfriend?"

"That's what she said, but I don't really think –" My eyes widened and I gripped Holly's arm as a horrible thought occurred to me. "Oh no! They're the pigeon people!"

"What pigeon – oh, you mean the ones who are hurting the little birdies?"

Fear roiled around in the pit of my stomach. "They have to be here to find Herbert. They probably followed Bess here, and must have figured she dumped Herbert with someone. Do you think they heard us talking about Fang?"

"I don't know, but even if they did, you didn't mention anything about a bird, so they can't know you have Herbert."

We hurried back to Holly's room, where we had left Herbert. "No, but the guy was being all snotty and using Fang's full title, and they could put two and two together."

Holly shook her head as I retrieved Herbert from where he was attempting to seduce a toilet brush. "I think that's a bit far-fetched, Emily."

"You'd better hope so, or we'll be on the lam just like Bess and Monk."

"Maybe you should tell the police," she told me a bit later as we were getting ready for bed.

"And have them confiscate Herbert? I don't think so. Bess was right about one thing – Fang is a vet. Herbert will be perfectly safe with us. You can't say that about some policeman who doesn't know squat about birds."

"I think you should talk to them. They can protect you from those pigeon-fighting people," she argued.

"I will if I have to, but until then, no thanks. We'll just lay low until morning, when I can get Fang to help me smuggle Herbert out of the hotel without anyone seeing him. Herbert that is, not Fang."

"I don't suppose you'd consider opening the window and letting him have his freedom?"

"He's just a little bird!" I said, pointing to where Herbert was cooing softly and trying to get busy with Holly's espadrille. "An innocent little creature of nature – oh, here, Herbert, let me take your guns off so you don't keep snagging them on the bedspread. He needs our protection. He probably doesn't even know how to forage for himself. No, sir, you have to harbor him – and me – in his time of need. It's part of your Buddhist oath."

"We don't *have* oaths," she answered with a little roll of her eyes. I settled into the far side of her bed, making sure that Herbert was comfortable in his nest of an extra blanket and Holly's shoe. "Fine, whatever it is you commit yourself to. I'm sure it calls for protecting the weak little animals, and Herbert needs your help. Plus, it's just for the night."

"It had better be," Holly said with a grim note in her voice, but she turned off the light and everyone went to sleep.

The next morning, I made Holly scout out the corridor in case the cops were lurking around just waiting to grab us, but luckily, we made it to Fang's room without seeing anyone.

Including Fang.

"I don't understand it. He should be here. We're getting married in –" I consulted my watch. "Three hours. Why isn't he here?"

"Maybe he passed out or something?" Holly suggested helpfully.

"He never drinks that much." I frowned. I was about to suggest that we go to the front desk and demand a key when Holly tried the door. It was open.

"Fang? We're here with – holy cow!"

Fang's room was a mess, clothing strewn everywhere, along with copious numbers of those little drink coasters they give you in chic pubs. The room was empty of Fang, however.

"It looks like a bomb has gone off here," Holly said, looking around in amazement. "Is he normally this messy?"

"No. Quite the opposite – oh, *merde*! It's the pigeon people! They must have him!"

"What?" Holly almost shrieked.

"Can you think of what else could have happened here?" I asked, waving my free hand around the room. The other hand was used to hold the wicker basket we'd confiscated from Holly's room to serve as a carrier for Herbert. Once we put one of my shirts in it, and draped her scarf over the top to keep him from escaping, he was as happy as a little feathered clam.

"Quite a few things, actually."

"Well, I don't have the time needed to tell you just how wrong they are. I know they kidnapped Fang in order to use him as ransom for Herbert."

"I don't know that they'd do that, Emily," Holly said slowly. "Kidnapping is a serious offense. Would they risk that for a pigeon?"

"A valuable pigeon? Of course! Criminal acts mean noth ing to these people."

"Well, you could always give them Herbert so they'd release Fang," she pointed out as I changed into a pair of jeans and a sweatshirt. I wished I had something to use as a weapon, but had to content myself with a pair of Holly's knitting needles.

"I'm not going to let those bastards have either my won derful Fang or Herbert. Come on, we have to go rescue my darling from the clutches of the evil pigeon fighters!"

Because I know you probably have to get up and pee by now, I won't bore you with the following half hour that it took me to convince Holly to help me rescue Fang. We'll skip over that and go right to the part where we were sneaking out the side door to the parking lot, when we ran into my mother and Aunt Tim obviously leaving the same way.

"Oh, Emily, there you are. I just left a message on your phone. Tim and I have to go to the train station to pick up the twins. Your father was supposed to do it, but he seems to have disappeared this morning."

Holly and I exchanged meaningful glances.

Aunt Tim laughed, and winked at me. "That must have been one heck of a bachelor party."

"We'll be back in less than half an hour, though. Are you girls going somewhere?"

"Er…" I hid the basket containing Herbert behind me. "Just out for a few last minute things."

"Ah. Well, don't be too long. We have to do your hair and makeup, and you know that always takes longer than you think it will."

Mom and Aunt T toddled off, leaving me staring in horror at Holly. "They have Brother, too!"

"Maybe they just went to do something together…"

I moved over to the window, and pointed at the car parked nearest the door. "That's our car. Would Fang go somewhere with Brother without his car?"

"No, I guess he wouldn't…you know, I wasn't at all con vinced that you were right about Fang being kidnapped, since it seems like the sort of wild conclusion you usually jump to that is almost always wrong, but that does seem odd that your father is missing, but not Fang's car." She bit her lower lip. "Em, I think we should talk to the police and let them handle this."

I hesitated. Part of me wanted to let the police take over, but the other part, the one that has had experience trying to explain stuff to police (and not had a lot of luck getting them to do what I want them to do), told me that it would take way too long to prod them into action. "And I have a hunkalicious vet to marry."

Holly blinked.

"Snap decision time. You talk to the police. Tell them what has happened, and that I'm going off to the abandoned abbey to find Fang and my father. If they get there in time, fabulous. If they don't, then I'll just let the baddies think they can have Herbert, and get Fang and Brother away from them."

"How are you going to do that?" Holly asked, looking startled.

I shrugged. "Don't ask hard questions. If my mom comes looking for me, tell her I've gone off to have a little meditation about the wonders of marriage or some such crap. I'll call if it looks like things are hairy."

"Your wedding is in three hours, you do remember that, yes?" Holly asked as I started down the stairs.

"Of course I remember. I can't very well have a wedding without a groom, though. I'll call if I – holy crap!"

I swear, Dru, I just about dropped Herbert when I saw the local swat team go racing past the bottom of the stairs. I ran back up to the top and pushed Holly aside to peer out of the window. The whole parking lot was filled with big police vans, and lots of police cars, and people milling around.

"How did they get there that quickly? They weren't there a minute ago!"

"Who wasn't? What are you holy crapping about? Oooh, more police!"

"I have to get out of here," I said, feeling trapped. Obvi ously, something big was going down at the hotel, and I needed to get far away from it so I could go save Fang. "They'll see me if I go out this entrance…maybe if I go out the back, through the kitchen, I can sneak around and get a taxi out on the road. Let's see what it looks like downstairs."

We trotted down one flight of stairs, but even before we had turned on the landing and started down the second, we could hear the outraged protests of one of the hotel patrons.

" – will be making my feelings known to your superiors, see if I don't," a man with a loud voice was saying as he stood with his back to us. "I don't see why you have to conduct your raid at a time when decent people are trying to have brunch!"

"I'm sorry, sir, there is a grave situation under investiga tion, and we must insist that all residents remain above stairs until it is resolved," a disembodied voice answered.

I grabbed Holly's arm and hurried back up the stairs to the second floor.

"Poop," Holly said, which as you know, is strong language for her.

"Double poop with sesame seeds on it," I said, thinking quickly. A sudden memory of my bachelorette dinner the night before came to me, and I spun around and ran the length of the second floor hall, saying over my shoulder, "Dumbwaiter!"

"Oh, Em, you can't be serious!"

You know me, Dru. You know how crazy I am about Fang. There was no way I was going to let some ghostly raid keep me from saving the man I loved. I won't say it wasn't a bit cramped in the dumbwaiter, what with me and Herbert both in it (although I had to take him out of his wicker basket to fit in there), but Holly finally agreed to send us down to the lower level, where the kitchen was.

Have you ever ridden in a dumbwaiter? It's not the most comfortable ride. It was hot and claustrophobic, and I worried that I'd get stuck in there, but at long last we bumped to an end. I shoved up the wooden panel in the wall, and oozed out, clutching Herbert to my chest.

Right into the middle of insanity. Insanity, Dru! A small group of people stood clustered near the kitchen door, a cou ple of them holding guns.

Naturally, I did the only thing I could do. I grabbed the biggest, sharpest looking knife I could find, and I started screaming.

Herbert freaked out at the noise, and flew like a deranged fool around the room. The second I started screaming, the people at the door spun around to stare at me, but when Herbert start swooping around them, they started screaming, as well. The two women in the group, and one of the three men, hunched over and covered their heads. The other two men waved their guns around and started shooting at Herbert.

"Don't hurt him, he's a valuable pigeon!" I yelled and threw a pan at the nearest man.

It missed him, of course (we all know I have a horrible throwing arm), but it made him mad enough to stop trying to kill Herbert, and turn his gun on me.

Luckily for the Herbster and me, the police evidently figured out that something was going on in here, and they burst through the door yelling all sorts of dramatic stuff straight out of CSI. It would have been awesome except they yelled at me to get on the floor.

"Not until I get my pigeon," I said, holding out my hand and whistling for Herbert. "Here pidgy, pidgy, pidgy. Come to Mama, Herbums."

"On the ground!" one of the cops repeated.

"I'm not one of them," I said, pointing. "I'm a bride. And that's my uber-valuable pigeon. Herbert! Come here this instant!"

Herbert evidently got tired of doing his swooping act, because he landed on one of the stainless steel counters and strutted over to a large metal mixing bowl, cooing at his reflection in it.

"Get on the floor, your hands over your head," the policeman yelled again.

"Look –" I plucked Herbert from the counter, lest he get into trouble with all the cops around. "I just told you I'm not with them. I came down in the dumbwaiter."

"You what?" the nearest policewoman asked.

"I have to rescue my fiancé! He's been kidnapped by a gang of bird thugs."

"I don't know anything about bird thugs," one of the plainclothes dudes said. He was obviously a head honcho. "But I do know that this ring of thieves pretending to be ghost investigators is now out of business. You can let her go, McK ay. She's telling the truth – she's not part of the group."

"I'm so glad someone realizes that. But wait, thieves? The ghost guys are thieves?"

Before someone could answer, more police poured into the room, and to my utter surprise, on their heels was Fang. My Fang! My Fang with a black eye, and bloody nose, and bruised, torn lip.

"Fang!" I screamed, and ignoring the cops, ran to fling myself on him. Unfortunately, I was still holding Herbert, who got a bit squished between us.

"I knew you'd be in here," he said, pulling back a little bit when Herbert started squawking. "Holly didn't have to say anything more than the word 'dumbwaiter' to make it all clear. What the hell are you doing here?"

"I was trying to rescue you." I touched his swollen, red nose. "You got away from the kidnappers yourself?"

"Kidnappers? What kidnappers?"

"The bird guys who overheard me asking for you at the reception desk. The same guys that are after Bess because she stole Herbert."

"I wasn't kidnapped, love. Things got a bit hectic after we went to that pub that Hugo recommended, and we all ended up in jail for the fight that my cousins started. Your father has a broken nose. Devon's missing a tooth. And my cousins are going to spend a lot longer than a night in jail."

"Then all's well that ends well," I said, giving him a gentle kiss on the part of his mouth that wasn't hurt.

"I don't know that you'd call a groom with a battered face, and a bride who was just about arrested for theft as ending well, but so long as I end up with you, it's all good."

"That is so romantic!" I sniffled and gave him my very best "I'm about to marry you and make you deliriously happy" smile.

I'm attaching a couple of pictures from the wedding. Ig nore the fact that Brother and Fang are kind of listing to the side (Fang ended up having a broken rib, while Brother's col larbone is cracked). Isn't Herbert cute as the ring-bearer? Holly said she didn't mind at all that he sat on her shoulder for the entire ceremony, even if he did poop on her best handspun tunic. And the swat guys making a little arch with their arms was just so sweet.

Love to you and Felix and Felix, Jr.

Hugs and kisses,
Emily

Timeless

by Wayne Jordan

For as long as he can remember, Wayne Jordan loved reading, but he also enjoyed creating his own make believe worlds. This love for reading and writing continued, and in November 2005, his first book, *Capture the Sunrise*, was published by BET Books. Wayne has always been an advocate for romance, especially African-American romance. In 1999, he founded www.romanceincolor.com, a website that focuses on African-American romance and its authors. Wayne is a high school teacher and a graduate of the University of the West Indies. He holds a B.A. in literature and linguistics and an M.A. in applied linguistics. He lives on the beautiful tropical island of Barbados, which, with its white sands and golden sunshine, is the perfect setting for the romance stories he loves to create. Of course, he still takes time out to immerse himself in the latest release from one of his favorite authors.

The central protagonist of my story is Byron Alleyne, a teenage who falls in love with a girl who is visiting Barbados, the island where he lives. Everyone loves an island romance. However, Byron lives in a time when interracial relationships where not totally accepted and prejudice still lingered. Byron, like my real grandfather, dared to fall in love with a white girl, knowing the fragility of any future with her. While Byron's story is a sad one, his love for the beautiful Abigail remains timeless, his heartbreak captured on the tear-stained pages of a journal.

Prologue

The Atlantic Ocean stretched before him like the essence of time. Already he loved Barbados. From the moment he'd stepped off the American Airlines flight, he had felt an unex pected sense of belonging.

The wind wafted the air, cooling his heated body, but he didn't mind. He welcomed the warmth, reveled in it. When he'd left Raleigh, North Carolina, the temperature had been 20 degrees Fahrenheit, typical March weather.

Now he stood on the beach, the sun's rays warm and comforting.

He turned in the direction of the house. He had been avoiding the inevitable. His father's funeral had taken place two days ago and he needed to read the diary, as the lawyer had instructed. He'd never known about his father until a few weeks ago. His life, his sense of self, had all been shattered by a single phone call.

He had been given a glimpse of his past from Mama, his father's mother, but there were other things he wanted to know. How had his parents met? How had they fallen in love? Why had they never been together?

These things he ached to know, but when confronted by his father's journal, he'd balked at discovering the truth.

He crossed the beach, the sand crunching under his bare feet, the coolness of it making him chuckle.

At forty-five he'd lived a comfortable life. His wife of eighteen years had passed two years before, one year after his mother. His only child, Adrian Jr., was married and living in Orlando. He had no plans of marrying again. He'd found a measure of contentment and happiness and still enjoyed his tenure as a professor of English at the University of North Carolina.

Oblivious to the chirping birds around him and the music of the wind through the trees, his mind focused on the task before him.

The walk to the house didn't take him long, but a thin film of sweat made him welcome the coolness of the air-conditioning.

The house, a massive structure, stood in the center of a sprawling acreage, nestled in the midst of vibrant mahogany trees. The house, despite the hint of neglect, wore its colonial dress with pride.

He walked along the hallway, stopping at the bottom of the stairs. He could use the elevator which had been installed for his grandmother now that she was confined to a wheel chair, but there was something grand about walking the wind ing staircase, the walls lined with portraits of members of the family and other family paintings.

One that caught his interest was a painting of a small wooden shack. His grandmother had told him that the shack was where his father, Byron Alleyne, had been born. How his father had moved from the tiny shack to the grandeur before him was a story he ached to know. Fortunately, Mama had promised to tell him.

He entered his room, tempted immediately to lie on the canopied bed. For the past few days he'd slept like a baby, an unusual thing when he travelled.

Adrian opened the diary, skimming through several blank pages until he reached the first page of writing. The handwrit ing was a strong masculine scrawl, bearing an uncanny resem blance to his.

He closed his eyes for a moment, breathed in deeply, and when he opened them, started to read…

Chapter One
1975

Byron watched as the young girl took her shoes off and threw them to the sand. She was white, but it was not unusual to see the occasional tourist on this stretch of beach. Like him, the tourists had discovered that this particular beach was not only beautiful, but the water was crystal clear.

For a while he watched her. She danced daintily, ballet, he knew it was called. Her toes pointed, her body rigid and straight, not like those of the girls in his class whose bodies gyrated sensuously to the local calypso. Yet, there was something incredibly sexy about her movement.

Involuntarily, his feet moved towards her, stopping when he was about ten meters away. He was surprised when she did not stop or look in his direction, but then he realized she was dancing with her eyes closed.

When she finally stopped, breathing in deeply, her eyes opened; beautiful, green eyes that sparkled with excitement and delight. Then, there was a glimpse of fear.

He smiled, reassuring her that everything was OK.

The fear dissipated and she smiled in return, a cautious smile that didn't exactly reach her eyes.

"That was beautiful," he said.

"Thank you," she replied softly.

"I'm Byron. You live around here?"

"My name is Abigail Larson. I'm staying at the Harrisons. My family is spending the summer here."

"My mother works for the Harrisons," he replied, acknowledging the irony of the situation. "She's their cook."

"Mrs. Hines is your mom. I like her. She's an excellent cook. I enjoyed the local breakfast she made this morning."

"Fish cakes and bakes?" he asked.

"Yes. I've never tasted anything as good as she makes and I've eaten in some of the best restaurants in the world."

"She's the best cook on the island," Byron said, the pride evident in his tone.

"I can tell she is. I totally enjoyed dinner last night too. She can cook anything well."

"Yes, she's the best!"

For a while there was silence.

"So where are you from?" he asked.

"I'm from North Carolina. Mr. Harrison is my dad's uncle."

The noise of a seagull flying overhead startled her and she looked up, watching the bird's graceful movement before it swooped down and dived into the water, appearing almost im mediately, a fish wiggling in its mouth.

She laughed, an infectious sound that made him laugh in response. He didn't laugh much, but there was something about her *joie de vivre* that made him feel soft inside. He winced. He didn't like the feeling.

She stopped laughing and turned to him.

"I want to go find some shells on the beach. You want to come with me?" she invited sweetly.

He hesitated, but then she looked at him with now warm, green eyes and he melted. For her, he would do anything.

She turned and headed up the beach. He followed. For a while they walked in silence. He wasn't sure what to say to her. His experience with white girls was almost non-existent. Most of the schools on the island where single sexed, and while his school had an interesting interracial balance of black and white, when school was over, the white, rich boys went their separate ways.

In June, he'd ended his last year in high school. He'd spent the past two years in sixth form and now he was awaiting the result of the Cambridge Examinations, which were still a few weeks away. But the end of August, he would know if he'd qualified to enter the Law Faculty at the University of the West Indies, here on the island.

"You're quiet. What are you thinking about?" she asked, stopping to look at him.

"My future," he replied.

"What do you want to be?"

"A lawyer."

"That's cool. You'll make a fine lawyer."

"And how do you know that?" he asked. He was sure that she was just being polite.

"It's your eyes," she replied. "I see intelligence and wis dom. They say that eyes are the windows to a man's soul and character."

He laughed. "I've never expected that idiom to refer to me. What about you? What do you want to do?"

"I want to be an actress on Broadway. I want to sing and dance and act." There was excitement in her voice, but he heard a hint of sadness.

"What's wrong?" he asked. He reached out and placed a hand on her shoulder.

She turned to him, her face startled by his perception.

"My parents want me to go to medical school. They think that my dream is not practical. But I don't know if I can give them what they want. As soon as I turn eighteen, I am heading to New York."

"Isn't that a dangerous place for a young girl like you?"

"Dangerous? New York is a wonderful place. I'm sure my dad regrets taking me to see *Funny Girl* when it opened last year. I love Barbra Streisand. She has an awesome voice."

He smiled at the look of wonder on her face. He'd heard about Broadway, but the theater was not his thing; though he would be willing to watch a play if she were in it. She would be good on stage.

"My dad always takes me somewhere special during the summer. Last year it was New York. This year it's Barbados. I wanted to go back to New York, but I love it here. I'm sure things will be even better now I've met you."

"I love it here too," he echoed, trying to ignore the implica tions behind what she said.

"You should. I could live here all year round. It's so warm and everything is so alive."

She glanced down at her watch.

"Oh dear. It's almost supper time. I promised my mom I would be back. And you must be here to see your mom. I'm keeping you back."

He frowned. What she said was true. He'd forgotten that he had walked from the village there, to his mom, to collect their supper. His dad wasn't well and since his mother lived in at the plantation during the week and only came home on her days off on Friday and Saturday, he had to make the daily trek to the house. He didn't come to the house often any more, but as a kid he'd spent many days and nights there.

It had been an exciting experience for a young boy. He was always awed by the way the rich lived, but the family treated him with the same respect they showed to his mother. He was allowed to roam the house, watch television, read the books in the den. Sometime in the future, he wanted a house just like the Harrisons.

She turned and headed towards the bushy path to the house.

"Are you coming?" she asked.

He followed her.

Chapter Two

The next day, Byron raced towards the beach, his heart pounding restlessly against his chest. He'd thought about Abigail all night, wondering if she would be there again. He wanted to see her.

His body, flustered and hot, tingled in anticipation.

Byron knew he was playing with fire; the memory of her soft, pale skin and the flowery scent of the perfume she wore only made him think of her more.

His feet barely touched the gritty sand. He came to a stop.

His gaze moved along the beach, coming to stop where the shadows played among the trees. As if sensing his presence, Abigail slipped from her hiding place. He hated that she was so far away. He wanted to see her reaction to his appearance.

He walked towards her, at first slowly, but his speed increased in anticipation of being with her.

She did not move, remaining motionless, as he strolled towards her.

Above, the dark clouds opened, pouring heavy drops down on him.

He'd had hoped it wouldn't rain, but the swirling mass of clouds suggested that the evening would be a wet one.

When he reached her, he smiled cautiously, but watched as her face transformed with childlike delight. His heart soared. She wanted to see him as much as he wanted to see her.

"I was hoping you would come again," she said, as they stood before each other, their bodies almost touching.

"I had to," he confessed. "I wanted to see you."

She blushed, but she continued to stare at him, her expres sion bold and flirtatious.

His heart soared again. He could see his own feelings, his own confusion, reflected in her eyes.

There was no color, were no differences…just a boy and girl experiencing the awesomeness of first love.

Today, he would push the reality of their situation into the background. He remembered the time he'd glanced at a white girl from the private school on the way to the school bus. His friends had caught him looking in her direction.

"Boy, what you looking at she for? She not in your class. All you can do is window shop," Philip, his best friend, had said.

He'd joined in the laughter, knowing that what they'd said was more truth than a lie, and he'd put that unexpected attrac tion to the back on his mind. Until now…

"We need to get out of the rain." Her voice drew him from his musings.

Instinctively, he glanced up, aware that the drizzle was now a heavy rain.

"There's a hut over there," he said, pointing in the direc tion of several weather-beaten huts which dotted the beaches on the island.

He knew the hut well. He'd seen George, the gardener, take his girlfriend there.

"You canna use it wheneve' you want," George had told him. "Ah willing to share but make sure me and Janice not in there."

Byron reached for Abigail's hand and together they ran towards the hut, her laughter echoing across the silent beach.

When they reached the hut, he pushed the door open, waiting until she entered, before he did.

The hut was unexpectedly clean, with a small makeshift bed in one corner and a table and two stools next to the only window. Light squeezed through a crack in the wall, bring ing brightness that lessened the shadows and dullness of the interior.

"You're not too wet, are you?" he asked.

"I'm fine," she said, looking up at him, "but I do feel a bit cold."

"Come over here and stand next to me. I can keep you warm," he dared to say.

She came to him eagerly, leaning her body against his and letting her head rest against his pounding chest.

They stood like that, oblivious to the drumming on the rooftop.

When she glanced up, he glanced down. The message in her eyes was clear and he obliged her, lowering his head to capture her lips with his. For a while they were contented with a cautious exploration, a hesitant touching of lips and tongue, but something in him stirred as some force inside him explod ed and heat radiated through him. He felt his body shake with his need for her, and it took all of his will to force his legs not to buckle with his excitement.

The kiss deepened and she groaned softly.

He raised his head, separating them, and he immediately felt empty inside.

"You are so beautiful," he whispered.

"I'm not. I'm pale. Not vibrant and exotic like the girls you know."

"You're perfect," he reassured, lifting a hand and tracing a finger across her delicate features. "I could fall in love with you, but it would make no sense. There is no future for us. Not in this time."

"What do you mean?"

"Do you think your parents would allow me to come by the great house and tell them I want to court their daughter?"

The expression on her face was priceless, but he'd expect ed it.

She lowered her head, as if embarrassed by her thoughts.

"No need to be ashamed about the situation. That's life. It's changing slowly here on the island, but it is not an easy thing. It's easier for the blacks who have money. When people like me try to cross the color line, we are considered uppity. For me, love isn't about color, or place, or time. It's timeless. It's about here." He placed his hand on her heart.

For a moment, time stood still, as if hearing his words.

"Maybe this is just an infatuation," he continued, "or just the need for us to do something bold and rebellious. What can we do about this? You'll be leaving and going back to the U.S. And me, I'll stay here in Barbados and support those who are trying to make a change in attitude."

She looked up at him, her eyes glistening with unshed tears. He knew that for the rest of his life he would remember this moment. He knew something else. He loved her. Would always love her. This woman-child, who, without even realizing it, had stolen his heart.

"When do you go back?" he asked, not wanting to hear her answer.

"We are here for most of the summer. And then it's off to college."

"Medicine, right?" he asked.

"Yes, I'll do my undergraduate degree first and then go to med school. I have my dreams, but I know my father will never allow me to do what I really want to."

"Promise me you'll find time to sing and dance?"

"I'm going to try, but I suspect medicine will take up lots of my time."

"I'm sure you will handle it. If you're planning to do medi cine, you must be very intelligent."

"I've been told so and my grades are pretty good. Studying comes easy for me. And what about you?" she asked. "What is your dream?"

"I want to be a lawyer. I want to own a house just like the Harrisons. I want to be happy."

She looked at him with determination. "I'm sure one day you will have all that and more."

He smiled. He knew that much of what he wanted were pipe dreams, his fantasy in a world that was changing, but still considered him a second class citizen.

"Kiss me again," she whispered.

He didn't need any encouragement to oblige her. He low ered his head immediately to take her lips in a kiss that did not possess the gentleness of before. His mouth assaulted hers, demanding the intensity they were both feeling. He plunged his tongue inside, capturing hers and suckling firmly on it. She moaned, that sweet sensual sound that stirred him and aroused him.

He pressed his erection against her, and was surprised when her hands snaked between his legs. She gripped him firmly and he groaned with the pleasure of her touch.

Her hand caressed the length of his penis and it jerked inside the confines of his pants. His body shuddered with the pleasure of her ministrations. He placed his hands over hers. If she continued to touch him there he knew he'd probably embarrass himself.

He glanced down at the front of her blouse. Her nipples pushed firm and upward under their covering and he ached to see them.

He reached for the hem of the blouse and pulled it up wards, pleased when she raised her arms to make it easier.

When she stood before him, her breasts seemed to be greeting him. He cupped them with his hands. They were just right, not too big, not too small. Just perfect.

He lowered his head, encircling one firm orb with his mouth, and suckled on it. Her response startled him. She screamed out in ecstasy, her hands gripping his head.

And then she stopped, pushing him away.

"Do you hear something?"

He listened and then he heard it. Someone was calling her name.

"I'll stay here. Go. They must have come for you because of the rain.

"I can't see you until Monday. We're going to St. Vincent for the weekend."

"I'll be here in the evening, around four." He kissed her fast and hard. "Go, before they find us."

She smiled and headed to the door, exiting just as someone called her name again.

"Miss Abigail, I'm glad you found somewhere to shelter from the rain."

He remained in the hut for a while after she left. Outside the rain was still falling. He felt alive. Instead of taking the path to his home, he headed in the direction of the beach.

The beach was empty, the waves pounding on the sand.

Feeling daring, he stripped his clothes off, flinging them to the sand.

He dived into the water.

Hours later, he walked home, his only thought of the girl who'd come into his life. Already he missed her. She was going to St. Vincent for three days and he didn't know how he would deal with it.

If he couldn't handle not seeing her for three days, how was he ever going to deal with her return to home?

Chapter Three

On Saturday, Byron waited outside the hut for her, his body already throbbing with his need. He wanted her. Of this he was sure. For days, Abigail had been the only person on his mind.

In the middle of the night, he would awake, his dreams of her anything but pure. This morning he'd risen with the sun, leaving immediately after breakfast, to get a haircut.

Evening had taken longer to come than he wanted. At two o'clock, he'd put on his best pair of jeans, and a new T-shirt he'd purchased that morning in the city, and he had sprayed on some of the cologne he used only on special occasions.

He was sitting on a damp log outside the hut when Abigail slipped from between the branches of the trees, her eyes scan ning until she saw him sitting there. He stood, too far away to see the expression on her face, but the way her footsteps quickened suggested she was as excited as he was.

When she was about five feet away from him, she paused, the tenseness of her body evident in her stance.

He opened his arms and she flew the rest of the distance.

He held her tenderly, loving the feel of her body against his. She smelt of peaches and apples, truly American, but when he tasted her lips, she was all woman, a budding innocent woman, and he felt a flash of regret that he would take that innocence.

His lips touched her gently, probing when they parted beneath his. Her response stirred him, as her body pushed against his.

"I want to see you," he said.

"See me?" she replied.

He could sense her hesitation.

"Are you sure you want to do this?" he asked softly.

"I'm sure," she replied immediately, the caution he'd sensed not evident in her voice. "Yes, I want you to make love to me."

She stepped back, allowing the sun-flowered dress she wore to fall to the ground. Underneath, she wore nothing, and immediately his penis jerked in reaction to her beauty.

He wanted her. Wanted her with an intensity he'd never experienced before. He was not a virgin. Had not been since his sixteenth birthday and one of the girls in the village had offered herself as a birthday present. He'd come a long way since that first awkward night, but tonight, he felt inexperienced and vulnerable.

He wanted to please her. What *he* wanted didn't matter.

"Are you going to stand there and think?" Her voice interrupted his brooding.

He moved towards her, taking her in his arms and hugging her tightly. He wanted this to be special for her, knew it would be special for him.

He led her into the hut. He'd come earlier that day and prepared it for them.

When they stepped inside, her gasp of delight pleased him. Hundreds of petals from the hibiscuses in the garden lay on the bed.

She turned to him, her hands folded across her chest.

He stepped to her, unfolding her arms and looking down at her. Her face turned red.

"Don't be embarrassed. You're beautiful."

She looked up, gazing into his eyes. Her lips parted, her face still flushed. Damn, he wanted her.

He lowered her to the bed, resting his body against hers. She felt small and delicate.

He bent his head and kissed her gently, his passion increasing as he was swept along by his need. He thrust his hips slowly, loving the feel of her. He hoped that his largeness did not scare her, but when her legs widened giving him greater access to the hot core of her being, he knew she wanted him as much as he wanted her.

Desire burned hot inside him. He wanted her, wanted to feel himself buried deep inside her, but he knew she was a virgin. Her pleasure was more important. He had to make her ready.

When his lips found the sensitive spot at her neck, she whispered his name.

His gaze lingered on her young breasts, firm and aroused, rising provocatively towards him. He took one dusky nub in his mouth and sucked deeply. Beneath him, she whimpered. He worked on one nipple and then the other, their hotness filling his mouth.

"I want you now," she moaned.

In response, he raised himself above her, placing his penis at the entrance of her vagina and slowly slipped inside her. For the briefest of moments, she tensed and he knew she'd experienced pain.

"I'm all right," she said. "Don't stop."

She held him tightly, drawing him deep inside. He almost lost control at the firm grip around him, but he breathed deeply, willing his body under control.

Her eyes were opened wide, filled with the pleasure she was experiencing. She gripped his buttocks, drawing him closer, until he was buried deep inside her. Unable to contain himself any longer, he started to stroke her at a slow leisurely pace. With each measured thrust he discovered a new sensation, a new height of awareness, a deeper meaning to the art of lovemaking.

Gradually, he increased his movement, plunging smoothly into her again and again, feeling the knowing tingle of coming release.

He felt her tense and then her body convulsed with spasm after spasm, and the intensity of her orgasm plunged him over the edge. The fire flowed through him until he screamed with the power of his release, as wave after wave of pleasure wracked his body.

As they continued to lie there, both breathing deeply, he drew her to him.

"I love you," he said.

She smiled, wrapping her arms around him and squeezing him.

"I love you too," she replied.

~ ~ ~

The next few weeks passed in a mist of beautiful colors. It was a happy time, but with each day Byron dreaded the in evitable…her return to the U.S. He loved her. He knew that as certain as he knew the sun would rise each day.

He wanted to spend his life with her, but he knew the im possibility of that happening. She was seventeen years old, still a girl. He was just a year older. He didn't know how to take care of a wife, and the reality of anything happening between them in this day or time was unlikely. Yes, things were changing, but he was sure that her father would never allow them to marry.

He sighed, watching her from where he stood. Her eyes came slowly open. He loved watching her come awake. Since that first time they'd made love, he'd met her here almost every day. He couldn't get enough of her. Even now, he wanted her again.

She smiled up at him, but the look changed to concern when she realized something was wrong with him.

"What's wrong?" she said.

He didn't reply at first, not wanting to share his fear.

"Please, tell me,'" she pleaded, as she raised her head and rested it on her elbow.

He turned away from her, his back tense with his apprehension.

She rose from the makeshift bed, moving to stand behind him, a hand resting on his shoulders.

"I wish I didn't have to go either," she said softly.

He turned to face her, seeing the sincerity in her eyes.

"I wouldn't do that to you, couldn't do that to you," he said. "We're just kids who happened to fall in love. We can't have a future. At least not now. Maybe when we're older."

She started to cry and he held her tightly, wanting to com fort her, not wanting to ever let go.

"What's going on here?"

They turned, both startled by the booming voice.

Byron held her close to him, protecting her instinctively.

"I love him, Dad," he heard Abigail say.

"Take your hands off my daughter, boy! I'm going to see that your mother is fired! Abigail, I can't believe what I'm see ing. Have you lost your mind, girl?"

"I love your daughter, sir."

"Sir? You defile my daughter and have the gall to call me sir? Abigail, go to the house!" he commanded.

Abigail stood firm, but her father turned to her and slapped her on her face. She screamed in pain.

Byron jumped forward, gripping him around his neck.

"Abby, go!" Byron shouted.

She raced away.

When she disappeared among the trees, Byron released Mr. Larson. The man had turned red with anger.

"I will see you locked up for this!" her father threatened.

"Feel free to do what you wish, sir. I promise the police will only know that I defended her. The mark across her face will be enough proof."

"Do you know who you are messing with, boy?"

"Don't particularly care, sir," he said, his emphasis on 'sir' laced with sarcasm and disrespect.

For a while they stared at each other until Mr. Larson averted his eyes.

The man turned to go, but before he did, he said, "I will die before I allow my daughter to be involved with a no-good yard boy like you." He spat on the ground and then scrambled away.

~ ~ ~

The next evening, he returned to the beach, but after an hour, he headed over to the big house.

He entered the kitchen, where his mother sat reading the newspaper.

She smiled when she saw him. He was surprised she was not cooking. As long as there were guests in residence, his mother had to cook dinner.

"I'm surprised not to see you cooking?"

"I have a free evening. Mr. Harrison took his guests to the airport and then they're eating out. I have some food in the fridge for you and your dad."

It took a while for the words to register, and then he turned and walked out, oblivious to the sound of his name.

He did not stop running until he reached the beach. It was only as he stood, his back against one of the many coconut trees which populated the beach, that he realized he was crying.

Shame washed over him. He couldn't remember the last time he'd cried. But for some reason, he could not control the flow of the tears.

He lowered himself to the ground. His body shook with the heartbreak ripping his guts out.

He allowed himself to cry until, spent, he stood. He should have been prepared for what happened. He'd known there would be no future for them, but for a time he'd allowed himself to dream.

Now, he would have to deal with reality. He'd never see her again. In time, she would forget about the island boy who had taken her innocence.

He would never forget her.

He remembered the words he'd spoken to her.

Love was timeless.

Whatever the circumstance, he knew he loved her, that Abigail Larson had taken his heart…and he would always love her.

He sighed, knowing that for a time, he would feel the pain. But in time, he'd be fine.

He stood slowly. He had to get back to the house. He would talk to his mother. She would understand. She always did.

In the distance, the sun was setting. Dusk was painting the sky with its most brilliant colors; shades of reds and orange tinted white clouds.

Sunsets in Barbados were glorious.

Tomorrow, the sun would rise again. A new day, a new beginning.

He was going to be fine.

Epilogue

Adrian closed the journal. He felt the sting of tears. Reading his father's words was surreal. He felt a great sadness for his mother and father. The journal explained so many things. Why his mother had never married, why his grandparents had always treated him with cool indifference, why his hair was not quite straight.

He'd only met Mama a few days ago and already he felt a love so powerful, it still amazed him. He could tell she loved him, was happy to know she had a grandson. His father had never married either.

Love was indeed timeless.

As he stood looking out to sea, in the shadows of the coconut trees, he thought he saw the lovers.

They kissed passionately and then were gone.

He smiled.

They were finally together.

The Hammer of Artemis

by Diana Peterfreund

Diana Peterfreund is the author of eight novels for adults and teens, including the *Secret Society Girl* series, the "killer unicorn" novels *Rampant* and *Ascendant*, and the post-apocalyptic *For Darkness Shows the Stars*, as well as several short stories and critical essays on popular children's fiction. Her work has been translated into twelve languages, and her short stories have been on the Locus Recommended Reading lists and anthologized in *The Best Science Fiction and Fantasy of the Year*. She lives in Washington, DC, with her family. You can find out more about Diana at www.dianapeterfreund.com.

Andrew Lyon is my first stab at a male protagonist after writing more than a dozen books and stories starring women. I received a letter from a teen boy who loved my killer unicorn series and wanted to know if there were ever any boys who were hunters. Andrew's story is the answer to that question. I'm fascinated by the idea of different kinds of strength, and what happens when they interact. My unicorn hunters – probably never more so than in the character of Margery Lyon – tend to be shoot-first-ask-questions-later types. Unlike Margery, Andrew's power is not physical, nor is it one of position like his noble brother's. But he does have a strength all his own.

To Donna Maria Isabella Leandrus
Cloisters of Ctesias, Rome,

Having come through the recent season of illness in my country, I am at last in a position to write to you. The sickness has carried off my noble father as well as my mother, a woman who once lived amongst you, before she was wed. My sister Catherine, betrothed in marriage to Lord Darnley, has also succumbed. It is this unfortunate news that now gives me cause to write. I require the return of my sister, Margery Lyon, who has been residing in your convent these last ten years, together with the portion allotted to your order that remains. As the girl is hardly twenty, I trust that the bulk of her dowry remains intact.

The agreement my mother's father had with my father upon her marriage was that my mother's second daughter be sent to Rome. Margery is now the only daughter of my late parents. She will come home to England, where she will be married to Lord Darnley, who has most charitably agreed to take her in the place of her sister.

Prepare her for the journey in all haste.

William Lyon
Earl of Maidenmere

~ ~ ~

To Andrew Lyon,

I require you to travel immediately to Rome, there to collect our sister Margery. There has been no response to my previous letters, and neither our sister nor the envoys charged with delivering my missives have returned.

Bring her at once to my estate. I do not expect much from a convent girl, especially given the unorthodox nature of the

Order of the Lioness, but do your best to impress upon her the nature of her duty, and to prepare her for her marriage to Lord Darnley.

As for you, you may rejoice that you can finally do some thing useful for your family. The money I have sent along with this letter should be more than enough to sustain you both for your travels.

William Lyon

~ ~ ~

Dear William,

I have shown our brother Andrew mercy; which is more than I afforded your previous messengers, in hope that it will inspire you to cease with your correspondence. Do not at tempt to contact me again. I cannot control the behavior of my charges when I or any of my sisters am set upon by strange men. You cannot hope to overcome us. We alone among our neighbors did not fall during the recent attack by the armies of the Holy Roman Emperor. We shall not fall to a boy of fifteen years with an ill-fitting overcoat and soot-blackened hands.

I am a sister of the Order of the Lioness, and thus beyond your dominion. I cannot take a husband, as I am a bride of our Savior. I am sorry to hear of Catherine's death, and hope that Lord Darnley can find himself a replacement wife, but he will not have one in

Margery Lyon

~ ~ ~

To William Lyon, Earl of Maidenmere,

I have enclosed the letter Margery had delivered to me for you after she drove me from her door. Brother, you have never seen the like of this convent. The iron gates which surround it are guarded not by men, but by beasts, the very kind our sister had been sent to Rome to learn how to kill. They prowl the perimeter, their spear-shaped single horns sounding omi nously against the iron rails, their mouths always open, with long teeth as sharp as daggers displayed proudly in warning. I have learned that the sisters of the Order have been taking such precautions ever since the sack of Rome by the army of Charles V. Apparently the miracles the sisters perform in the woods and fields are not limited to killing these creatures. They even keep some as guards, the way you keep your fighting dogs.

The white-clad girls within the convent taunted me as I stood, and threatened to open the doors and let the beasts free. I believed they would, too, but their hands were stayed by our sister. She did not recognize me at first, but I knew her. She has the countenance of our dear mother. I had never thought to see it again, and could not remain composed. It was as if she read my feelings on my face, for she made a motion with her hand and the animals fell away. She beckoned me near, and when I approached, she called me by name. I cannot fathom how she knew, for I am not the baby she left behind in England. I tower above her now in fact, but she still frightens me. She is so small – hardly larger than one of the swords I've forged – yet like a sword, I am sure she'd find it no great hardship to cut me in two. Indeed, in that moment she held me there with her eyes alone, and before she dismissed me, I did not know which I feared more, my sister or the beasts she held at bay. She has grown into a fearsome creature herself, and I do not doubt that your previous envoys are dead – if not at her hand, than by her command to these unicorns that carry out her will.

I will not be able to bring her by force, and so, I wait here for word from you that you've either relinquished her to the Order of the Lioness or by what inducements I might convince her to return with me.

Andrew Lyon

~ ~ ~

Andrew,

I was mistaken to send you. It is clear from your last letter that the cowardice that has plagued you since youth was not beaten out of you by our father nor worked out of you by the laborers on our northern estate. There does not seem to be a purpose for fourth sons. You are too stupid for the court, and too weak for the army. You are such a large man, and yet you seem to have the spleen of a mouse. You spent so much time at the blacksmith's knee, and yet you know nothing of the sword.

I have wasted a year on useless messengers. I shall not waste another. You are relieved of this duty. I have sent my finest captain to retrieve our sister. You may return to England with them, but do not expect a place at my table until you have demonstrated some reason that you deserve the slightest rec ognition from

William Lyon
Earl of Maidenmere

~ ~ ~

My dear Brother,

I send you this letter, along with the crest that once be longed to your captain, John Lorry. I have seen to it that what remained of his body was given a proper funeral here. His corpse was delivered at my door, as he still bore your letter on his person. I have divined its meaning as best I could through the bloodstains. The unicorns, it seems, are quite thorough.

As you gave no further instructions should the captain fail, I will still remain. I know you will be happy to learn I require no money from you, as I have found employment with a local jeweler these last six months. Goldsmithing is evidently not so very different than blacksmithing, though I am sure you have even less love for a brother who makes earrings than you did for one who made swords.

I am tracking the movements of our sister, in hopes that one day soon I will find her beyond the convent walls and away from the protection of her deadly animal guard. The girls of the Order of the Lioness remain in their convent at all times unless they are sent on a hunt, but these requests have, I have learned, been very sparse since the sack of Rome. The rumors in the neighborhood are split. Some argue that a hunt would do much to replenish the coffers so depleted since the army laid waste to the city. Others say his Holiness should refuse any re quest originating from the land of his enemies; that those who hurt Rome should suffer the sting of the unicorn as penance.

I have not offered my opinion on this matter, as I am far too stupid and fearful to speak on matters of politics and pillaging.

Do offer my condolences to John Lorry's wife. I believe she was with child when I left for Rome.

Andrew Lyon

~ ~ ~

My Brother Andrew,

Word has reached me that you remain in Rome, and have been asking questions about the living fortifications of the Cloisters of Ctesias. I hope you are merely concerned for the safety of myself and my sisters. Mayhap it will put you at ease to know that the unicorns pose no danger to us. We are all maidens, graced by God to be shown tenderness by even these, most wild, most blood-thirsty beasts. They will nibble food from my hand, and I'll feel no more than the velvet touch of their lips upon my skin. But were you within their reach, they would eat you without hesitation. Indeed, it is for this reason that we never allow a man or married or widowed woman within the walls of the Cloisters. I have seen a single unicorn tear a man limb from limb before he had a chance to draw his sword. I must warn you that a similar fate will likely befall you if you ever approach our walls again. And probably something more terrible still, as we possess no fewer than twelve unicorns.

It would pain me to learn of your death.

With most tender affection,
Your Sister Margery

~ ~ ~

My Beloved Sister Margery,

I have sent along this letter with the maiden daughter of my employer, in hope that it will be delivered safely into your hands. Do not think me insensitive to your desire to remain. I have been now a year in Rome, and I see its charms compared to England, even though everyone tells me it has been bad here since the troubles with the Imperial Army. Here I have met more people than I did in my whole life in England. Here there are people from the Holy Land and from Africa. Here there are people who speak languages I've never heard, and create art such as I have never seen.

But you don't see that, shut away in the Cloisters. Do you not wish to emerge?

My most earnest love,
Andrew

~ ~ ~

To Andrew Lyon,

I know not what demands our noble brother has placed on you, nor how you do so far away from your home and everyone you know. William's cruelty to you now seems as great as that he shows to me. Do you think that I, as devout a Christian as any in my Order, desire the death of so many of my brother's men? William might have spared their lives had he relinquished me to the Church, as was the agreement our father made with our mother upon their marriage. I am for the Order of the Lioness, forever and inviolate.

Even if it were not so, did you think I would happily consent to such a change in my life? You, who see for yourself the glories of this city, would you be content to leave this place and travel back to cold, gray England, there to be sold like a breeding mare to Lord Darnley? Here I have been taught history, and languages, and most of all, how to use the miracle my holy sisters and I have been granted in service to our Savior. Before she died, our sister Catherine could not even read and write. I know my letters to her were read by her priest, and her responses were inscribed by him as well. Is that the life you wish for me? Is it the life you would wish for yourself if you were

Your Sister Margery

~ ~ ~

To Davide de Levi of the Via de Recti,

I entreat my most honored master to be forgiving, for now, after these twelve months of your kindness to me, I must depart your employ. My sister has at last made a mistake, for the acolyte she sent with her missive shared with me that several of the members of her Order shall soon depart their protected Cloister and head north for a raid against a den of wild unicorns in the mountains. This might be my only chance to detain her, though she and her holy sisters shall be armed.

I go with heavy heart. It is a duty I owe my family, but my sister has leached all the joy from my actions. I go now, sure that triumph for one of my siblings will almost certainly equal treachery for the other.

If I do not see you again, it is because I have either secured my sister, and will depart with her immediately to England, or because I have failed in my attempt and this time Margery has shown me no mercy.

Andrew Lyon

~ ~ ~

To Davide de Levi of the Via Recti,

Honored master, by the Grace of God, I yet live, though I remain in the house of a farmer, who has given me a place to sleep and food in exchange for gifts of nails and horseshoes and other items I might craft for him by forge. I hope to return to Rome soon, when my leg has mended enough to withstand the trip.

I write to you now to request your help, as I believe that you alone possess the knowledge I need to help me accomplish my goal. It would be to your credit, signore, and I believe it may also be to your very great fortune.

But let me tell you what I have discovered. The informa tion given me by the acolyte Joan was not wholly correct. My sister and a company of other nuns departed the Cloisters of Ctesias armed only with bows, arrows, and hunting daggers and from there traveled north of Rome, but they did not do it on the day Joan had reported to me. Thus it was that I could not apprehend my sister in Rome. I followed the party, how ever, and at last overtook them in a lonely wilderness not far from this very farm where I now reside. They had stopped, I thought to rest, and dispersed among the brush and trees at the base of a small rocky outcrop. I concealed myself behind a tree and waited for an opportunity to isolate Margery and overpower her. Though she was armed, I had little doubt that my superior size and strength would triumph over whatever training her female companions had given her.

I was never to know the truth of this matter, however, as soon, the whole party was set upon by a corps of wild unicorns. I had thought the ones the holy sisters use as guardians of their convent were the fiercest of all creatures, but I was mistaken. I wonder now at all the painters and sculptors in your city who liken these beasts to the Lord Jesus Christ in images on canvas or carved in stone. These beasts are demons. They are difficult to see in whole, since they move so fast. Their bodies blur like a sword in the hand of a master. They are the color of black smoke, all except for their horns, which are white as bone and curve like the tusk of the beast they call elephant, and their eyes, which glow like candle flame.

I braced myself for death, but they rushed past me and into the company of holy sisters as if I were not even there. Beasts are well known to prefer weaker prey, and a group of women, even armed, must be much weaker than a man like myself. That is what I thought, but I had never seen the mem bers of the Order of the Lioness beyond the walls of their convent. The name of lioness suits them well, for no great cat could be as ferocious and deadly as they became in that instant. By the miracle granted these holy sisters, they grew just as fast and as strong as the monsters who closed in on them. The air was filled with the sound of screams and the smell of blood, but all of it seemed to belong to the unicorns. As each beast fell dead, I could at last see it clearly. In form they most resemble a large black horse, but with fangs like a great viper, and beards which twist down their chests. Their coats are rough and longer than even the winter coat of a horse, and their legs are that of bucks, with tufts of fur around each cloven hoof. Their tails are like whips, and as with snakes, twitch long after the beasts themselves are dead.

As the unicorns realized the women would not yield, they retreated. I felt unsafe and attempted to hide. The obvious location was the rocky outcrop, in hope that the unicorns would not be able to climb. In this, I was also mistaken, for they are as nimble as sheep. I was barely three stories in the air when I heard their hoofbeats closing in. Fearing for my life, I shoved my body into a crevice between two rocks, but even this did not keep me safe, as they still pursued.

Because of the narrow opening, they could not follow me into the crack, but they slammed against the stones with their heavy heads and slid their deadly horns in as far as they could reach. The screech of bone against the rock seared through my ears and sent me scrambling as deep as my shoulders and the walls of my ribs would allow. The walls of rock closed around me, cool and firm, but just beyond my flesh, I could hear unicorn-cry and the sound of their hooves and horns as they beat against the stone, beside me and above me and even below. I could feel the puff of their heated breath as they tried to force themselves into my hiding place. The assault continued, and I kicked out at the creatures, mindful of their horns but even more scared that they might breech the sanctuary, when I felt movement among the rocks. The force the monsters had put upon the stones had shifted them, and the earth was tilting. In a rain of rocks, we all fell – man and stone and unicorn.

My leg was crushed, though I know not if it was by a boulder or a beast. I dragged myself away from the pile, as several unicorns, still alive, thrashed about with horn and hoof. Perhaps, like me, they were too injured to stand. Some never moved again. There was great pain in my chest and my limbs were wet with blood, but still I fought to crawl, to slither if

I must, away from these animals. The floor beneath me was damp, bare earth, and here, the light did not penetrate. My nostrils burned with the scent of fire and rot. As my eyes adjusted, I saw that we had somehow fallen into one of their dens. Piles of bones surrounded us, and I grabbed the largest one I could find to use as a club.

Not all the sounds came from the injured unicorns at my back. So intent was I in escaping the unicorns that had fallen with me, that I crawled right into another. This one was a kid, its flank pressed against the wall as it cowered away from the mess of stones and thrashing bodies. Like me, its leg had been crushed, and even more than its leg, I think, the rear portion of its body. It keened most pitifully and in its eyes, I saw mirrored my own terror. In the center of its brow, where the others' horns had erupted, there was a giant, red boil, pulsing and seeping bright blood. At first, I thought it was yet another injury, and yet, the boil elongated as I watched, transfixed, heedless of the pain in my leg and of the other unicorns even now shaking off dust and pebbles and rising to meet me. And then, before my eyes, the boil burst.

This seemed to be too much for the beast, however, as it collapsed, mewling, its eyes flickering shut. On the ground before it lay a congealed lump of blood and tissue that glowed with an impossible inner fire. The kid was too weak to lift its head but it opened its mouth and out spilled its long pink tongue, probing weakly in the dirt for the lost flesh as if its life depended on its repossession. Where the boil had been I could now see the point of its newborn horn. Somewhere in my wrecked mind, I recalled the stories I'd heard of the healing properties of unicorn. I reached out and snatched away the lump. I expected it to be soft in my hand, like meat, but instead it felt pulpy, like a cherry squashed around a pit.

The kid's breath grew shallow, and then stopped. I opened my mouth to swallow the vile boil, but then realized the surviving unicorns had overcome their injuries and were once more standing, looking about in the rubble for me. They advanced, horns lowered and I raised my hands to fend off their expected blow.

It never came. They shied away from me. Emboldened, I swung at them with the bone I held, and they parried me easily with their horns, but came no closer. The flesh I'd stolen from the dying kid pulsed in my hand, retaining the life its owner had lost. I held it forth, and the beasts shrank from it. I know not why. The only knowledge I have of unicorns is that the holy sisters make from their bodies a panacea against all ills, a Remedy from all poisons.

But there are other stories I have heard, of pearls from the mouths of vipers, of stones from the root of an elephant's tusk, that has in them the power of a talisman. The unicorn pearl is hard and shiny now, like amber made from blood. Perhaps this jewel is not a cure, but a weapon. You who are a jeweler, can you tell me more of this? Have you made for anyone a talisman like that?

Your humble servant,
Andrew Lyon

~ ~ ~

Dear Andrew,

Never was I more pleased than to receive your letter. I had gone so long without word from you, though I know your sister returned to her Cloisters. I had feared the worst. Please do not delay in returning with my son in the cart I have procured for you.

In my long career, I have crafted necklaces strung with the teeth of saints. I have made earrings from iron that once shackled the feet of martyrs in the Coliseum, and even once, I bought and sold at great profit an arm cuff set with, it was said, a piece of the cross that held your Christ. Never have I experienced the magic their owners said the jewels possessed, but they always attributed that to my lack of faith. I kept my tongue, and forged their relics. I cannot tell you more than that.

Therefore, I do not know if the pearl in your possession contains such worthy charms, but I do know this: the horn of a unicorn could ransom a king, so valued are its properties.

The pearl might fetch a similar price, if you seek to make such a talisman.

I have shared your story, except for the portion about the pearl, with all of our friends. Everyone is riveted and wonders how you escaped alive. We cannot wait for your return so that we might hear the rest.

With utmost respect,
Davide de Levi

~ ~ ~

My most honored Master,

Your son has taken ill and so we dally in this town until he is well enough to continue our journey. We had some difficulty finding Jacopo an apothecary initially, but do not be concerned, for he improves in condition and the man I secured believes our delay will last no longer than a week.

In the meantime, I will distract your mind from this misfortune with the conclusion of my tale.

I feared that I would sit forever in the den of monsters, my leg on fire with pain, my life's blood draining away while the unicorns surrounded me, held at bay only by the miraculous power of the pearl clutched in my fist. But it was not to be. There was a quick sound that I did not at first recognize, and then one unicorn dropped, and then the next, as sudden and neat as if their lives were candles waiting to be snuffed. By the time the third fell, I knew the sound. It was an arrow, released from a bow. I looked up at the spot from where I fell and there, her body half hanging through the hole, was Margery. But it was Margery as I have never seen her. Her white cloak was torn asunder, leaving bare her arms. Her wimple was torn free, and her dark hair fell wildly about. Her hands held tight to bow and string, and in her eyes was fire to dwarf the flames I'd once imagined in the monsters' stares.

She killed every unicorn in the den, then pointed her next arrow at my heart. We were both as statues, staring at one another in silence. I had been spared by the unicorns, but I would not be spared by her, I knew it.

Her voice came to me. She might have whispered, but in the stillness of the cave, I heard every word. "Andrew," was what she said. "Leave me in peace."

And then she hauled herself out of the hole in the roof and was gone.

I know not if she left me to die in that cave. By the time I had pulled my broken body out of the den, she and her company were long gone, with nothing but the burnt, hornless bodies of the unicorns left behind. I made it to a path and eventually was found by the farmer. And in these months of waiting and healing, I cannot forget her countenance as she saved my life, nor the plea she made before she vanished again.

Most of all, I cannot forget her actions. I was wrong to think I could ever overtake her. She is mightier than any of my brother's soldiers. She is stronger even than the unicorns she uses as guards. I no longer wonder that she does not wish to marry. It is more than her distaste for returning to England or submitting to William which fortifies her defiance. Margery told me once that only maidens are graced by God to overcome the unicorns.

I sit here alone on the side of an ancient road, a lame blacksmith clutching a single bright pearl that I hope to use to change my fortune. But all along, my sister is the one with the real power.

Before your son and I departed from the farm, I entreated him to return with me to the unicorn's den. I could not navigate into that dark underground space myself, but Jacopo had no trouble. The unicorns' corpses were untouched but by worms, and so your son brings back more than merely

Your humble servant,
Andrew Lyon

~ ~ ~

To my sister Edith, daughter of Roland Hornley, Essex

At last I have had the opportunity to write to you, my dearest sister. Please give a kiss to each of the boys, and relay my fondest love to our father.

My studies continue at a great rate here. Truly the amount of knowledge Donna Isabella requires of her charges is far above any that I would have thought necessary for a woman in holy orders. There is Latin, of course, but also Greek, and history, and natural history, and even mathematics. And when I am not enclosed with books, I must partake of the bodily training which forms the bulk of my duties here at the Cloisters of Ctesias. My instructor in the unicorn arts is still the Englishwoman Margery Lyon. I feel fortunate that they have chosen an English tutor for me, as others in my rank of acolyte do not share a native tongue with their instructors.

I was surprised to learn in your last letter that Margery's actions have even reached your ears. I know it has been years that her family has been requesting her return to England. I suppose they will not give her up, though I must assure you most fervently that my honored Sister will never return to England while breath resides in her body. I do not understand it myself. I do not dislike my work here, and have even found a sort of affection for the beasts, though their odor and bloody ways are still offensive to me. However, to be given the opportunity to marry would be a most desirable lot in life. I wonder that Margery disdains it so.

On this front, I have just witnessed a most interesting development. Perhaps you will remember from my last letter the time Sister Margery entrusted to me a journey beyond our fortified cloister walls to deliver to her brother a letter. If you recall, at that time he procured from me Margery's plans for leaving the Cloisters. When she discovered my betrayal, I was whipped, which I still do not believe was right. After all, Margery was not detained by her brother at that time.

Despite my punishment, I bore Andrew Lyon no malice, as he is a most well-looking man, taller than any of these Italians and with broad shoulders and a fair face. Were our father to change his mind about my placement here and seek for me a husband, I would wish him to be a man such as Andrew Lyon.

After that occasion, for many months Andrew did not return to our convent. Before, he had visited nearly every day, remaining a safe distance from the house unicorns who stand always as guardians of our gates. Indeed, it was this familiarity that loosened my tongue when I delivered the letter to him. But this is of no account anymore. For today, after many months, he has returned.

He was not the same man who had come before. Now, he walked with the help of a stick, and even then, he mostly limped. When he approached the gates, the unicorns, instead of lunging forward and gnashing their teeth, as they have here tofore done with any man who treads too close, they instead reared back, hissing and growling their displeasure. My fellow maidens all stopped and stared at this, for no one, not even the oldest among us, has ever seen these fierce creatures show such fear.

With our single, impenetrable security gone, Andrew sim ply opened the latch and walked inside. Into our Cloisters. Into the place where all men have ever feared to tread. Not even the priests come hence, but Andrew Lyon limped through the doors like it was any courtyard in Rome.

It was to me he came, and he stopped and called me by name, and entreated me to bring him to Margery at once.

Dear Edith, what was I to do under these circumstances? I went as quickly as my feet could carry me to Margery, fearing the worst, but she was too overcome with surprise to punish me again, and ran even faster than I did back to where Andrew now waited for her inside. Inside our convent! In the center of the hall beneath the great dome. All around him were my holy sisters, intermixed with their guardian unicorns. Unicorns I have seen rip even armed Imperial soldiers into pieces. And yet they stood silent, even cowering, before this simple man with the twisted leg.

Sister Margery stared at him, fiercer than the beasts, and despite the circumstances, I saw no fear in her eyes. This I dreaded more than anything, for it was clear to me that even defeating the unicorns would not help Andrew Lyon. Margery is deadlier still. I would have cried out for him, Edith. I think I might have even put my body between his and the others. But he spoke. These were his words, as best as I remember:

"I have come, Margery. I have breached these walls at last. Your beasts stand helpless before me. Your defenses are laid waste. And yet, as you see, you still have more power than me, than any man alive. And so we need not be enemies, you and I. I have brought you a gift."

At this, he held out his hand, and on one of his fingers, he wore a large golden ring, intricately carved, and set with a single stone the color of blood. I have seen prettier rings, but its power did not lie in beauty. The unicorns beheld it and hissed, and I was overcome with the ecstasy one feels in church, or, since I have become a hunter, in chase. It was a miraculous thing.

Andrew Lyon then said, "This ring holds the power to allow a man past these gates, that gives a man or woman not graced by God as you and your company are the ability to stand against the unicorns. And I shall send it to our brother William so that he too might enter the Cloisters and take what he wishes, unless you agree to my demands."

Demands! Demands made by a man to a sister of the Order of the Lioness! Not even His Holiness sounds like this when he graces Donna Isabella with his requests. He dare not with the unicorns about. But Andrew Lyon demanded, and these were the things he required:

To embrace his sister, for whom he had come to Rome so many years ago, but whom he had barely spoken to for all this time.

To remain here, in an apartment in the Cloisters, further to study the relics we collect and see what use can be made of them.

To be allowed the use of a forge by which to create for us weapons that might help us in our duties.

When he was finished speaking his demands, there was not a sound in all of the chamber. Brother and sister Lyon stood as still as the marble statues that grace our courtyard and every woman and creature there waited for we knew not what.

I have never before this day seen Sister Margery smile. Yet after that long moment she smiled, and when she did, the whole room breathed again. I do not know if Donna Isabella will agree to allow a man such as Andrew Lyon to remain here, as we are a convent of women. And yet, it seems impossible that she should not, when he offers a miracle as to rival those of the hunters ourselves.

The Lyons must be formidable family at home in England, for the two we have here are as commanding as kings and queens, as mighty as ancient gods. On one side stood the lame blacksmith, as proud as Hephaestus himself, and across from him, his fierce sister, the maiden huntress.

What marvels they could create together!

All my love,
Joan Hornley, Cloisters of Ctesias, Rome

~ ~ ~

To William Lyon, Earl of Maidenmere,

We have received your latest letter. The answer to your request is no.

Regards,
Sister Margery Lyon of the Order of the Lioness
and
Andrew Lyon, Hammer of Artemis

Lady's Man

by Tanya Anne Crosby

Tanya is a *New York Times* bestselling novelist and an award-winning journalist. Friends and family sometimes refer to her as "Pollyanna," but the name-calling is usually dispensed with a healthy helping of good will, so she's OK with it. Those who know her best, however, know that Pollyanna is just half her personality – she's a Gemini, after all! She's a five-time nominee for a Romantic Times Career Achievement Award, and her next novel, a romantic suspense as yet untitled, is due to be released early 2013.

Instinct brought Annie Franklin to Folly Beach, South Carolina to say good-bye to her grandmother. As a parting gift to her beloved gram, whose greatest wish was for Annie to live a less guarded life, she decides it's also time to take gram's advice. She hopes her moment will come with the symbolic release of her grandmother's ashes into Charleston's beautiful wetlands, but thanks to one very intuitive dog and a perfect stranger, Annie discovers that "letting go" has as much to do with embracing the future as it does with shedding the past.

Chapter One

Annie Franklin inadvertently stumbled upon the address to Heaven: It was a two-story beach house at 1776 East Ashley Avenue on Folly Beach.

For months, she had researched to find the perfect place. Apparently, on this tiny spit of sand, the houses were booked sometimes years in advance. Just as she was about to give up, she'd gotten an email from the owner. He had recently remodeled so that the house was rentable both upstairs and down, and he would personally be occupying the other half on the week of the Fourth. He wanted to know if Annie was interested in taking half the house at half the price.

Two words: "Hell yes!"

And much to her delight, the house looked exactly as it had in the photos.

Trying not to trip over her dog as she dragged her suitcase up the stairs, she dumped her luggage inside the nearest bedroom and patted the bag lovingly. "OK, Gram, so you were right."

Sometimes good things come when you least expect them.

Lady, her yellow Lab, cocked her head and whined.

"I'm not talking to you," Annie reassured as she adjusted her glasses to inspect the room.

Throughout the upstairs, the windows were open to the breeze, letting in a mix of scents – not all of them wonderful.

With Lady close at her heels, she made her way to the back deck to do a little reconnaissance. They were literally surrounded by water, from the Atlantic Ocean to the Folly River and she didn't need Lady's keen sense of smell to scent it – except that the one place water was supposed to be, it didn't appear to be.

From the deck, Annie contemplated the waterway that wasn't there. According to Google Maps, the river was supposed to be accessible from the back yard, but alongside a weathered dock sat a small boat, nearly grounded by the low tide. She couldn't imagine throwing her grandmother into that trickle of water and just letting her float there in the muck.

Considering the possible necessity of a Plan B, she made her way back inside from the upper deck, grabbed a book from her bag and settled into one of the deep, comfy chairs in the upstairs den to wait for the owner. Although he didn't seem to care whether she took the upstairs or downstairs, she decided to give him the courtesy of asking and waited to unpack until after he arrived.

Lady sat dutifully at her feet and Annie opened her book with a contented sigh. She was thirty-two pages into her newest Pamela Morsi novel with her dog stretched comfortably under her feet when Mr. Heywood arrived. Somewhere in the back of her mind, she heard the knock but the sound didn't register until he was already climbing the stairs.

"Hello?"

A dirty blond head emerged above the landing.

Annie blinked. He was much younger than she expected. Second homes were not luxuries people her age usually had at their disposal. She stared at him dumbly, the weight of her feet preventing Lady from rising to greet him.

He eyed the dog and Annie slid her feet off Lady's back and Lady immediately jumped up to greet him, tail wagging furiously.

Annie got up too, but without quite the same enthusiasm. For no reason at all she took an instant disliking to the guy. He was certainly cute, but that wasn't working in his favor as far as Annie was concerned. "She doesn't usually take to strangers so well," Annie said, eyeing her dog with a bit of annoyance.

"Pretty girl," he cooed, shifting his gaze to Annie and lingering a long, awkward instant before returning his attention to her dog.

It was a perfectly harmless glance, but his waggish smile brought an immediate blush to Annie's cheeks. Annie watched the muscles in his forearm flex while he stroked her dog and unwanted images popped into her head.

"What's her name?"

"Jesus!"

His head shot up. “Jesus?”

Annie swiped her palm across her thigh. “Uh, no. Lady.”

He smiled and returned his attention to her dog.

Little doggie ho.

He spent an inordinately long time rustling Lady’s hair, petting her, cooing to her and somehow it only served to annoy Annie all the more. Finally, he peered up at her and said, “Amazing animal. I always wanted a Lab. You can really see the intelligence in those big brown eyes.”

Annie lifted a dubious brow. Like a giddy little cheerleader, Lady wagged her tail, shamelessly loving the attention and not quite ready to be dismissed. He came all the way up the stairs, extending his hand in greeting. “Jamie Heywood,” he offered. “Good to finally meet you. I’m guessing you chose upstairs?”

Annie shook his hand, opening her mouth to confirm, but he wasn’t finished talking.

“I got here this morning and tossed my bags into one of the rooms downstairs, but I’d be happy to move them if you’d rather be down there?”

Annie shook her head. “Honestly, I couldn’t wait to see the view and came straight up. Hope you don’t mind.”

“Works for me,” he said, winking. “I prefer the bottom anyway.”

Annie’s brow rose. Was he actually flirting with her? “Great,” she said. Typically guys like him were not interested in girls like her. She didn’t wear tight Gucci skirts and three-inch Manolo Blahnik heels.

“Only the downstairs has access to the kitchen,” he went on to explain, “but there’s a fridge built into the wet bar up here and the outside stairs lead to the deck upstairs. The key works on that door as well, so you can lock your door to the interior if you want … or not.” He winked again and before Annie could ask if he had a tic with his eye, he turned to leave, heading back downstairs, dismissing her. Amazing how some men could flirt so mindlessly. Annoyed, she sank back into the chair and picked up her book again.

“Don’t waste the entire week holed up in your room!” he shouted from the bottom of the stairs. And the last thing he said before closing the door was, “Lady’s not the only one who needs a little sunshine!”

From the top of the stairs, Lady stared after him. Once the door closed, she turned those “big brown eyes” on Annie.

“What does he know?”

Lady continued staring, those dark, soulful eyes seeming far too knowing and Annie slammed her book shut and set it down on the armrest.

Seriously, what could some guy she just met know about her outdoor habits?

~ ~ ~

Annie was still bristling over the insult when she ventured downstairs hours later to find Jamie hauling a hose into the back yard. Lady bolted to his side the instant she spotted him and he dropped everything, stooping to pet her.

Annie approached the pair, both so engrossed in their display of mutual affection that it seemed she was completely invisible. He didn’t appear to notice her, but his gaze met hers the instant she opened her mouth to call off Lady.

“Find everything OK?”

“Yeah, it’s great,” Annie assured. “Thanks.”

He stopped fondling her dog and stood. “Glad to hear it!

Of course he was. She was a customer, she reminded herself. “Well, I’ll let you get back to work,” she said, and started away, expecting Lady to follow.

“Plans?”

Surprised by the inquiry, Annie turned to find Lady lounging at his side, tail wagging happily, but this time his attention was centered on Annie. Something about the way he looked at her sent goose bumps racing down her arms and she rubbed her arms absently. “Not really.”

He smiled, a lazy smile that reminded her of Elvis. “Good. Thought maybe I’d ask Lady here out on a date … if it’s OK with you.”

Annie’s brows collided. “You want to ask my dog … on a date?”

“Sort of. I was going to see if it was OK to take her out on the boat. Labs were bred for water, you know.”

He was going to educate her about her dog?

"So how 'bout it?"

Annie shook her head. Sharing the house with him might be part of the plan, sharing her dog was not. "I … don't know … really … Lady's never been on a boat. I don't think it's a good idea."

"You can come too," he cajoled.

The sheer ridiculousness of the conversation made Annie crack a smile. "Let me get this straight. You are asking me to be a third wheel on your date with my dog?"

He laughed, giving her a glimpse of high-dollar dental work – that, or he was way too blessed in life. "When you put it like that, I suppose I am."

Annie just looked at him, unsure how to respond. Some part of her wanted to jump at the opportunity to check out the surrounding marshland, but the word "yes," stuck some where in her craw. It wasn't simply that she hadn't expected the invitation, or feared being out on the water for the first time. Something about the guy made her feel more awkward than she had felt in years … but he was just some dude who hap pened to own the house she had rented. So what harm could there be in going?

His grin turned lopsided. "If I didn't know better, I'd say you were scared."

Annie slid her hands into her back pockets and straight ened her shoulders. "Of you!"

"Actually, I was thinking maybe my boat?"

"Hah!" Annie exclaimed. "Why would you think that?"

His hands went to his hips as he scrutinized her and even his stance seemed a bit of a challenge. "So you've been on a boat before?"

Annie felt a little cornered, but she'd started down this path and she wasn't backing down. "Of course!" she lied. "Big boats. Little boats. I like boats!"

He chuckled. "Alrighty then, give me about thirty minutes to get things ready and then come on down and prove it."

"Yeah… OK."

He eyed her speculatively. "Thirty minutes," he said again as though it were a challenge he didn't believe she'd rise to.

"I'll be back!" she said and found herself grinning stupid ly as she turned to go inside. She was pretty certain he'd just asked her out.

It didn't occur to her to call for Lady and Lady didn't come.

"Don't worry. I'll watch your dog until you get back," he called after her.

Startled at having forgotten her dog, Annie spun about, walking backward, marveling at how Lady had taken to him so quickly. She was on her back squirming happily while he rubbed her belly. Like children, dogs had very good instincts when it came to people. "Don't let her out of your sight, alright?"

He gave her a spirited captain's wave. "She'll be fine. Don't forget your bathing suit."

"All right!"

"Watch where you're going!"

Annie spun about and grazed her cheek on the back deck column. Yelping in surprise, she caught her glasses and ducked around the brickwork, hurrying inside, her pride injured slight ly more than her cheek.

Chapter Two

Exactly thirty minutes later the sun was already beginning to go down, turning the horizon a coral pink – the perfect camouflage for bruises. Lady was settled into the boat wearing a bright yellow life vest.

"You had a dog vest? I didn't think about that!"

"I have gear for all walks of life," he said with a wink and bent to retrieve one lying at his feet. He tossed it over to Annie. "Remember how to put one on?"

Annie caught it. "Sure," She said, but her cheeks warmed as she tried to find the right holes for her arms. Fortunately, if she was blushing, he probably couldn't see past the blossoming bruise on her face. He watched for a moment, and then smil ing a little, stopped what he was doing to come to her aid. "It's been awhile," she offered sheepishly.

"I figured."

Annie contemplated his motives as he righted the vest and allowed him to guide her into it. He already had her money. Maybe he just needed company, she decided. Even cute guys were bound to have lonely moments. He finished snapping her in and brushed a finger across her cheek, so lightly that it sent a jolt down her spine.

Lady sat patiently in the boat, watching her human companions with a certain canine awareness.

"Let's not keep my date waiting," Jamie teased.

The tide was coming back in, lifting the dory nearly to deck level. Annie stepped into the boat with confidence only to shriek in surprise. It happened so fast. The boat flipped. She heard Jamie shout her name as she and Lady both went tumbling into the river, dispatching a furor of protesting birds from the surrounding marshland.

Luckily, the water wasn't deep.

Somehow, Annie managed not to lose her glasses. Spewing water from her mouth, she found her footing and instinctively reached for Lady who was thrashing about awkwardly. She peered up at Jamie, mortified, until she saw the look on his face. Morphing quickly from alarm to a look of pained restraint, he was trying desperately not to laugh.

Standing waist-deep in the river, cradling her dog in muddy arms, with her glasses seated precariously atop the bridge of her nose, Annie couldn't quite hold back a peal of horrified laughter.

Laughter exploded from Jamie's lips.

Giggling a little in consternation, Annie waded with Lady to the side of the dock, and with Jamie's help, lifted and pushed Lady up out of the water. Once on the dock, Lady shook herself vigorously, eyed Annie distrustfully and waddled out of reach.

"First time on a boat?"

Annie smirked. "How'd you guess?"

He busted out laughing again and Annie couldn't blame him. He hauled her out of the water and she was suddenly glad she hadn't chickened out of wearing her bathing suit. She considered shaking off a layer of muck much as Lady had done, but yanked off her lifejacket and soggy T-shirt instead, too wet and muddy to care how she looked in her suit. "That was painful!"

His laughter ended abruptly when Annie squirmed out of her wet shorts. "Wow," he said automatically. And then added a little awkwardly, "You look … great."

Their gazes met over the unexpected compliment.

Annie couldn't imagine looking more unkempt than she did at the moment, but he was being serious. The twinkle re mained in his eyes, but she recognized a serious compliment when she heard one. Her brows twitched in surprise. "Thanks."

Abruptly, he began to laugh again, apparently coming to his senses. "I'm sorry," he said. "How 'bout we leave the boat ing for another day and head out to the beach to rinse you off?"

Annie scrunched her nose, embarrassed. "So sorry for spoiling your date with my dog!"

"On the contrary," he reassured, "you made my night."

He hauled the little dory out of the water to hose down later and together they walked to the beach with Lady ambling sullenly behind them.

As the sun disappeared to the west, the color of the sky deepened to crimson and plum. Annie didn't think she could have planned a lovelier evening for a first dip in the ocean. The breeze was balmy, the sand still warm and Jamie's presence was strangely comforting. Not that anything would happen, she reasoned, but if anything did happen, she sensed he was the right guy to have at your side.

She watched as Lady fell into pace beside him, but at the moment, it didn't seem to bother her. "I think you've won over my dog."

He responded with a crooked grin. "One down, one to go."

Before Annie could register what he'd said, he demanded, "Watch this." He stopped and faced Lady, slapping his hands to his knees before turning and sprinting out to the water.

Lady hunkered down playfully and barked and then bolted after him. She watched in amazement as her dog chased him into the surf completely without fear.

She thought about joining them, but a lifetime of pru dence kept her rooted to the spot.

You can't always wait for the perfect time, her grandmother's voice coached from the grave. *Sometimes you have to jump, Annie.*

"Just do it," she whispered, and for once Annie didn't think. She took a deep breath, banished all thought from her head and sprinted in to join them.

It was the most fun she'd had since she was a child. They spent about an hour playing in the surf and then walked on down the beach.

"They call this the Washout," he explained as they reached what appeared to be just that – a washed out road and the abrupt end of a row of houses. "Some serious surfing goes on right here." For a moment, Annie lost his attention to the sea. With the waning sun casting long shadows over the ocean, the water looked far too calm to surf, but she took his word for it.

"So you're a surfer?"

He nodded. "Yeah, but not sure why I was so hell bent on coming this weekend." He peered down at Annie, seeming to study her. "I guess sometimes you have to go with your gut … know what I mean?"

Annie didn't. Her inner voice usually only said, "I told you so." But she nodded anyway and sat down on the sand. "My grandmother was big on living by her internal compass," she offered.

Lady plopped herself down at Annie's side, scenting the salt air.

Jamie sat down next to her. "Unlike you?"

Her brows drew together. "Why would you say that?"

"People don't usually preach to the choir," he offered. "Were you close to her?"

"My grandmother? Very. Mom and dad divorced when I was nine," she told him. "Mom died when I was ten. My grandmother left everything and came to Nashville to raise me. I guess she did it hoping my father would turn his attention from trying to become the next Hank Williams long enough to get to know his kid."

"Did he?"

Annie picked up a tiny shell, inspected it and then tossed it away. "Nope."

He nodded and asked point blank. "So when did she pass away?"

He was a little too intuitive maybe.

Annie averted her gaze. "Six months ago." As comfortable as she was beginning to feel around him, there were some things she just didn't want to share. She changed the subject. "Why do they call this the Washout?"

He turned again to look out to sea. "Because right where we're sitting there used to be a row of houses. Hurricane Hugo changed the landscape drastically, but it makes for awesome surfing when the wind is good."

"How long you been coming here … to surf?"

"Folly? All my life," he said. "I grew up here." And for a moment, he seemed to consider what more to say. Then he stated matter-of-factly, "Mine was one of those houses Hugo washed out to sea."

Annie's brows shot up. "And you bought another property? Seems …" She wanted to say stupid. "Reckless."

Again he contemplated her, but Annie couldn't read the thoughts behind those intense blue eyes. After a moment, he offered, "I have a few properties actually. Life is all about risks, Annie. Sometimes you just have to jump."

Annie's heart leapt a little at hearing her grandmother's words come out of his mouth.

He picked up a small bit of debris and tossed it into the surf. Lady scurried after it, sniffing at the water where it landed. She nosed it, trying to pick it up.

"My grandmother lived somewhere around here," she revealed, her eyes stinging a little … maybe from the salt breeze. "She talked about coming back … but never did." She stood, feeling suddenly a little self-conscious and very bare in only a swimsuit. "It's getting a little nippy out here. Should we go?"

He didn't budge. He just sat there, peering up at her, his dirty blond hair ruffling in the twilight breeze and Annie told herself not to expect too much from him. Just because they'd spent an afternoon together didn't mean a thing. She fidgeted uncomfortably, brushing sand from her palm onto her thigh.

"Only if you'll agree to join me for dinner tonight?"

Surprised, Annie rubbed her arms self-consciously, eyeing Lady. "I-I don't know … what about Lady?"

"She can come too. This is Folly. Nobody minds. I know just the place. Do you like oysters?"

"Yeah …"

He gave her a skeptical look. "Uh, you've had them before, right?"

Annie laughed. "More often than I've been on boats," she assured and lifted a brow. "So you found a way to make me a third wheel after all?"

He stood finally, grinning down at her.

The wind whipped her hair into her face and he reached out to brush it away, but didn't actually touch her. "I think it's the other way around."

Chapter Three

Life is all about risks, Annie.

Sometimes you just have to jump.

The words rang like a litany in Annie's head. It was as though her grandmother had sent Jamie to whisper in her ear and she couldn't quite determine if it was serendipity, or simply annoying.

In her room, she took the time to unpack while Jamie gave Lady a much-needed bath. He'd offered and since Lady would probably end up in her bed tonight, Annie wasn't about to refuse.

At the bottom of her suitcase sat a blue velvet satchel.

Gingerly, Annie took it out and laid it on the bed, leaving the gold drawstring tightly drawn. Within the satchel, inside a silver urn, were her grandmother's ashes.

Annie had brought her home.

But this wasn't just a tribute to her grandmother. Some where deep down she understood the importance of letting go and it was the one thing she knew her grandmother desperately wanted for her – independence from her past. It was partly why she'd chosen July Fourth to do this thing, and when she'd spotted the house in the ad, with the bright blue house numbers in sync with the holiday, it seemed meant to be. She had been so disappointed to learn it was already booked, and then she'd gotten the email from Jamie.

She was still mulling over the serendipitous aspect of it all as she made her way downstairs, sans glasses, wearing a bright orange button-up halter dress and a pair of white short-heeled sandals. The sun on her face, and a little artfully placed makeup, hid the bruise on her cheek.

"Wow!" he said when she descended the stairs. He peered down at Lady, talking to the dog in a conspiratorial tone that made Annie smile. "Suddenly, I feel we should have used fancier soap!"

Lady cocked her head and whined pitifully.

Annie rolled her eyes and laughed. "You're a silly man," she told him. "But thank you."

He took her to a little spot on Bowens Island, a tiny island not far from Folly. The restaurant was, as most people would describe it, a dive, but with some of the most amazing food Annie had ever eaten.

In the days that followed, the three of them spent nearly every waking moment together. Although none of it was part of Annie's original plan, it was too easy to spend time with him and avoid what she had come to do. He made her laugh.

On Monday she went shopping, leaving Lady at home to nap while Jamie tested the surf. The winds had kicked up and he didn't want to miss the opportunity to "catch some air."

On Tuesday, Annie took Lady on her leash to the Washout to watch him surf. It was a little windy and the sand stung as it whipped her in the face, but she couldn't have cared less. Surrounded by laughter and little kids running around with red and blue plastic shovels, she couldn't remember a more contented moment in all her life.

Jamie spotted her and came ashore with his faded orange surfboard under his arm and dropped it onto the sand beside her. It was the first time she'd seen him actually look annoyed. "Did you see that guy drop in on me out there! Too many kooks today! So," he said, changing the subject, "ready for some fireworks?"

Annie shielded her eyes with a hand as she peered up at him, grinning. "Why, are you gonna beat someone up?"

He chuckled. "I meant tonight. I know a prime spot to catch the best of Charleston's pyrotechnics."

Annie was beginning to get the distinct feeling he was enjoying her company. "Sounds great!"

He sat next to her and leaned in to whisper in her ear and Annie's heart lurched a little. He said, "I don't want to hurt you-know-who's feelings, but I was thinking maybe just you and me tonight?"

Until now, everything had been a little flirty, but completely platonic. Feeling his warm breath on her skin gave Annie goose bumps of the sort the wind could never have produced. Swallowing the lump that rose in her throat, she turned to look him in the eyes.

He was waiting for her answer, staring at her mouth, anticipating words.

Their faces were so close now that the slightest lean forward would have brought their mouths together. Annie held her breath and didn't back away. Neither did he, but he didn't kiss her either.

He was still waiting.

"OK," Annie said finally.

"Red or white wine?"

He was still staring at her mouth.

"Red," she said and dared to move just a smidgen closer, her heart skipping a beat. Hoping he would kiss her, she waited for what seemed an interminable moment while people milled about them in a blur of movement.

He smiled and backed away, rising to his feet and brushing sand from his body, careful not to sweep it in her face. "I'll come by to get you at six."

Annie didn't have a chance to respond. He picked up his surfboard and ran off down the beach.

Lady barked a complaint at his retreating back.

Luckily, Annie was sitting on the leash. She reached out to stroke Lady's back and let out a shuddering breath. "He's pretty hard not to like," she agreed and rose to her feet to walk Lady home.

~ ~ ~

As promised, Jamie showed up at six with a basket and a giant bone for Lady. "To keep her occupied," he explained, and before she could protest that maybe they shouldn't leave Lady alone with a bone she could choke on, he took Annie by the hand and dragged her out to the beach.

"This end of Folly stays pretty quiet. You can't really swim because of the currents so we'll have the beach mostly to ourselves."

They passed the remains of an old building that had become a canvas for graffiti artists. Jamie explained that it was an old deserted World War II Coast Guard Station. Once beyond the dunes, the beach itself was bordered by rocks and nearly deserted as well. He took her by the hand and led her to the top of a dune and then put the basket down and spread out a blanket, gesturing for her to sit. "I've never actually brought a girl on a picnic before."

Annie was amused he felt compelled to tell her so. "We're even," she said. "I've never been on a picnic before."

He cocked his head and said in an exaggerated manner, "Oh, really?

"Annie smiled.

"I guess we'll figure it out," he assured her. "And look … I brought you this!"

Laughter erupted from Annie's lips as he pulled out another bone.

"Oh, no, that was in case Lady whined and we had to bring her." He reached back in the basket. "This!"

This time, he pulled out a beautiful multicolored crochet shawl and set it around Annie's shoulders then reached back into the basket without waiting to see her reaction. "I wasn't sure what color you'd be wearing tonight so I picked out something that would go with everything."

Annie's breath caught as she admired the gift. "Thank you," her eyes misting. She couldn't remember the last time anyone had given her anything besides a birthday card.

"And this …"

He pulled out a bottle of Silver Oak cabernet, which he proceeded to open, then he handed the bottle to Annie. "Hold that, please," he said and took out two wine goblets, handing one to Annie. Annie was a little stunned by the amount of thought he'd put into the evening. He took the bottle from her and poured them each half a glass and set the bottle back in the basket holster and raised his glass. "To unexpected surprises!"

Annie couldn't have put it better. "To unexpected surprises," she agreed and found that, for the first time in her life, she actually meant it.

They sat for hours, talking, as the sun retreated to the west, leaving the sky a beautiful blend of dusky hues.

"This is the highest point on the beach," he explained. "From here, we should be able to see the fireworks downtown."

"It's lovely."

"Not as lovely as you," he countered with a smile. And without waiting for a response, he asked, "See where that lighthouse is? Behind it, that's Morris Island. It used to stand on the middle of three islands. Now it's about a thousand feet offshore. That's how gnarly the currents are out there." He pointed to an area offshore where waves were breaking, churning up whitecaps. "I've always wanted to surf out there – can't imagine feeling closer to heaven. There's a fine line between life and death and I think there's a part of every surfer who wants to own it."

Annie shuddered. "Sounds dangerous to me!"

"Only if you don't know what you're doing or you make a stupid call.'"

Annie studied him. There were no worry lines etched into his brow – not even faint ones – although they were close to the same age. Only a few laugh lines were etched deeply into his cheeks. "Don't you ever worry you'll do – or say the wrong thing?"

He shook his head, not even considering her question. "Nah. I agree with the idea that whatever doesn't kill you makes you stronger."

Annie shuddered. "I guess I'm just not that fearless."

He stared at her curiously. "Of course you are. You're stay ing in a house with a strange guy you just met and you don't bother to lock your door at night. What made you just trust that everything would be OK?"

Annie blinked in surprise. "You tried the door?"

"The first night," he confessed. "Your dog was whining and I let her out to pee then let her back in."

Annie sipped self-consciously at her wine. "That wasn't smart, was it?"

Jamie shrugged. "But you're fine, right? And now we're having fun … and maybe we actually like each other a little?"

Annie smiled a little too readily and ducked behind her arms to conceal it, swirling the wine in her glass. "Maybe."

They continued to talk as they polished off a second bottle of wine between them. Jamie brought grapes and cheese and they munched on finger sandwiches while they waited for the fireworks to begin.

Staring at the darkening sky, Annie laid back on the blan ket, feeling a little guilty for turning this trip into a complete 'me fest.'

She couldn't put off dealing with her grandmother forever.

Lying there contemplating exactly where to set her grand mother's ashes free, she asked, "Jamie … do you ever think about what might be out there?"

"Sometimes," he admitted. "But I'm much more interested in here and now. He rolled over, looking down at her. "One thing I know."

"What's that?" Annie spotted the first of the fireworks go off in the sky above his head, but she didn't alert him. If he hadn't heard them, she didn't want to spoil the moment. More than anything, she wanted him to kiss her … right now.

Her heart beat so loudly it seemed to drown out the fireworks.

"I think loggerhead turtles have exactly the right idea," he whispered, slurring his words a little.

Annie's brows collided. That *wasn't* what she had expected to hear. "You do?"

"Uh huh. They listen to their inner voices and it leads them right back home … so they can make their babies on this beautiful beach." And with that, he laid his head on her breast and went very, very still.

After some time, Annie could hear his smooth easy breathing.

It took her awhile to realize he was sleeping.

She didn't move.

She lay there feeling his weight with every rise and fall of her breath; all the while spectacular fireworks went off over head, lighting up the sky in a celebration of color. She slid her hand around his neck, feeling the strong pulse of his heartbeat beneath her fingertips and sighed with the realization that at this moment, there was nowhere on earth she'd rather be.

Chapter Four

The following morning Annie expected to find Jamie nurs ing a hangover, but he was gone early. So was his board. She guessed he was out surfing, hangover and all.

She was glad he wasn't there. As much as she enjoyed his company, she was running out of time to do what she'd come to do and she needed privacy in order to do it. She left Lady in her room and wandered out to the dock where the dory re mained grounded. It was a small boat, probably easy to handle and the river didn't look all that scary.

It certainly wasn't deep.

Life is all about risks, Annie.

Her grandmother was worth it.

Making sure the paddles were in the boat and her lifejacket was on, she set the blue velvet satchel inside and maneuvered the boat back into the water. Once settled into the dory, she took the paddles and rowed herself downstream. She was gone maybe an hour and when she returned, she found Jamie pacing the dock.

"Where the hell have you been?"

Annie was startled at how angry he appeared. She didn't in tend to answer so flippantly, but she wasn't ready to reveal her private affairs. "Sightseeing," she replied with a smile. "Why?"

"Do you understand how dangerous that was? You have absolutely no idea how to handle that boat!"

Annie thought she had handled it just fine.

While he stood glaring at her, she carefully guided the boat up along side the dock. He didn't bother waiting for her to show him how well she could do. He got down on his knees, reached out to grasp the side of the boat and jerked it close enough to strap a mooring line to it. Then he helped her out, yanking her up rather rudely.

Annie clutched the blue satchel so it wouldn't fall into the river. "Damn it! Why are you so angry? I thought you were all about taking chances!"

"I'm OK with *me* taking chances – not you! Does it make any difference to you that I'd be horrified forever if you wan dered out into the channel and got yourself killed?"

Annie didn't think his anger was very rational. She raised her voice just a little. "Obviously, it wouldn't have been your fault!"

"It's my damned boat, Annie! What the hell were you try ing to prove?"

"I wasn't trying to prove anything! I was trying to find a place to bury my grandmother!"

His gaze shifted to the satchel in her hand and he took a visible step backward. He ran his hand through his hair in what appeared to be frustration and when he looked at her again the anger had vanished from his expression, replaced with some other emotion. "Look, I was just worried."

They stared at each other.

Annie's eyes stung though she wasn't sure why.

"Ashes?"

Annie nodded and swallowed hard, fighting back tears.

He held out his arms and she went into them automati cally, throwing her arms around him, burying her face into his chest.

He patted her back gently, but that only seemed to make it worse. Annie began to sob in earnest. "I was going to do it right here from the dock! It didn't feel right! The tide's too low!"

He stroked her back. "Shit, I'm sorry. I didn't know, Annie."

Annie held him tighter, grateful for his presence. It seemed every bit of emotion she'd held back since her grandmother's death suddenly burst forth.

"I know an amazing place," he said, stroking her back. "Will you let me share it with you?"

Annie clung to him, soaking the front of his shirt with her tears, not wanting him to see her face. She cried until she couldn't anymore.

"Annie?"

She nodded and he put a finger beneath her chin, lifting her face, forcing her to look up at him. She knew her nose was red. Her cheek was purple by now and her eyes were probably blood-red as well. He bent to kiss her bruised cheek.

"Your grandmother must have been an amazing woman," he said. "I'm glad I met you, Annie Franklin."

Annie forced a smile and hiccupped. "I'm glad I met you too."

"Get in the boat," he directed.

Tearstains on her cheeks, Annie got back into the dory and sat patiently with her grandmother's ashes in her lap while Jamie untied the mooring line and pushed off into the river.

He took her to a beautiful, unspoiled island deep inside Folly's winding wetlands. They dragged the dory ashore and wandered just a short distance inland. "This way … I want to show you something." He said nothing more until they reached a little clearing. The first thing he showed her was an unham pered view of the Morris Island Lighthouse in the distance. The second thing he showed her was a small weathered plaque on a nearby tree that wasn't visible without brushing aside the spartina grass. About three inches by three inches, it was made of some kind of metal and screwed to the tree. It read simply: James Arthur Heywood Jun 2 1921 - Sep 22 1989.

Annie blinked and peered up at him.

"My dad," he explained. "It's a just a memorial. They never found his body."

"What happened?"

"Hugo. At least that's what we think. He left a message for my mother that he was driving out and would meet her at my place in Raleigh … but I don't believe he ever left."

Annie stared at the plaque. "Why would he do that?"

Jamie sighed. "He was diagnosed with cancer a year before. His health was deteriorating. I guess Hugo handed him an easy out."

Annie didn't know what to say.

"Like I said … they never found his body. This was just my way of getting closure. I haven't been back since so I think I understand how you're feeling."

Annie's eyes stung. "I'm honored you would share this place with my grandmother. She would have loved it here."

"You never know, Annie. Maybe this is exactly where she wanted to be. I don't believe all things are simply coincidence. He reached out to place a hand behind her back. "Ready?"

Annie nodded. Somehow, knowing they shared this in common gave her the necessary strength. She chose a place not far from Jamie's father's tree and just as with a Band-Aid, she told herself, no hesitation, she had to do it.

Silence was her only prayer as she removed the urn from its satchel. Jamie stepped out of her way when she broke the sealed container. Her heart constricting a little, she squeezed her eyes shut and cast the ashes into the air. When she opened her eyes, for just an instant, a cloud of gray seemed to congre gate before her – a final farewell form – and then it dissipated, scattering into the wind.

For a long moment, Annie just stared at the beauty of the wetlands, feeling acutely her grandmother's presence.

But the surprising thing was … she didn't feel alone.

She peered up at Jamie. He opened his arms and she went into them eagerly. "I'll make her a plaque," he said soberly. "You can pick a tree."

Annie nodded and peered up at him. "Thank you, Jamie! Thank you for everything!" She gave him a heartfelt squeeze.

He tightened his embrace and Annie felt her eyes burn. "All I did was listen, Annie. When the Universe talks, I try to pay attention." He bent his head close to hers and said quietly, "Funny thing is, the closer you listen, the more it seems to say."

Words caught in her throat.

He gave her a gentle squeeze, put his arm around her shoulders and walked her back to the boat.

~ ~ ~

That night, Annie awakened to the sound of rain pattering her window.

The bed was empty and she could hear Lady whining downstairs.

About a week before she'd died, her grandmother had held her hand, squeezed it and said, *"It's true what they say, Annie … it's never the things you did that haunt you most … ."*

At the time, Annie had thought it was her way of reassur ing Annie that she'd had a full life, but this instant, as she lay there listening to Lady's insistent whines, it seemed more of a warning.

For once, she listened to that inner voice and got up to go downstairs.

Lady peered up at her guiltily as she descended in bare feet.

Annie opened the door that separated the upstairs and downstairs. "Go on," she whispered conspiratorially.

Lady didn't need further encouragement. It was dark, but Annie didn't need light to see where she had gone.

The same place Annie was going now.

Jamie's bedroom door was cracked enough for Lady to scamper in. Pushing it open, Annie took a deep breath and followed the dog into the room.

Jamie seemed to sense her presence. He turned groggily and sat up, peering through the shadows. "Annie?"

"Is there room for one more?"

Sleepily, he raked his fingers through his hair. "Are you OK?

Annie wasn't sure how to respond. "I think so. Maybe. I don't know."

There was a long stretch of silence as he seemed to con template her request. "I'm not wearing clothes," he said finally.

Annie smiled. "That's OK, I'm not wearing glasses."

He chuckled. "Right. Come on in."

She didn't hesitate. She crawled over Lady to the other side of Jamie and laid her head down on his pillow, curling up next to him. "I needed a warm body and Lady abandoned me hours ago to pine for you at the bottom of the stairs."

He adjusted his covers and pulled them over both of them, drawing her closer. "I see. And any warm body will do?"

Annie laughed softly. "Not quite."

"Good answer!" he said and she could hear the approval in his voice. "Your grandmother?"

Annie slid an arm around his chest. "In a way." But not really, and yet she couldn't get the words out to tell him that it was more about him and the prospect of leaving Folly.

It's never the things you did that haunt you most …

Rolling over, Annie kissed him firmly on the lips. He slid strong arms around her, kissing her back.

Grunting in complaint, Lady jumped off the bed and found a quiet spot on the floor free from unwelcome nudges.

Jamie stroked Annie's hair. "I think someone's jealous."

"Too bad," Annie said, emboldened. She slid a leg over his thighs and kissed him again, wanting to make love to him.

This time, he resisted her advance, placing a hand between her breasts and gently pushing her back. "Annie," he said soberly. "That's one way I never throw caution to the wind."

Confusion swirled through her head. "Are you saying no?"

His hand shifted slightly, covering her breast and Annie held her breath. But his words were not in tune with his actions. "I'm saying I've had my fill of one-night stands and I don't want you to sleep with me only because we're both here."

"Then why are you holding my breast in your hand?"

He hesitated only a moment and said huskily, "Admiring perfection." He kneaded gently, flicking his thumb across her nipple over her T-shirt and Annie moaned as he kissed her. Her skin burned, aching for more. She leaned into his touch, pleading, "we might never have another chance."

"In that case, we *definitely* shouldn't do this."

He kissed her one last time, then shifted her from atop him, making room for her at his side, pinning her hands at his chest. "Go to sleep, Annie."

Confusion wove cobwebs through Annie's thoughts as she lay there trying to determine exactly what had happened.

Sleep eluded her … so did the answers.

Chapter Five

Annie awoke in Jamie's bed, but he wasn't in it. In his place was a hefty yellow dog curled up in his warm spot. Sometime after he'd gone, Lady must have crawled back into bed and settled in beside her.

Apparently, they were both pining over the same man. Amazing how easily he had wormed his way into both their hearts.

When she saw his board was gone, she presumed he was out surfing and after getting dressed and wolfing down a few of the leftover sandwiches, she and Lady made their way out to the Washout to watch.

She sat on the beach and studied the surfers. It was crowd ed and difficult to make out faces at this distance. She was there nearly an hour when she realized Jamie wasn't there yet.

With the wind kicking up the waves, she was sure he would want to surf, and thought maybe she knew why he was com pelled to do it. Right here at the Washout, somehow, he con nected with his father. This is probably where he felt his dad's presence the most and eulogized him by surfing the waves.

Yesterday, on the island, he claimed he hadn't been back to that place since his private memorial to his father. He'd stated it pretty matter-of- factly, without any visible sign of emotion aside from his concern for her, and she couldn't help but won der what sort of emotions swirled just beneath the surface of his skin. He didn't seem to let many through. Anger, maybe – he had shown a bit of anger when he thought she might be in danger. But then he'd put up an immediate barrier when she'd reached out to him last night – despite the fact that he had been the one to pursue her since the moment they met.

So how did a man like Jamie Heywood deal with a storm of overpowering emotions?

As she sat there, the wind picked up, sweeping in a ceiling of gray that turned the water the color of mercury and drained the color from the beach.

A grim thought bore its way into Annie's brain.

She glanced down at her watch. 1 p.m. If he wasn't here, where could he be?

She stared at Lady, who whined, seeming to sense her unease.

There's a fine line between life and death … I think there's a part of every surfer who wants to own it.

Annie bolted to her feet.

Without stopping to think about why, she ran toward the east end of the beach, dropping Lady's leash as she ran. She ran, tripping through the sand, up through the street and past the coast guard station, her chest aching from the effort.

Leash dragging behind her, Lady kept pace at her side.

A tremendous sense of urgency nearly overwhelmed Annie. Going on instinct, she shouted at Lady, "Get Jamie!" She pointed to the beach beyond the dunes. "Go get Jamie!"

It seemed somehow Lady understood and doubled her pace. Passing Annie, she loped through the sand toward the surf. Her chest ached, but Annie kept running, something deep down pressing her forward – all the while, a horrible sense of impending doom followed her like the incoming black clouds. She stumbled past the dunes in time to see her worst fears realized.

Lady sprinted across the sand and dove into the surf.

Jamie was on his surfboard, but he wasn't alone in the surf. A monster wave rolled in, lifting him up high on his board and for an instant, he looked like he was king of the sea, riding high on his mercurial wave. He road it about three seconds on his haunches before another surfer appeared on the crest alongside him. Suddenly, the surfer next to him fell, launching his bright yellow board into the air toward Jamie. Even from this distance, Annie could see that it smacked Jamie upside his head. He wavered and for a dizzying moment, she thought he might stay up. He tumbled headlong into the water, flipping his board up behind him, leaving it floating ominously amidst the whitecaps.

"Jamie!" she shouted.

Lady was already halfway to where his body lay bobbing.

Annie knew it was stupid but she didn't care. Fully dressed, she ran in after her dog, after Jamie, her heart pounding furiously. The shoreline fell away immediately and she stumbled into deep water. The currents swirled dangerously around her and she swam with all her might.

Her heart hammered as the ocean took on a life of its own and for a terrible, awful moment, she didn't see either Lady or Jamie and she realized there was a distinct possibility they would all drown. And then she spotted Lady's head bobbing furiously toward a black spot in the water near Jamie's orange surfboard.

Oh, God, was it Jamie? She couldn't tell! He wasn't moving. His hair was too dark. God, it wasn't Jamie!

Finally, Lady reached the surfboard and kept going, dragging a body in the direction of the lighthouse.

"Jamie!" Annie shouted, gulping in water. She tried desperately to follow, but a fearsome current threatened to suck her under and she instinctively turned back toward the shore, realizing she wasn't strong enough to make it. She reached the beach, sputtering salt water from her mouth, gagging on emotion.

People came running out of nowhere, helping her the rest of the way out.

Someone had already called the Coast Guard. She could hear the engine's roaring in the air.

From the shore, they watched as Lady swam toward the lighthouse, holding fast to her burden. Emotion welled like a tidal surge from the bottom of Annie's gut. Her eyes burned with unshed tears as she watched her dog reach a sliver of shore behind the lighthouse, dragging a limp, dark haired body up the beach with her.

People around her chattered feverishly, but she didn't understand anything they were saying.

Someone nudged her. "Who is that?"

"My dog … and … my boyfriend," she said, choking. She added quietly, "I think."

There was no sign of the other surfer anywhere on the horizon. Whitecaps stippled the channel.

"Lucky bastard!" someone declared.

"His guardian angel earned her wings!"

"Angel, hell! Did you see that dog?"

Annie focused on the choppers in the air.

She waited, standing ankle deep in the surf, watching Lady hover over the body on the distant shore. And the moments while she stood there were the longest of her life.

~ ~ ~

News of a dead surfer made the six o'clock news. The body of a twenty-year-old College of Charleston student washed ashore on Morris Island.

Annie sat beside Jamie's hospital bed, watching over him as he slept, thankful it wasn't him.

All afternoon, reporters remained outside the door, want ing an interview with the dog that had saved a man's life. Lady was being treated to VIP status and given free reign of a small waiting room near the E.R. while Annie waited to see if they planned to admit Jamie. If he would just wake up, they planned to release him. Aside from the lump on his head, he seemed fine. Apparently, his surfboard tether had kept him afloat long enough for Lady to reach him.

When he opened his eyes, Annie was right there to greet him.

"Hi," he said groggily.

Annie gently brushed the hair back from his forehead. His blue eyes gleamed a little feverishly, but the smile that followed was every bit as waggish as she had grown accustomed to. Her voice held none of the censure her words did. "So which is it, Jamie Heywood – stupid, can't read, or have something to prove?"

He groaned. "All of the above."

Annie laughed softly. "You scared the hell out of me. For a minute, I thought I was going to lose the two souls in my life I care about most."

The twinkle in his eyes brightened. "You mean that, Annie?"

Annie kissed him fully on the mouth. "I do, Jamie – what are the odds?"

"Definitely better that we would have met and walked away," he said. "It happens every day." His expression sobered, the glimmer fading from his eyes. "The other surfer?"

Her hand went to the angry red knot on his head, caressing it. "He didn't make it. You almost didn't either. Lady dragged you out."

His Adam's apple bobbed. "I guess I owe your dog two debts …."

Annie bent to kiss him on the lips. "Shhhh."

"Never shush a dying man," he chided her.

Annie smiled. "Except that you're not dying." She brushed the back of her knuckles over his cheek.

"What do you think about marriage, Annie?"

Annie screwed up her face. "I think that's a weird question and you took a nasty blow to the head!"

"Not so weird if you just saw your life flash before your eyes."

Something in his expression told her he was completely serious.

"I meant, to me, Annie." He stared at her expectantly.

Annie blinked. "Are you … asking me … to marry you?"

He shrugged. "Sort of. Maybe." His eyes glistened slightly. "I guess I am. I've been around long enough to know a good thing when I see it, Annie."

Annie stared at him.

Who in their right mind signed up for a lifetime after a single awesome week? There were jobs to think about. Geog raphy – they lived in different cities – and what did they really know about each other? Marriage was not something to be taken lightly. Neither was leaping in to suicide waters to save a stranger's life, and yet both she and Lady had done it without hesitation.

Annie searched her heart, banished all thought and gave him the only answer that felt right.

Two words: "Hell yes!"

Acknowledgments

We'd like to thank Carolynn Carey, Julie Compton, Tanya Anne Crosby, Shannon Donnelly, Ann Jacobs, Marianna Jameson, Sylvie Kurtz, Ann Lethbridge, Diana Peterfreund, Deb Stover, and Carol Umberger for the help they offered copyediting this anthology.

We'd also like to thank Julie Ortolon for her beautiful cover design.

Thanks, too, to the 2011 Novelists Inc. board – President Donna Fletcher, President-Elect Lou Aronica, Treasurer Marcia Evanick, Secretary Denise Agnew, Newsletter Editor Marianna Jameson, and Advisory Council Representative Jean Brashear – for their help in getting this project underway, and the 2012 Novelists Inc. board – President Lou Aronica, President-Elect Laura Castoro, Treasurer Trish Jensen, Secretary Denise Agnew, Newsletter Editor Marianna Jameson, and Advisory Council Representative Pat McLaughlin – for seeing it through.